BLOOD IN THE WATER

THE LOST TALE OF CAPTAIN HOOK

M.A. KERSH

Dedicated to my husband, Daniel, for it was his sea of love and devotion that taught me that wishes really can come true.

CHAPTER ONE

A LOST BOY

The late night's quiet was interrupted by the splashing footsteps of a dark-haired woman running upon the wet cobblestone street. Once she safely arrived at the door of The Moore Orphanage, she glanced around furtively, before carefully lowering a large basket she'd kept hidden under her cloak. Upon the steps outside the door, the basket stirred and revealed the tiny face of a baby boy. A mother's tear fell upon his innocent face as she bent down to kiss his soft cheeks for the last time. "I hope one day you can forgive me," she whispered, wrapping him tightly in his thick red blanket. Holding his tiny hand in hers, she cried, "I pray you will be safe now. Goodbye, my sweet James." She looked into the dark streets around her once more, closed her eyes, and murmured a wish for her baby. Gathering her resolve, she steeled herself and loudly knocked on the door. After three hard raps, she ran into the pouring rain and disappeared into the darkness.

Minutes passed, and no one inside had heard her knocks as the tiny baby lay quietly upon the steps. Normally, the absence of seeing his mother's face would bring him to tears, but somehow the image of the storm in the sky left him calm and unafraid. Soon his basket became soaked from the rain, causing him to slide down on the watery doorsteps. One by one, the basket slipped down and began floating down the streets. As it was very late at night and as everyone was inside, nobody noticed the little basket sailing upon the flooding streets. He began to laugh and coo with joy as the water carried the basket thrashing around upon the bumpy roads.

Finally, the water led him into a dark alley, and as the water went down into the sewer drain, his basket got stuck. Frustrated, he tried to wiggle and squirm around, but it didn't work. Peering up for help in the darkness, he suddenly felt scared. He started to cry, but no one could hear such a tiny voice through the powerful storm. He cried out for his mother, hoping she would come to find him, but she didn't come, no one came.

Truly in the dark now, James felt an unfamiliar emotion: fear. He cried out in that special baby language that mothers understand, pleading for her to comfort him, the way she always had. Unfortunately, the storm drowned out his cries. For the first time in his young life, his mother was not there, and he was alone. Then, the storm and darkness receded as a brilliant ball of blue light approached him.

"Well aren't you quite the little adventurer?" Asked a tiny voice. Surprised, baby James wiped at his watery eyes to discover a small fairy with vibrant azure hair and large pearlescent wings floating above him.

She smiled and whispered in a reassuring tone, "Don't cry, little James. I have come to help you."

He watched with amazement as she danced gracefully in the air. The fairy's dance was indeed like another language, communicating with James that he was safe. He cooed happily and kicked his feet as her glittering blue dust began to fall upon his basket. With each of his giggles, the basket began to rise into the air and floated in her direction. She encouraged his eyes to follow her as she danced her way through the streets and back toward the entrance steps of the orphanage. After guiding the basket to the top step, she flew up to the bell next to the door. James watched her grab the clapper and push it. She tried to hit the bell, but it barely made a sound. Again, and again, the fairy couldn't make a ring. James giggled in amusement as she contemplated her next move. She whipped up her hand, revealed a dazzling silver wand, and sent a blue blast of energy upon the bell. James gasped at the force and winced at the loudness of the banging. The clapper began to swing wildly, and the clanging was so loud, it seemed to vibrate through the building. When she suddenly heard footsteps coming towards the door, she quickly flew away, and the storm resumed as if it had never stopped.

A kindly nun opened the creaky door to discover a tiny baby boy with beautiful blue eyes. No one else was in sight, so she picked up the wet basket and brought the baby inside. "My goodness! You are soaked to the bone, my child," the nun said as she lifted him out of the basket and cradled him against her chest. She took him to a large nursery with five rows of old baby cribs filled with the soft cries of orphaned children. She took him over to one of the empty cribs and laid him down. He started to cry, and as she unwrapped his wet red blanket, she noticed a name stitched into the top right corner. "Baby James," she read quietly.

Eventually, all the other babies were silent, asleep in their cribs throughout the room, all except for James.

Finally, the nun came back over to him. "You are quite the fussy little thing," she said as she picked him up and brought him over to an old rocking chair sitting next to the only window in the nursery. When she sat down, she held him tightly in her arms. He looked out the window, watching the rain stream down the glass as the nun slowly rocked him back and forth. She hummed a sweet tune until he finally drifted off to sleep.

In the next few years, the baby that had been rocked to sleep every night was now being moved into a room full of older boys. He exchanged glances with the other young children being transferred into the room with him. They looked frightened and nervous, but James was excited and eager to play. Some of them were playing games, others were playing with toys, but most were running around the room. Then he noticed two boys throwing a small rubber ball back and forth. The boys were only a few years older than him. Suddenly, one of the boys missed a catch, and the ball went flying across the room and under one of the beds. He ran towards the ball and dived under a bed to retrieve it when suddenly somebody grabbed him by his ankle and pulled backward. Once he was all the way out from under the bed, he looked up to see one of the older boys angrily standing above him. The boy was a little taller than him, with light auburn hair, golden-brown eyes, and a sneering face.

"What do you think you are doing, you little runt?" Demanded the boy.

James stood unafraid but was somewhat stunned and confused. "I was getting the ball. I thought I could play catch with you."

The older boy laughed rudely, "You hear that boys? This baby thinks he can play with us!" He shouted. The other boys in the room slowly approached them, laughing along.

"I am not a baby!" James shouted back bravely. This surprised the older boy, and all the surrounding children began to cheer.

The boy leaned down close to his face and asked, "What's your name, runt?"

He thought for a moment. The nurses had always called him Baby James. That had to change. It had to be something scary. He looked out the window next to him. Down below were the docks with a giant ship was coming into port. Suddenly, it hit him. He bravely leaned in close to the smug boy's face, and stated with a strong voice, "My name is James Hook!"

5

The boy bent his head back and roared with laughter. "What? Were your parents' pirates, or something?" The boy asked mockingly. The room was quiet as all the other boys looked down into the severe and fierce eyes of the new little boy.

Still, he did not flinch. "And what is your name?" He asked in the scariest voice he could muster.

The boy raised his left eyebrow, mildly amused and replied, "Peter. My name is Peter."

After that day, all the children in the boy's room stayed away from James. But he didn't mind. He spent his time reading or looking out the corner window that was next to his bed. At night, when the stars were bright above in the dark sky, he enjoyed seeing all the different types of ships coming into the dock. He would imagine all the mysterious places they had seen, and what incredible adventures laid out beyond the horizon. Every night, when he drifted off to sleep, he would dream of being a tall and ferocious pirate with long hair and a captain's hat. He dreamt he was aboard a large ship, riding the waves, and hearing praise from his vast adoring crew. Then every morning, he would wake from the screams of the nuns. He would look around him, still stuck in these wretched walls that he couldn't wait to one day escape. He knew he didn't belong here, and so did the other children.

One day, while James was reading one of his books, the other boys suddenly grabbed him by both arms and pulled him down to his knees. He tried to free himself, but it was no use. There were too many of them. He looked up at the ledge to see Peter pulling something small out of his pocket. Before he could see what he had in his hand, Peter jumped down and approached him with a rusted old fishing hook between his fingers. He was frightened now and tried harder to break free as Peter bent down to pull something from his left shoe. It was a matchbox he had stolen from one of the nuns that smoked. Peter was known for his skill of stealing things. All the boys knew of Peter's collection of items he kept hidden under his mattress. *What was he going to do?*

Peter slowly lit a match. James looked into the tiny bright flame as Peter held the hook over the flickering fire. "Do it, boys!" Peter shouted. The boys began to pull up one of his pant legs, exposing his pale skin. He tried to scream for help, but one of the boys stuffed a rag into his mouth, silencing him. No one would help him. He was all alone. After a few moments went by, Peter smiled as he leaned in and pressed the rusty hook hard against James' skin. He screamed in pain, but Peter held the hook there until it cooled. To James, the time seemed like forever. Peter laughed as he slowly removed the hook and peeled away melted flesh with it. Feeling very pleased with himself, Peter calmly ordered the boys to let him go, dropping him to the floor. He looked down to see the charred mark of a hook embedded into his skin. His hands trembled. The burning felt like it would last forever. Taunting him, Peter said, "Some pirate you are, crying like a little baby!"

Suddenly, a nun walked in. "Lights out, boys! Get in bed!"

Peter and James looked at each other. Peter waited for him to cry and tell on him, but he didn't. Instead, he crawled his way back to his bed by the window, and as he weakly climbed his way onto the mattress, he heard the boys snickering quietly. "Goodnight, Hook!"

James didn't say anything. He forced himself to climb under the covers and focus on the roaring sounds of thunder outside. Nothing could match the storm that was building inside of him as his tears fell like rain upon his pillow. In that dark room, while all the other boys slept, his pain kept him wide awake. He wished he could escape this place. He wished he could fast forward time to a future out on the sea. He wished he had a friend. But, most of all, he wished he would never again have to set eyes on the hated Peter.

CHAPTER TWO

THE SCARLET FAIRY

After enduring more torturous behavior from the boys in his room, James had a restless night of feeling more alone and hopeless than usual. He peered out his window, as was his custom when things seemed bleak, and watched the moon's reflection on the water. Suddenly, a bright red light out of the corner of his eye caught his attention. When he tried to look directly at it, the small ball of light would move out of view. James tilted his head as he heard music tinkling and chiming. It was beautiful, but unlike any he had heard before. The red light in the room became brighter but didn't touch any other part of the room except for his own bed. Although he did not realize it, he was under its enchantment and felt no fear.

"What are you?" He whispered toward the light but received no answer. Instead, the small ball of red light came directly into his view. It was a tiny woman with large wings. Her long hair was the deepest shade of scarlet red. Every strand of her hair floated in the air around her as if she were underwater. He tried to look into her eyes, but she avoided eye contact. Her skin was very white, almost translucent, and her wings were disproportionately large for her small body. Still, he was in awe of their beauty. As if she had read his thoughts, she smiled proudly, the way one does when given such a compliment. Silence fell over the room. The music, the breathing of the other boys, and noises from men working at the docks below all went silent.

Then the fairy began to talk. "Hello, Sweet James," she said in a soothing voice. Somehow a warm calmness had enveloped him.

"How do you know my name?"

"My kind has a great fondness for names. Yours is a name I learned many years ago. I've been watching you. I've heard your dreams and wishes."

His eyes grew wide. He felt violated. His dreams and wishes were all he possessed as his own. He had never shared them with anyone.

"Don't worry, James. I am in the business of wish granting. I know of your loneliness, and I only desire to give you happiness."

Despite being under her enchantment, he quietly replied, "My dreams are none of your business." Then, he drew his brows together and asked: "How do you know of my dreams?"

Surprised, and a bit offended by his impertinence, the Scarlet Fairy lifted her chin and looked straight into his eyes. The lull dropped, and James suddenly became very afraid. Her eyes were black and deep. He tried to look away but couldn't move. Time seemed to stand still with him stuck in her haunting black gaze burning through him.

Finally, he managed to find his voice. "I am so sorry, ma'am. I meant no disrespect; I was just curious. Please do not be angry with me." Unable to blink his eyes, the burning sensation increased, and tears began to stream down his cheeks. "Please stop; it hurts!"

She nodded and squinted her eyes, releasing him from her power. He closed his eyes and gently rubbed his sore eyelids. Unsure of how long he'd been locked in her black eyes and afraid to open them again, he thanked her for her mercy to avoid upsetting her any further. With his eyes still shut, he began to wonder if she was still there until he heard a giggle that was both soft and deceptively sweet. "Now that things have calmed down, sweet James, I must insist that you do not ever address me in that tone again. Are we clear?" She said in a scolding voice.

He nodded slowly.

"Good. Then I shall answer your rude question. I know about your dreams because the dream world is, in fact, another realm. It is a realm that is much closer to my kind than it is yours. Out of all the realms, my kind can enter the Dream Realm the easiest. We can hear and see what humans dream about: hopes, memories, fears, and no one dreams as much as a lost child. I can hear your dreams even when you are awake. The clearer the dreams are, the more drawn we are to them. I know what you wish for more than anything else in the world: to be a fearsome pirate."

James gasped, opening his sore eyes, but she had already disappeared before he could say anything else. Instantly, he felt immense relief, though he dared not think about it, for now he knew that no thought was private, and though he resisted sleep for fear of the Dream Realm, he eventually drifted off to sleep to helplessly dream again.

CHAPTER THREE

THE HALLS

The next morning, he woke by the usual daily shouting of the nuns entering the room. He thought for a second that maybe the terrifying incident he had endured the night before was just a nightmare, but as he glanced around the room, the lingering pain in his eyes convinced him that the Scarlet Fairy *was* real, and she was watching him. He sat in his bed for a while until it was time for the nuns to take the boys into the classroom for lessons. Peter and the other boys acted foolishly, as usual. They were always utterly uninterested in learning. Usually, James found their behavior annoying, but today he saw it as an opportunity. When the teacher sat down, and it was time for the boys to begin reading, he looked at Peter and his gang playing and laughing, and quietly got up to approach her desk. She looked up curiously at him. "Yes, what can I do for you?" She asked suspiciously looking behind him since this was a usual tactic of one of the other boys to distract her and get away with some nasty scheme.

"Yes, ma'am, I was wondering if I may go to the library? I have read all the books within our room and would enjoy something new to read," he said politely.

She sat straight up in her chair. "I do not intend to go out of my way to take you to the library, just so your friends may get away with whatever it is you are planning!"

He shook his head. "No, ma'am. I really do just want something new to read. Believe me; those boys are no friends of mine," he assured her.

She suspiciously raised her left eyebrow, "What kind of book?"

He looked down, suddenly realizing he wasn't sure. The teacher's face grew impatient.

When he froze, she merely nodded with a smirk. "That's what I thought."

He turned to go back to his desk when the words hit him: "Fairy tales!"

"Did you say fairy tales?" She asked sounding slightly stunned.

"Yes, ma'am. I would like to learn about-*fairies*," he said before clasping his lips shut. Fairy *tales* was what he meant to say, but the truth slipped out. He instantly worried if anyone else had heard him.

She looked at him in such a way that struck James as fear. "You've nothing to gain from such nonsense! Go back to your seat, young man!" She demanded. James didn't understand, but he did as he was told and walked back to his small desk in the back of the classroom. Though she remained quiet for the rest of the class, he was sure he could see her watching him out of the corner of his eye. It was only a short while longer until the class would be dismissed, and all the boys quickly ran to the door almost trampling each other to leave. James was the last, but just as he stepped outside the door, the teacher grabbed his shoulder. At first, he was startled. His mind wandered, worried and afraid that maybe the Scarlet Fairy would know he had been trying to learn about her kind and would punish him. His breath came back to him when he realized it was just the teacher.

"Yes, ma'am?" He asked looking up into her eyes, and again he could see a tinge of fear. She guided him back into the room and closed the door behind her. It was then that he worried he might be in trouble.

"Sit down, boy," she said coldly. He sat down in a desk directly in front of her. James had never been alone with one of the nuns. They were intimidating figures, cold and harsh. At this moment, her fear exposed her as being as vulnerable as he was. They both sat quietly for a few minutes; a fact that was making James' anxiety grow by the second. "I want you to dismiss this recent interest of yours completely. No good can come from it. Do you understand?" She asked in a stern tone.

"Yes, ma'am."

"Good. Now go to your room," she said as if she instantly felt relieved by his obedience.

James got up and made his way to the door, but as he opened it, he thought of something and looked back at her. "By the way, ma'am, my name is Jam-."

"Your name is immaterial and therefore will be of no importance to anyone here. So, you need not parade about, announcing it as if you are royalty," she said very harshly.

James nodded and walked out into the hall, but before he got to the door of his room, he realized something. The nuns were known to be cold, but her abrupt halt of his name had made something quite clear. She knew something, and he was going to find out what. As James entered the boy's room, his attention focused on Peter and his friends. They were all crowded around Peter's bed admiring his newest stolen treasures. The boys did this like clockwork every day. In the past, he wished he was included in Peter's trickery, but now he found it stupid and childish. After all, the things they stole were nothing but random pieces of junk. Sometimes they would acquire something of value, like a pocket watch or chocolate from the kitchen. But, most of the time, it was something small and useless, such as one of the nun's toothbrushes or pieces of silverware. Peter was always immensely proud of his stolen items and collected them under his mattress. All the nuns knew it was Peter that was responsible for the petty thefts, but none had ever caught him in the act, nor could they figure out where the objects were hidden. James didn't understand how they couldn't find them. It was not like it was a clever place. Every so often, one of the nuns managed to catch one of Peter's friends in the act, and they were punished, but never Peter. He was never caught. When James sat on his bed, he suddenly noticed something as he watched Peter showing off his latest victory. He had held up an unfamiliar book. He must have stolen it from the library or maybe even from one of the nun's rooms. None of the other boys would dare such a venture, but Peter thrived off such a challenge.

Suddenly, Peter looked up as if he sensed he was being watched. James quickly looked away and gazed out the window. In the distance, a large ship was going towards the horizon. *They are going off on an exciting adventure,* he thought. *I need to be brave and daring if I am to ever become a pirate sailing the open seas. I need to watch and learn how Peter is stealing these things. I need to know more about fairies, and I certainly cannot ask the red one directly.* The mere thought of the Scarlet Fairy made his eyes burn. He needed to find the library, but he had to be very careful not to be caught. Everyone knew the nun's punishments were severe, but in the end, James was more afraid of what the Scarlet Fairy could do to him. He had to know what she wanted from him- no matter the cost. As the day passed, James remained very focused on Peter, trying very hard not to think about the fairy. Not only because the thoughts were frightening, but also because he feared she could hear them somehow. Just as dusk fell, James could see that Peter was growing bored and restless. He watched as his friends began to approach quiet old Sister Mary, sitting in the room. There wasn't always a nun in the room to watch them, but if there was, Peter saw it as just another obstacle. It was not a risk any of the other boys would take alone, but they were always willing to be a distraction during one of Peter's daring escapes.

James slowly got down on the floor by his bed. It was dirty and old. He couldn't help but see all the broken cracks and filth on the floor as he slowly moved his small body towards the door. He couldn't see anyone's face but instead kept an eye on Peter's feet. Peter had been given the same shoes as all the rest of the boys, but he was always barefoot if he could get away with it. James didn't know why anyone would want to walk on the floors barefoot. He felt sick just thinking about it. Still, he knew he had to be quick if he was going to get on Peter's tail. James was only a few feet away hiding under one of the beds closest to the door when he saw it slightly open. It was then that he watched Peter's dirty bare feet slide swiftly into the dark hallway, and within a moment, he was gone. James looked up very slowly; his eyes reaching barely above the mattress. No one was looking, and Peter's friends were still crowded around the old nun. James crawled towards the door and gently twisted the doorknob. He could feel his heart racing and sweat starting to trickle down his face. He felt both afraid and excited as he opened the door just enough to slide his body into the darkness on the other side. James let out a quiet breath. He was out.

He looked left and right looking for any sign of which way Peter went, but the orphanage was big, and he had never explored it before. He did not want to get lost and be unable to get back to his room before anyone noticed his absence. Suddenly up ahead, he spotted something. It was very dark, but as James' eyes adjusted, he could make out the faint shadow of a boy. He knew it was Peter and started to walk towards him when suddenly he heard his own shoes squeak against the floor. He froze immediately. Then he saw the shadow quickly run and disappear down the far-left hallway. He slowly squatted down and reluctantly took his shoes off, but he couldn't bring himself to take off his socks.

He decided to start walking around on his own. There was no need to follow Peter anymore, as there was no telling where he was going. James was unsure which direction would lead him to the library. So, he just kept an eye on all the room numbers. He seemed to be going to the older part of the building, as the numbers were getting bigger and that's where the older children's rooms were located. That meant that the next hallway was where the staff's bedrooms were. James knew he needed to be extremely careful. Peter must have been heading down towards the kitchen at the farthest part of the second hallway, at least that's the direction he thought he saw him going. There was very little light, and it was hard to see anything. His eyesight was not the best, but the children in the orphanage would never be given glasses, no matter how badly they needed them.

At the end of the long hallway, there was a set of double doors, but there were no markings or windows on them. He put his hand on the door and tried to turn the knob, but it was stuck. It didn't feel as if it was locked, just difficult to turn. He put both hands on the knob and twisted with all the strength he had in his arms. Finally, the door flew open and something very heavy fell on top of him. James hit the hard floor, causing a loud booming sound to echo down the narrow hallway. He had just begun to reach his hand up behind his throbbing head when he suddenly heard a groaning noise above him. When he opened his eyes to see what had fallen on top of him, horror-struck him. *It was Peter!* They looked into each other's eyes for a second. before they both heard the dreaded sound of all the doors in the hallway creaking open around them. Peter and James both looked up to see all the nuns coming out of their rooms, walking towards them with candles lighting up the dark hallway. Both boys stood up, but there was nowhere to run. They were both caught. James fearfully looked up into the cruel eyes of the boy he hated. The uncatchable Peter was caught, and it was all his fault. Two of the nuns approached them and grabbed them both tightly by their ears and began to pull them down the hallway. James should have had a billion thoughts racing through his mind, but at this moment, all he could think was: *Peter is going to kill me!*

CHAPTER FOUR

THE FAIRY RULES

The boys were dragged back to their room, but only James was thrown inside, leaving Peter and the nun holding his pinched ear in the open doorway for everyone to see, gaining the embarrassing attention from all the boys within the room. James could see what they were all thinking: *What was he doing with Peter?* The nun that had thrown him yelled in a stern voice, "Get in your bed, boy! You will be dealt with in the morning!" Then she turned and looked at Peter... everyone did. James half expected him to look embarrassed or afraid, but he just glared right back at the nun with a smug smirk on his face. James had never seen him look so calm and devious before this moment, and it seemed only to intensify the nun's anger. "And as for you! I have waited for this moment a long time. I knew we would catch you in the act one day. We'll fix that devil smile on your face! You are coming with us!" She said before slamming the door closed. James sat on his bed stunned and afraid. He knew the worse this was for Peter; the worse things would be for him.

There was no clock in the room, so he could not tell how long Peter had been gone, but he did know it had been a long time. The next few hours went by slowly. When it was time for all the boys to go to bed, each fell sound asleep, while he lay wide awake for fear of both the wrath of Peter and the possible return of the Scarlet Fairy. He didn't know which would be worse. His stomach began to ache from the fear and worry. He could not do anything but just lay in bed and cry until he eventually drifted off to sleep. He began to dream of many voices. Many were telling him how worthless he was; how nobody in the world loved him, and how he would never become a pirate. This kind of dream was unusual for James. They were usually filled with adventures upon a large beautiful ship with a crew that both feared and loved him. His dreams had always been an escape from this horrible place, but this... this was a *nightmare*.

Suddenly, he could hear Peter's voice in the distance: "Wake up and face me! Wake up and face me! You're going to pay for what you've done! Wake up and..." Suddenly James woke up to being shaken back and forth. Then something hit his stomach hard, knocking the wind out of him. "Wake up and face me!" Peter screamed right in his face.

James' eyes shot open! Peter was sitting on his stomach, straddling him and was shaking him by his shoulders. "Get off of me!" He shouted over and over, but Peter didn't listen. Then finally, as if maybe his arms were tired, Peter stood up on top of the bed. For a second, James thought he was going to get down, but then Peter started bouncing on the bed, kicking his sides, his stomach, and even his face. He screamed in pain, "Help! Somebody, help me, please!" He cried trying to look around, but there was not a nun in the room tonight. Then suddenly Peter stopped, letting him think it was over, but it was just a cruel trick. *This was not over.*

"Come on, boys!" Peter shouted out of breath. He jumped off the bed as his friends approached James crying and bleeding all over his bed. By this point, James was quiet as each of the boys got their hits in. All the while, he could hear the cruel laughter coming from the bed next to his, and though he could no longer see out of either of his swollen eyes, he knew it was Peter. It was a wicked sound he would never forget. After all the boys had worn themselves out, they all went back to their beds, but Peter just sat on the bed next to his. The pain had left him numb to all but one thing- Peter's psychotic stare. James' body soon gave into the darkness of exhaustion. It had been so hard to breathe; he feared he would not wake up in the morning. As he slipped into a fitful and broken sleep, his face swollen and covered with the uncomfortable sensation of blood drying and cracking upon his skin, James' head was ringing. Whether his ears were still chiming from the slamming of their fist or it was the ominous bells of the Scarlet Fairy approaching, he would never truly know. He did not dream about anything that night, but he had lived a real nightmare.

He woke the next morning to a loud gasp. He couldn't open his eyes, but he could hear a nun's voice: "Oh, my poor child. Can you hear me?" Her voice sounded horrified. James could suddenly feel all the pain surging through his body. He couldn't move. All he could let out was a weak cry as a single tear fell out from one of his swollen eyes and down his beaten face. "Poor dear, don't try to move. Sister Lois, call for the doctor right away!" She ordered, her voice cracking as if she might cry. It suddenly became clear that she thought he might die, and honestly- he wished for it. He felt her hand pick up his and hold it gently. "It is going to be alright, child. I will not leave your side; I promise."

James had never felt this cared for, but this moment was too horrible for him to feel anything but severe pain. He began to fall in and out of consciousness, only waking to a spike of pain from someone examining his mangled body. It would only last a moment before he would fade back into the darkness. This went on for the rest of the day, and James felt sure he would die, but the next morning he woke to the same sweet voice he had heard before. His eyes could still not open, and his body felt strange and fuzzy. He was neither able to move or in any pain. He tried to focus on the nun's voice. It was so calming and nurturing. She didn't leave his side all day, just as she promised. In and out of consciousness, he could hear her kind voice singing or even reading to him. James wished he could see her. He knew every part of him was broken, but somehow this had brought him a mother. But as he fell asleep, his feeling of joy disappeared when the sound of her singing slowly changed into something sinister and whimsical. It was both beautiful and frighteningly familiar. Then through the darkness, he saw a small red light coming towards him.

"Poor Sweet James." The silhouette of a fairy began to form in front of the light when his eyes started to burn. Then suddenly he woke up, his eyes opening as he could feel two streams of blood running down from the top of his eyelids.

He looked above him to see a doctor holding a tiny blade. "There you go, son. Now doesn't that feel a lot better?"

James couldn't reply but was able to barely nod his head.

Then he listened as the doctor told the nuns of his condition. "He will need to be on bed rest for quite some time, many bones are broken, and I fear one of his broken ribs may have punctured his left lung. I will distribute pain medicine so that he won't be too terribly uncomfortable, but I make no promises for a full recovery. Have you found out who did this?"

"Yes, we have," the nun answered. Her voice trailed off for a second and James tried to listen harder. "I fear we are to blame. We should have known that the devil child would do something, but we never imagined he would retaliate as far as this. He has been moved into Room 714. I'm happy to say that these two boys will unlikely ever see each other again."

"Mm-hmm," the doctor replied. "Well, thank our good lord for that."

James should have felt happy or at least relieved, but he couldn't feel much of anything. He couldn't stop feeling such utter exhaustion. His body felt fuzzy, and his mind was in a fog, but he didn't want to go back to sleep. He almost wished they would stop giving him the medicine. The pain would at least keep him awake with the nun that was taking care of him, instead of the Scarlet Fairy that would surely be waiting for him in his dreams. He heard the doctor's footsteps as he walked away, and the nun sat back down in the chair next to his bed. She picked up his small hand with hers. He could barely feel it, but it helped that her hand was cold. His eyes were still very swollen and very tired, but he was determined to see her face. He slightly tilted his head towards her and opened his eyes as wide as they would go. His vision was a bit blurry, but within a few seconds, she came into focus. To his surprise, it was the same nun that had taught his class the day he had asked to go to the library. *Why had she seemed so different?* He had been so sure she would be a stranger to him. Her eyes, once so cold and harsh, were now so concerned and loving. James saw her smile at him in an encouraging way, and he tried to smile back.

She must have seen it because her smile widened, and she leaned in to whisper to him. "There you are," she said sweetly. She suddenly looked around her, as if making sure no one would hear her. "I know what you were after the other night. I know why you were trying to sneak into the library. I don't blame you, child; I blame myself. If only I had been honest with you, maybe you would not be in this horrible state. But you must understand, I was just trying to protect you. I'm afraid your misadventure was doomed from the beginning. You see, all of the fair..." Her voice broke off like she dared not say the words. "The stories you seek were taken out of the library long ago, in the hope that if children didn't know about them, maybe those evil things would stay away," she said sadly. He could hear the guilt in her voice, but he did not blame her or any of the nuns for this, just Peter and his friends. Just the thought of Peter fueled a fire of hatred deep inside of him that he knew was the beginning of something terrible. She collected herself and began to speak again: "I know things seem hopeless right now my dear, but you must not give in to those thoughts. The evil out there can sense it, and I fear that not I, nor any other nun here can protect you. I've looked over your small body all night, and I know you must have been very desperate if you were willing to put yourself in such danger. Well, I have decided not to let your effort go unrewarded, though I pray that what I'm about to tell you does not put you in more danger. Blink your eyes twice if you can hear what I am saying. I want to be sure you understand and heed my every warning."

James blinked twice.

"Good, now listen carefully, for we do not have much time before you will be given your next dose of medicine, and it will surely put you asleep." She bent forward as to whisper close to his ear. "Let me begin by asking: have you been visited by one of them? Blink twice if you have. It's important that I know what has already happened. I know you cannot talk right now, but please; I need you to answer my questions okay?"

James blinked twice, eager to reveal his dark secret. He heard the nun sigh sadly as if she still had some small hope that he hadn't.

"Now I want you to answer my next question honestly. Have they offered any promises to you yet?"

Yet? He thought back to the conversation with the Scarlet Fairy. He did not think so. He wanted to be sure and answer the nun honestly. He must have been taking too long because the nun said his name urgently, worried what his hesitance meant. But he needed a moment to think about it. The Scarlet Fairy had mentioned his hopes and dreams and said she had been watching him, but he did not recall any offers being made. *He blinked once.*

She let out a breath of relief. "Thank the heavens, my dear boy. In that case, I may still have help to offer," she said, pulling her chair closer to his bed. "Alright, I must keep this short, because your previous dose of medicine is wearing off. I need you to follow these very important rules, for they may revisit you tonight. I've had children tell me about the visits in their dreams, and while I promise I will not leave your side tonight, I do not pretend I know how to protect you in your dreams. I shall spend another restless night praying the words of god next to you. Are you ready for the rules?" She asked in a more serious tone.

James quickly blinked twice.

"I must tell you that these rules apply whether you are awake or not. Even if it does not seem real, you must know that it always is. The hidden people can easily trick you, so you must be very- very careful to not do any of these things: First, never accept a gift, even if it appears free. It never is. Second, never eat or drink anything they offer you. It may look delicious. You may feel very hungry or extremely thirsty, but you must not accept it. Those who have, have gone mad. Human food or drink will never again sate your appetite again, forcing you to go to their realm if you want to survive. Third, be polite, very polite. They are easily offended, but you should never say thank you. These words to them mean that you owe them something, or it is just taken as an insulting too little reward for what they have done for you. And last, no matter what they promise or how hopeless they make your life seem... Do not ever follow the music. Now blink twice if you heard and understood every word that I've said?"

James blinked twice.

"Good, my boy- good," she said using her sweet tone again. Suddenly, James began feeling fuzzy all over, and he knew she had given him his medicine. His eyes instantly felt heavy, but this time he didn't fight it. He closed them, ready to bravely face the Scarlet Fairy, with his mother holding his small hand again, letting him know she would be right next to him.

CHAPTER FIVE

FAIRY DREAMS

James' mind went to the sea. Beautiful waves crashed against the sides of a large ship as he looked straight ahead at the horizon. In the distance, there was a beautiful island. He heard cheers roaring from the faceless men aboard. They chanted his name, but it was not 'James' he heard. It was 'Hook! Hook! Hook!' James turned his back to them, for he dared not show them his smile. Even in dreams, James did not want to appear weak to anyone.

As they sailed closer to the large island, he saw it was almost completely covered in trees. Not palm trees as he had seen in many pictures, but many different types of trees, standing very tall above the shore. Everything was green and alive, and the water glittered like diamonds under the sun. It was a magical paradise. James had seen many places in dreams and storybooks, but none like this one. Within minutes, the waves carried the ship close to the shore, and the crew jumped down onto the beach. When James made his way onto the shore, he noticed the sand was neither brown nor white. Instead, they were specks of gold. He bent down to gently scoop a handful of the shining grains of sand and watched as they fell back to the ground through his fingers. He smiled as he stood. The men ran around, greedily stuffing their pockets full of the golden sand, shouting: "Captain! Captain, you must take these riches! Take some! Take some!" They insisted. "Put some in your coat! Take as much as you'd like!"

He smiled and bent down to take some of the sand for himself when a sick feeling came over him. He heard the nun's voice in his head: "Remember the rules, James."

Quickly, he dropped the sand and rubbed his hands against his long coat to be sure not a single grain was left on his person. "I want none of it!" He shouted, looking towards the forest of trees. He watched as the forest darkened and the woods turned as black as night. The darkness spread out onto the sand, getting closer to him and his crew. It was now clear that this was a dangerous place. For a moment, he could have sworn he heard bells chiming from the forest. Suddenly, a narrow trail appeared out of nowhere. He was not fooled, but his men began following the music.

"Come, Captain! We should all follow the music and find its source! I want to see more of the island. Don't you, sir?" Asked one of his mates.

But James did not move a muscle. He felt the music pulling him, and decided it was time to leave. "Come, men!" He shouted, but the crew continued forward. "Men! It is my order that you remove all sand from your pockets, and be sure to leave all of it, for it has come to my attention that the riches from this place is a cursed treasure! Hurry, men! Let us leave this cursed paradise far behind us!" He demanded. Suddenly, the crew's faces rapidly turned to him with pitch black eyes. The horrific sight shot him wide awake. He groaned in agony.

"He's awake! Get his medicine now!" His mother screamed. He continued to whimper in pain, but he wanted to see her face after such a challenging night. She smiled at him as she bent down to look him in the face. Her eyes were sky blue and very kind. She caressed the side of his cheek. "Did you remember the rules?"

James nodded gently.

"And you didn't break any, did you?"

James' body burned with agony as he blinked once.

She smiled happily. "Thank God, my child. I wish I could say this was over, but I know that it is not. You are such a brave boy. I promise I will help you to the best of my ability. I will tell you everything I know."

James was exhausted. Every day and night became a battle. Here he was, almost beaten to death, bedridden, and tormented with nightmares each time he slept. He didn't know if he could handle much more of this. He felt agonizing pain coursing through him with each breath. He worried that he might never heal. A nurse gave him more medicine. He tried to shake his head to tell her, no, but he still couldn't speak. He was utterly helpless as the dose flowed through him. It made him feel heavy and numb, but he kept his eyes wide open. He couldn't face the horrors in his dreams again. Fearing he would fail the next time; he began to cry. He thought himself a coward, but he couldn't help it anymore. He could feel himself giving up. Nobody could truly help him; the magic was just too powerful and played by its own rules. It was unfair.

His mother stood over him and used a small cloth to wipe away his tears. "Shh," she whispered. He looked up into her eyes as tears welled up inside of them. "Don't give up, James. Please, don't give up," she said with tears streaming down her tired face. He could see she was tired and frightened. He wasn't in this battle alone. She was doing all she could to fight by his side, and it meant everything to him. They had become very important to each other, and he knew he would have already given up without her. She began humming to him as she continued to dry his tears and caress his small face. "Oh, how I wish you knew how much I admire you. You've been so strong and brave. I need to be brave too." She looked down as she gathered her courage. "Through the many years I've been here, the nuns have heard many stories of fairies. At first, I admit I thought it utter nonsense. That is until the children began disappearing. People said the children must have just run away, and that's what the people out there still believe. We let them believe it. The children were never found. Some of the staff began to notice a pattern surrounding the odd circumstances of how those children behaved before their disappearances. We heard them talking to thin air, and when we questioned them, we heard about offerings and gifts from a beautiful fairy. The description of the fairy varied from each child, but consistently, there were the inevitable dreams. Sometimes a child behaved as though everything in the world was hopeless and told us a fairy would soon take them somewhere to be loved and live happily. One by one, they disappeared. The staff took measures to ensure security: windows were locked, and doors were chained. Still, children disappeared. The police never found any of them. When other children asked about their missing friends, we simply said they were put in another room. We didn't know what was happening. You must understand that it was difficult for us to believe something so strange. After all, I had never actually seen a fairy, but when impossible things continue to happen, one must wonder. I decided to learn about them. I read every book I could find, and I discovered very quickly that all the things those children told me were real. Once the fae have their wicked heart set on you..." She began to cry.

James didn't know why he had become so special to her, but he knew this was the first time she had talked about this. Her tears pulled at his heart. He would be brave and fight for her sake. "Aww, sweet James. Let's not give up now. We must have faith," she said straightening herself in her chair. "I will bring some books from my room. There are many stories concerning fairies and children. They hold important information. I'll be right back," she said before leaving the room. James laid on the bed, closing his eyes.

When the door opened again, he jolted in alarm. "It is just me, dear. I brought my books. There is one I think you will particularly like. It is an anthology of fairy tales: stories of brave knights that fight ferocious dragons, and lovely damsels in distress. These stories prove that if you are brave- good will prevail! Evil is always defeated in the end. That's what we shall do. You must continue to be strong and brave. Will you do that?" She asked sweetly.

James lowered his eyes: he wasn't ready to be brave again. No, he couldn't blink his eyes to signal 'yes' to her yet. She waited for his eyes to show any sign of hope, but she saw none. She believed he needed more reason to feel confident, so she leaned back in her chair and opened a large blue book. The leather was worn, and the pages were old and fragile. She carefully turned the first few pages. James listened as she read aloud stories ending in '*happily ever after.*' Soon, he was completely lost in her stories. With every tale, she read from her large book, and every sweet caress from her nurturing hand- he felt safe and loved. Throughout the pain of healing and the nightmares, she'd made him believe in happy endings. In moments where his fear returned, or his pain increased, she reached for the book and eased his mind. His imagination was so carried away with her stories; he didn't notice the exhaustion in her voice. In the passing hours, her voice had begun to trail off, and she began to fall asleep. He was afraid to be alone, but he could see now, that she no longer had the strength to stay awake. James didn't utter a sound to wake her. He kept very quiet in an attempt to give her peace. He felt it was his turn to be the hero and watch over her.

The ticking of the clock was the only sound James could hear besides the occasional steps of someone passing in the hallway. The room was now well lit from the morning sun coming in through the windows. This fact and that he knew everyone else in the orphanage was wide awake and walking around brought him comfort, but soon, his medicine had worn off, and his pain returned. Each breath he took was like a fire being set in his bones. Still, he would not wake her. He distracted himself by thinking of the stories she had read to him- of heroes and villains. *They all ended happily, but how did he get involved in such a story like this? He was no prince or knight. He was a small orphan boy. How could he become a hero?* He pondered that point and eventually, the sound of the clock ticking was the last thing he heard before falling fast asleep.

At first, he couldn't see anything. It was pitch black, yet he felt very alert. He felt as though he were standing in a black hole with nothing around him. He couldn't hear or see anything. There was a feeling deep in his gut that he was in a terrible place. The darkness was bringing a feeling of despair that started to crawl within him as if this feeling was alive and sentient. Up ahead, he saw a small light. It was bright like a piece of the sun had pierced through the darkness and it was the only opening in sight. The light grew bigger and brighter as he drew closer to the opening of what now appeared to be a tiny keyhole. He reached out his hand looking for a doorknob, but as soon as he touched it, he screamed. It burned him. He realized if he wanted to get through the door, he'd have to burn his hand- badly. It was the cost to get out of the darkness.

James braced himself as best he could and grabbed the doorknob with his small right hand, a decision he wished he had thought through since he was right-handed. The knob was difficult to turn as if it hadn't moved in a long time. He didn't let go, for he knew if he did, he would not be able to bring himself to do this again. He felt his skin searing. The smell was terrible. Finally, the door cracked and as James went to let go, some of his singed skin remained on the knob. The pain was horrific. He screamed in agony as he grabbed his wrist to look at the gruesome sight in front of him.

Suddenly, he could hear laughter coming from behind him. He stopped screaming as he slowly turned around to see an endless number of tiny eyes glowing in the darkness. He quickly moved the edge of the door the rest of the way with his arm and walked through it. When he kicked the large door shut, he realized that the door wasn't attached to anything. It was just standing there on the sand. He turned around to see that he was now in a desert. The sand went on and on with no grass or water in sight. There was not a single cloud in the sky, and the air around him was sweltering. He walked through the hot sand. His eyes began to burn from the sun, and his clothes were now completely drenched in sweat, and he realized he was very thirsty. He continued forward, despite not knowing where he was or how long he'd been walking, but the sun didn't change to indicate any time has passed. He knew he had been tricked and didn't know what to do next. If only he knew the right direction, he wouldn't feel so helpless. There was nothing in sight.

Then suddenly, he saw something move. It was his shadow, playfully dancing in front of him. He stopped walking, completely in awe. It waved at him and then continued dancing around, taunting him. He felt angry and quickened his pace, pretending he didn't see it. As more sweat dripped from his tired body, he felt his body weakening. He needed water, and there was nothing in sight... nothing but his playful shadow which seemed to be getting more excited and energetic. It was as if it was gaining the very energy he was losing. He needed to rest.

Eventually, he gave in, sitting down on the hot sand and trying to keep his eyes open. Feeling himself burning in the hot sun, he silently wished he had stayed in the darkness. He looked at his hand; it was a gory sight and extremely painful. He wanted to cry, but he couldn't. His body had no more liquid to give. Suddenly, his shadow stopped dancing and sat in front of him. The shadow's head tilted slightly, and James imitated it without thinking. Then the shadow looked to the left, and James followed it. There, a few feet away, was a small pool of water. The top of the water was shaded, and James noticed the sun was not in the water's reflection at all, yet the water was shining all on its own, illuminating from within. With all his strength, he crawled weakly towards the water, following the shadow. He watched as it picked up a small bit of water and brought it slowly to its mouth. James suddenly realized how dry his mouth was. He bent down to touch the water, but something stopped him. He wasn't sure what it was, but something powerful within him told him not to touch it. But as he opened his eyes to see the glittering water again, he couldn't help himself any longer. He leaned in to take a drink when he heard a voice screaming his name from behind him.

"James! James! No!"

He turned to see it was his mother. She was standing there on the sand behind him. James froze as he looked up at her. There was a cool breeze coming from her direction. *How was she here? Was this another trick? This couldn't be real,* he thought. There was something different about her face. There was a serenity about her. He had seen her look stern, worried, sad, and kind, but through almost all her expressions, he had felt love, and that was more apparent now than ever. She reached out her arms for him. Although James didn't know what to make of this strange turn of events, he walked into her arms, and let her hold him. He closed his eyes as he laid his weak head upon her shoulder. "I cannot stay long, my child. I wanted to see you one last time," she said as she caressed his cheek like she always did when comforting him.

James shook his head in confusion: "What do you mean, one last time?" He asked feeling his chest become tight.

She tilted her head slightly and smiled at him. "Don't worry, James. You are safe now. When we couldn't get you to wake, I summoned the fairy myself and made a wish to protect you. No fairy can harm you in any way again. The Scarlet Fairy and I struck a bargain, and not even the fairies, with all their powers, can break a deal. It is magic's most Absolute Law."

He didn't understand, now feeling a sharp pain in his chest, like he could actually feel his heart being ripped apart. "Deal? Bargain? What did you do?" Panic overtook him as he screamed in a hoarse voice: "No! This is just a dream! I just need to wake up and this horrible nightmare to come to an end. I will wake up, and you will be there, waiting for me," he said with his voice shaking. But deep down, he knew he was wrong.

She shook her head slowly as she gently held his small face in both her hands. "Goodbye, James. Be safe," she whispered, pulling his head down so she could gently kiss his forehead, causing him to wake instantly.

He was back in his bed. He quickly looked over to her chair, but she wasn't there. A surge of horror came over him as he looked down to find her lifeless body lying on the floor next to her chair. James screamed and cried out for help. Many nuns ran into the room to see what was wrong. They gasped at the sight of her. He reached out for her screaming and crying. His body ached, but that couldn't stop him from crawling off the bed and hitting the floor. Every bone in his body burned in agony as he crawled over to her dead body. He wrapped his arms around her. It took five of the other nuns and the doctor to pull him off and carry her away. He used all the strength he could to keep her, but they had overpowered him. Suddenly, he felt the pinch of the doctor giving him a shot that brought him down and then everything went black.

CHAPTER SIX

THE LAST DREAM

In the darkness, James soon realized he was in the middle of the woods. As he looked to the left, he saw an impenetrable fog, but when he looked towards the right, he noticed the air was completely clear. The top of the trees was dead, with the cold touch of winter, whereas the bottom and the brush on the ground were full of bright green leaves. Despite the thick fog, he decided to walk down the trail of the path on the left side of the forest. He began to see the beauty in these strange woods, but he did not trust any of it. He didn't understand why he was here, or what he was supposed to see, but he suddenly felt like he was being watched.

It was them.

He could see their breath in the fog around him. They were close, but he couldn't see them. "Show yourselves! I know you can hear me, you cowards! I demand you show yourselves!" He screamed into the open woods. Finally, the Scarlet Fairy appeared. Her red glowing light intensified with anger as she flew towards him. He attempted to grab her as quickly as he could, "I'm going to tear off your wings and rip out your heart!" He shouted in ragged breaths, trying to grab her, she just ascended higher in the air- to remain safely out of his reach. She stared down at him vacantly. He knew she wanted to hurt him, but her efforts were worthless. The fairy no longer had power over him, and they both knew it. Unable to resist, a smirk appeared on James' face.

"What makes you so happy, boy? Do you not mourn the loss of the old woman? How is it the *'lost boy with no one to love him'* is smiling at me?" She asked sardonically. Her choice of words was precise and aimed to hurt him where it would hurt the most. He imagined his revenge, remembering the tales from the book. All the while, staring at the Scarlet Fairy flying anxiously around him. He could tell she was greatly agitated that he didn't respond; that there was no fear spread across his face. Something deep within him had changed. "I see the fire burning within you, boy. Your hatred radiates brightly from your bitter little soul. I can almost taste it. I almost regret taking that pitiful, kind-hearted soul of hers," she said smugly.

"Oh, trust me. You will regret it," he said in an eerily calm voice.

The Scarlet Fairy froze, stupefied in one place. At that moment, James felt the weather change. Everything suddenly moved more rapidly, as if stirred by her fury. It wasn't what he had said that bothered her, but the absolute certainty in his tone. Suddenly, James could hear whispers from all the hidden people around them. Looked around, she screamed: "Silence!" The red light illuminating from her was now beaming brighter than he had ever seen it before. She was livid.

Still, he continued, "You can no longer hear my thoughts or see my dreams. You can't touch me! You have absolutely no power over me!"

"You should be grateful to the woman who gave up her soul in exchange for your protection from us- for if she did not, I would..."

"That's right- she did! But you have no such protection from me!" James rebuked. "And I will spend the rest of my life hunting you and your kind to annihilation."

"Then you shall have a very lonely and bitter life, for my kind will never tell you where we are, and we will not seek you out ever again. So, this is where we part ways, James. I am sure we are unlikely ever to see each other again," she said with her eyes fixated on his.

"Then why are you sweating?"

She quickly wiped her pale face, also hoping to remove her discontent. Collecting herself for the sake of the many eyes on her, she giggled. "You are still very young, James, but it is of little matter. For you fragile mortals, time is so short. You will have long forgotten me in the days not far beyond."

James smiled and whispered, "If it takes my entire lifetime... make no mistake about it; I *will* kill you."

After a heavy breath, she turned her back to him and said, "Then you'd better hurry, for the clock is already ticking against you." Before disappearing into the darkness, she couldn't resist looking back once at the boy. James stood bravely and waved goodbye to her with his insufferable smile still on his face. When James awoke, he remained quiet and listened to the clock ticking. He didn't respond whenever someone spoke to him. He wouldn't even look at them. He stared into nothingness, always ready for his next dose of medicine, ready to return to sleep. Night after night, his dreams would take him to a strange place, but he was always alone and never in danger. He was not discouraged, for he now looked at the dream world as something to wander and explore. He knew he would find the fae eventually. All he needed to do was listen for the sound of bells, and then- he would follow the music. As each day and night went by, James healed more and more. He was asked to stand and move around the large room several times a day. Then one day he heard a couple of the nuns talking about him far off in the corner of the room. They were whispering, but James' senses had heightened somehow, making it possible to understand most of what they were saying.

"The boy will be ready soon."

"But he seems so- you know, after seeing Sister Roger die like that."

"I know. I know. I heard that she left a note asking that her books be given to the boy, but I think the very idea is nonsense, and will only cause the child more damage."

"But Father Michael has insisted that we obey her last wishes."

There was a moment of muffled words that James couldn't quite make out, but then suddenly he heard one of the nun's voices speak up again: "They are going to put him in the room for disturbed children. After all, the poor child is absolutely broken, and we can't have him talking about those evil creatures to the other children and putting them in any danger."

"That is, if he ever talks again," said the other voice.

"At least in room 714, anything he says will just be declared the crazy ramblings of a troubled child."

"Yes, it's for the best.

CHAPTER SEVEN

ROOM 714

When the nuns were done talking, they opened the door and walked out of the room. James' heart began to race- not out of fear, but rather thrilling anticipation. He was getting his mother's books. He could learn all the things his mother had known about the fae, and maybe even summon one as she had done. Then, there was Peter to consider also. *Ah, Peter- Peter- Peter.* The very name was like fuel feeding a deadly fire. James had never imagined he would see him again, let alone, have the chance to exact revenge upon him. Yes, he was truly pleased with this news. The thoughts of what he would do to him stirred wildly in his mind. After all, James did have an excellent imagination. Not even Peter himself could fathom the darkness that dwelled within him now. There was nothing he, nor any other children could do to harm more than he'd already suffered, and people with nothing left to lose are the most dangerous people of all. He had been to hell and back both physically and mentally. And now, he felt invincible.

That night, he dreamed of Peter. He was chasing him with a large metal rod broken off from one of the beds. Peter ran from him, hiding in different rooms, but he always found and beat him again and again until his body was covered in bumps and bruises. Through this bloody haze, he realized it was not only about killing Peter himself but what he symbolized: a reminder of the sad and vulnerable boy he once was. *It was Peter who started all of this. If I had never met that demon then I would not have been a lonely boy with only my dreams and wishes, thus attracting terrible evil. If not for Peter, Sister Roger would still be alive. Yes, it is all Peter's fault, and he will pay dearly.*

James woke up the next morning, laughing wickedly. There was a nun in the room watching over him, and she looked at him as if he had gone mad. Today, the doctor was expected to come and evaluate him once more before moving him out of the sick ward and into the room that all the children feared-Room 714. As he waited, James listened anxiously to the ticking clock. It was a sound he had come to hate, for it represented something that had become his enemy- *time.* James had found that time had always been against him. It would linger, sometimes stretching a mere second into thousands. When he needed it to pass quickly, it would spitefully standstill or take moments that were the most precious and rip them away instantly. Time with his mother had been too short, yet his moments of torture felt like they would last forever. Yes, he hated time. It was an unbeatable force that wore you down. *When I am grown, I will destroy every clock I see. I will not be taunted by the constant reminder from its instrument of cruelty, the ticking-tock of the clock.*

The doctor arrived early in the afternoon. He examined each of his ribs, arms, legs, and collar bone. Everything was fine. Then, the doctor asked him to stand and walk around the room once more for good measure. James silently obeyed. His body had healed very well, and as expected; the doctor decided it was time for him to be moved. He instructed one of the nuns to escort him down the hallway into the left wing of the orphanage. Room 714 was the last room on the right. It was very far away from the room he had previously been in with the rest of the other boys his age. They had all heard the disturbing screams and strange voices echoing down the hallway whenever the door cracked open. Most of them had heard stories that the room was filled with the ghosts of children that had misbehaved too many times and were then locked away to starve to death. All the children were afraid to go near the room — all, except for one. James stood fearlessly in the doorway. He saw right away that the conditions in this room were far worse than any of the other rooms he had seen. There was a vile stench in the air from all the old soiled mattresses that were lying on rusty bed frames. Dust blanketed everything in the room with a grey layer of shed skin and cobwebs. Nothing was organized, and all the room's toys were old and broken.

Scattered aged books were sitting in the far-right corner. It seemed everything inside this room was filled with all manner of unwanted and unloved things.

There were no pillows on any of the beds, and only half of them had rags for blankets, with torn edges and no color. It was as if they had been worn down to their last layer of thread. And there, sitting on the floor next to the only window, was Peter. He glanced towards the door in surprise. James stepped forward, locking eyes with the boy for a long and intense moment before blocking the closing door behind him with his shoe. Without taking his eyes off Peter, he whispered to the doctor holding the door, "Would you kindly bring me my books, sir?"

The doctor's eyes opened wide in complete shock. He had not heard James speak in so long that he didn't expect he ever would again. He was also taken aback by his demeanor, for it was not like a child at all, but rather a mature adult with authority. "Books?"

"Yes, sir. I would like the books Sister Roger left for me."

The doctor understood his words, yet still felt confused. He wasn't aware the boy knew of the books being left for him. "Yes, sir. I mean, *yes*. She did leave books for you, but we thought it better- or more appropriate if we gave them to you upon your departure as an adult." The doctor felt sheepish. He didn't know why, but he didn't want to upset the boy.

"No, that will not do. I would like to have them now. They are my property now; are they not?" James asked, his stern voice deepening.

"Um, yes, sir, they are, but we don't want the other children to..." The doctor couldn't finish his thought, as he was struck by the fierce intensity of the young boy's eyes. "I will get them."

"Thank you, sir," James said as he removed his foot from the doorway, allowing the door to close. He sauntered across the room, going in between some of the crooked beds spread out chaotically throughout the room. Peter stood, and although he looked neglected and filthy, he held his head high and walked toward him. Most of the children moved out of their way, and the ones that didn't were shoved. As he pushed more of the children around, a familiar psychotic smile spread across his bony face. Finally, he stood before James. He was weaker and thinner, but the evil spirit inside him was still very much alive. Peter noticed something different about James too, but he didn't understand what it was. The tension between them was thick.

Peter spoke first, ever eager to taunt him, "Hello, Hook. Bet you thought you'd never see me again, huh?"

But James didn't say a word. He just stared at Peter. Still, the thoughts of all the horrible and nasty things he had in store for him did manage to bring a sinister smile to his face. In silence, he stepped away to pick up a large candelabra. It felt nice and heavy in his hand. He looked back to verify that he still had his attention- he did. As he looked into his eyes, he blew out the first flame. Peter glared at him. He blew out another; still, Peter didn't say anything as if waiting for what was going to happen next. But once he blew out the third flame, he heard a familiar psychotic laugh. It was a sound that sent chills down his spine. The cold room was now wholly pitch dark as the smell of smoke from the wicks of the candles filled the room.

"Do you really think blowing out those candles will hide you from me?" Peter asked as he walked across the room towards him.

James kept very quiet and still, adjusting his eyes to see his enemy's outline coming closer.

"You better run," Peter taunted.

James smiled as he quietly lifted the candlestick. Peter reached out his arm. *Wack!* Peter fell to the floor, having been struck hard on his head. He reached his hand behind his head and found he was bleeding. Before he could say anything... *Wack!* James struck again. "Oh, Peter, I wasn't hiding from you. I wanted to hurt you without burning myself with hot wax. Though, I'd have gladly burned you with it, if you hadn't taken so long to get over here." *Wack!* "You've rather disappointed me. But, don't worry, this next part is where the real fun begins."

Peter now felt afraid, not being able to see where the next attack might be coming from. Suddenly, he was startled by a loud banging noise, like two metals crashing into each other. He heard it again and again, coming closer. He crawled backward on the floor, trying to get away, but James kept coming towards him. He crawled through the maze of crooked beds around the room, moving as quickly and quietly as possible. But wherever he went, the banging followed him. It wasn't just Peter that was afraid now. James was hitting the bed frames with the candlestick so loudly that it was upsetting the other children. They began to scream and cry. Then suddenly, he saw Peter's panicked silhouette ducking under one of the beds to hide. It was a pathetic effort from James' point of view, as he could hear every breath and see every movement that his prey made. He had expected Peter to be more of a challenge. *This is laughable.*

"Hahaha!" James laughed mockingly. "Come now, Peter. Are we not having fun? Come out and face me!" He screamed while banging the beds even louder as he drew in.

Thinking this was his only chance, Peter carefully slid out from under the bed to regain the upper hand. His breaths were racing, and his heart was pounding, but something about this was thrilling for him too. He had never experienced anything like this before. He was afraid, yet he felt more alive than he did the night he nearly beat the young boy to death.

James smiled as he watched Peter's silhouette come slithering out of hiding and stand. The other children's screams had faded into the background, making James and Peter feel like there was no one else in the world but them. He leaned in and whispered: "Here comes the next part of the game! Are you ready?"

Peter stepped forward bravely and let out a tiny chuckle. "Yes, yes! Let us play!"

But James hadn't only trained his ears to hear Peter; he'd also been listening for any sounds coming from the hall. Peter hadn't heard footsteps coming toward their room, but he had. He left the candelabra on the closest mattress and whispered calmly in Peter's ear again: "The candlestick is on the bed. Take it and give me your best shot." Knowing that Peter would take the bait, he walked back towards the opposite wall and sat on the floor. He watched Peter's silhouette pick up the candlestick and take a few steps forward. He had just managed to bump into one of the beds just when the door to the room opened.

The doctor had returned with James' books and three nuns behind him carried in candlelight. "What is going on here? Why is it so dark?" They all asked, looking around the room. All the children were on the floor screaming and crying — all of them except for Peter, who was looming over them with the candelabra in his hand. "You! I should have known it was you!" One of the nun's said. The other two grabbed him by each of his arms. "Yes, we'll deal with you!" One of the others said as they dragged him out of the room.

James let out a little chuckle as he and Peter's eyes met. Surprisingly, Peter didn't seem angry. Instead, he nodded, as if he was impressed. He did not put up any fight against being dragged out of the room, but he did notice the box stacked with books being brought inside. As the door closed, the nuns continued scolding as they dragged him down the hallway.

No longer concerned with Peter, James watched the doctor bring the box of books to his bed. "Will this be alright for you, sir?"

"Yes, that will be fine, thank you," James replied as he looked around the room. "Doctor, since my body is still in recovery, wouldn't you say it is necessary that I have the proper bedding: pillows, sheets, and a fresh blanket?"

The doctor again found it uncomfortable that this boy not only spoke as an adult but as his superior. He was not frightened of him, but there was something to this boy. The doctor knew about the boy's experience with the fairies, and for a reason unknown to him, Sister Roger had died. The boy had survived the encounters with the little people, but he had come back changed. The doctor understood that the boy's eyes had seen too much, had his heart broken, and survived a fatal beating, but his soul had experienced something no doctor couldn't fathom. The boy hadn't asked for anything unreasonable, so the doctor found no reason to deny his requests. "Yes, I will get better bedding for you. Will you be needing it tonight?" Immediately, the doctor felt like a complete fool for asking such a question.

The expression on James' face indicated he also thought the question was ridiculous, but he remained polite, "Yes, sir. I should like to have them when I sleep tonight."

"Of course," the doctor said before leaving the room.

CHAPTER EIGHT

THE BOOKS

James didn't waste any time. He picked up the first book; the one his mother was reading to him before she died. Holding her book pulled at his heart. What he wanted more than anything right now, was to feel her presence.

The other children were calm again; it was time to search for what he needed. He put the fairy tale book back in the box and reached for an old green book. Its leather cover was so worn that the title wasn't legible. Once opened, he read the title on the old page: *Lore of the Irish Fae.* James carefully turned the delicate pages and began to read tirelessly. Chapter after chapter, he read frightening stories about goblins, elves, changelings, leprechauns, banshees, and the many other types of the fae. With each story, he learned more and more about their history. His obsession and bitterness grew the longer he read. He hated them, that was certain, *but why do they hate mortals?* He wondered as he flipped through the pages. There was one thing that remained consistent about the fae; what they deemed most precious, most valuable- the human soul. Each one is born, not given, and are not easily stolen. Souls hold more power than the life itself. A soul can be moved, traded, or even get stuck, but it cannot die. The fact is that there is always someone or something hiding behind one of the veils, watching and scheming to get its hands on one. Creatures of the Nine Realms are born from magic and resent humankind. They see humans as merely a pathetic race of pests, undeserving of the magic that dwells inside their mortal souls. Long ago, earth was considered the Tenth Realm. It was a beautiful place full of wonder. Magic filled the air, the trees, and the water. The doors between realms were open, allowing animals, gods, and all beings to travel between them freely. That is until humans were created.

At first, the gods argued about which of them were responsible for such a creation, but as time passed, what had once seemed extraordinary, soon became a danger. In the beginning, various gods tried to guide the humans, teaching them to use tools, make fire, play music, and use magic. But to their dismay, humans became destructive to each other, to nature, and animals. Disappointed and repulsed by them, the gods left the Tenth Realm, and humans continued to abuse and ruin nature. Not all of the magic beings agreed to leave.

Some stayed out of hope, some out of spite, but the more powerful used their magic to make the doors between the realms invisible and thus limited the mortals to one realm. Humanity cut down trees, polluted the air and the ocean, and hunted animals. The magical creatures cried out in horror and rage with each falling tree and murdered animal. Men built homes upon their death and destruction. At first, the magical creatures tried to protect the lands and sea but had little effect. Humans forgot the magic they were taught, and the relationship between men and magical creatures deteriorated into hatred and bitterness. Despite the doors being closed, the actions of humans threatened magic beyond just the Tenth Realm. This threat affected the magical creatures in many different ways. Some of the animals became violent. Other creatures made appearances to humans, in hopes of bringing back a spark of magic and love of nature in men.

But humans were selfish and chose to exploit such magic to grant their wishes. So, the fae were forced to leave or hide. As their resentment grew, they decided they'd use their magic to grant wishes, but only for a trade. Yet again, things did not always go as the creatures planned. Mortals were capturing the fae, caging or even killing them.

Soon, the fairies developed a great fear of being seen and imprisoned. Now, when a magical creature roams this realm, they do their best to remain hidden. But the fae were not completely defeated. A new idea came to them: the perfect prey for them would be a child. The soul of a child would be pure, hopeful, and loving. Mortal children can still access magic within themselves. It is in the dream world that a child's imagination roams free. All their deepest desires, fears, and hopes are exposed there.

Adults believe their dreams are harmless and they couldn't be more wrong. The things seen and felt in dreams are actually quite real and dangerous. Once asleep, the soul rises out of the body, thus leaving it unprotected. A soul can be driven mad, or even scared to death before it can re-enter the protection of its body. It's a land where the hidden veil doesn't exist. The rules can be broken, monsters can creep, and the dead may visit. Magical creatures can try to trick you, trap you, and if you die before you wake- you are theirs to keep.

The last book from the box was the smallest of them all. It was dark brown, and hand sewn. It felt strange. He wasn't sure what it was made from, but it wasn't as smooth as the other leather covers. He had never felt a cover like this before. It had no title printed on the cover, and as he opened the book, he saw that it was handwritten- like a diary.

James' face contorted with confusion as he flipped through the pages. It consisted of long passages of what appeared to be instructions. The pages were ancient and worn. The book looked as if it had been read many times. The words were beautifully written but faded and difficult to see. He squinted his eyes to read one of the pages and gasped- this was a book of spells.

He flipped through the pages looking for the one word he needed to see most. Then the door opened just as he had found it- the summoning spell. James looked up to see two nuns bringing a tired, beaten Peter into the room. He looked utterly exhausted. One of the nuns brought him to a bed halfway across the room, while the other walked towards James' bed.

She was holding a folded sheet, a wool blanket, and a small pillow. It was the same bedding he had in the sick ward. She placed it all at the foot of his bed, without giving him so much as a glance. James watched as Peter collapsed on his bed across the room.

As soon as the nun turned her back, Peter smirked and winked at James. Peter stared at him with his trademark smile. Suddenly, the book in James' lap caught his eye. James quickly put the book under his mattress to hide it. Peter watched as James laid his head down upon his pillow and unfolded the small sheet and blanket. He pulled them up upon his tired body facing the right side of the room, leaving his box with all the other books completely unattended. Peter couldn't help but admire the boldness of James turning his back to him as if he was utterly confident nothing would happen. He almost respected the boy.

Once Peter was sure James was asleep, he quietly walked barefoot towards James' bed. Peter thought of waking the boy up with a beating, but he had already done that, and it no longer seemed fun to him. James was very different from the other children. Peter had become bored terrorizing the children in room 714. James was a challenge.

He'd taken Peter by surprise, and he was not accustomed to being tricked. When he reached the bed, he leaned across the bed to see James' face. He was in fact: sound asleep. Peter let out a sigh of relief. His heart was racing. Peter smiled as he quietly crept down to the floor next to the bed. He slowly lifted his hand to the edge of the mattress. His heart pounded so hard; he thought it would burst out of his chest as he slid his hand under the bed and slid the book out carefully. His eyes lit up with excitement- he had done it! Peter quietly jumped up and tiptoed proudly back to his bed utterly unaware that the stolen book he held in his hands would change both of their lives forever.

CHAPTER NINE

THE GREEN FAIRY

As Peter sat down, he laid his head back quietly on his bare bed. He had no pillow, no sheet, no rag, yet he kicked up his legs like he was on top of the world. This victory was just what he needed. He loved this feeling: the thrill, the excitement, the win. He had missed it being stuck in this wretched room of cracked stone.

He turned his head to look at James sleeping in his bed, wondering what would happen now. *Sure, I might get out of the orphanage one day, but what then?*

Peter thought of it all as he looked around the dreary room. He missed being the boy in charge of the orphanage; the boy that came up with schemes and got away with everything. He truly loved being who he was, but he couldn't live here forever. One day, he would leave, and on that day- he wouldn't be the leader of anyone or anything. He'd lose everything that made him *'him'*. The very idea made him feel truly sad as he lost himself in his thoughts.

A depression settled over him like a heavy blanket weighed down with anger and regrets. Peter didn't like imagining life as a man. He knew that manhood meant all the many banalities that stole one's soul. He didn't want a job. Working every day would be boring! As for a wife, well- he'd heard of love and marriage, and it all seemed very dull, which led to the next problem: kids. Little monsters to run around and remind him of all he had lost. Yes, he would hate them. Everything he was- would be forgotten. Tears welled up in Peter's eyes. Here in room 714 is where he would spend the rest of his childhood.

As he realized he would never again see his friends, be the cunning leader, or play mischievous pranks, tears fell down his cheeks. "I don't ever want to grow up," he whispered, looking up at James again. *What was so important about this book?* Peter thought, turning his back to James before opening his prize. He noticed how strange the cover felt to his fingers. He'd never cared much for reading- it was boring. But this book was strange, and he somehow felt drawn to it. As he looked at the beautifully written passages, his eyes grew wide. *This book is about magic!* A spark had lit within him, but as he feverishly read through the faded pages, his eyes became heavy, and against all resistance, Peter's tired punished body finally fell asleep.

When James awoke, he looked at Peter and saw him sleeping. He quietly rose from his bed and lifted his mattress to find that the book was gone. "Oh, Peter, you are so predictable. I knew you wouldn't be able to help yourself," he sighed, pleased with himself. It was all too easy. Still, he needed to know if Peter had found the summoning spell. He crept toward Peter's bed and looked for the book, hoping he'd see a sign that it had been read rather than stashed away with other stolen objects. Then he saw it! The spellbook was laying in Peter's lap with one of his hands still resting on top of it. He peeked down to see how far he had read. *He did not make it to the right page!* He stepped away, anger welling inside him. *Useless!* He hadn't gotten as far as James had hoped, but he had read enough to get himself into trouble. "I'd say you should be getting a visit from one of them soon. I cannot wait to watch them break you. Whether you are stolen or killed, I will rejoice."

When Peter finally woke, he quickly felt around and grabbed the fallen book. Then a look appeared on his face that James didn't quite understand. Peter turned to see him staring at him. They both rose from their beds and walked toward each other. As James came face to face with Peter's gleaming eyes, the more confused he became. He had always been one to talk, so James waited patiently to hear what he had to say. "I guess I should say thank you," Peter said as he roamed the room.

James was stunned, "Thank me for what?"

"Because of your book, they have found me."

"They? You were visited by more than one?"

"The first thing I remember when I fell asleep was the feeling of immense pressure. When I opened my eyes, I was underwater. I don't know how to swim, and I admit I panicked. I tried as hard as I could to reach the surface. Flailing my arms and legs, I tried to get to the top before I drowned. Just when I thought I couldn't take anymore, my head burst through the water and I could see a large island in the distance. But the waves were rough and dragged me down again. This went on for a long time. My body was becoming very weak, and each time I broke the surface and looked at that Island- I could see that I was no closer to it than before. I was losing hope as I felt water filling my lungs, but then, I saw something else in the water. Through the dark sea, was the shadow of a giant sea monster. I couldn't exactly make out what it was. All I could see as it circled me was its large jagged teeth and small yellow eyes. It made a growling sound as it swam closer, snapping at me. Its razor-sharp teeth cut deeply through my skin. The pain was unbearable, and I was sure I was going to die. But then through the cloud of my blood, I suddenly saw three other creatures swim towards me. I'm not sure when it happened, but the other creatures drove away the giant beast. They carried me out of the water and onto the island. That's when I saw what they were."

"What? What were they?"

"I don't know what your little books call them, but they were the most beautiful creatures I have ever seen. They were young- majestic women with long hair that shined like the brightest colors of the rainbow. Their skin was pale. Their faces looked human, but below their waist were long fish tails with gills that glimmered like stars in the moonlight."

"Mermaids! You are telling me that you were saved by mermaids?"

Peter nodded and chuckled. "Mermaids, huh? You sure are smart, kid. How do you know so much about this and I don't, eh?"

"Because I would rather read and learn than play childish games."

Peter nodded, admiring his boldness. "Anyways, the mermaids left me bleeding on the shore. I felt agonizing pain all over my body, but I was so happy to be on dry land. I ran my hands slowly through the soft grains of sand below me in relief. I coughed up as much of the salty water as I could. My blood and the water that had only moments ago threatened to be my grave dripped down onto the beach. I inhaled each breath of air deeply. Then I heard music coming from the dark center of the island. The area was covered in so many tall trees that it made me feel suspicious. The music sounded lovely and all, but there was something else about it. Suddenly, the music stopped, and the forest became silent. The leaves and branches on the trees stopped swaying, and the waves on the beach stopped. It was as if time had frozen. I didn't feel afraid of going into the dark forest, for I knew that waiting behind me was the ocean, and there was nothing I feared more than that. Then, I heard the faint sound of what seemed like a hundred whispering voices echoing in the trees. I couldn't make out anything they were saying, but they were all around me. I suddenly saw tiny balls of light above me. They were all different colors, and some were bigger than others. I watched as the small figures appeared flying around me. I tried to snatch one, but they were too fast. It must have frightened them, because one by one, all the balls of light disappeared, and the forest faded to black again. Soon, everything was silent. When I couldn't hear any of the voices anymore, I got upset. I yelled that they were cheating! That wasn't fair! Then suddenly, one of them appeared in front of me. It was a small green light at first, but as she came closer, I saw that it was a tiny woman. She was wearing a dress that was made from some type of leaves. She wasn't very pretty. In fact, she looked wicked and foul. Her skin was milky white and almost transparent. The only thing about her that was nice to look at all was her wings- they were tremendous and graceful. She looked young, but then again, I don't know how old they get. I only say so, because before the others fled, I got a good look at them. They all looked a lot older than the little green one. I could see from her face that she was angry with me. She flew around, circling me, taunting me with her wretched chiming sound. I admired her spunk. I asked what her name was, but she didn't answer me. She just kept circling me, ringing like a bloody bell. The chiming grew louder as her attempts of intimidation failed. She floated down to a tree branch in front of me. I said, "Are you gonna tell me your name or am I just gonna have to name you myself?" But she just glared at me with her big coal black eyes. Her face was red with rage, but as her little body began to shake, I could hear the faint sound of tinkering bells again. "Well, since you won't tell me, I guess I'll just have to call you Tink. Tinker Bell!" I told her. Honestly, I found annoying her very amusing. She moved around, using her hands and feet in dramatic gestures. I excitedly began to guess what it was she was saying. It was a fun guessing game. There was something about her- we felt connected. I understood everything she said! It was incredible, and I could see that she felt it too. I no longer found it funny, and she no longer looked angry. I realized she was telling me about the book. When she was done, and she knew I understood, she snapped her fingers, and I awoke."

"What did she say about the book?"

Peter smiled wickedly, turning the fragile pages to the page with the folded corner. "Maybe you're right, Hook! Maybe it is time I learn something myself, eh?"

James glanced at the page and scoffed at his arrogance, "You think that you can summon a fairy?"

"You think I can't?"

"Oh, you might be able to summon one, but they are cleverer than you. I'm afraid that even the great Peter will find himself tricked!"

"Me? Trick Me?"

James laughed. "You are out of your depth, Peter! They thrive off your fear, and I long for the moment when you find yourself drowning in the deep water you hate so much!" He said, strutting back to his bed.

Peter's nose flared as he huffed with anger. "We'll see who has the last laugh, Hook! We'll just see!"

James just smiled- enjoying Peter's frustration. He raised his hand gesturing for him to *go ahead.* Peter sat down, crossed his legs, and began to read. Still, James wasn't worried. Even if Peter truly had learned all that he had, then maybe he would be smart enough not to make a deal for his soul, but the harsh truth was yet to come. For he had already caught the Green Fairy's attention and if he rejected her efforts, he would surely suffer her wrath. Peter could feel him watching him from across the room, but his eyes never strayed from the book. He wanted to learn every single detail. It wasn't just James' that made him so diligent; there was something else. He felt with every instinct that he needed to be careful.

He knew this would be the most important thing that ever happened in his life. Room 714, the orphanage, the town, this world- he wanted something more exciting than what this it had to offer. And maybe now, if he played his cards right, something better could be within his grasp. James had been right about everything else, but he wasn't right about this. It was not the end for him; it was only the beginning. Peter didn't see fairies or the magical realms as something to fear, but rather an opportunity for the life he wanted; the life he was destined to have. He couldn't wait for his moment of glory, but mostly, he couldn't wait for James to see him win.

As the hours passed, the rain stopped. The moon shined bright in the clear sky. Peter had finished the last page, and both boys' hearts raced as he closed the book. He looked at James and smiled.

"Finally!" James exclaimed. "I wondered if you would ever finish."

Peter straightened his back, still sitting with his legs crossed, but didn't say anything.

"Am I to take your silence as a sign of defeat? Surely, you see now that you cannot win this game, Peter! No matter what you do, you- will- lose," James said in a proud and arrogant tone. This was a moment he would always treasure. Peter's demise would bring him one step closer to his vengeance and justice for his mother. His heart was pounding as he waited for the boy's next move.

Then a sinister smile spread across Peter's face. "They must have really hurt you bad, huh? I mean, they must have done something truly terrible!"

Now, James was irritated. "What are you talking about?"

"You have a lot of hatred for these creatures. I can see it in your eyes. What did they do?" Peter asked, bending forward with anticipation.

When James did not respond, Peter leaped off his bed and tapped his finger against his cheek. "Hmmm," he said, starting to pace back and forth in the center of the room. "Ugh, you're right! It doesn't matter, because what I really wonder is... if one of the fairies had their eyes on you- how are you still here? Come on, lad. We both know I am doomed; won't you tell me? Come on! Come on!" Peter repeated annoyingly.

"If I tell you, would you please just get on with the summoning spell?"

Peter walked over to the foot of his bed and gave a slight bow. "I give you my word."

James sighed. "I have had many encounters with one the fae. She invaded my dreams, and even after you and your friends almost beat me to death, I still rejected her offers of granting wishes. Then the dreams and visits turned dark, intense, and torturous. In a matter of days, I was so broken mentally and physically that I thought I would die."

"Well, that is a shame! Why didn't you?"

Hook glared up at Peter's excited face. "Because someone sacrificed themselves to save me."

"Sacrifice? You mean... the nun that died here. That was about you?"

James began to charge him, "You don't ever get to talk about her! Ever!"

It was then that Peter's racing thoughts came together. "It was she who gave you all these old books? Wait, the book under your bed! You knew I would take it. You set me up!"

James smiled. He had no issue admitting the truth to him now. The damage was done. "You're correct, Peter. I knew you would steal it. I probably know you better than anyone else here, including your little cronies. I know you hate it here, and I know you need excitement. You thrive off the pain and misery of others, so you don't have to admit your own. While you have successfully tricked everyone around you into thinking you are something special, you couldn't trick yourself. So, you occupied your time with stealing and doing your silly little pranks. You've been admired and respected by all the boys in the orphanage, but you and I both know that at the end of the night, you are just pissed off because deep down you know there is nothing extraordinary about you! I like to imagine that's exactly how the nuns treated you away from your adoring crowd. Did they remind you of how insignificant you truly are? Did they laugh about how pathetic, wretched, and weak you are?" He asked, making Peter's face glow red with anger. He could see he had touched a nerve and reveled in it. "Wow, they must have done a real number on you that last night."

"They called me worthless! They didn't stop whipping me until I screamed! Until I cried! It went on for hours! I was humiliated!" Peter screamed as a tear streamed down his cheek. In a moment of breath, he heard the unmistakable sound of a snicker. When Peter looked up to find a smug smile on James' face, he leaned in and whispered: "There is another thing you don't know. The nun that you love so much came in here after my attack on you. She told me that you were still alive. When she saw my disappointment, she told me that I was nothing, and that I would always be nothing. She promised that if you died, she would send me to the most wretched workhouse to live until the day the devil comes to collect my evil soul. Kind of ironic right?"

"What is?"

"Is it not obvious, book boy. Everything she said would to me- happened to her. She is the one who is nothing now. Why, I do believe she even got her soul taken, if I am not mistaken. In any case, I'm glad the old hag is dead!"

"Enough talking! Just read the bloody page!"

Peter laid back down on his bed, quickly flipping through the pages. Then at long last, he reached the page with the folded corner. He raised his head with a sinister grin, "Yes, you are right. Let us begin:

From the gates of hell to the heavens above
To those who hate and those who love
Creatures of the Nine Realms
I summon thee
Hear my wish
Bring me a fairy
Open a portal on the land, stars, or sea
Through the magical veil
Come to me."

CHAPTER TEN

PETER'S BARGAIN

Suddenly, a strong gust of wind blew open the small window and extinguished the candles. Everything went dark as Peter watched all the children in the room, including James, fall into a deep sleep around him. Peter hesitantly walked toward the window; his eyes drawn to a twinkling star in the sky. A ball of light came from the star, heading out of the dark night towards him. Peter chuckled as his eyes caught the bright hue of green. *Tinker Bell.* She was coming in very fast, and before he knew it, she was through the window and had tumbled to the floor causing a clashing of bell sounds. "Are all fairies as clumsy as you, Tink?" He asked in good fun, but her red face made it clear she did not find it funny. "Oh, come now, Tinker Bell. I was just poking fun. I really am glad to see you. I mean, I hoped the spell would summon you. Aren't you happy to see me?"

Tinker Bell stood, and as she looked into Peter's eyes, her anger subsided. Soon, her skin was illuminating her natural green glow, and she gave him a pleased smile.

"I'll take that as a yes. So, how long does this summoning spell last? I mean, how long will they be asleep?"

Tinker Bell didn't speak but communicated with gestures. The fact that he understood her perfectly made him feel clever. He observed her as she used her dramatic gestures to answer his questions. She made it clear that all the boys that were under the sleeping spell would stay asleep until she left since her kind didn't like to be seen if they could avoid it. Then she used her magic to make a cloud that resembled a clock. She pointed to the hands to show that time was standing still, but they did need to hurry since the magic wasn't hers- but rather the work of witchcraft. Then she displayed a wand. It looked like a long-manipulated piece of green wood. She held it up and tapped the top of her wrist as if to say, '*hurry up.*'

"Alright. Let's begin." His face became grave, as he knew how important this was. One mistake could take away his life, or she could trick him out of his soul. He knew that was what she wanted. They all did, but he had his own trick up his sleeve. "I would like to make a wish, Tinker Bell," he said as serious and direct as he could. "I wish to have powers like yours. I wish to live within the Nine Realms. I wish to freeze the clock- to remain a boy forever. But most of all... I wish I could fly."

Tinker Bell flew up to his face and pointed her finger, scolding him as if to say, "*Listen here, we have never given such powers of the gods and magical creatures to a human- ever."*

"Look, Tink! I have summoned you here, and I know that you can grant any wish I have," he said pointing his finger at her. "And don't you try to bully me again! I am no fool! I know what you can do! I know that you can do this!"

Tinker Bell lowered her arm slowly, and her face went calm as she gave him a small smirk. She crossed her arms, then waved her hand as if to say, *"Very well."* Then she went on to say that those were many wishes and therefore he would need to give up something of equal value. She created a clouded figure of him in her hand. *The price would be his soul.*

Peter shook his head but remained calm and firm. "I know that what I ask is a lot, and I understand there is a steep price, but if you grant my wishes, then I too will be a magical creature. So, my offer is this: to pay my debt not with my soul, but with the souls of the children I steal for you."

Tinker Bell squinted her eyes and raised her brow. He could see he had spiked her interest, but she remained uncertain.

"Take me to the Nine Realms, give me my powers, and I will spend my immortal life collecting souls for you. Do we have a deal?" Peter's heart raced, anxiously awaiting her answer. "Tinker Bell? Do- we- have- a- deal?"

She gave a sly smile as she lifted her wand. Suddenly, a bright light blasted throughout the room. The candles were relit, and all the children slowly woke from their enchantment as James opened his eyes and rose from his bed still feeling groggy. He looked around at all the confused faces that filled the room, but there was one face he didn't see- Peter was gone.

James looked at Peter's bed and saw the book still open to the page with the summoning spell. He searched the room for any clue, anything at all, to bring him the certainty that it was indeed done. *They have clearly taken him, but where? Was he even still alive?* James paced the room for hours pondering the fate of Peter. He imagined him being tortured out in the middle of the sea somewhere, screaming in pain as the monster ripped him apart as he drowned. *Yes, he was definitely dead- he must be. If he'd made a deal, his soul would be theirs. If he hadn't made a deal, then may his torture be truly agonizing. I shall sleep better at night dreaming of Peter's suffering, and when the morning comes, I shall rejoice as I journey across the seven seas to find the door that holds my greatest treasure: The Scarlet Fairy!*

As James was resting on his bed feeling triumphant, Peter and Tinker Bell were flying through the clouds in the starry sky. Peter didn't know where they were going, but he didn't care. He followed closely behind Tinker Bell with his arms opened wide. Peter looked down and found that all he could see were clouds below. The farther away from the world he was, the freer he felt. Above him, Tinker Bell pointed at two stars. The one on the right twinkled brighter than the other. Instinctively, Peter resisted its pull, but the smile on Tinker Bell's face enticed him onward. Suddenly, everything around them changed. The sky became a tunnel of sorts- its walls changing colors from pink to purple and blue to green. As they flew through the passage of swirling colors, Peter began to feel transformed. He felt invincible.

He had done it. His wishes had come true. He was everything he wanted to be- superior, immortal, and free. It was at this moment that he thought of James. He had succeeded where James said he would not. If only he could show him and laugh in his face.

They approached nine openings in the walls of the tunnel, but as they flew closer toward them, the openings began to close. Peter looked to Tinker Bell and saw alarm on her face as she raced toward the only opening that remained, afraid it would close any second. He did his best to keep up with her, but she was very fast. To his horror, she went through the steadily closing portal. Quickly, he stiffened his body, clasped his arms tightly at his sides, and focused all his energy to burst through the portal in time. He let out a massive breath of relief as the portal closed that very second behind him.

"Did you see that?" He asked, laughing as he looked for the little fairy. "Tink? Where are you?" He called out for her, but she was nowhere in sight. Now, he was beginning to worry. She had looked terrified before she cleared the tunnel. It was dark, but there was a full moon. As he looked for her, he discovered he was flying towards the island from his dream. He desperately looked towards the trees and saw a tiny flicker of green light. "Tink!" He shouted. *She is okay!* He smiled with relief, and immediately went towards the beach, lowering himself onto the golden sand. Peter looked at the familiar forest in the center of the island. There were no trails on the ground, but a single clearing leading towards the lighted area. As he crept toward the beautiful lights, he heard several voices. Suddenly, he felt he was not meant to hear their conversation. The clearing became narrower, with large thorn bushes on each side. Peter winced as the branches cut his arms and legs as he continued forward. The voices grew louder and angrier in tone. He felt nervous. *What was happening?* Finally, he recognized a familiar bell. *Tink. She is in trouble.* Something felt very wrong.

Peter hurried forward and saw a steep hill. All the colored lights were coming from the top. As he slowly made his way up, he couldn't help but notice the voices seemed louder than humanly possible. The tree branches above whipped as if reflecting the hostility in the air. He looked around; the entire island began to move with fury.

When he finally reached the top, he saw Tinker Bell standing opposite a large group of fairies. She was inside a small iron cage. Peter looked upon the others with discomfort. Some of the creatures had wings, and some didn't. Some looked old, while others looked like small children. A few were hypnotizingly beautiful, while most appeared vile and disgusting. But through them all, there was an unmistakable power. Although Peter had never respected authority of any kind, there was now a fear within him that he had never felt before. There was a strong aura of supremacy that made him feel inferior. It was as if he had no free will at all; like he was unable to be disrespectful towards them. Peter moved to the other side of the hill, so he could face Tink and have the other fairies' backs to him. He crawled a bit closer and peeked his head up into the light. Tink spotted him. Hiding behind the tall sycamore trees, he began to inch closer to her, but she subtly waved her hand for him to stop. He knew she wanted him to stay hidden and she wasn't issuing an order- it was a plea. So, he remained still and quiet, concealed by the dark shadows surrounding the glade. *What is wrong? Why are they angry with her?* He tilted his head and leaned in closer, desperately trying to hear what was being said.

"What you have done cannot be undone!" Shouted one fairy.

"You dared give a human boy our powers!" Roared another.

"Banishment!" Was echoed by the rest throughout the trees. The word was enough to bring Tinker Bell to tears. She begged for forgiveness, but Peter could see from her distraught face that it was no use. He had gotten her into trouble with her own kind. He didn't regret his wishes, but he did feel guilty on her account. One of the oldest fairies amongst a secluded group that stood upon the midlevel of trees, lightly tapped his wand against a branch. The rest of the fairies became quiet, leaving only whispers. Now, all he could hear was a faint chant echoing: "The Elder... the Elder... the Elder." It was then that the oldest one lifted his wand high into the air, and all noise ceased. Everything was eerily quiet as everyone waited to hear what the elder would say.

"Silence! Judgment must be made, and I pass it now! There are rules set in place! Not just for our protection, but for the protection of all the Nine Realms! By bringing this human to our world and giving him our magic, Ahnee, you have betrayed us all. Did the mortal survive the wall?" The Grand Elder asked in a loud commanding tone, but Tinker Bell just stared at him in silence. Peter waited for her to point to him, but she didn't. She remained perfectly still. "I asked you- did the boy survive the wall!? Did- he- get- through- the- door?!" He asked, but Tink remained still. This time the Grand Elder trembled with rage. "Where is the human, Ahnee? If you do not tell me, then you will suffer the eternal death!"

"No!" Peter screamed running into the light, waving his arms. The fairies gasped as he stepped up to the Elder Tree and boldly faced them with his fists on his hips. The Grand Elder was ancient and wise. He stood only a foot tall and had a long white beard that rested near his feet. He wore an elaborate crown of leaves upon his head and an incredibly long cloth robe covered in beautiful leaves. The train of his robe nearly reached the ground. His skin was grey like stone. His nose was large, and his ears were pointed. But the most extraordinary feature about him was his shoes. They were curled up to a point, adorned in breathtakingly beautiful gems, and too large for his feet. As they sparkled in the reflection of the gathered fairy lights, Peter realized that the twinkling lights he had seen earlier were not coming from the fairies themselves, but from the Elder's jeweled shoes. He glanced around the hill at all the fairies. All of them wore shoes; each beautiful and unique. Peter looked at Tink, and noticed for the first time, that she too had shoes. Suddenly, he felt an overwhelming sense of shame and tried to hide his dirty bare feet, but it was no use. The entire hilltop began to echo with whispers. Back at the orphanage, he was known to be the only boy who walked around with bare feet. Before, being different made him feel proud and rebellious. This was different. Now, he felt as if his feet were proof that he didn't belong here. He felt all their eyes judging him. They stared at him as if he was a repulsive bug that needed to be squashed. While he didn't dare move or say anything rash that would get Tink and himself killed. He stood tall and turned up his chin as he locked eyes with the Elder Fairy, who raised his wand once more- silencing the hilltop. All were silent except one. Peter heard Tink banging her fists against the iron bars. But Peter didn't turn to look at her. He knew she wanted him to fly away and hide, but he refused to leave her here to die. Peter had bonded with Tink in a way that he had never been with anyone or anything, and her willingness to sacrifice herself to give him a chance of escape awakened something inside him that he never knew was there. He cared for her. The Elder fairy gracefully floated down from the tree toward Peter. As he came close, he gazed deep into Peter's eyes, making him feel uneasy.

"Well... well! So, this is the human, I presume? So, you are here." His voice echoed as he cast an angry gaze toward Tinker Bell.

"Leave her alone!" Peter demanded, gaining the Elder's full attention.

The Grand Elder chuckled to himself. "Am I to understand you wish to save this fairy? You, a human?!"

"Yes, I do," Peter replied sternly. The hilltop echoed with whispers again.

"Settle down, settle down. This human does not truly care for her. He is only a human," the Elder said dismissively, as he flew back onto the tree branch with the other Elders. Peter turned around.

"Don't worry, Tink, I'm gonna get you out of there," Peter said as he looked upon the frightened pixie in her tiny cage.

The Grand Elder laughed at them. "I see. So, you believe that by saving her, you will ensure you keep your wishes. Well, fear not, child. Her death cannot void the deal. You have your powers, and we cannot take them away. The deal cannot be broken. It is our law. Now, step aside!" The Elder said sternly.

But Peter didn't obey him. He stepped up to the small iron cage and tried to open the door, but as his fingers touched the bars, he heard the entire hilltop of fairies' gasp. Peter repeatedly pulled on the lock, trying to force it open, until he heard the Elder speak again: "Hmmm, how interesting," he said as he slowly ran his fingers through his long white beard. He whipped up his wand and sent a surge of power blasting towards the cage, breaking the lock and opening the door.

"Come on, Tink!" Peter called as he snatched her up and was about to fly away when Tink pointed to the trees around them. They were completely surrounded, and the crowd of fairies was closing in on them. Peter held up his hand with Tink standing on his palm. He looked into her eyes and said sadly: "Thanks for teaching me how to fly."

Suddenly, they both heard the Grand Elder's laughter echoing throughout the trees as he slowly approached them. He put his small arm around Peter's shoulder in what appeared to be a friendly gesture.

"Well, it seems Ahnee may have found something of value," the Elder said cheerfully to the crowd.

"Me?" Peter asked.

"Yes, boyo, you! Now, let's settle down and come to some sort of understanding? After all, you are the first human to be granted such wishes," the Elder said as he directed Peter and Tinker Bell into the center of the crowd below the Elder tree, before returning to his branch. "Boy, what is your name?"

"Umm, Peter."

The Elder lifted his arms to the sky above as he closed his eyes in pause. "You will no longer be called by your human name, as you are no longer mortal."

Suddenly, Tinker Bell moved about, gesturing things rapidly. She made impressions of Peter- sneaking around, running wild, and free. She zapped her tiny wand making a small clouded figure of what appeared to be half boy and half goat. Then she giggled so hard she accidentally bumped into Peter.

"What is *that?*" Peter asked, feeling offended.

The Grand Elder chuckled upon the tree. "Pan. She is saying you remind her of the god Pan. I must admit, the name is quite fitting."

Peter angrily looked at Tink: "Now listen here, I'm no goat boy!"

Tink wrinkled up her nose, flying close to his face. She stomped around, throwing a fit, scolding him in return: "That's not fair! I've accepted your name to me!"

Peter's face grew long. He felt a tinge of remorse for angering her. "Alright, if it means that much to you... Pan is my name," he said, looking glum.

"It is a fine name, boy. Pan is the god of youth, the wild, nature, and music. So, you see, the name is perfect for you. I believe your fairy has chosen it well. Do you accept it?" The Elder asked.

Peter looked at Tink with a smile, before nodding.

"Then it is official. The boy is one of us!" The Grand Elder announced. But the crowd of creatures huffed in discontent. "Calm yourselves, for it is not my final word on the matter. The boy does possess our magical powers, and in return, he has promised to spend his immortal life collecting souls from children of the human world. Some of you might wonder how he could do any better than us. But I assure you- he can, and he will! For it has come to my attention that while this boy has the powers of the fae, he still has a human body that makes him invulnerable to iron and the other things the mortals have used against us. With this boy- there will be no child we cannot reach!" The hilltop suddenly roared with cheers that made Peter smile with pride. The Elder tapped his wand against the tree, hushing the excited fairies. "Now, there are still rules."

"Rules?" Peter scowled.

"Though you wished to live within the Nine Realms, you will only be allowed in one: this one. You may come and go from the island, but only to collect the souls for your debt. If you should, at any point fail to retrieve them as promised- your deal will be declared null and void. You will lose your powers, and we will devour your soul. And as for you, Ahnee, your punishment for endangering us and all the creatures of the Nine Realms is banishment! You shall also be restricted to this realm with the boy. You shall be responsible for living with him, helping him, teaching him, and supervising him here in both here and the human world. If he should fail in any way, know that both you and the boy will die. Do you both understand?"

Peter and Tinker Bell both nodded as the large crowd of brightly glowing fairies slowly began to rise high into the air, disappearing from the hilltop. Peter and Tinker Bell looked at each other silently until the moon was the only light left shining down upon the Lost Island that was now their home.

CHAPTER ELEVEN
THE WINDOW

The Grand Elder waved his wand, opening the realm's portal and all the fairies followed him into the brightly colored tunnel that led to the other realms. Each fairy went into whichever realm they called home, all except for one. Instead, this fairy would return to where it all began- the Moore Orphanage. The Scarlet Fairy flew through the portal, past the hidden veil with an overwhelming sense of urgency and fear. Her mind raced through her memories. *The boy that had been given the powers and immortality of the fae had looked so familiar. He couldn't be the same boy, could he?* Her worry and anxiety were at its peak when she finally arrived at the window. Searching the boys' room, she didn't see either of the two boys she remembered. Frustration and panic overcame her as she raced to every window until she came to the tiny window of room 714. She peered through the old battered glass, frantically looking for the only two faces able to give her any solace. It was still early in the evening within the human realm, but the room was so poorly lit, it was nearly impossible to see anything. As she squinted and wiped at the glass, one by one- the children's faces became clear. Finally, she saw one familiar face. There, sitting on a bed nearest to the window, was James. At first, the sight of him locked safely away brought her relief, but the feeling was short lived as she realized the other boy was not there. *It was him! The same boy she had seen in so many of James' thoughts and dreams was the boy 'Pan'! He must have used the same summoning spell that meddling woman used to summon me. But how did he get it? She knew that somehow James was involved in all of this. A human child bestowed with fae magic now lived in one of the magical realms.* Suddenly, the threats James had made that night in the forest struck her heart with terror. She fled the orphanage, but the distance didn't seem to ease her fear.

She needed a plan to steal the spell book from James. He needed to give up this vendetta against her. She had to take care of this situation quickly. If the Elder fairies found out this was all her fault, death would be a mercy. The dark forest below her appeared so beautiful and serene. Its tranquility calmed her. She decided to stop here and think about what to do next. She slowly floated down to rest on a fallen log, but as she gazed down at the fallen tree below her, she was suddenly struck with a marvelous plan. Quickly looking about the ground, the excited fairy flew over to another large piece of dead wood laying lifeless in the forest. As she hovered over the broken tree, she waved her right hand, gracefully sprinkling red dust upon the tree. The wood instantly began to move, like something inside was about to hatch. She coaxed the tree. "Come on, come on," until the wood cracked open. Smiling as she reached down, she gently opened the wooden cocoon to reveal a young boy's shadow. "Now, you know what you must do," she whispered in a motherly voice. "You won't be a shadow for long. Go to the boy's bed. Even a child as ruthless as Peter cried when he thought no one could see. Lay on the bed and let his tears touch you. Then, you will have his appearance. But heed my words-there will be one that will try to talk with you, but no matter what he says, do not utter a single word to him. Now, fly away darkness, and slip into the room where my enemy sleeps."

CHAPTER TWELVE

CHANGELING

It was an unusually dark night when the shadowy figure approached the small window of room 714. A shiver came upon James as the creature deftly reached in and opened the window. His eyes immediately shot open, but something inside him told him to remain very still. He couldn't determine what it was; only that it was a flat shadowy figure in the shape of a boy. It flitted around the room playfully from one bed to another until it reached the only empty bed- Peter's bed. James watched as the shadow laid down upon the mattress, and before his very eyes, the dark figure began to transform. Suddenly less transparent and flat; this thing was somehow becoming a *person*. James gawked in terror as bones and flesh slowly attached; the creature making itself as real as any other boy in the room. He wanted to hide under his blanket, but he couldn't move. He was completely paralyzed with fear. Within a few moments, the figure's transformation was complete. It was then that James saw the figure's chest rise and fall. *It's breathing!*

The creature slowly turned its head towards him. "It's just a dream, wake up! It's just a dream; wake up!" James whispered. Collecting his breath and his bravery, he looked towards the creature now sitting upright on Peter's bed, staring directly at him. All the hair on the back of his neck and arms rapidly stood on end. His heart pounded in his chest, and his palms began to sweat from adrenaline as the shade rose from the bed and started creeping towards him. James leaped from his bed, expecting an attack, but to his surprise, the creature bent down and grabbed his box of books. Outraged, James grabbed the creature by its wrist, ready to kill it for touching his things. Now that he and the creature were eye to eye, shock suffused him. *It was Peter! A complete copy.* It had his body, hair, and eyes- but James knew it wasn't the real him. This was fae magic trying to trick him. He didn't know what to expect next, but in an instant, his fear had been wholly replaced with anger and vigilance. The creature walked back to the other side of the room, set down the box of books, and seized the same candlestick that James had used to terrorize Peter. James braced himself to fight the imposter, but when it bent down and brought out the summoning book, his heart sank. "No!" He screamed, running across the room, but he was too late. The old and fragile pages burned to ash in mere seconds.

The creature threw the candlestick onto the bed, setting the tattered old mattress on fire. James raced to retrieve his mother's fairytale book, saving it from the flames, while the creature went about the room, throwing everything it could onto the burning bed. All the children in the room began screaming as the small flames grew into a deadly fire. They ran to the door, beating and begging to be let out.

By the time the staff opened the door, they were trampled on by all the children fleeing. Fire and smoke quickly filled the room, leaving only the creature and James standing inside. Suddenly, a nun grabbed him by the shoulders and dragged him out of the room. Everyone throughout the orphanage bolted outside as fast as they could. James held his mother's fairy tale book tightly in his arms as he raced outside with the others. The staff did all they could to unlock all the doors and get everyone out, but James knew by their screams that not all could be saved. He looked around at all the crying, frightened faces. *Why in the face of such horror, do I not shed any tears?* He felt inhuman. The nuns wailed and prayed at the screaming inferno before them. James suddenly realized he hadn't seen the imposter outside. All his instincts told him it was time to leave. He didn't want to see the final carnage.

He slowly backed away from the chaos and turned toward the docks and his new life. Suddenly, a chill ran down his spine. Something terrible was behind him.

What he saw next would haunt him for years to come. There, in the small window of room 714, stood the imposter staring at him through the flames that engulfed its body. It never screamed or moved, and though James forced himself to turn and not look back, he was sure it never did.

He walked towards the harbor, knowing that every step would bring him closer to the sea and farther away from the horror and heartache of his past. The black smoke and smell of death filled the air, and the horrific screams didn't seem to fade with distance. Every wailing cry sent a violent chill up James' spine. A part of him felt guilty. He knew the creature had come for the spellbook, and if it hadn't, then all those children would not be... burning alive. He fought the urge to cry as he forced his legs onward away from the place where he had been beaten, tortured, and afraid. The orphanage was his past, and the ocean before him was his future.

CHAPTER THIRTEEN

THE SHIP

The harbor was dark and dreary under the smoky black sky, and the wood below his feet was wet from the waves splashing upon the wharf. There was only one ship anchored, and it was the most glorious vessel James had ever seen. He felt incredibly drawn to its magnificence. With each step forward, he found himself admiring the ship's every detail. The wood was painted pitch black, and the large sails were red as if stained from blood. All the sails he had seen from his window before had large shredded tears from raging storms and blasted holes from cannon fire, but these were in pristine condition. Large lanterns were hung across the ship. Two larger lanterns in exquisite brass design, both swayed ever so slowly, back and forth illuminating the ship's stern. They cast an orange glow, revealing hundreds of what appeared to be golden human skulls. The sides were lined with long rows of gun ports and within them held large cannons ready to blast down any ship who dared cross its path. In excitement, James quickened his pace. He was eager to see this grand ship's crew. He looked up at the captain's quarters. Long red velvet drapes lined all the large windows. Though he couldn't see inside, the glow of candlelight from within the room outlined the dark silhouette of a tall man pacing back and forth. James gasped! He was sure it was the captain, as the man wore the infamous large hat symbolizing his rank.

James' admiration was suddenly interrupted by the loud sound of smashing glass. He moved closer to the docks where he finally laid his eyes on the crew. He was instantly disappointed and repulsed by their filthy appearance. *How could these men belong to such a grand ship?* He wondered as he watched the men scurry around the docks, picking up barrels and supplies in an unorganized drunken manner. James tiptoed closer and squatted down behind one of the large barrels in an area to see them more clearly. Their eyes were glassy in a way James had never seen before. They were filthy and smelled as if they had not washed in months. He sneered at the stumbling fools in disgust.

One of the men was drawing closer to the barrel where he was hiding. He was a short, fat, and greasy looking man with a matted beard surrounding a nasty black mouth holding three rotting teeth. He was the last of the crew on the dock and James needed to get on the ship. He quickly looked around, grabbed some of the large rope laying upon the ground, and pulled it up tight. The drunkard tripped, fell hard to the ground, and was rendered unconscious. James mustered up his strength to lift the large barrel the man was carrying. His arms trembled as he struggled to carry the heavy wooden barrel that was nearly as big as him. He tried not to draw any attention to himself as he made his way across a long wooden ramp, and aboard the grand ship.

As James entered the vessel, he followed the other men into a large supply room. The drunken crew stumbled as they stocked heavy sacks, crates, and aligned the barrels. All were too intoxicated to notice James. They moved about in a way that made them seem visually impaired as they bumped into things and each other. Many of them accidentally dropped their load, causing crates to break and barrels to spill. The foul-smelling liquid spilled out across the floor. They cackled loudly and cheered as two of their shipmates laid their heads on the floor trying to lap up the drink.

Suddenly, they heard loud footsteps coming down the stairs. Every man in the room froze, quivering in fear. "It's the captain." The crew watched in horror as two large black boots stepped down below the deck. The man wore a thick black coat with red threading. His large tricorn hat was black leather with golden buttons sewed along the edges. The only thing missing was a feather, James thought. He stood beside the cowering men as they watched their captain walking towards them.

James tried to see the captain's face under the hat, but the room was so dark that the man's face merely appeared leathery and scarred. His eyes were small and tight as he glared around the room. With every puff of his pipe, you could see their fiery yellow color almost glowing. The captain scowled at his trembling crew as he made his way toward them. He looked down at the dark liquid pooling around his boots.

"Tsk, tsk," he uttered shaking his head as he surveyed all the broken crates and spilled barrels. So much of the cargo and supplies had been ruined, and there wouldn't be another shipment for weeks. "You fools!" He shouted with a thundering voice that inspired more terror than his appearance. "What it cost to pay for all of this is worth more than anyone of your insignificant lives! But one of yours will have to do for now!" His face was now red with fury. Some of the men dropped to their knees begging for mercy. Others began to argue, pointing their fingers at each other as the captain ran his hand across his belt and grabbed the handle of his sword. As he drew his blade, he pointed it straight out towards his groveling crew. Suddenly, he noticed one person not clamoring in fear. There, standing tall and unafraid was a young boy. He brought the tip of his blade to the boy's neck, but his anger turned to curiosity as the boy exposed his neck further and glared defiantly at him. His bravery amused him. "And just where the hell did you come from, lad?"

"I snuck aboard, loading supplies on your ship after leaving one of your drunken men unconscious on the harbor," James replied in the same disconcerting voice he'd used with the doctor from the orphanage.

The captain chuckled at the young child's spunk: "Well, well, lad. You are either very brave or very stupid."

James slowly raised his hand and moved the sword away from his neck: "It is your crew that is stupid, Captain."

"You dare insult my ship and my crew, boy? It might be the last thing you ever do."

"On the contrary, sir. I do not disparage you or your magnificent ship- only your crew of incompetent, drunken fools unworthy of working aboard such a grand ship," James said, each word causing the tip of the sword to move, nicking his throat up and down without him showing any sign of discomfort. As the captain watched small streams of the boy's blood run down his collar and onto his raggedy shirt, he dropped the sword. He suddenly felt respect for this strange boy whose manner and nerve were more mature than any of his crew.

The captain leaned his head back and laughed. "You're right, lad. They are a bunch of worthless cowards," he said, putting his arm around James' shoulders. "So, you say you snuck aboard my ship, ey? And you be able to lift a full barrel of rum with that puny little body of yours? And you say you did all this without the notice of any of my men?" He asked as he turned James around and bent down to look him in his eyes.

James leaned in, looking into the yellow eyes of the fearsome captain once more without a glimmer of fear: "I *managed.*"

"Hmmm. You managed. I see. Fine choice of words," the captain said as he paced the floor. "You *managed* to knock out one of my crew. You *managed* to carry supplies aboard my ship without anyone seeing you, and you *managed* to get all this done without causing any damage?"

The men remained silent, staring daggers at James with their hate, but didn't dare look into the captain's burning eyes. There was a tense pause as the captain glared at his crew waiting for any of them to utter a word, but none did.

"Yes, I did," James said boldly.

The captain turned, facing the boy once more: "And what are your plans now? You wish to work upon my ship?"

"I require a means to travel, as I am searching for something."

The captain roared with laughter again: "All pirates are, me boy! Well, I am no child keeper." He sighed as if thinking for a moment. "If you travel aboard *my* vessel, you must earn your keep. I must admit, your mission tonight has impressed me, and I would be lying if I said I am not in need of someone with your skill of management. So, here is what I offer you: a job aboard my ship. You will not be given any pay or leeway just because you are a child. It will also be your job to keep a watchful eye on these worthless idiots. Do we have a deal?" He asked as he reached his out his hand for the boy to shake. James looked

101

down and shook the captain's hand. "What's your name, boy?"

James thought for a second. He opened his mouth to say, but something stopped him. He didn't feel like James anymore. It was as if James died in the fire- lost in the ashes. It was in that moment that he realized something: he had been reborn. "Hook."

The captain smirked. "You indeed have the dark soul of a true pirate, lad! Well then, Hook, I am Blackbeard, your captain. Welcome aboard the Queen Anne's Revenge."

CHAPTER FOURTEEN

THE PIED PIPER

As the years went by, Hook became quite the pirate. Working his way up the ranks, he had become the very bosun and right hand of Captain Blackbeard. Hook had grown tall and strong, and though he was still a young man, he had made quite the name for himself. Many men and women across the sea had heard of the stealthy pirate able to steal any treasure, win any battle using only his sword, and under the teachings of Blackbeard, Hook had learned how to command the crew.

Sadly, his cold heart hadn't healed with time, for in all his travels, he had still not found a way into the Nine Realms. With each passing day, he would watch as another sunset dropped below the horizon, bringing him no closer to his vengeance. Time had only brought him more bitterness and anger, making him one of the most ruthless pirates amongst the seven seas.

At night, when Hook lay in his private quarters, the mere memory of the Scarlet Fairy still haunted his dreams. He had never told a soul about his mystical torment, not even Blackbeard who had become both his mentor and his friend. It was no secret amongst the crew that Hook preferred to be alone, and though Blackbeard did not know the real anguish he kept hidden.

He had always considered the boy's behavior a sign of focus. There was nothing about Hook that the captain didn't admire in some way. In the years past, he had grown to look upon the boy as his kin. They had fought many battles together, and Hook had taken some of the deadliest wounds, to protect him. Hook had survived them all and earned Blackbeard's trust.

Every time they would drop anchor on land, the crew would run across the docks and into town to drink and enjoy the company of women, all except for Hook. He would spend his evening in the captain's quarters, enjoying a glorious feast with Blackbeard, discussing where to set course next. Hook may not have found a passage into the Nine Realms, but his extensive research with books and maps had made him into quite a worthy adversary to have. Hook had led Blackbeard to so many wonderous lands and treasure, that Blackbeard had overtime given full course to the boy, never questioning his decisions.

After their dinner, Hook would often go walking late into the night, and tonight was no different. The town streets were dark, as all the lights from within the small houses had already been blown out for the night. Hook suffered from severe insomnia and though he had a great love for the sea, whenever he found himself awake and alone, a walk upon land into the dead of the night seemed to mirror his soul perfectly.

The air tonight was so full of fog; he could barely see anything around him. Luckily, he had learned a long time ago to not rely on only his sight.

He could hear every movement around him: The townspeople shutting their windows, a child's cough, and the sound of bottles breaking upon the stone as the unfortunates passed out drunk upon the ground. But eventually, all sounds of man ceased, leaving only the sound of his boots and the sound of something Hook hated- the ticking of the tall clocktower in the center of town. One of the best things about being on the ship was there was no clock in sight.

The captain had a golden pocket watch once, but Hook had secretly smashed it a long time ago. The captain never knew it was him, but he didn't seem to care. Hook tried to distract himself as he walked onwards, but the sound of the ticking clock had become so relentless and rhythmic, it was if it was impossible to not somehow move in sync with it.

Then suddenly the ticking sound stopped. Hook froze as he looked up towards the clocktower. The fog in the air was thick, but he could see that the hands on the clock's face had indeed stopped. Something wasn't right.

The winter air had somehow suddenly become warm, and the ocean breeze no longer smelled of ice, but rather salty like the tropical waters. A strange feeling washed over him that he hadn't felt in years- *magic was here.*

Suddenly, a frightening sound touched his hearing- music. It wasn't the sound of chiming bells, as he had expected, but pipes. It was undoubtedly magical, as there was something in it that was alluring. The music began to get louder, echoing down the streets. Suddenly, windows and doors started to open, but it wasn't adults coming out to see what it was- *it was children*. One by one, they playfully skipped and ran down the streets, following the beautiful song. Hook couldn't believe what he was seeing.

He had heard stories of a fairy entering orphanages and homes, but only one child would go missing at a time. But these children were not being taken; they were running right into the magical creature's grasp. Hook didn't know what this thing was, but it was no fairy.

He desperately raced towards them, trying to stop them, but as he looked into their eyes, he could see it was no use. The magic had complete control over them. He screamed and used all his strength to try to force them still, but there were too many of them.

Then suddenly, a distant voice sent a violent chill down his spine: "It's no use, Hook! They belong to me now."

Hook's heart thumped loudly inside his chest as he spun around quickly: "Peter?" He said as he turned to gaze upon his old foe. He looked at the young boy up and down. He was on top of a street lantern and next to him was a small flickering ball of green light.

106

He walked arrogantly across the air as he played his pipes. He was wearing all green, though it didn't look like human clothing, but rather some cloth covered in dark leaves. He wore a pointed hat like one of the elf people and funny looking shoes that curled up at the top. He was still a little boy. It was as if no time had passed at all. He looked exactly like he did the last time he saw him: the same childlike face with the sinister smile that made his blood boil. Hook was speechless. He had so many questions and yet, not a single word escaped his mouth.

Peter's head bent back with sudden maniacal laughter. "Your eyes do not deceive you, old friend. It is me. I've waited a long time for this moment old' boy. And I must say, the look upon your face has made it all worth it."

Hook scoffed angrily: "How?"

"Don't sound so surprised. I have done what no other mortal has. I have gained the power of the fae!" Peter said putting his arms on his hips proudly.

Hook felt a lump in his throat as he struggled to speak again: "The fae?" He asked zoning in on Peter's appearance. But upon seeing the revealing color of Peter's eyes, Hook suddenly began to laugh. There was not even the slightest flicker of green with them. "Oh, Peter. You truly are just a pathetic child! You haven't changed one bit. You think by covering yourself in green clothes and green shoes that it somehow makes you a true magical creature?" Hook laughed coldly.

"I am a magical creature! I have powers! I can even fly! I am immortal! I live in the Nine Realms! I outsmarted you, and I outsmarted the fairies!" Peter screamed in a tantrum.

Hook's left eyebrow raised as he glared up at Peter curiously: "I see- and just how did you do that?"

Peter smiled, raising his wooden pipes to his lips to make the magical song echo its beauty through the streets once again. He peered his evil eyes upon the children dancing foolishly towards him. Hook looked around at all the children's faces. Suddenly, through all their empty glassed eyes, he saw the dark truth. "*These children.* You are stealing children's souls for them." A fiery rage quickly welled inside of him as Peter laughed again. It suddenly felt as if guilt, anger, and hate would finally destroy the last essence of his being. "You are the devil! I'll send you back to hell!" Hook shouted as he whipped out his steel blade from his belt with murderous rage. Peter laughed, flying high into the air before swooping down and circled him beyond the blade's reach.

Peter laughed wildly, feeling so proud and happy with himself. "You know, I have had such fun these past years, but nothing quite as thrilling as this; how I've missed these little moments of ours. Come now- admit it. You've missed me too!"

"How did you find me?" Hook demanded in a harsh tone.

"I've been looking for you for some time now. I went back to the orphanage once, but it was gone- burnt down somehow. But I know you... I knew you had survived, but alas, I could not find you. Then through the whispers of fears and dreams, I heard the tales of a fearsome pirate going by the name of Hook, and I knew it was you. Now, look at you- so grown up and dignified. I must admit, you haven't disappointed me. Though I must ask, did you choose a life on the water just to hide from me?"

Hook scowled: "Hide from you? Why would you think that? Oh- because you are afraid to go anywhere near the water like an infant. No, Peter, I assure you I am not afraid of anything, and I am most definitely not afraid of an arrogant little brat like you! I am not the small lonely boy that you tormented all those years ago. That boy's heart and soul died with the orphanage. Time went on- I chose the life I wanted. After all, not all of us are afraid to grow up, Peter!"

"My name is not Peter anymore! I have been given the name of the god, Pan! Pan is my name now! You are not the only one that has changed, Hook!" Peter yelled as he slowly took in a large calming breath and closed his eyes for a moment before letting out a small chuckle. "Come now, old friend. Let's not be sore about the old times. After all, it was all just fun and games."

"I am not your friend, Peter Pan! I never was! You were nothing more than a sadistic psychopath striking fear into the minds of a bunch of lost little boys. Running around, trying to make everyone around you believe you were anything special, but I saw through you then, and I see through you now! Even with your new powers, you are still just a bully, preying on the weak. Well, I am not a little boy anymore. Fight me now, and I will strike you down! And when I'm done killing you, your little fairy is next!"

Tinker Bell stopped firmly in the air, shooting a burning stare at Hook. The intensity on her face grew until her entire body glowed a fiery red. The violent sound of loud chiming bells banging should have struck him with immense pain, but it was as if it fell upon deaf ears, leaving her confused and frustrated. She tried again, but still- nothing happened. Hook sneered up at her with a sly smile. Finally, her rage got the best of her. She whipped out her magic wand and shot her deadliest blast of magic towards him, but the magic disappeared before hitting its target. The spell vanished into thin air, leaving both Pan and Tinker Bell utterly stunned. Tinker Bell looked to Pan, making gestures of pointing and death. Hook could see Pan was somehow communicating with the disturbed fairy. When she was finished, they both looked back at Hook. She looked alarmed but Pan merely looked amused at the interesting turn of events.

"You're not the only one here with a trick up their sleeve, Peter Pan! You may indeed have the immense power of the fae coursing through you, but you see, that leaves you with quite the disadvantage!"

"Does it?" Pan asked smugly.

"It does! You see, a long time ago- another small fairy made a very grave mistake. She struck a bargain for the cost of one soul. In exchange for that one soul, I am protected by all fairy magic! No fairy creature can harm me in any way magical, and I guess now- that includes you! Now I will make the same promise to you that I made that wretched creature all those years ago. No matter where you go or what you do, I will find and kill you!" Hook roared. His promise struck pure terror into Tinker Bell's heart, but even as her fear overwhelmed her, she remained by Pan's side, waiting for his cue. But Pan didn't move, nor did he look bothered by the pirate's deadly threat.

"You may be right, James Hook. Maybe my kind can't harm you, but you and I both know that I am not one to follow the rules! I will find a way to beat you! Until then, you will remain here working, aging alone with only your bitterness and your books to keep you company. Find the magic you need to get into the magical realms, and when you do, I'll be waiting for you with an army!"

"What use is an army of fairies against me?"

"I speak of the soulless children in the land where time *never* flies, where games *never* end, and a place where you will *never- ever-* win!" Pan said in a fierce, confident voice.

"Oh, and just where is this Never- Neverland?" Hook asked enticed.

Pan chuckled lightly: "Neverland... I like that. It is my island! You will find it through the veil of the Ninth Realm." Pan waved his hand to Tink, before lifting the wooden pipes to his lips once more, playing the magical song as the small fairy spread sparkling green dust upon the dancing children. They slowly lifted into the air flying closely behind Tink towards the stars. Peter turned to follow when suddenly he turned his head back to look upon Hook's face once more. "Until that day, my old friend, I want you to know that with every child I steal, every soul I take, every power I have- I owe it all to you."

Hook raised his sword: "And I'll be the one to take it all away!" Hook screamed towards the sky as Pan, and his small green fairy flew away. After they had all disappeared, the winter chill returned to the air, and as he made his first step upon the stone road, Hook heard the loud ticking sound of the clocktower return.

CHAPTER FIFTEEN

BLACKBEARD'S CURSE

It was still late in the night when Hook boarded back upon the ship. Most of the crew had likely passed out somewhere in town, having spent all their money on rum and women. The Queen Anne's Revenge was dark and quiet. Hook stepped lightly, as he entered his private chamber. The bright moon shined its way through the foggy night air, into his window.

Hook had spent many years down below deck with the crew, but he had paid his dues. Working long hours on deck, sometimes going days without sleep, he had gained the respect of the captain. With his keen sense of direction and the finest skill of thievery, he had earned himself a high rank. He had mastered the art of sword fighting, winning many battles alongside his legendary captain, and had even been speared twice during a battle with Long John Silver. He had created an epic reputation for himself, and though he was still young, he had a strong presence. Throughout the lands and seven seas, Hook's name had become respected and feared.

After leading Blackbeard to massive amounts of treasure, he was finally given his cut of the crew's profits and his own private quarters. It was the first place he considered his home: It was well kept, with a large bed covered in thick blankets and pillows. There were large windows with the most beautiful and terrifying view. He laid awake many nights, enjoying the most magnificent storms. Hook spent most of what spare time he had within his grand room, reading. The walls were lined with anchored wooden shelves covered in various books of lore that he had collected throughout the years. But upon a small table next to his bed, laid his one prized possession, his mother's fairy tale book. It was the one thing he had when he arrived on this ship, and it was the one thing he would take with him when he left. He walked towards a small desk in the farthest corner of the room, next to the window. It was where he did most of his work and planning.

Blackbeard had counted on him for years for direction. He had braved the most violent of storms, always overpowering the deadliest of waters, leading the captain and his crew to mysterious islands hiding the most spectacular of treasures. Tales of the pirate's fearless spirit had become something of legend, saying not even Poseidon himself, could conjure up a storm strong enough to stop him.

Rumors had spread across the seas, that other captains wanted him, but he had never left Blackbeard. He reached down into a small drawer to grab his matchbox. It was one of his finest treasures, for it had been given to him as a gift from Blackbeard a year ago after they had won a fierce battle. It was small and tarnished, but it was made entirely of gold and on the top, was the engraved symbol of a pirate's hook.

Through the years past, Hook had acquired many pieces of gold and silver, along with offered tributes from the grateful crew, but this piece was different somehow. It was special. Hook had never celebrated a single Christmas, nor did he even know his birthday. He had never been given a real gift in his life before this one. He laid his eyes upon a candle and lit a match. He grabbed his maps and books, but the idea of leaving his home caused such anger that he violently threw it all against the walls. Though he was a master of the compass, he had no idea of where to start.

He had looked for another book of spells for years now with no luck. Magic wasn't a subject he could just utter wandering around town, for he could have been charged with conspiring with witchcraft and would ultimately be put to death. The whole matter had to be dealt with very carefully, but he never had the proper time to investigate the matter deeply.

Having heard the crashing commotion, Blackbeard barged in thinking someone was trying to rob his ship. The room looked as if a tornado had torn through it. Hook's knees hit the floor, burying his face in his hands. Blackbeard knelt in front of him, putting both of his large hands on Hook's shoulders. Blackbeard sat there silently amongst the dark destroyed room, waiting patiently for him to speak.

Hours went by, and the sun was already starting to rise upon the horizon. Blackbeard and Hook both looked out at the burning red sky, leaving both with a bad feeling as they knew the pirate's warning of such a day's greeting.

"I must leave," Hook said plainly.

Blackbeard shot him a look of surprise and dread: "What? Why?!"

Hook didn't answer, but Blackbeard wouldn't give up.

"Listen, whatever or whoever you are looking for, we can find it together. If anyone has dared crossed you, they have also crossed me. They will meet their end upon our swords!"

Hook shook his head, giving his vengeful captain a slight smile. "Where I am going, I cannot- I will not take your ship, your crew, or even you with me," Hook said sternly. He and Blackbeard stood from the floor. "I learned some time ago that you are more than just my captain. You have been my mentor, my most loyal ally, and above all- you have become my truest friend. So, I ask you to trust me."

The captain stood still. His face looked fierce, and his presence in the darkroom had become bigger somehow. He had never directed such anger at him before now. He wasn't surprised though. After all, Blackbeard was not the kind of man you should challenge, and he wasn't the kind of captain one could dare tell what he could or couldn't do. Blackbeard raised his chin, making his intense yellow eyes glow under the dark shadow of his large hat: "Now, look here, boy! You may be a fine pirate. I'd be a fool to

116

have not seen your skill on the ship and with a sword. But you are a fool if you think there is anyone, anywhere, or anything my ship, my crew, or I- Captain Blackbeard, couldn't handle!"

Hook humbly stepped towards him and put his hand upon his shoulder: "I meant no disrespect, my friend. I know you have the grandest ship and crew, and you are indeed a more fearsome captain than I could ever hope to be- but what I seek and where I must go will mean certain death. I will not be the man to set you and your ship's course to its doom."

Blackbeard remained silent for a moment as he watched Hook walk about the room, grabbing a large brown bag, only to put his mother's book inside. He had seen it many times over the years, yet its importance had never been discussed. After all, he was not a prying man, and Hook was not an open person.

In every way, Hook had been a mystery to him: his family, where he was from, and even his real name. But now, at this moment, he needed at least one answer from him. "Hook, if what you say is true, and I have indeed become a friend to you in any real way, then tell me what you're after! Give me the chance to help you, if I can," he spoke in a tone Hook had never heard before. It was both caring and concerned.

Something about his voice has somehow reached down into the depths of his bitter soul. It wasn't a welcome feeling for him, and everything within him wanted nothing more than to fight it off, but he couldn't. For that small bit of light left deep inside his tortured soul cared for Blackbeard. Hook couldn't walk away denying this one request.

He slowly placed his bag down upon his bed. "Come, Captain, let us sit at your table to enjoy one last meal together. We can talk, and I will tell you a tale- a *fairy* tale," he said looking into the captain's yellow eyes. He expected a look of shock or disbelief, but neither came. Instead, Blackbeard nodded gently before lifting his arm to the door. Hook left the bag on the bed and made his way to the grandest section of the ship- the captain's quarters. When one entered the room, their eyes were immediately drawn to the stacks of gold coins and three trunks full of beautiful gems and jewels that the captain had acquired over his many adventures at sea.

The room itself was not clean or tidy like his, but rather dirty. The air was musty and thick. His treasures were never touched and covered in dust. The windows were draped with thick red curtains and were never to be opened on pain of death.

Whenever Hook had asked about it, Blackbeard said it was bad luck for the fish to see your riches. For if Poseidon learned of your vast treasures, he would use all the power of the sea to devour your ship, taking all of it down into its depths to claim the marvelous loot for himself. He had also warned him to never chase after Poseidon's sunken treasure, for it would be cursed and damn the ship and all its crew until every piece was returned into the sea.

Hook had always taken heed to everything Blackbeard had ever told him, and it made him a better pirate for it. Blackbeard wasn't much of a paranoid man, but when it came to his room and his treasure, he couldn't be more careful. None of the crew besides Hook dared to go anywhere near it. There was a time some years past when he still lived below deck with the crew.

Late one night, the men had gathered around, drinking, playing dice, and talking. As it is with most pirates, it doesn't take long for the subject to turn to treasure, and although the captain paid his crew decent enough, most of the men would squander their profits quickly on drinks, gambling, and the company of a woman, leaving them once again penniless. But it was on this one particular night, after a little too much liquid courage, one man dared to sneak into the captain's quarters while he slept and made the fatal attempt of stealing a single piece of Blackbeard's gold.

No sooner had his dirty fingers wrapped around the shiny coin did his severed hand hit the floor. In the next terrifying moments, Hook and the crew watched as the traitor was dragged out onto the main deck. The man clutched his bloodied arm, screaming in horror as the frightening captain towered over him. Blackbeard commanded the attention of the rest of his crew, demanding their assistance with tying the man to the main mast with rope. The man screamed, begging for mercy, but Blackbeard was not a forgiving man. Even asking for a quick death from Blackbeard was like waiting for a miracle that would never come. After some roaring words of anger, it was all just a blur of screaming, whipping, and slicing.

When the man finally died, the ship went so silent, the only thing you could hear was the sound of blood dripping down from the man's mangled body onto the deck. Hook had watched the whole thing without a single flinch or a second of pity. For the entire crew knew the rules about the captain's quarters- just as everyone knew if you dared cross Blackbeard, your death would be long and severe.

Hook and Blackbeard entered the room and walked towards a large wooden table far off by the windows. There were so many drapes around the walls; it was as if you were sitting in a red room. There was a gigantic iron chandelier hanging above the table filled with small white candles that brightly lit up the room.

When they sat down at the table, Blackbeard leaned over to a large bowl upon the table; it was full of cigars and matches. He grabbed one of each, lifted his boot and scratched the match, lighting its flame. He took three puffs of smoke off the cigar before he began to speak: "So, my dear boy," he puffs. "Am I to understand you are in search of- magic?" Hook was stunned. "Don't think me a fool boy, for I have been around a long time and have encountered many things. I could tell you tales that would make your blood run cold... ghost, witches, and curses. I've seen haunted ships sailing the same waters as I. I have even fought against an army of the living dead," Blackbeard boasted, taking in another large puff of smoke.

"What about fairies? Have you ever encountered a fairy?" Hook asked in a deep voice.

Instantly, the captain's yellow eyes flickered with fear. It was as if the very air in the room had changed. Blackbeard dropped his legs from the table and sat up looking very uncomfortable. He didn't say anything but rather just gulped harshly as if the word itself was difficult to swallow. There was a moment of silence between them, but the answer was clear. The frightened look in his eyes was unmistakable. "You have."

Blackbeard shuffled his hands together as if preparing himself for what he was about to say. Hook leaned forward as Blackbeard put out the cigar into a small wooden ashtray sitting upon the table between them. "It was many years ago. I was just a lad back then, though I remember it like it was yesterday. When I was a young captain, I was far too risky. I was foolish and obsessed with treasure. I went on daring adventures. Many of which, resulted in vast amounts of legendary treasure. My wealth and power made me arrogant. I was always searching for a bigger challenge-this was a mistake. I was like you Hook. I wasn't keen on reading books, but I was incredibly fond of stories, and through my travels, I had heard of the most legendary treasure. It was hidden in a place known as the great black cave on the Isle of Man. It was said to be guarded by some otherworldly creature called the

Nightman. Now, if you had asked me at the time if I believed in curses or magical beings, I would have laughed right in your face, but I was wrong- very wrong! I set sail for the Isle with a full crew. I remember the day was clear. There were no clouds in the sky, and the hot blazing sun beat down upon us. I remember the sweat pouring down my face and back. The waves were nice. My hand was steady at the wheel. Everything seemed a little too easy, but as we drew closer, I couldn't shake the feeling that I was somehow being tricked. I tried to shake it off and kept going forward. I remember the moment I looked through my spyglass to gaze upon the Isle. At first, there was nothing out of the ordinary, but we drew closer, the foam from the sea raised into the form of a man. Not believing what I had just seen was real, I looked back up into the spyglass. The creature was still there. It looked to made up of foam and mist. I could see the great black cave behind him. Then suddenly, this thing started making this horrific howling sound. It didn't sound as if it was angry or afraid; it sounded like it was calling something. The crew panicked, begging me to turn back, but I couldn't. I knew if I did, my name would be ruined. I wouldn't be deemed a coward. I just couldn't- so I kept forward. The air began to change. The winds blew cold and hard, and the waves began to thrash with rage. The sky soon filled with black clouds, bringing forth the most powerful storm I had ever seen. I looked through the spyglass again, trying to see the howling creature again, but the storm had made it impossible to see anything. It was as if this creature had called upon a monster in the clouds, and it wasn't going to stop until we turned away. Violent crashing waves threatened to tear my ship apart. We were heading right for the cliffs, and I knew if we went any further, we would crash right into them. To save my ship and my crew, I used all the remaining strength in my body to turn the wheel as hard as I could. I could hear the screams of my men. I thought it was the unforgiving sea from the storm that had consumed them, but then I heard something else in the water. Men were being ripped off the ship one by one. I wanted to save them, but I knew if I let go of the wheel even for a second, the ship would give, and we would all die. I'll never forget the sound of their screams! I will never forget the sound of that howling creature! And I will never forget the chilling silence upon my escape! When I had sailed far enough away from the Isle of Man, the howling stopped, the clouds went away, and the air became clear again. I'll tell you, Hook, I've never been so happy to see the sun in all my life. But my moment of relief was short lived as I looked down at the deck to see I had no surviving crew. There was blood everywhere! But- there- were- no- bodies! I sailed in silence for weeks after that. I wasn't sure how or why I had survived, but it was then that I realized the curse of guilt I would be left with forever. Their ghosts haunted me in my dreams. Their screams tortured me every night. Then one morning, I woke to the sound of that awful howling. It wasn't long until I could see and hear them when I was awake. I thought I must be going mad. I tried to drown them out with rum. It worked at first, Hell I drank so much, I was surprised every morning that I woke up. But as time passed, it got worse. Their screams were getting louder. The rum wasn't helping anymore. I was starting to see the mangled corpses of my crew around me. I became so haunted that I had lost count of my days on the sea. I should have died from lack of food or water, but somehow, I didn't. The relentless howling came for me every night. I couldn't sleep. One day, I reached for a bottle of rum, but they were all empty. Out of hopelessness and frustration, I smashed the bottle. I tried to use the broken glass to end my suffering, but as I looked down waiting for the blood of life to pour away, but it never came. I wasn't bleeding at all! In a sort of panic and confusion, I ran below deck to grab a gun and fired a shot to my head- again nothing. There was gun powder on my hand, and I heard the gunfire, but I was not wounded at all. My legs buckled then. I hit the floor weeping, begging for mercy- begging for death, but it never came. As my haunting days went on, my sorrow turned into something else. I became angry, wrathful, and overcome with determination. If I wasn't going to die, then I was going to find a way to kill that creature. I sailed ashore looking for the same thing you are searching for now. I was looking for magic- and I found it! As it happened, my name was not ruined, as there was no one left alive to tell the tale. I kept quiet about everything. I have never told a single soul about that day until now."

"You said you found magic. How?"

Blackbeard huffed: "I looked day and night for something to end my suffering. Then one night, I

124

came across an old man in a dark street. He uttered something to me quietly. When I leaned in closely, I heard him say that I was cursed! I thought it odd, so I began asking him many questions. He told me of a witch in the woods that could help. I was in Ireland; there were wooded areas everywhere. The man refused to guide me, but as I am a pirate, searching for hidden things is what I'm good at. When I finally found the odd old bat, she invited me into her little cabin. It was as dirty and as strange as she was. I dared not show her any disrespect, as I desperately needed her help. We sat down at a small table with two damaged chairs. I started to tell her of my predicament, but before I could say more than a few words, she raised one of her tiny hands to silence me. She stood up and walked over to a rather extraordinary shelved area, much like yours. It was covered in books, candles, and clouded old jars. She took down a large green book and brought it over to the table. As she opened it, a cloud of dust appeared, causing her to cough harshly. She ran her long fingernails down the pages. She went on doing this page after page, her forgetfulness testing my patience, but just as I was starting to doubt her and get up to leave, she cackled loudly to herself as if she could hear my thoughts. I felt my temper burn at that moment. I demanded to know if she could fix me or not! When she looked up at me, her eyes were fierce and bright green. I have never seen eyes like that before; they were both beautiful and enchanting for one so old. She told me she could not lift the curse of the Dooinney oie, but for the right price, maybe she could change it.

She said that I would continue to be immortal, but that she could turn my curse into a gift. She said she would silence the noises and give me a blind eye for the ghost, but that should never suggest that they are not still there, watching me every moment. I admit I was so thrilled, that I screamed, 'Yes! Name your price! Anything you want, it is yours!"

She gave me a wicked smile and simply said, "Good."

"Then she stood up, waving her arms in the air, muttering words in a language I had never heard or understood. Then suddenly, as I looked around, all the wailing ghost and distant howling were gone. I was so thrilled that I thanked her incessantly. She said there was no need to thank her, that there was just the matter of payment. I asked her what she wanted, and her answer will torment me forever."

"What did she want?" Hook asked feeling his heart racing.

A tear welled up in Blackbeard's eye as he answered: "My first-born child. I remember feeling both a bit of confusion and relief, for at the time- I did not have a child, nor did I ever think I would. I agreed, thinking I had gotten off easily. She said that I didn't need to bring the baby to her, that something would come and take it away. I remember how those words sent chills up my spine. When I asked what would come to take it away, she cackled."

"A fairy of course," she said.

"Her answer surprised me, yet I had another question to ask: What about the mother?

Again, the witch laughed. She said I did not have to worry about such things. She said- 'just don't have anything red around the baby. That it would be switched in the dead of night, and that the mother need never know.'

I couldn't help feeling overwhelmed with terror with what she had said, but you have to understand, I couldn't bear the thought of being haunted for eternity."

Hook nodded feeling both alarm and pity for Blackbeard: "Of course, I understand. This *Wood Witch*, is she still out there?"

"I don't know. I have tried to go back many times to find her, but the little cabin in the woods is gone now, with no trace that it was ever there. I know she is still out there, for, in my many travels, I have heard different stories of her. For every person, her location has changed. I tell you all this hoping that in some way my story helps you, but I urge you to let whatever this is go. Whether for vengeance or out of desperation, the cost of magic will bring you nothing but further torment."

Hook shook his head as he stood up from the table. "I'm sorry, Captain, but like you- this is just something I must do." Blackbeard buried his head as Hook walked to the door about to leave the chambers when suddenly a thought crept up inside of him,

127

forcing him to ask: "Captain, did you ever have a child?"

Blackbeard raised his head slowly: "Yes, I did."

Hook suddenly understood his captain's dark soul. "And did the fairies take it?"

Blackbeard looked across the room at all his piles and trunks full of treasure. "I don't know. I did meet a nice girl once. We fell in love, and when I learned she was with child, I couldn't bear the guilt. In a drunken rage, I told her the truth. Her poor heart broke right before my eyes. I promised her I would make it right. I collected as much gold and jewels as I could and searched tirelessly for the witch, hoping she would accept my riches in exchange for my unborn child's freedom, but I could never find her. I covered my ship entirely with red, but when my son was born, his mother became overcome by fear. She took off with him one night while I was sleeping. I never saw either of them again. Years have passed, but I've always held on to some hope that the fairies never found him."

Hook's heart fell to his stomach. "Him?"

"My son."

"What... What was your son's name?"

Blackbeard looked up and smiled weakly: "James. My son's name was James."

CHAPTER SIXTEENTH

THE WOOD WITCH

Hook stormed out of the room without another word, leaving the captain alone with his grief. Quickly grabbing the bag off his bed, Hook left the room and the ship that had become his home, and the captain that had been a father to him, through both sea and blood. Hook didn't know how to feel or what to say.

Everything had become so unbearably clear; it was impossible to process a single thought. It all made sense: why his mother had given him up, why the Scarlet Fairy had come after him, why he had such a profound connection with the captain, and why he had such a great love for the sea. Being a pirate was in his very blood, and somehow fate had brought everything together.

A part of him wanted to be angry with Blackbeard for everything that had happened, but somehow, he just couldn't. For he had seen the genuine sadness that had flooded the captain's heart. And though Hook was not one to let go of a grudge, deep down he had seen Blackbeard's remorse and that his ghost though invisible, still haunted him to this day,

If he told Blackbeard the truth of who he was, he knew it would only bring the captain more anguish, for no matter how many years had passed, or how hard Blackbeard tried to avoid it, the truth was that the fairies had found him, and though Sister Roger had saved him, it was Blackbeard that would unknowingly lead him to the very Wood Witch he had promised him to all those years ago.

But none of that changed anything, Hook would find this Wood Witch, and when he did, he would discover the magic that would lead him into the Nine Realms. And once Peter Pan and the Scarlet Fairy had met their bloody end, he will have made the wrong things right.

It was all up to him.

Just as Blackbeard had said, tales of the Wood Witch had traveled far across the lands of Scotland, Ireland, and Wales. Her house had always been found by a wandering traveler lost in the woods, caught in some dreadful weather of fog or rain. Ultimately, they stumble across an old cabin. While many left her cabin with good fortune, others had barely managed to stay alive.

Hook listened carefully, studying every detail of their terrifying encounters, trying to find that one detail that would help lead him to her. Most of the story's details surround merely her frightening haggard appearance: a hag with hair as white as snow and skin cracked like old stone instead of wrinkled and worn. The cabin itself has only ever been seen in the woods and always surrounded by large black birds. It's never seen in the same place twice and only visible in the

wee hours of the morning and the darkest hours at
night, luring in the lost and desperate.

But there was one legendary song, that might
ultimately give Hook the key to finding her:

Deep in the woods lives an old witch
Far beyond the trees
Her skin so cold and grey like stone
With eyes of emerald green
Through the thickest of fog
Or the hard-pouring rain
When you are at your weakest
And your body aches with pain
Look and listen for her crows
Circling above in the sky
For whenever you should see them
The Wood Witch is always nearby
Should you ever be so unlucky
To be lost by the hour of three
You'll surely be lured to her cabin
And invited in for tea
Should you sit warm by her fire
And hear her beautiful song
You better repay her kindness
Or you will not live for long.
However silly or severe your bargain
How much time has passed, or how far you go;
If you should ever break your word...
The Wood Witch will surely know.

Hook had been so careful and precise in his search for the Wood Witch, he realized now, that is why Blackbeard had never found her again. For only the lost and desperate would fall victim to the sight of her welcoming cabin, offering warmth and shelter to those with lost hope. He had been going about this all wrong, waiting for the right time, the right weather, and the right direction, but this was a place only found by the lost, and he had not been either of those things in many years. Feeling discouraged and frustrated, he wandered into a small pub off one of the large dirt roads near the forest. Many looked up at him in marvel, for many knew of his fame.

"What would you like to drink tonight, sir?" Asked a young barmaid.

Hook thought to himself for a second as he looked down at his compass. Tonight, he was going to do something else- he was going to be someone else. He snapped the compass and put it away in his bag. "Sure, miss, get me a glass of port. Better yet, bring me the bottle." He spent the next extended hours of the night drinking more and more. He wasn't much of a drinker, as he always liked to remain focused and in control, but none of that would do for now, and he could think of no other way of becoming what he needed to find her. Every sip of alcohol that ran down his throat brought with it every torturous memory that he had successfully suppressed for years. The feelings brought forth both a mighty rage and terrible sadness. It was all so horrible; he couldn't understand why anyone would want such an experience. He tried with all his power to fight off his demons, but the venom coursing through him made it impossible. His head felt heavy, and his body felt hot and sick, but he had to keep going. After the pub closed, Hook stepped down the dark dirt road, heading straight into the deep black forest. he wandered off the narrow trail drifting farther into the darkness. Everything was a blur as he stumbled through, his skin being cut by the crowding brushes and his head spinning as he fought the unbearable urge to throw up. It didn't take long for him to realize he was indeed very lost, his body growing sore as the hours brought dehydration. Uncertain of the hour or having even the faintest idea of where he was, he looked around completely disoriented and began screaming out into the darkness in frustration.

"Where are you? Why won't you show yourself? Appear before me!" His voice echoed loudly throughout the dark woods. After each exhausted breath, his body drew closer to collapse. His body was growing weaker. *Why can't I see the cabin? Am I not weak or lost enough?* Tears began pouring down his pale cheeks, as he couldn't bear the thought of ever doing this again. *This is it! I must find her tonight! I must! For if this doesn't work, nothing ever will.* His thoughts and desperation swarmed him. The volume of the surrounding animals of the forest increased. This was not a time for bravery: he needed to be helpless, and he needed to be afraid. Letting an overwhelming wave of a panic crash over him, he began to run. He tore through the trees as fast as he could move. Suddenly he tripped over a broken log of wood in front of him, hitting his head on a large rock on the ground. Blood began to drip down from the open gash. His eyes were barely able to open. The forest had gone utterly silent as Hook looked down to see a single raindrop fall upon his blood on the stone. Then all the sudden he looked up to discover a large black crow land upon the bloody rock right before his eyes. It stared at him for a moment before flying away in the rain. The crow was heading towards a small wooden cabin on top of a hill. The cold rain soaked him as he stumbled towards it still bleeding and utterly confused. With each step, he couldn't help but notice a murder of carrion crows. They were suddenly everywhere: on the tree branches, on top of her roof, and circling the stormy sky above. It was both a strange and creepy sight, even for him. Smoke from her chimney and the light from her cabin was such a welcoming sight to see. He couldn't help feeling so relieved, and he knew that that's exactly what she wanted. He hated that he was in such a helpless state, as he needed to talk to her with a sound mind and reason. He drew closer to the door. As he reached for the wooden post on her porch, he bent down and purged. The poisoned sickness within him came out upon the ground. And with each violent breath, he felt much better, and though he was still not entirely sober, the thoughts inside his head were rapidly becoming clearer. Once he caught his breath, he pulled himself up. He reached his hand to knock, but before he could, the door suddenly creaked open, revealing a small old hag.

"Come in, child; I've been waiting for you." The old woman said with an eerie crooked smile. She turned and sauntered towards a small stone fireplace within the room. She reached her hand out guiding him to two old wooden rocking chairs sitting warmly in front of the calm flames.

Hook looked around, taking in all his surroundings, everything seemed so petite and beautiful, it was not at all as Blackbeard had described. Maybe this was not the witch at all; maybe this was just some harmless old woman. The very thought was delusional, yet he couldn't help feeling succumb to the charming little cabin. Everything was so clean and neat, small trinkets displayed so carefully in a special place. Suddenly the words she had said at the door shook him to his very core, a feeling of such alarm that his blood ran cold, a moment that sobered him quickly. Hook closed his eyes still standing within the doorway. *I've been waiting for you.*

Her voice echoed in his head. *It is her.*

He opened his eyes to find the beautiful illusion that he had found so safe and charming only a moment before, now appeared damp and wretched. The walls were tattered, and grey, the shelves that had previously held such beautiful trinkets and treasures were now stacked with clouded jars of herbs and candles. The place suddenly carried the smell of death within its decrepit walls.

It was damaged and worn. The witch turned back towards him; her appearance much more haggard than before. She wore a large light grey cloak that covered her hunched back, with a hood that laid upon her head of long hair the color of the first frost of winter snow. Her skin looked like old clay, damaged and cracked with age. Her mouth was small, and her cheeks were high. She seemed very short and bony, she walked with a wooden cane, and her body shook like that of a weak old woman, but as he looked upon her frightening face, his eyes were immediately drawn to her eyes. For within them was the undeniable burst of green. Each were as bright and vibrant as a wild garden in spring. The green wasn't her entire eye color, for she was merely a distant descendant of the fae, but the flicker of magic hidden behind the surface of a mere witch was still very much alive with fae blood and was undoubtedly the reason she has lived so long.

"Come, James, sit down by the warm fire with me."

Hook stepped forward. "I can see that you think you know who I am, but I am not James. He died a long time ago. And though I know of Blackbeard's promise to you, you must know that that is not why I am here."

The witch choked on her cackling laugh as she sat down and began rocking in one of the chairs by the fire. "Yet you are here, and I assume you didn't come here just to stand in my doorway. Come and sit down.

You need not be afraid of me; I am not going to hurt you, my dear boy."

Hook sneered at the thought as he sat fearless in the chair next to her. "I am not afraid of you, witch. I am here for your help, and while I do not trust a single bone in your body, I am quite confident I will leave with the answers I seek."

The witch rubbed her bony hands together and gave the young pirate a slight smirk, amused with his arrogance. "I see. Well, as you should know all too well, my help comes at a cost."

"Not for me," Hook interrupted.

The witch's face turned and went still and fierce, angered by his blatant disrespect. "Foolish child! Do you not know who and what I am!?"

"Oh, yes, I know exactly *who* and *what* you are, which is how I know you are going to tell me exactly what I want to know!"

Her stone face cracked with fury. "How dare you! I'll blast you!" She exclaimed as she rose up from her chair.

"I assure you, witch, I am no fool. I know that for magic, there indeed must be a trade, but what I desire is not your magic. But fear not, for our little trade tonight will benefit you as well as I, for I am willing to offer you something should you be wise enough to answer all of my questions to my utmost satisfaction."

His manner had now awoken her rage. "I shall curse thee!" She screamed, dropping her cane and raising her arms up high. The green in her eyes glowed as she roared violently in a language Hook had never heard. The front door swung open, and a mighty wind came crashing through the cabin blowing out the fire and circling around, but nothing touching him. He stood watching as the violent wind began to demolish the cottage. The wind had turned into a frightening storm within the cabin, yet he stood calm and untouched as her furniture began to thrash about the room violently. The look on his face was as if he was merely waiting for her poor pathetic attempt to be over. The witch screamed in horror as her face and arms began to crack rapidly. She weakly sat back down in the rocking chair out of breath.

"My name is not James, it is Hook, and I have absolute protection from all fae power and seeing as we both know that you are a descendant of the fae, that means that you too cannot harm me. So, you see, your curses are nothing more than a waste of both our time. So how about we sit back down, and I will explain the terms of our agreement." The witch looked uneasy and bothered by whatever had just happened.

"All trades are done at my table. We must sit there."

Hook stood back up and nodded. "That is fine by me."

She sat down in one of the rickety chairs. As she did, one of the crows flew down upon her shoulder. It had suddenly occurred to him that through all of this, the crows had just been there watching quietly somehow. Hook walked over to the dingy table and sat down in front of her. But both remained eerily silent- just staring at each other. The witch's face was covered in confusion and hatred; she wanted so badly to understand why her spell had not worked. It didn't even touch him. She had never felt so disturbed. He sat in front of her, reveling in her moment of failure.

Squinting at him with a hateful glare, she finally decided to speak. "Well, are you just going to sit there? Explain yourself! What sort of magic is this?!" She asked in utter frustration.

Hook gave her a wicked smile and leaned forward. "Let us rather discuss the terms of our trade. After all, we both know how much you love a good bargain."

"I don't make trades on terms that are not my own! I won't!"

Hook chuckled at her defiance. "Oh, but you will. See, what I offer you is something that you hold most dear- your life!"

"I have lived an awfully long time, boyo. What makes you so sure you can end my life?"

"I sit here across your table with as much desire to kill you like all the rest of them, and on behalf of all the lives you have cursed and destroyed, I'd say you more than deserve it. Alas, I need your help. So, let me make this very plain. I have questions- questions I know you can answer. Tell me what I want to know, and I will let you live. I will walk out of that door, and you will never see me again. Do we have a bargain?"

"How do I know you won't just kill me once I have told you what you want to know. Our deal is not one bound by the law of magic, you could easily break your word."

Hook nodded his head. "True, you don't know if I am lying. I imagine someone who has spent all their wretched life using trickery and deceit couldn't possibly feel anything but as unbearably skeptical as you are now. Yet, I ask this: what other choice do you have? If you don't tell me what I want, I will indeed kill you. But if you should answer my questions truthfully, then maybe you will get to live. I am not going to sit at this table and implore to you that my intentions are honorable, for I must admit I find true pleasure in your agonizing concerns of doubt."

With a regrettable sigh, she submitted. "What is your first question?"

Hook smiled wickedly. "My first question is about the fairy you sent after me when I was born. Was is her true name?"

The witch shook her head with worry. "I do not know the name of the fairy herself, only the name of the type of fairy she is. It was the Duoine Sidhe that came after you. It is their job to steal children, and until you, I have never known them to fail."

Hook hummed displeased with her answer.

"I assure you, if I knew the rightful name of the fairy that failed me, I would have dealt with her myself."

"Her failure to capture was not her only mistake, nor will it be only her that suffers for it."

"And what makes you think I won't warn the fae if given a chance?" She asked bravely, though her body shook afraid.

"Oh, I hope you do."

"And why is that?"

"Because unlike you and your kind, it is not my mission to cowardly hide. Let them know that death is coming for them! Let them try to hide! It makes absolutely no difference to me because I will still find and kill all of them. Yet, I must say it is rather unwise for you to give them such a warning."

The witch's face distorted, cracking once again in anger. "Why?"

He laughed evilly. "Because it is you that is going to tell me how to find them, of course." With every gasp of his laughter brought with them a dark black cloud over her heart. She could not see a way out of this. It was to be her actions that would set in play the very end of magic itself. She felt weak and completely broken, for at this moment what could she do.

"How do I find the realms? And remember, I will slice you dead if should you lie."

It was then under the stress of the blade that she started to sing:

"Seven veils to the Nine Realms
you will find here on Earth
Never knowing which was last
And which one was the first
Through the gardens
you will find the small gnomes
And through the old wardrobe
are the wild creatures of summer, spring, and snow
Through the Great Labyrinth
you will find many goblins
And through the second star to the right,
you will find the Lost Island.
Through the looking glass
lies the opposite of everything,
leaving everyone inside it
utterly insane
Through the woods are the Fair Folk
Dancing at their ball
Usually dressed more fancy
Then any perfect doll
Across the bridge, you find the trolls
of the tale the Billy goat three
And the Realm of Monsters you will find
Deep below the sea
Only by your end,
will you find the Realm of the Dead
And it's in the Land of Dreams,
Where they'll find you in your bed."

With the last word of her rhymes, her voice cracked in a sad whimper, so saddened that it was to be her that would be the one to lead him to them.

"And what if you couldn't fly through the stars, is there another way to the island?"

The witch was alarmed by the frightening tone in his voice. "Well actually, there is another way to get to the Lost Island, but it is almost impossible to achieve. If you were to travel upon the sparkling road on the longest night of the year, the moon would light the sparkling road that will ultimately lead you there. But there are creatures to guard each veil between this world and theirs, and the monster in the sea is by far the evilest. You would need to get to the island before a single spot of light from the sun touched the top of the horizon. For if you don't, the Lost Island will disappear, and you will have to wait for another whole year." Her words were rhyming back and forth as if she was somehow breaking down in a fit of insanity. Her heart filled with horror as she watched her words of guidance bring a wicked smile to his face.

"Oh, don't look so sad- I'm sorry, what is your name? Out of all the tales I have read, it never seemed to be quite clear."

The witch weakly lifted her head to answer: "I have been called by many names over the ages: Mother Molly as of late."

"You don't deserve to be called the mother of anything."

She looked up as another crystal tear fell down her cracked face. Her voice choked as she sobbed, begging him to remove his blade, for though he had not cut her, it was somehow burning into her cracking flesh. He lifted his sword but kept it ready as if that was a mere warning. She bent her head back down looking upon his sword. "Iron. Your sword is made of iron?"

Hook gave her a single yet a clear nod.

She gathered her breath and wiped her face. She needed to pull herself together if she was going to survive this. "It was your father's arrogant actions and greed that cursed him. Though you choose to only blame me for where we are now, you must understand that you would not be here right now if it weren't for him. You would have never set eyes upon a fairy if it wasn't for him. You wouldn't be spending your life with only hatred and bitterness in your heart, desiring only vengeance and death if it wasn't for him! Your anger blinds you from the truth. Humans are not victims; they are the killers! They must be punished for their crimes, and should you smite me down right here, and now, I want you to remember what I've said!" She said sternly with sincere passion in her voice.

Hook sneered at her as he slowly laid his sword on the table, the handle still in his hand. The blade so close to her, she could feel it like a scorching heat all over her body. "Stealing babies, destroying souls, and luring unsuspecting people to a fate worse than death, are not moral weapons of war. True, Blackbeard, amongst many other mortal's actions are that of sin and greed, but don't think your kind superior when you hide, steal, trick, lie, and kill for nothing more than sheer pleasure."

She nodded slowly. "You asked how you find them- the Nine Realms. How did you find me?" She asked as if her question was somehow his answer.

Hook looked around the cabin, and then back to her. "The crows. In my brief moment of desperation, it was the crows that led me to you. Why crows? I thought cats were a witch's thing?"

She looked to her shoulder stroking the black feathers of one of her darling pets. "Many believe that, but cats are other-worldly creatures, tied neither to this land or the next. No, it is the crows that belong to me. Mortals think that all the animals here are all from this realm and are easily hunted down and killed, but not every creature from this land is the prey; many are the predators. Should you see the faintest glow of green in their eyes, it is a warning that you are too close to fae territory. You may see mortals as saints, moral, and honorable, but it was the humans that started this war, and with every amount of destruction and every death they cause, the animals will watch- and the fae will know. There is but one animal that is the truest friend of man. The vile creature can see and even smell creatures of magic or the dead, yet it remains at the human's side, loyal and true."

Hook looked intrigued. "And can this creature see through and could even guide me through a veil?"

145

She nodded hesitantly.

"I see. And just what is this loyal creature of man?"

The witch looked as if she had just swallowed something sickening as she opened her mouth to answer. "The dog. Filthy beast!"

He smiled at her displeasure. "Hmmm- a dog. How interesting indeed. How has such information gone so unnoticed? I am a well-read man, yet I have never seen or discovered this special sight of dogs you speak of."

The witch scowled as if it was an impertinent question. "Because humans believe only with their own eyes. The language of an animal is completely unknown to them, leaving the humans to believe they are the superior race and treating even their most loyal of allies as mere slaves. Meanwhile, the animal fights us and protects humans despite their poor treatment. I will never understand that foolish animal's loyalty."

Hook's face was still, taking in her every word and gesture. He reveled in her hatred for the little animal. *How curious.* "Well, you have been most helpful, witch! I think I will be off now. Tell or warn whoever you wish, though I fear it will only bring you harm. Pray, we never meet again", Hook said as he stood up from the wooden table, feeling the cold stares of the cabin's surrounding crows as he walked towards her door.

She nodded in relief. "I will not forget this! That you were a man of your word," she said in a grateful tone, feeling better with each step he made towards the door, putting more distance between her and his iron.

He turned to face her as he put his hand on the doorknob: "Goodbye then, witch. Shall we never set eyes on each other again." As he stepped out the door and off her porch, a whishing sound behind him, Hook turned around to find that the cabin wasn't there anymore. The crows, the rain, the Wood Witch: it was all just gone.

REVEAL

The search for the Wood Witch was over, and time was of the very essence now. It was time to send word to the Queen Anne's Revenge -to its captain! Hook was ready to tell Blackbeard everything. But with his new knowledge of the Nine Realms and how to get there, the rest was merely the difficult task of planning. To achieve his goal, he would need Blackbeard's help with the means to buy a ship and crew.

Hook knew he would require much more extended study on time before he could set course on the sparkling road, but in the meantime, there were other realms to visit. Not all the realms would suffer the pirate's deadly wrath. He could neither reach the Realm of the Gods nor could he enter the Realm of the Dead without being dead himself.

So, for the next few weeks, he wandered about looking for every book that contained ancient tales of lore and the other creatures that the Wood Witch had mentioned in her moment of manic rhymes. He wanted to learn all about them; every portal and the realms behind each veil.

Hook was going on his third sleepless night when suddenly a knock came at the door. He rose frantically, drawing his sword from his belt. But before he could open the door, a small letter slid in from underneath. He heard footsteps as the person who delivered it walked away. Hook bent down to pick up the small envelope. On the top was the same symbol that had been engraved into his matchbox. The letter was from Blackbeard. He walked over to sit in a large comfy chair in the corner of the room to open the letter.

I was most happy to hear from you, old friend.
I have already set sail for Wales and should
be there to meet with you in a little more
than a week. I proudly await the tale
of your latest victory.

Your true friend,
Blackbeard

Hook crumbled the letter and threw it into the trash bin. He couldn't help but feel he had somehow let Blackbeard down, for he knew what he was hoping for some sort of knowledge of the Wood Witch that would lead him back on the path to finding his lost son. But the answers that awaited the cursed captain was more than he could possibly imagine. A week felt like it would be forever to Hook. It was all he could do to keep calm within his room of tight walls full of books. Each page within them fueled his fiery rage. He wanted to burn them all- every evil creature hidden within a magical realm. But the journey to one could take an entire lifetime, and time here on earth would stop for no mortal. He had to find the sparkling road and travel to Neverland while he still could. The lore of the various creatures mounted higher and higher, yet he couldn't find anything about the sparkling road. It just didn't seem to exist.

Hook was exhausted, having stressed alone for days in a small room with no food and nothing to drink but well water from the outside. The portals, the creatures, and the countless souls that had fallen victim within the legendary stories had begun to haunt his every waking hour.

One night, after endless hours of reading about trolls, Hook finally passed out, when suddenly a loud knock came at the door. At first, it wasn't enough to wake up the tired pirate, but the knocking continued growing louder. The booming sound woke him up in a fright. It was the middle of the night, and Hook was furious that someone had dared disturb the rare amount of sleep he had. He stormed to open the door, ready to beat whoever it was, but when the door opened, he was instantly overwhelmed with relief as his eyes set upon Blackbeard.

"What happened, my boy? Your face is pale as a sheet. You look like you've seen a ghost."

Hook smirked at him, quickly trying to hide his troubles. He didn't like anyone being able to read him like that. He walked over to sit down in a chair to put his boots on. "Come- let us go somewhere we can talk," Hook said as he grabbed his coat and walked out the door.

As they made their way out to the stone road, Blackbeard grabbed Hook's coat. "Stop, lad. You must tell me what is going on? Did you find the Wood Witch?"

Hook looked back at his former captain. "I know you have waited a long time, my friend, but let's walk up a bit farther. There is a pub that is open very late and may very well still be open. I have not eaten a meal in days, and I am sure I will be able to think and talk better once I have a little something in my stomach. But don't worry, Captain, there is much to say," Hook said as he turned to walk on down the road.

After a few miles north, they had finally come across a small town where the nightlife seemed to be wide awake. Hook knew this was a place where men like themselves would feel right at home in this drab town. Sure enough, there was a pub nearby with lights still on. There were crowds of hollering men inside. When Blackbeard opened the door, all the loud cheers and laughter went silent as their eyes looked up at two of the most feared pirates of all the seven seas. It was a feeling that both Blackbeard and Hook secretly loved. It was nice being that feared and respected. The people that were already sitting there quickly grabbed their stuff and scurried out of their way. Once they sat down at a table, Hook raised his arm to summon a waitress. Words about the young pirate's kindness towards women had spread around. It was something that made all the barmaids in the area feel a little safer. Blackbeard however, still sent chills down everyone's spine. He was in all manner, a heartless bastard, but only Hook knew why.

A young barmaid approached the table. She must have been nervous because she kept giggling after every word she said. A character trait that was starting to get under Blackbeard's skin. Soon she had brought some drinks, hot soup, and warm bread to the table.

"Thank you, doll. That will be everything. Now leave my friend and me alone. We have important matters to discuss, and I won't have any interruptions. Now take this and be on your way," Blackbeard said as he gave her more than enough pieces to cover her services.

Her eyes grew wide in delight as she gazed at the shiny coins in her hand. She started to giggle until she looked down to find Blackbeard turning his head to glare at her with an irritated face. "Oh... yes, sir. Right away, sir. I will not disturb you or your guest again." She turned to walk away when suddenly he grabbed her tiny arm roughly.

"Maybe you didn't understand me," he said harshly. Hook subtly coughed, giving him a look suggesting he calm himself. Blackbeard took in a breath as he cracked his neck sideways. He reached down into his pocket bag for more coins. "Listen carefully now, lass. I want this entire place empty. Tell your boss if you should think it would make it go faster. Just get it done. I am not a patient man. Should I be made to wait, my kind gestures... such as what you hold tightly in your hand will can go much differently, and honey you don't want to see my bad side."

The waitress ran into the back of the pub. Within seconds, her boss came running out, demanding that every other guest get up and leave immediately. Within minutes the entire place was silent.

"Now that we are alone, lad, let us talk of your travels," Blackbeard said in a rushed voice.

Hook knew what he wanted to hear, and he knew that Blackbeard wouldn't be able to talk about anything else until he had covered the topic of the Wood Witch. *Should I tell him about the witch or the truth about who I am first? Should I tell him the truth at all?* He wanted so badly not to cause him more heartache, though he feared that might be impossible, for he had no good news to share with him in the end. Hook took in a large breath, not knowing what should come out of his mouth next. "I found her."

There were a few seconds were Hook couldn't gage the look on Blackbeard's face. It was a look of both amazement and fear. "Did she mention my son?" He asked as tears welled up in his eyes; each unable to fall until he knew the answer.

"Yes, we talked about your son," Hook answered.

Blackbeard's tears fell down his dark leathery cheeks. "Did she take him?! She took him. I know it!"

Hook scooted his chair closer to him. "Captain, there is something you must know. I cannot let you go on any further not knowing the truth about what really happened to James."

Blackbeard found the words he had just said and the way he said them very curious. He couldn't tell if he was about to hear good or bad news. He loved everything about the mysterious pirate, but right now he found his behavior to be utterly confusing.

"Your son was left at the Moore Orphanage wrapped up in a red blanket. His mother hoped it would protect him, but-"

"-They found him?" Blackbeard interrupted.

Hook sighed. "Yes, they found him. A fairy tortured him; tried to trick him into their world. Yet, even in his deadliest of nightmares, he rejected her charms. It was more than any boy should have to survive, but as bad as that was, there was another he was facing."

"Who?"

"A boy. He was a sadistic child much bigger and stronger than James. He and his friends ganged up on him one night, and nearly beat him to death. Though he survived, the medicine his body would need for the pain left him in a constant state of projection. The fairy took every opportunity to torment him beyond the reach of sanity. James tried to be strong. He fought so hard, but in his final torturous nightmare, the fairy broke him."

Blackbeard's swollen red eyes were flooded with the saddest of tears. "My poor little boy. If only he hadn't been alone."

"He wasn't alone. He had a wonderful nurturing caregiver that truly loved him and looked over him. She told him about the fae. She did everything she could to help him, but in the end, it was her love for the boy that would cost her... her life and soul." Hook's voice trailed off as he remembered that fateful morning when he found her lifeless next to his bed.

"What happened to her?"

"She struck a fatal bargain with the fairy."

Blackbeard shook his head as if he couldn't bear to hear anymore, but he had to know. "What was the bargain?"

"She sacrificed her soul for a shield that would protect him from all fae magic."

Blackbeard stood up, blasting out of his chair. His eyes went wide with shock. "That's incredible! Then my boy is alive! James is alive! I must find him! Let's see, how old would he be now?"

"Twenty," Hook said looking down.

Suddenly, Blackbeard's heart sunk as he slowly sat back down in his seat. "How do you know all this? Do you know my son?"

Hook stood up from his chair and took a deep breath. "I *am* your son."

Blackbeard stood back up: overwhelmed with questions, doubt, joy, and anger. "No, that's impossible! When I found you; you were..."

"Ten. The Moore Orphanage was burned down by what I can only assume was a changeling. I believe it was sent to the orphanage by the fairy to destroy the bit of magic I had in my possession: a spell book. Inside it was the summoning spell that the nun used to save me. After she died, I was given the book. But the creature was too late. I had used the book's power to take down my enemy, but it all went tragically wrong. The boy outwitted me and struck a bargain that gave him all the power of the fae. Because of me, he has stolen countless souls. It is a wrong that I intend to right. The night we met was the night the orphanage went up in flames. I snuck off behind the smoke and wandered down to the docks. I had admired the ships from my window so much as a young boy. So, when I had no other place to go, its where my feet took me. I had no idea they would lead me to my father, but as fate would have it... they did."

Blackbeard's eyes welled up as he began to pace the floor. His thoughts raced with memories of that night, and all the times past on the ship. But as more and more memories spun in his mind, the more things seemed to become clear. The boy had never revealed his true name, and there *had* always been an undeniable bond between them. He was the right age, he had dark features, and his skill as a pirate was as famed as his own. *Could I really have spent the last decade with my long-lost son? It just doesn't seem real, but why would Hook lie to me now?* He rubbed his face in frustration. "How long have you known this?"

"I had no idea until that last day on your ship... when you told your tale. It was the way you described what happened with your son. I felt the truth deep in my soul. Still, I just couldn't believe it. That is, until I asked you your son's name."

Blackbeard's thoughts stirred wildly in his mind. *Could I really have found my son by chance? Out of all the ships that night, the boy boarded mine.* Then everything inside him changed as he turned to take a deep look into Hook's eyes. They were the same ocean blue color as his mother's. The truth had been right there in front of him all this time. "James. My boy." Blackbeard pulled Hook in tightly, hugging his son. "Come, let's go aboard my ship. We can sail anywhere you want to go together. Now that I know the truth... that the fae cannot harm you in any way. I am free from this curse at last! Tell me, where do you want to go? What do you want to do?" Blackbeard's joyous news of his son had somehow blinded him to the other disturbing facts about his son's frightening past.

"You haven't been listening to everything I've said, Captain. Though it is true the fae did not take your son away; I was beaten and tortured in that horrible place. The fae did find me! And because of me and you, a kind woman lost not only her life but her eternal soul. An evil little boy now has the power of the fae because of a mistake I made. You may be free now, father, but I am not."

"Okay, son, okay. I can see how important this is to you. Tell me how I can help?"

Hook looked down to the floor before taking in a deep breath. "I need a ship and a crew!" Hook and Blackbeard exchanged a sinister smile.

Something about his son's dark motives gave Blackbeard a sense of pride. "That's my boy! Captain James Hook!" He roared, patting Hook's back. "You shall have a fine ship indeed, and the finest crew money can buy. Come, let us go back to my ship where I will give you all the riches you require."

The two pirates left the silent tavern just in time for the sun starting to rise into the dark sky. Blackbeard wrapped his arm around Hook's shoulders, feeling a sense of pride and joy like he had never felt.

CHAPTER EIGHTEENTH

THE DOCTOR

The town was eerily quiet as they walked down the narrow stone roads. There was a thick fog in the air, but above most streets were large lanterns that shined down on the path ahead. The fine details were never in Hook's focus. For in his eyes, almost everything was a blur. It was a fact that seemed always to heighten his sense of hearing. They had nearly made their way to the docks when suddenly Hook heard a snarling growl coming from one of the alleys behind them. Something about the sound made him stop. He turned and began to walk towards the dark alley.

Blackbeard looked at him confused. "Where are you going? Did you see something?"

Hook put his finger to his lips. "Shhhhh." He wanted to catch whatever this creature was by surprise. But as he stepped closer, he heard another noise: the sound of men laughing cruelly. There was something about their laughter that bothered him. He began to pace faster down the street. Blackbeard curiously followed him with his hand ready at his sword. When Hook made his way down the alley, he saw something that infuriated him. Three drunk men were kicking a dog that was tied up by rope to a heavy barrel. The vision of senseless torture was a sickening sight for him. With each kick and punch, the memory of his last night in the boy's room flashed through his mind. It took mere seconds before he stormed in. Blackbeard charged with him, assuming Hook had some torrid history with them. Truth be told, he was in no need of his help, for the young pirate was beating down the three men with incredible force.

Each man begged for mercy: "What did we do?!" They all screamed!

"We're sorry! Please stop!"

But it was no use, for Hook didn't hear a word. All he could see was Peter and his little gang of followers. "Hahaha! Is it funny now: beating up someone so helpless? Three against one, huh?! Cowards!" He roared as he continued to swing.

One of the men tried to limp away, but Blackbeard stood in his way of escape. The desperate man looked up at the tall captain. "Please- help me?"

Blackbeard sighed as he slowly squatted down to look into the pleading man's eyes. The man quivered as the captain drew his boot knife. Panicked fear suffused the sobbing man as he slowly drove the short blade through his chest. The man fell to the ground dead, his blood running down the dark alley. But for Hook, there was no end. Each brutal blow upon them brought him a sense of justice. It wasn't until Blackbeard pulled him off, that his vision of reality came back into focus.

"Stop, son! They're gone now. Do you hear me? They're gone," Blackbeard said trying to calm him. Hook looked over to the beaten bloody dog; now unconscious on the ground. "Come, son. It's over now. There is nothing more you can do for the poor creature."

Hook bent down and laid his hand gently upon the dog's side. He could feel a faint pulse through the creature's broken body. He thought of Sister Roger. "No, he will live!" He said, gently picking up the dog. Without a breath of argument from Blackbeard, Hook carried the pup down to the docks. Once they arrived back on the ship, he demanded one of the crew go and find the town's best physician.

It didn't take long before a frightened little man appeared in the doorway of his chambers. The man was short and middle-aged. He had clearly been dragged out of bed, as he was still in his pajamas and nightcap. He had tiny round glasses that seemed to barely stay on his face. His small beady eyes stared down at the floor as his body shook. The crewmate that Hook had sent out was standing behind the little man with a pistol pointed to the back of his head.

"What are you doing? I didn't tell you to terrorize him! Off with you!" Hook screamed. The pirate nodded and quickly made his way out of the room to join the rest of the crew on deck. "I must apologize for your treatment. It was not my intention to frighten you so severely, but I must insist on the importance of your help. Come here."

161

The little man looked hesitantly at the pirate, too afraid to move.

"Make haste, Doctor!" Hook screamed impatiently.

The little man hurried over to the corner of the room where Hook was standing. There on the floor below him was a dog covered in splattered blood. The doctor looked confused as he looked down at the little creature. "The dog? I am here to treat the dog?"

It was a question that seemed to irritate Hook profusely. "Don't be a fool! Yes, the dog! I need you to save him. Treat his wounds, and nurse him back to health! Save him!" He demanded loudly, startling the little man. "Now!"

"Yes, sir." The doctor squealed, dropping to the ground. Upon closer observation of the animal, a chill of horror crawled up his spine.

"Oh, don't worry. That blood is not his," Hook said alarmingly calm.

The little man gave a nervous chuckle. "Oh, I see. Well to treat him, I will need my supplies. But first, I would like to clean him off so that I may see the severity of his wounds."

Hook nodded. "I see. Well, let us not waste any time then. I will send for your supplies. Meanwhile, do what you must to clean him; though I implore to you to treat him well. Be as careful with him as you would your children."

The little man fixed his glasses dropping down his large nose. "I do not have any children, but I will be as gentle with him as possible, sir."

Hook nodded. "Good man! I will have one of my mates bring you some water and rags."

"-But..." The little man interrupted.

Hook glared down at him fiercely. "What?!"

"It's just that such a task could take quite a bit of time. I thought I would be taking him to my offi–" His words cut off as he saw the frightening pirate's head shake.

"No, Doctor. Seeing as you have no family to speak of; I see it only fitting that you come with me instead."

The little man looked stunned. "Here? On board this ship? But I-"

Suddenly Blackbeard stepped into the room, causing the doctor to stop speechless as he gazed at the infamous captain. "So how are we doing, son?"

"Son?" Smee whispered.

"Seems our dear doctor feels hesitant to stay here on board while he treats his new patient," Hook said.

Blackbeard looked down at the small man cowering before them. "I see. Does he need a little more persuasion?" He asked pointing a long dagger to the little man's quivering neck. "Really, Hook, you are

163

just too kind: asking him, letting him think he has a choice in the matter at all. Look here, Doctor! The fact that you are here on my ship upon my son's request should make you feel incredibly grateful and cooperative. If it had been I that sent for you, I would have simply just used you and then killed you. Lucky for you, my son is far more patient and generous than me. I would not make matters difficult if I were you," Blackbeard said in an alarmingly calm voice before leaving the room.

"Doctor, I need you to hurry now," Hook said urgently.

"Yes, sir."

"I don't know if you have other patients, but I assure you that you will be paid handsomely for your services. Now, where do I send for your supplies Mr.-?"

The little man looked up at the young pirate. "Smee, my name is Smee."

It wasn't long before one of the crew showed back up with Dr. Smee's supplies. Meanwhile, Smee had been gently washing the dry blood and dirt off the small dog's coat. Many rags had to be used to clean the dog off and with each cloth covered in blood. Smee's nervous mind raced, imagining who the blood belonged to, and after such significant evidence of severe blood loss, there was little doubt that who so ever endured such brutality could possibly be still alive. Hook watched over Smee and the unconscious dog's activity for hours, only ever looking away to read, never quite attending to his hunger or exhaustion. He waited with agonizing patience to see the weak animal's eyes open. It was a moment both the pirate and the doctor waited for most anxiously. Smee could feel the pirate's fierce eyes hovering over him with each passing moment. The only thing more terrifying was when Blackbeard would enter the somber chambers to check status. After the small doctor had cleaned off the dog to the best of his ability, something was suddenly revealed.

"Um..." Smee whispered.

Hook looked over alertly. "Yes?"

Smee looked over at him with such terror behind his eyes as he spoke: "I see now that this dog is not a small breed, but rather that his size is due to age, he is just a puppy. I cannot know his exact breed. Nevertheless, being so young will make it much harder to survive his injuries."

Hook stood up and walked over to examine the dog closer, before setting his sight again upon the trembling doctor. "Then you will just have to try harder to make sure he does! For the penalty of his death is your own. Understand!?"

Smee nodded: "Yes, sir, I will." The doctor put in a line into one of the puppy's small legs, giving him fluids, hoping with each drop that it would provide him with strength. But the hours turned day to night with still no change or sign of hope from the pup. The tireless hours of effort from Smee, without any food or water had left him tired and weak. Late into the night, it seemed that only Hook alone was awake, with only his desperation and the memory of Sister Roger to keep him awake. Seeing the puppy in his fragile state, barely above death was a feeling of memory too close to home for him. But now it was he who was in the seat where his mother sat. But like her, he would not give up on the creature.

The bright moonlight shined in through the same windows that Hook had always marveled at in all his years within his room on Blackbeard's ship. But tonight, the light seemed to cause a dreadful stirring inside of him. Hook looked out the window at the full blue moon above in the dark sky. Its luminescence was indeed beautiful and shone its glorious reflection onto the calm waters below. His gaze fell upon the long glittering line glowing on top of the ocean's surface. A feeling of epiphany welled up inside of him: "It's the sparkling road." Suddenly the silence broke within the room; it was the faint sound of a familiar growl. Smee shot up awake as Hook looked over to discover the small pup's eyes opened with alarm. The dog was alive and wide awake, though the puppy was still too injured to lift its weak body off the pile of blankets. The small dog managed to raise his snout into the air and began to sniff as if he was ready to hunt. Whatever the little dog was smelling was close enough to cause the weak creature great frustration. The growling intensified, and it was the most welcome sound. Hook smiled as he walked over to the small dog. "You can feel it, can't you boy?"

Smee looked about the room completely confused. He couldn't see anything. "What is close?"

"Magic, my dear Smee- magic," Hook said as he gently patted the dog's head, praising him.

"Magic, sir?" Smee asked thinking the young pirate must be joking, looking to his face for a laugh or even the faintest sign of sarcasm, but none came. Hook looked over to the confused doctor with a frightfully serious face. Smee didn't know what to say. The fact that the pirate who stood beside him believed in magic made his captivity even more frightening. In his moment of pause, he noticed Hook glaring at him as if waiting for some reaction. "Ah yes, sir. The magic. Is it close now? In this very room?" Smee raced through his many questions, trying desperately not to say the wrong thing. It was a badly failed attempt — a fact quite clearly written across the pirate's sneering face.

"Do you think me mad, Mr. Smee?"

"No, sir! Not at all, sir!" Shuddered the small man.

"Then do you think me a fool?" Hook asked, his voice growing louder and more frightening. Smee didn't know what to do, his body shook with terror, unable to speak another word to the furious pirate. He wanted so desperately to be somewhere else- to be someone else. Smee was now speechless. "Well?!"

Hook screamed, leaning his face in close to the shaken doctor, this time his horrifying voice sent Smee into a frantic breath that left him with tunneling blurred vision as he fainted upon the ground. Hook rolled his eyes at the pitiful being upon the floor. But somehow the pause had given Hook a moment to look upon Smee with pity. He knew he couldn't possibly expect every man to believe in magic, but he wasn't going to tolerate being treated as if he was one of the insane. He walked over to his desk to pick up a glass of water and threw the drink in Smee's face, waking him immediately. Smee opened his bitty eyes in a state of fog. "Come along now, Smee. Get up and come talk with me at my table- where I will reassure you of my sanity and give you some piece of mind. But I should tell you now that what you will hear will not be pleasant, but nothing you will hear out of my mouth will ever be untrue! Are you ready to listen to me now?"

Smee nodded gently.

"Good! Then come sit and let us talk."

After spilling a speech of horrific detail, Hook stood up and walked out of the quiet room, hearing no reply from the doctor at all. Smee felt a stirring of thoughts. Many things the pirate had said left him at a loss of thought. His words sounded insane still, though the way he spoke was that of sound mind and wisdom.

Smee didn't know what to think of it. He walked back over to the weak little dog. "Now listen here, pup. I am going to try to feed you some real food, so if you would settle down that growling, I could attempt to make you better yet." But the dog never lost its alert growl, its face and eyes fixated on the windows looking out to the moon. Smee quickly remembered that before he had fainted, the pirate had praised the dog for his behavior and spoke as if the dog could sense magic. Suddenly, he heard something just outside the windows. It startled him, but he nevertheless made his way slowly over to the windows to investigate the noise. Down below the pirate's quarters, were two figures that were pushing a small boat onto the water next to the anchored ship. Smee could see one of the men was Hook. The other man began to row closer to the moon's line across the water. But what happened next was something that would change him forever. Smee watched below as Hook ever slowly reached out his right foot onto the moon's sparkled reflection, only his foot never went below the surface. It was as if the road was somehow whole, and strong enough to carry the full weight of his foot. In mere seconds, the pirate stepped out of the small boat entirely and onto the sparkling road, heading north towards the full and glorious moon. He watched as Hook walked farther into the distance, with the boatman following closely beside him. Imagining driving his sword through Peter was enough to make Hook's feet fly fast forward at full pace. But suddenly he heard a sound that stopped him dead in his tracks. It was a sound that not even his boatman noticed.

"Halt," Hook said sternly to his boatman. His crewmate followed his command and stopped rowing immediately.

"What is it?" The boatman asked startled.

Hook's eyes zoned in on a disturbing motion in the water circled them. His mind flashed back to the Wood Witch's warning. The guardians of the veils. "Go now!" He screamed to his boatman.

"I can't! Blackbeard would surely kill me if I left you here alone!" The shaking boatman replied rapidly. Hook could see he was afraid of the mysterious creature, but he was more fearful of their frightful captain.

"Then let us be brave, and venture onward as fast as we can, surely the creature will grow bored and give way to other prey below," Hook said hastily, though it was a lie only too obvious. He sped forward, his heart racing as the sea monster followed at an alarming speed. It became clear right away that this creature was enormous, for as it sped through the surface waves, its large Though Hook never dared look directly at the monster, it's frightening features were not lost on his sight. It looked to be over twenty feet long, with large ugly scales and barely above the surface, were two bright yellow eyes that seemed to glow fiercely in the dark night. His legs were growing tired, but he kept forward, pushing harder and harder through the pain aching in his thighs and legs. Ignoring his pounding heart and racing breath, Hook looked behind him to see how far from Blackbeard's ship he had gone. The ship was increasingly small and far away. The monster from the water began to snip at the small boat beside him, small and timid at first, as if it was deliberately trying to taunt both, showing off its incredibly large teeth. The boatman tried to shove it away with one of his rows, but it was of no use. The boatman's weak attempts seemed to amuse the creature. Hook didn't look over but instead ran as hard as his legs could go. The pain was intensifying as if his legs would fall off if he continued, but he wouldn't give up, and he wouldn't be stopped- even by the sea monster. Suddenly the path started to move. Hook remembered that it was already late into the night when he had first seen the path, and that surely the sun would be greeting the day before long. Sweat poured down his body as he hurried on, trying desperately to achieve his goal. He wasn't sure what he would do if should he arrive in Neverland, in this state of exhaustion, he would not be fit to fight Peter, but logic couldn't stop him now. The path continued to move unsteadily, and the sky's darkness began to change with it. The boatman began to panic, as the sea monster raised its massive head above the surface of the water and had now become more aggressive. It didn't seem to be angry, but rather enjoying itself. Hook lost his footing for a second and tripped, falling into the water. Hook opened his eyes under the water. Suddenly, he heard the muffled sound of screaming from above him. The surrounding waters became red. Hook quickly thrashed around, trying to locate the monster. Only it seemed the monster had had the same desire, for when he turned his head, the monster's two yellow eyes were staring right at him. He froze in fear for a moment but quickly attempted to draw his sword from his belt, though his eyes never left the monster, and his frightful glowing glare. He raised his sword, also trying to maintain his breath under the water, afraid that if he should raise his head above the surface than the monster would surely rip him apart. Hook tried to swipe his sword under the water, but the movement was difficult, for though his form had always been flawless in a battle of man, the water seemed to work against him. His frustration grew, but through the movement of the waves he was causing, he could see more and more of the creature's enormous body. It was a gigantic crocodile! The sight was indeed a horrific one, but he was not a stranger to such terror. He continued to swipe the sword, as if in slow motion through the water, when he began to feel his lungs starting to panic, forcing him upward against his will. Without time to think, Hook thrashed his body above the water to take in another deep breath, but once he did, the monstrous croc charged in and bit his leg. Hook screamed in pain but did not dare drop his head below the water again. He looked next to him to find the floating bloody parts of his boatman on top of the water. The crocodile had grown excited and tried to thrash him in its wild frenzy, he kicked the creature as hard as he could manage, causing the creature to lose its grip momentarily. Hook quickly grabbed one of his boatman's floating legs and shoved it below the water to confuse the crocodile's next attack. It worked, the crocodile began to shred into the detached leg excitedly, like a dog presented with a fresh bone.

Hook quickly thrashed his arms, swimming towards the small wooden boat, desperately pulling himself up to safety. The blood from his wounded leg gushed out onto the wood, as he reached for the two rows that had somehow survived the monster's vicious attack. His adrenaline was sky high and was probably the only thing holding the pain from the monster's bite at bay. He used all the energy he had to row the boat backward- safely back aboard the Queen Anne's revenge. Hook kept his eyes on Blackbeard's ship. However so far, with each row through the bloody water, he would be that much closer to the ship and farther away from the silver path's guardian. Hook didn't dare look towards the moon, for fear of seeing the hungry creature following him. He didn't hear anything besides the rhythmic crashing of the rows hitting the water again and again, with each second becoming more desperate as he could feel himself getting weaker with each drop of blood that left his body.

Finally, he had reached the ship, though he was too weak to pull himself on board, he yelled up to the crew. Two pirates poked their heads off the side of the ship to see who was about when they saw him covered in blood sitting in the small wooden boat. His body was about to give out. They threw down some rope and began to lift him from the boat, and as they stood him up, Hook looked towards the water. The sparkling road was gone, but far off in the distance, he could have sworn he saw the crocodile smiling as if he knew they would meet again.

After a few days went by, both the dog's and Hook's injuries had already started to heal. Hook had spent his time entirely on his bed, reading and calculating hours on end. But he was not alone, for one night the little wounded dog had crept from his pile of blankets and had successfully leaped onto his bed and had not left his side since. It was as if the dog had known who had saved him and destroyed his attackers. Smee did his best to mend Hook's leg, though it was still a gruesome sight to behold, with over a hundred stitches aligned around what flesh had survived. It had become almost an hourly requirement of Smee's to make every attempt to clean and remove all dead tissue for fear of rot and infection, a process that was both difficult and extremely painful. But Hook would not endure his pain alone, for his faithful dog was also in the slow process of healing on the bed next to him, while Smee would suffer all the wrath from the pirate's pain. On one rainy afternoon, Smee rushed into his chambers after hearing the wounded pirate screaming in agony.

Blackbeard came sprinting behind him, shoving him hard into the room. "Fix it, you fool! Help him!"

Smee had fallen to the ground but quickly made his way to his feet, grabbing his medical bag and sat gently on Hook's bed to see what was wrong. Hook's hands grabbed both sides of his wounded leg, blood and pus pouring down them.

"What is it? What's wrong?!" Blackbeard yelled.

Smee looked behind him, into the yellow eyes of the captain with terror. "It's infected, sir."

The captain's ears flooded with his son's screams. The thought of losing him now was too much to bear. "Can you fix it? Tell me you can fix it!" Blackbeard said with such sad desperation that it made the doctor's eyes well up. For he knew that if the young pirate died, so would he.

"I can try. I have tears of the poppy and a poultice of my own invention. I had thought to use it on the dog, should one of his wounds be open and become infected, but it never happened. I can use it on his leg to help the inflammation and help draw out the infection, though you should know it will cause him a great deal of pain."

Blackbeard looked into his son's weak eyes and nodded. Smee opened his bag and retrieved a small brown poultice. With great hesitance, he brought it above Hook's leg but paused. "Do it!" Blackbeard commanded loudly! Smee jumped startled but rapidly placed the poultice on Hook's open wound. What followed was the horrific screams of torture until finally, the bliss of darkness came over him and his body fell back on the bed. "What happened? Is he?" Blackbeard couldn't finish his words. He couldn't speak of such a significant loss.

"No, sir, he is still alive. He had just fainted under such great pain. He needs water and air; you must open a window."

Blackbeard had never allowed anyone to tell him what to do or open a window on his ship, but at this moment, he hesitated for neither. He quickly ran over to one of the windows closest to Hook's face and started to yell out for water.

"Shhh, we must not wake him. For if we do, he will be in severe pain," Smee said sheepishly under Blackbeard's striking glare. Without another word, Blackbeard left the room quietly, though never losing his gaze. The second he had left the room, Smee let out a breath of relief, though how much longer he would have breath left was uncertain. Smee's fear kept his heart at a constant race of alarm.

An old pirate came through Hook's chamber door quietly with a small cup and bowl of water. The pirate handed the items to the doctor slowly, though his snarling glare left Smee with chills of fright. When Smee reached to grab the bowl of warm water carefully, the pirate didn't let go but instead leaned in to speak in Smee's ear.

"The captain wants you to know that he will consider forgiving your blatant tone of insubordination, but you best pray for his son's survival." The pirate then let go of the bowl gently and walked out of the room. Smee cleaned up Hook's leg with gentle ease, all the while keeping a hand on the poultice. The height of the burning had subsided, and the swelling had already gone down. Once all the pus and blood had been carefully washed away, Smee took the chance to cut and re-sew where he could. Smee's hand was steady, though his heart pounded hard with anxiety within his chest. But it wasn't before he had finished, that a chilly gust of wind came in, and with a gentle brush upon the sweat of his face, did he wake. Smee had not noticed, for his full focus was still on the leg, but something in the winds had changed for as Hook watched Smee work, he was now in far less pain and overcome with the gracious feeling for the small man that had saved his leg and ultimately his life. But before Smee could spot his gaze, he closed his eyes pretending to be asleep, for before he could succumb to trusting the doctor, he wanted to see what Smee would do in his absence. Hook used his immense sense of hearing to listen to Smee's movements once he had finally finished sewing and removed the poultice from his leg. Smee dipped the white cloth into the bowl, submerging it in the remaining water. He listened as Smee ringed the fabric, the water dripping back into the bowl. Smee then silently lifted the rag to wipe Hook's forehead, cooling him down and removing his former fevered sweat from his face. He remained perfectly still. Then he felt the balance of the bed start to shift as if Smee was reaching for his dog. He barely opened his right eye, just enough to squint a view at the doctor. Hook was about to grab his arm when suddenly he heard him whisper.

"Forgive me, but I have seen you read through this book many times, and it seems to be the only thing you possess that brings you some sort of comfort." Smee pulled over the fairy tale book towards his lap, opened it gently and began to read the first story out

177

loud. As each page turned, Hook suddenly came a realization. Smee had gone above his charge and duty. This action came purely from kindness, and though Hook had no room in his heart for friends, with this one act, Smee had reached him and had earned his undoubting trust. Smee had proved himself a worthy asset to the ship. He had taken such desperate care of two patients with the utmost urgency, though it had been pressed upon him by Blackbeard. But under such frightening terror, Smee had become a somewhat permanent wreck of nerves. The crew found great joy in the added teasing and torment of the little doctor, with no interference or help from Blackbeard. Smee had lost his dignity, his freedom, and his sanity. The only thing Smee had left was his life, which seemed always to be hanging in the balance with every miserable day. Hook was the only man on board that treated Smee with kindness. Smee spent as much time as he could in Hook's chambers, always trying to avoid the awful hazing of the crew and the death threats from Blackbeard. But their time together could sometimes be awkward, for a while Hook could go days without speaking a word to anyone, Smee couldn't seem to shut up, always inquiring about the current book Hook was reading or trying to make random small talk. But somehow as the days and nights went on, through all the dim-witted questions and rambling, Smee had somehow become a welcoming presence for him.

Then one day Smee asked the burning question: "When you and the dog are all well again, will you or Blackbeard kill me?"

Hook stopped looking at the mountain of books and paper upon his bed to look upon Smee's sad face. "Why should I kill you, my dear Smee, you saved my leg, my life, and of course you saved my new friend I find by my side. Your kindness should, in fact, be a matter of which you are owed, for your services have been beyond what I could have imagined. For that, I cannot thank you enough. You should not think about such horrible things anymore. But if you still feel a lingering cloud of fear hovering you while you are on board this ship, then sleep well my friend, because you are under my protection. No great harm will come to you. *That* I can promise."

Blackbeard regularly checked in with Hook. It seemed that his health was all Blackbeard could think about, his fear going far beyond the level of paranoia he had always held for his treasure. For Blackbeard, finding out the truth about Hook was bittersweet. True, he was happy for his son's life, and that fate had been kind enough to bring him back to him years ago. And above all, he was proud of the pirate he had become. There was a time that he and Hook could talk, but it was always about their next venture- not about feelings or matters of the heart. It was torture that his son should be so close and yet so far beyond his reach, but it was even more torturous to see a dim-witted doctor get through his son's thick walls.

"Your leg should be healed soon enough, son, and I was thinking that in that time, you could begin making sketches," Blackbeard said.

Hook looked up at him with mild confusion. "Sketches of what, Captain?"

Blackbeard's face fell. He so desperately wanted him to call him father- to see him as a father instead of a captain. But there was hope yet, for he was willing to do anything to reach him. "Well for your ship of course! We will not simply buy a ship, but rather have one built! You will design your own magnificent vessel, and when you are finished, I have commissioned the finest men to build it."

Hook's eyes grew wide. "Wow, Captain! That is a most gracious offer but..."

Blackbeard raised his hand to silence him. "Do not object this, Hook. I have acquired more gold and silver than I could spend in a lifetime. It was always meant for you, and this is only the beginning. I have missed so much and still have so much to atone. I will do all I can to help you on your missions. But I fear that while I am immortal to all weapons of man, I am not immune to magic like you. And while I would gladly go into any battle with you- magical or not, I want to be sure that while I lived on this earth, that I gave you all I could."

Hook nodded as he looked straight into his father's piercing yellow eyes. "Alright, father."

Blackbeard closed his eyes for a moment, to embrace that most precious word before speaking again. "Good! Then get to work on your ideas, be sure to make it a grand vessel, one worthy of Captain James

Hook!" He shouted proudly, before turning to leave the room. As he shut the door behind him, a single tear dropped down his dark leathered cheek.

"Fetch me some ink and paper, Smee," Hook commanded. Smee ran over to the desk to get what he requested when he heard Hook speak again: "When I have my own ship, Mr. Smee, do you desire to travel back to Wales?"

Smee turned around slowly. "No, sir, for I have rather grown quite fond of the sea. I should like to go with you if you should want a physician on your ship."

Hook gave him a slight smile. "I would gladly employ you, Smee, but I should tell you that I fear whosoever is aboard my ship will always be in grave danger. You might be better to stay aboard this ship. I know Blackbeard will employ you, should it be upon my request."

Smee gave an uncomfortable chuckle as he walked back over to the bed, handing over the paper and ink. "No, sir, for it is you that is my captain, and I will gladly face every dangerous adventure that awaits in your future." Smee held up the inked feather to Hook's hand and smiled. "It's a pirate's life for me."

Throughout the next week, Hook worked tirelessly on the sketching and measurements of his ship, combing over every meticulous detail carefully and quietly. Smee tried hard not to disturb him, though there was something quite majestic about watching Hook work, he had such a diligent process and focus about him, every man aboard couldn't wait to see the final result. And after three long weeks, he had finished.

"Fetch the captain, Smee!" Hook commanded.

"Right away, Si-sir!" Smee stuttered as he went to raced towards the door, tripping over his own feet and falling to the floor.

"Get up you idiot!"

Smee stumbled to his feet and quickly made his way out the door to find Blackbeard. Hook looked down next to him, at his loyal companion. "Look, boy, this will be our home."

The dog looked up at him excitedly, unaware of what his master had said, but happy as always to be addressed. It wasn't more than a moment before Blackbeard came through his chamber doors with Smee following closely behind him.

"The doctor has just informed me that you requested my presence. Have you finished?"

"I have," Hook replied, handing his stack of papers to Blackbeard. Smee adjusted his round glasses on top his big nose, behind Blackbeard's shoulder, hoping to gaze upon his final creation. Blackbeard saw him and struck him in the face with his shoulder. Smee squealed and retreated to the far corner of the room. Blackbeard stepped back, making his way over to the small desk within the chamber, already admiring the pages as he sat down in the chair. Hook laid out each page on the desktop, his eyes slowly and carefully observing every detail. He waited anxiously for Blackbeard's thoughts or words, but the captain was utterly speechless, carefully grazing his hand down the pages as if it was already real, and he desired nothing more than to touch it. There were scribbles and words, and numbers, all very precise and drawn with perfect detail. There were four huge masts with two rows of pitch-black sails on each. The ship itself was to be painted in deep red, black, and bright shining gold. On the back of the vessel, the captain's quarters, revealed a giant golden skull, with a golden captain's hat leading up to three large lanterns hanging down from the top deck. There were to be two sets of windows, in the circular shape of the skull's eyes, with thick red curtains draped down inside and out, and another set of thirty windows in the shape of a nose. There was a large opening below was in the form of a red large gaping mouth that appeared to be giving an evil grin. The wood that was painted red, black, or gold seemed to be a dark cherry colored wood. Each color would surround a row of twenty-gun ports. The figurehead was a glorious marbled mermaid, her body made of bones and a skull instead of a face, with four golden spears going through her sides. And above all the ship's frightening glory was a waving black flack with white skull and crossbones. Blackbeard admired every piece. It was the most magnificent ship he had ever laid eyes on, exceeding even his own.

"What's her name, son?"

Hook tilted his head upward and stern. "Look to the end, father."

Blackbeard sorted through the pages again. There on the last page, he saw the name that would make its mark on history forever, as the most feared, infamous, and immortal ship that sailed beyond the seven seas: *The Jolly Roger.*

TIGER LILY

While Hook slept, dreaming of blood and vengeance, Pan was far from such thoughts. In fact, Peter had all but long forgotten him. For some time, Peter and Tink had both waited for his arrival; Peter had even instructed his growing population of soulless children in the ways of battle. Playing with the lost boy's day and night on the Lost Island had at first been great fun for Peter, but like most children, he had grown tired of his toys. He was always seeking out new things, places, and souls to steal, but the game had grown old, and far too easy. The job bestowed upon him had become just that- a job, both tedious and unchallenging. Neverland was indeed a magical place full of extraordinary wonder. He was worshipped by all that lived there, but what had once felt like his kingdom had now become like a prison. Tink had explained the rule of fae secrecy. Rules that stated to only travel at night, as to not risk being seen. But the silence of the night proved to be most boring. The mere sound of his pipes was enough to call every child to the windows, sometimes even bringing them to the streets leading right towards him. Peter missed the thrill of breaking the rules: those moments where you find yourself almost caught but get away in the nick of time. Living in the corner of one's eye was what he missed the most, and though his life should be everything he wanted, something was missing. Tink pleaded with Peter to dare not enter the Tenth Realm while the rays of the sun still shined. But Tink's fear and constant protest breaking the fairy rules, only increased his desire to break them.

One night, Peter and Tink flew into the night, traveling far across the seas. Seeing new lands was his one remaining luxury he still enjoyed. The ease of stealing children from the highly populated cities had become a bore, and he had taken more than enough to keep the Elders off his back for now. He wanted to see something new- to do something new.

The moon and stars were clear on this night, a fact that was less favorable to him, as he enjoyed racing around the earth's clouds with Tink. But tonight, they would fly through the crisp, clear air, leaving any hope of excitement or play down below them. Off in the distance was an island. The night's darkness pierced by an orange glow and the sound of beating drums coming from below the trees, spiking Peter's interest. Giving each other a mutual nod, Peter and Tink quietly flew down into the surrounding forest to look more closely. Their sight soon gazed in wonder at what seemed to be a gathering of people dancing around a great fire. Peter craned his head curiously. He had never seen people like this before: their features were strange yet mesmerizing to him somehow. Their skin was dark with painted markings on their faces and bodies. Their clothes were unusual, and their hair was long and dark, covered in beads and feathers. They made strange noises as they danced. Both children and adults were present. Peter scurried through the tall trees wanting to look closer. The sound of the drums reverberated through the trees and ground. It seemed as if they were having some sort of celebration. In the distance, there were many tiny huts and other kinds of pointed clothed houses built by what appeared to be long sticks of wood. The cloths were painted, each with different colors and symbols. Some of the strange homes were bigger than others but somehow complimented each other thus. Suddenly the beating stopped, and all the dancing ceased as they turned to face the largest of the pointed houses. A tall man slowly walked out from behind the cloth. His clothing was more decorated than the others, covered in beads and lined with stripped colored leather, but that was not what struck Peter's sight. For on top of the giant man's head of long glorious black hair was a large headdress of magnificent feathers and incredible beads, and behind him followed a beautiful young girl. The previous group of dancing people began to cheer most oddly, placing a hand on and off their mouths while making sounds. It was all so odd, yet Peter couldn't take his eyes off the young girl. It appeared the people were cheering for her, though he didn't know why. The large man slowly raised his hand, bringing silence to the group. He gently placed a band upon the girl's head, it had few feathers, but they were tall and beautiful. She raised her head high with pride as the large man behind her began to speak. His deep voice thundered upon the people. He spoke strongly in a language Peter didn't know or understand, but the people cheered again, this time more loudly and a line of more adults brought out food and drink for everyone. The large man lowered his hands firmly upon her shoulders as a young man approached them. They spoke again, though it still foreign to Peter, he felt a sense of concern at this moment. He wasn't sure what it meant; all he knew was he wanted the young man to go away. The girl looked nervous as she swallowed a deep breath. The large man spoke again, this time the crowd roared with their hand motions upon their mouths once more before everything went back to what it was before; with the group chanting and dancing strangely around the high fire to the music. Many began to approach the glorious feast, but it appeared the young girl wasn't allowed to go near it. The large man stood before her, waving his finger and shaking his head, looking upon her sternly. But she turned up her face, with a single stubborn stomp upon the ground before turning away to wander off through the crowd. The large man made his way towards a large carved wooden chair observing the entire celebration. But through the feathered haze of dancers, the young girl subtly wandered slowly away from the crowd unnoticed, all except by the one that had been watching her the whole time.

Peter whipped through the darkness following her. She had snuck around the clothed houses and was now crawling on the ground towards the food. He watched as she stole a tiny bit of everything, all without notice. She was quiet and quick. Peter slowly lowered himself to the ground, when suddenly... snap! A small branch of wood snapped under his left foot. Peter's heart jumped as he quickly whipped around one of the trees, the sound causing one of the nearby men to strike his gaze towards the woods in suspicion. He remained perfectly still for a moment, waiting for the man to return his attention towards the others. Peter slowly peeked his eye back towards the ground where the girl had been, but she was gone. Only the tiny pieces of food she had stolen remained on the ground. Peter's face fell, his eyes rapidly searching for her, but she was nowhere in sight. Peter quietly flew up high into the trees when he spotted her. She was now a bit far away from the others, sitting on a log near a small stream in the darkness, away from the amber glow of the fire and lit only by the clear night sky full of moonlight and stars. She looked like she was crying. Peter looked over at Tink, she gestured that they should leave, for though she did not feel the sense of iron nearby, there was the unmistakable force of magic in the air, and it was powerful. Typically, he would go along with her, but there was something about this girl that made him hesitate. He looked at the young girl again before flying away... but not out of the forest as Tink expected, but instead flew low to the ground and proceeded to steal bits of food in his hands slowly. He did so quickly, and then flew over towards the girl, landing before her. Tink's eyes widened in shock as he approached her. The young girl looked up startled.

"Uh, here is the food you wanted. I am sorry I interrupted your chance earlier," he said.

She looked him up and down curiously.

"Do you understand any English?" He asked, but she still just stared at him suspiciously. Peter sighed: "Alright well, I guess I am going to leave now that you have your food." Peter turned and began to rise into the air when suddenly he heard a voice.

"Thank you."

He turned back towards her and lowered back down to the ground. "You do know English then?" He replied pleased.

She nodded. "I know a little; it is important to know the white man's tongue in case they ever take us... Are you taking me?" She asked sounding afraid. Peter looked up at Tink hiding high in the trees. She gave him a slight nod, but again he remained uncertain. If she were to be taken, it would not be because he was a man.

"No, I am not going to take you," he said. The girl smiled in relief. Peter came and sat down in front of her, crossing his legs as if mirroring her. "What are you?"

She giggled. "I am what the white man calls an Indian, though I would just call myself a girl. What are you?"

He thought about his answer as not to frighten her away. "I'm a boy."

She raised her eyebrow in suspicion. "A boy that can fly?"

190

Peter smiled smugly. "That's right!"

Her eyes widened with wonder and awe. "What other magic can you do?"

Peter raised his head with pride, eager to brag: "I am Peter Pan! I can do anything!"

"Peter Pan... Where did you come from? I have never seen you before on the island?"

"I flew here from my island," he answered growing her interest. For the first time in a long time, Peter could feel real admiration. It wasn't through magic or spoken from a hollow vessel. He had used an effort to hide and steal tonight, and it was more fun than he remembered.

"What do you do on your island?" She asked enamored by his magical charm.

Peter stood up, putting his arms on his hips. "I do whatever I want. I create my own rules, I can stay up all night, and I play games with all my friends. I am the best at games!" He boasted arrogantly.

The young girl stood up and placed her hands on her hips too. "I am the best at games on this island!" She said proudly.

Peter gave her a sinister smile. "Let us play a game then to see who the best of both is, shall we?"

She nodded. "What game should we play?"

"Do you know how to play hide and seek? One of us will hide while the other counts to ten slowly while keeping their eyes covered. I will hide, and after you finish the count, come look for me. Should you find me, you will then be declared the best. Agreed?"

The girl looked at him with a sly smile: "Agreed." She slowly backed up and turned her head to face a tree. She covered her eyes and began to count aloud. Peter quietly rose into the air, looking for the perfect spot. There was a lot to choose from towering trees, bushes, and boulders laid upon the ground. But he wasn't going to leave it up to chance. He knew that flying gave him an incredible advantage. Quickly as she reached the number seven, Peter dashed behind a tall, thin tree with no branches. She will never think to seek me here.

The girl reached the number ten and emerged her view from the tree. She began to look around the big boulders and then some of the bushes. Peter giggled silently at her efforts, his arms wrapped around his belly and his knees bent to his chest when suddenly he heard her.

"There you are!" She shouted. His eyes grew wide, he looked down, and sure enough, the young girl stood below him with her finger pointed right at him. A wave of anger sparked within him as he slowly lowered himself back to the ground to face her. "I found you! That makes me the best!" The girl began to laugh, but she wasn't the only one, for up in the trees was another giggle. Suddenly they were interrupted by movement in the trees. Voices and bright bits of glowing orange began to head towards them. The young girl gasps. "They are looking for me. I must go now."

Peter grabbed her hand suddenly. "This isn't over. I will be back tomorrow night to play again." The girl smiled looking down at her hand in his. Peter quickly let it go nervously. She reached up to her headband and took down a single red feather and placed it in his hand. Peter smiled, placing it upon his green hat. She started to walk away, heading towards the others when she heard him whisper from above. "Wait- What is your name?"

She looked up to see him in the air. "I am Tiger Lily," she said before running off into the woods back to her people. The next night Peter and Tink returned to the island, dropping down to the same location they were before. And as he expected, the girl sat next to the night stream glittered by the stars, only shadowed by the covering trees and framed by moss from the ground. She smiled as she saw him. Peter saw that she had already stolen some food; it lay on a cloth half eaten next to the log. Peter had forgotten her face and was struck in awe by her beautiful young appearance as if seeing it for the first time. Neverland had that kind of effect on memory, though Peter had never quite noticed it before. He remembered the existence of her, he even remembered playing the game and conversation, yet somehow the image of her had become a mere blur in his mind.

Tiger Lily approached him unaware of his lacking recollection. "I told my father about you. He forbids me from seeing you again. He said he could sense the magic of the little people. He said that you are- evil."

Peter looked at her slightly stunned, though didn't deny a word. "Yet here you are," Peter stated feeling a shiver of thrill go down his spine. But her words raised a question: "How does your father know about the little people?"

Tiger Lily smiled: "My people have their own ways of magic. Are you ready to play again, Peter Pan?" She asked sweetly, snapping him back to reality.

"Yes, I am."

"Shall I be the one to hide this time? Do you think you can find me?" She asked playfully.

"Bet on it, girl," he said arrogantly.

She looked at him concerned by his manner. "What is wrong?"

Peter shook his head. "Nothing; go hide. I will start counting now." Peter closed his eyes and faced and tree. After counting to ten he looked for her, and though she hid well, he ultimately found her. They played like that throughout the night, each taking their turn and never failing to find the other, leaving no winner still as the night came to an end. Peter did not like to lose; he had always prided himself as the best at all games. Usually, Peter would just enjoy watching the boys swarm the island looking for him like idiots, only to burst out of the trees at the right moment to frighten them, pointing and laughing at their stupidity, but this young girl always managed to find him. Tinker Bell watched and laughed at Pan's growing frustration, making Peter even more desperate each night to win.

Peter promised to return the following night to play, just as she was always there by the stream waiting for him next to a stolen bit of food, and always seeing her face as if he never had before. After three nights of games had passed, Peter returned the fourth night to find Tiger Lily crying by the water. Rushing down to see her, he noticed something different: a small detail he had managed to convey to memory was now changed; there was no cloth with food next to the log. Peter had come here for fun, but instead, it was tense and growing more awkward with her silence. *Girls are so annoying.* Contemplating just flying away and leaving her crossed his mind, but he had still not succeeded in beating her in their little battle of hiding, and he still couldn't figure out how she always knew how to find him.

Letting out a sigh of irritation he asked: "What is wrong?" But she didn't say anything. Growing more frustrated he pressed again: "Is this because you do not have food? I will go get you some food if we can just get back to playing."

Tiger Lily glared up at him with her swollen red eyes. "No, this is not because of food! I didn't have to steal food tonight! I am crying because it is the last night of the Moonlight Ceremony and tomorrow everything will be different!"

Peter looked at her curiously. "What is a-Moonlight Ceremony?"

Tiger Lily stood up from the log and looked down into the water at her reflection: "It is my rite of passage into womanhood. I am to marry and will carry the burden of age. I will play no more, but rather perform my duties as my future husband sees fit."

Peter shook his head in disbelief. "But if you are a woman then... No! What do you mean you cannot play anymore?! Husband!? No! I will not allow it!"

"Everyone has to grow up," she replied sadly.

"Not me!"

Tiger Lily snarled at his rudeness: "Goodbye Pan! I have to go. They will be looking for me."

A feeling of sheer panic suffused him, the idea of her old and with another felt painful somehow. This wasn't just about losing a game- this was about losing her. He flew in front of her. "Tiger Lily, wait! Come with me!"

She looked up at him with confusion: "Where?"

Suddenly three balls of glowing orange lights began to move towards them with mumbling voices calling her name. Peter rushed frantically: "To my island: a place where you can be young forever like me." Tiger Lily looked at him shocked. The lights were drawing closer, making Peter start to panic. He grabbed her by the shoulders and leaned in close to her, "We can play games together- you and me. I can take you to a place where you will never have to grow up! You have true magic inside you, so you need not fear me. I promise no harm will come to you!" More of the lights drew closer; the voices grew louder- they were almost there. "Tiger Lily! Say yes! Please just say yes! I need you to say the word! Say yes!"

The chief's thundering voice roared her name as the tribe of Indians came bursting through the tall surrounding bushes, but it was too late...

"-Yes."

CHAPTER TWENTY

CATCHER

Even with the employ of hundreds of skilled craftsmen, building the Jolly Roger would still take likely two years to finish, and while Blackbeard was in no hurry for his son to leave and venture off to his deadly travels, he knew that Hook couldn't idly stand by and wait years for the blood he so craved to spill. Hook's thirst for a kill was growing by the day, leaving everyone in his presence utterly afraid. Only Smee and his dog were allowed in his company. Blackbeard kept himself busy, supervising Hook's creation, making sure every inch of its glory would be to his son's utmost satisfaction. Still, the job was a tedious task indeed; not a touch of paint could be uneven, or a piece of sculpture miscalculated. It was to be the most terrifying and perfect vessel on the sea. But as hundreds of men worked day and night on his ship, Hook was not wasting a single minute of his own. Reading and studying the art of horology became a crucial part of his plan if he was to attempt the difficulty of reaching the end of the sparkling road. Every night he studied the ever-changing phases of the moon, but he soon discovered that like most things, it does follow a pattern, and that made it ultimately predictable. But while the road could only be solid if there were a full moon, its color was also important, for it is not only the sparkling road on the water that reflects the moon but by ways of magic does the moon reflect the water's road. Should you see a full moon in the sky and its color has the tint of red, then you can be sure it is the reflection of the road covered in blood.

Hook thought of all the times he had seen a red moon, and how many lives that must have been taken by the crocodile. Even after his horrific encounter with the monster, he couldn't allow himself to fear the water as Peter had. After all, he had always loved the sea, but every time he thought of the crocodile, his blood ran cold. "Smee! Is my father on board?" He shouted.

"Yes, I believe so, Captain."

"Go then and fetch him! I need to speak to him," he said staring at his leg in a daze.

"Is everything alright, Captain?"

"Don't question me, Smee. You must only ever do as I say."

"Yes, sir," Smee replied before walking out of the room. He hated approaching Blackbeard, for it always felt as nerve-racking as climbing into a cannon that was ready to fire. Thus far, he had been able to avoid it, but now he had no other choice. It was by the request of his own captain. He could see that it was of some importance, though he didn't understand why. His leg was well into its healing period, and otherwise, he was in perfect health. Still, Smee could never quite shake the feeling that he may have done something wrong or displeasing in some way. Whatever his offense, he knew his death would inevitably be the result. The thought of death seemed to never be too far in the back of Smee's nervous mind. The crew teased him with countless tales of brutal deaths and unthinkable torture at the hands of Blackbeard; each giving him enough vivid images to cloud his mind beyond the point of sanity. He had grown to live in utter fear; never quite knowing what was real and what was a nightmare. He approached Blackbeard quickly, though his body cringed in fear as he spoke: "Uh, excuse me, sir?"

Blackbeard turned rapidly upon hearing Smee's shaky voice, for it was a very uncommon one to address him directly. Usually, if the doctor had something to discuss, he would ask one of the crew to deliver his message. "What is it? Is my son alright?"

Smee stuttered in reply: "Y-yes, sir. He just requests your company."

Blackbeard had to pause for a moment, turning his head to look upon his son's chamber door. Hook's daze was still lingering when he entered the somber room. Smee tried to follow behind him, but Blackbeard rapidly turned and shoved him out of the doorway. "Get out! He wants to speak with me, not you, Mr. Smee!" He shouted as he slammed the door on the small man's face. The room was dark and gloomy. Though the sun was still high, all the drapes were closed over the windows, making the room as dark as night. Blackbeard's heavy boots echoed off the wooden floor as he approached the bed. He could see from Hook's eyes that he was troubled and was happy that it was he and not Smee, that he requested to pacify his sullen spirit. "The doctor said you asked for me. Are you alright?"

At first, Hook did not answer. He had not even acknowledged his father's presence in the room; his eyes still locked on his leg. His silence concerned Blackbeard, but before his hope fell, he tried again. This was the first time Hook had asked for him on a personal level, and he didn't want to fail him.

Blackbeard's large beard lifted as he gave him a slight smile. "Do you want to hear word about your ship? It's magnificent, son. I cannot wait for you to see it. It will be a glorious day indeed, and I am only too proud to share it with you."

Hook finally blinked, as if coming back to it all. He looked haunted somehow. It was a look that was all too familiar to Blackbeard. Hook looked into his eyes, though he still hadn't said a word.

His father raised his hand and put it firmly upon his shoulder. "You are going to get them, son. I know you will. You will have your revenge, your spill of magical blood, and I know you will not stop until you have seized your victory of vengeance."

Hook's eyes welled up with tears, though he did not allow them to fall; a skill he mastered years ago. "Father..." He paused. "After your encounter with the

Nightman, how were you able to go back out on the sea?"

Blackbeard looked at him a little confused.

"I mean- how were you not afraid?" Hook asked shamefully.

Blackbeard's smile grew; his face appearing sweet. Hook had never seen this look from his captain before, but the look lasted a mere moment before the face of his captain turned stern and fierce as it had always been, and it was precisely what Hook needed. "Listen to me, son. I know more than most what true fear is. I could have cowered on land after my curse. I am immortal after all. I could have kept safe forever- just as you could choose to cower here on earth. You would never have to see or be harmed by any creature of the Nine Realms. But we..." Blackbeard grabbed Hook's chin: "I mean *you* and *I*- are not cowards! We are pirates! We are captains! Now, you must push on with your purpose- just as I did. The ocean can be a man's heaven or hell, and I am a god at sea! You shall be too! You should never be afraid! Do that, and nothing and no one can stop you! Do you understand me?"

Hook jerked his face out of Blackbeard's tight grip and replied harshly: "Yes, sir, I do."

Blackbeard gave a proud chuckle as he stood up and walked towards the window and thrashed open the heavy drapes. "You know, I got these red curtains to hide you once, but I'm not going to do that anymore.

You are strong. You will heal. And when you do, you must fight!"

Though his methods were harsh, Blackbeard's speech was precisely the inspiration Hook needed. He knew that had he expressed his concerns to Smee; he would have just blubbered sympathy and praises. To Hook, such sweetness could only turn one soft and weak, and those were things Blackbeard was not capable of expressing. To be and do what Hook wanted, he needed to be just like him: frightening, brave, and deadly brutal. So, he did as his father commanded. He stopped hiding behind his fear and pushed forward with his purpose with full force. He sent letters to the cleverest of horologists in various parts of the world, studying the ways of time around the world, meanwhile keeping his notes and charts of the moon's phases and colors.

As the next days and weeks went on, the small dog that remained at his side had grown and proved to be a promising hunter. Hook had become quite fond of his company. He would often set time aside to offer his new pet some token of his affections: petting him, talking to him, and yet making every possible attempt of training or preparing him the best he could. He would make detailed sketches of various creatures or merely show the dog pages of his book, all while expressing extreme measures of hatred towards them and encouraging aggressive behavior from the dog, should he see one of them. Smee found it all to be a rather amusing form of training. But whatsoever made his captain feel productive in his mission, proved to be beneficial to them both, for it put the healing pirate in high spirits.

One night, as Smee was tending to the dog's long-haired coat. His fur was no longer stained with his attacker's blood, but now looked quite beautiful and soft, having been given such ample pampering care. His coat was white with large patches of dark and light brown. His eyes were kind and golden. He had rather large paws, which only further proved how much bigger he would ultimately become. As Smee cleaned him, he looked him over thoroughly. There was a cool knock at the door, though by the familiar sound of his heavy boots, Hook already knew who it was. "Come in, Captain."

Blackbeard walked through the door. "How are you feeling today, son?"

"I am well, father. You are kind to ask."

Blackbeard gave Hook a slight nod before looking over at Smee and the small dog. "And what of the dog's health?"

Smee eagerly responded: "He has healed, Captain Blackbeard, and is now in perfect health."

Blackbeard nodded, "Ah, well, then he is a lucky one indeed. I expect that when we should drop anchor in Yorkshire within a few weeks. You should do well to find him a suitable home, Doctor. Find one for yourself as well, since my son is almost on his feet, and we are in no further need of you."

Smee looked struck with shock. "B-bb-but I thought..."

Hook closed the book on his lap and set his gaze upon the captain, sternly. "They are to remain here with me. When my ship is ready, they will be but the first to board."

Blackbeard didn't reply hastily but instead gave a disgruntled huff. "The sea is no place for a dog, lad. And while I find your gratitude most admirable, this doctor was but a means in a desperate pursuit. But I see now that he is, in fact, nothing but a dim-witted fool that should only be used in incidents of last resort. He is most certainly not fit for a permanent charge on your ship. If it is your wish to have a physician on board the Jolly Roger, then permit one of my men to find one more suited for such a...."

Hook raised his hand to interrupt. "I find your words and temperament a most ungracious one, father. This doctor managed not only to save one life on the brink of death but two. He has saved something precious of mine and has managed to do so all while you and your crew continued to torment him. It will not do any good, to neither him or my conscience to repay him by sending him out on the streets penniless and with no home. The doctor has asked to work for me, so he shall," Hook said patting his hand hard upon his bed beside him, and the dog rapidly jumped upon the bed and laid by his side. "And as for the dog, he is mine. He has become as precious to me as my mother's book. His purpose in my life is of great importance, for he can smell and see beyond the veil. He could be the very key to me finding and destroying my enemies of magic. He has been a comfort to me when I had none. He is my treasure, father, and should anyone or anything be so cruel or foolish as to try to take away my treasure; then I will cut off the very hand that dares to touch him."

Blackbeard grunted as he approached the bed, "Very well. Far be it from me to go against your conscience or deny ye your treasure. Does he have a name then? Your pet?" He asked reaching his hand out to pat the dog but hesitated after hearing the undertone of the dog's sneering growl.

Hook chuckled, "Don't mind him, father. It appears as if he is only loyal to one master. It's quite amazing isn't it, that two souls that don't share the same language, can reach such a profound bond?"

Blackbeard retracted his hand quickly. "Indeed. Well, does your beast have a name?"

"I have not thought about it thus far, but I will put my mind to it," Hook replied.

Blackbeard nodded and walked back towards the door. "I look forward to hearing it. I also came to inform you that there looks to be quite a storm coming tonight. The darkness stirring the clouds predicts it to be a wicked one. The thunder and lightning tonight should make for the kind of magnificent show you love. But I'll be off now, no doubt someone strong need be at the wheel for such beautiful chaos.

Goodnight then, son, Mr. Smee, and *dog*," he said as he walked out.

Smee let out a breath of relief, as he always did when Blackbeard left the room. "Thank you, Captain. I was scared there for a moment."

Hook huffed displeased. "Well, then you must do better not to question the honor of my word, in the future, for I do not offer it lightly. Understand?"

Smee nodded with a face of such remorse. "You are right, sir. I will never question it again. So, what are you going to name this guy?" He asked, hastily changing the subject as quickly as it came into his scattered brain.

Hook looked down at the dog. "Hmmm, I do not know. I mean how does one give a name to another? By the way they look, by the way, they act, or by what they do? Human names are so different. People name a vessel before knowing its soul. I want to be sure I pick the right one, for I have learned that in every world: a name can be of great significance. Let me think. You are white and brown in color and coat."

Smee's head popped up. "You could just call him Patches or maybe Fluffy?"

Hook's face contorted in disgust. "No! He will not be given such a ridiculous name. Then suddenly Hook had a marvelous idea. He opened one of his books of sketches. Each page was covered in the detailed picture of a fairy. Hook held one up in front of the dog. We are going to catch them together."

Hook crumbled the piece of paper and threw it across the room. "Go catch it, boy!" He yelled. The dog rapidly jumped off the bed and attacked the paper. "You know what your name is? It is Catcher, because that is what you are... my catcher. Do you like it, Mr. Smee?"

The doctor looked overzealous with agreement, nodding rapidly like a fool. Thunder crashed suddenly all around them. Smee yelped and cowered on the floor in the corner during storms like this. He didn't have the stomach for it. "May I have some ale, Captain? It will help with the nerves."

Hook waved his hand. "Of course, Smee. Help yourself."

But the trouble with Smee getting drunk was, you couldn't get him to shut up. Hook tried to ignore the drunken ramblings of the doctor, but he just went on and on. For the most part, Hook managed to block him out; never entirely paying his words much attention, but then Smee said something: "What if... I mean since we are to go to York. Maybe we can go to the woods that have those- you know- fairy rings? Do you know what I am speaking of, Captain? The circles with the little mushrooms around it? I thought, I mean- I was thinking you and little Catcher could..." Smee said pointing his finger up, before falling to the floor unconscious.

Hook chuckled. "How about that, Catcher? Our poor blubbering Smee comes up with good ideas made of sense, while he is full of the drink. Most interesting, don't you think so, boy?" Hook asked his dog. *Well at least now he will shut up, and I can truly enjoy this storm.* He leaned back on his bed and just watched nature's hard power in awe.

With the help of Smee, Hook was up and out of his bed in the next few days. His leg had healed nicely, though the heinous scar on his leg would forever remind him of that night's failure, much like the small burned scar of a fishing hook next to it. When the ship had finally docked in Whitby, Hook was eager to see the progress of his ship. It was already a glorious sight to behold. To see it gave Hook such pride and purpose.

"What do you think, son? Is she to your liking?" Blackbeard asked standing proudly beside him.

Hook gave him a sly smile. "It is marvelous indeed, father, but it needs a little something."

Blackbeard looked at him curiously. "Ah, and just what do you think it needs, lad?"

"A touch of color- red *perhaps.*"

Blackbeard bent his head back with malevolent laughter. "And just where do you intend to find this red?"

Hook took out of his blades of iron, stroking the edge with a sinister smirk. "In the woods, Captain. In the woods." Hook turned back towards

209

Blackbeard's ship and whistled loudly, "Catcher! Come on, boy!"

CHAPTER TWENTY-ONE

THE WOODLAND PARTY

Though the area of Scarborough was full of hunters and traders, there were still entire woods that were untouched by man. Hook was careful to inquire about the best hunting grounds, but he had no interest in hunting animals today. No, he was interested in a very different kind of prey. He would find it in the most sacred of forest; the kind of lands that were so dangerous that no man would dare to venture into them alone. But Hook was no ordinary man. With his protective shield, he would not be in any danger at all. All he needed was for Catcher to lead him across the veil. The time of spring was already upon the year, though the coldest touch of winter had not yet left the land. The air was still blistering cold, and the grounds and trees were covered in the brightest of glittering snow. For most, the idea of being outside in such weather with no hope of fire would seem unbearable, but Hook's determination and focus was enough to keep him warm. Catcher was happy to be on land and showed nothing short of the pure joy of a puppy as he pranced about in the snow.

After a few hours, they were deep into the woods. Trees laid frosted on the ground, broken from the harshness of all the previous winters. The sun's rays were blasting out from behind the trees like orange colored beams. The forest was indeed beautiful; made more so by the presence of wild animals. There were rabbits around some of the bushes and what looked to be both elk and deer off in the distance. It struck Hook as rather odd but was accepted as merely a good omen. The trees were chattering in the cold wind above them. There was an ominous uncomfortable feeling about it; a feeling that only grew heavier upon them with each step forward. He marched with awareness, listening intently to every scuffle on the ground and every creak in the trees. His posture was that of a man entering battle, with his arms at his side and his hand ready at his sword. But this mission would still prove to be difficult, as the forest was very dark and his vision very poor. Still, Hook stepped onward with deadly ambition.

He made his way deeper into the dark forest covered in tall shadowy silhouettes from the trees and cold air. He had Catcher, yet somehow, he had lost his bearings. He reached into one of his pouches, taking out his compass to get a better sense of his direction. His eyes squinted to focus, but as his view finally narrowed in on the pointer, he saw that it was moving. It was not pointing north as it should be, but instead just going in slow-moving circles. Anger and frustration began to flood his thoughts. *It was them and the magic surrounding their hidden veil.* Hook looked up, giving the woods a sinister smile. *No matter what you do, I will find you.*

But the following hours brought only more confusion and painful misery from the cold. Hook saw a large broken log up ahead and decided to rest his wounded leg for a moment. Maybe taking a few minutes would help. As he sat, he tried harder to see his surroundings, but the forest looked darker somehow. He had always relied on his keen sense of hearing, but he suddenly didn't hear a thing. Even the trees had become eerily still. Not even the wind made a whistle. He wasn't going to be able to go on much longer if he didn't warm himself up. He reached in his pocket and grabbed his engraved matchbox. He took one out and used the bottom of his boot to light it; a trick that Blackbeard had taught him years before. There wasn't any blustering wind about, so the flame burned nicely and maintained its fiery glow. Hook looked around to find pieces of broken wood to put in a pile on the ground, but even as the flames grew higher, he felt no comfort in its warmth. The unwelcome forest had become darker somehow, and he felt his edginess increasing more by the second. He felt the need to turn around over and over as if suddenly aware that there was something behind him. He reached down to grab two of the larger branches from the fire, and decided to walk onward, taking what light the fire had to offer with him. But as he went forward, his paranoia only seemed to increase, making him run and trip down the forested slopes. Still, he never once slowed down.

He continued to race on for what felt like forever, feeling more terror with each passing second.

Suddenly up ahead, he saw a light. Its vision stole his breath. It was the fire- his fire. *How is that possible? I should be far away from the fire by now. I couldn't have been running in a circle. That is impossible.*

Suddenly, Catcher began to growl just as Hook heard footsteps coming upon the snow behind him. Whatever it was, it sounded massive. All of the sudden, the growling sounds of Catcher went silent. Hook rapidly turned around to discover his dog had disappeared. It was then that he realized more were coming. He was being hunted. Fear suffused his body and mind as he couldn't resist the terrified urge to look behind him. What he saw when he did, sent chills down his spine. There were largely wooded figures on what looked to be down on four long-limbed legs. They were each covered in snowy wooden twine. Hook didn't dare turn his back on them but instead looked down to the snow below. But what he saw next was even more alarming. There were no tracks on the ground, not even one. *How could that be?* There should have been many since the snow was deep and soft, but there was none. His heart began to race as if it were trying to pound right out of his chest. *How am I to ever get out of here without knowing where I've been? I am lost.*

He finally decided to turn around, bracing himself to run away. It had to be now while he still had his nerve. Then suddenly, he heard the echoing sound of his full name in various voices around him: "James-James Teach... James! James Teach!" The voices continued until he suddenly felt this overwhelming awareness that something was standing right behind him. "Hello," the voice said as a small gust of wind put out the last bit of flame he had left. His body shook in the darkness as he slowly turned to face the beast that called for him. But when he looked up, he was rather stunned to find a young woman standing before him. She was holding up a small glowing lantern that shined upon her enchanting features. She had tumbling locks of dark hair going down her left shoulder; each with several small glittering flowers in perfectly designed braids. She had pale skin and eyes that looked grey. She was wearing a white lace dress that was formal and long, with a train that dragged across the snow. She was beautiful and somehow even struck him as familiar, but he knew that was impossible. Her voice had been calm, and she gave him a smile that was so sweet, it made him blush. She giggled. "I said hello." Something about her laugh was perfectly symmetrical to her delicate features; it was musical and bell-like. He slowly reached his hand down to the handle of his sword as she walked past him. "Are you coming?" She asked in a flirtatious manner.

"Where?" Hook asked, pretending to be just another victim in the forest.

She turned to look at him again, holding up a masquerade mask over her face. "To the party, of course," she said with a crooked smile.

He followed behind her, struggling to keep up. His arms were getting cut by the frosty thorn bushes and his pants caught on random roots sticking out of the ground. The beautiful woman somehow walked through it all gracefully, as if floating along on some invisible path that only she could see. Then all the sudden, they were surrounded by the echoing sound of whispers. *They were everywhere.*

The beautiful woman stopped suddenly, lifting her lantern. He waited anxiously for her to say something, but she didn't. Instead, she made an eerie giggle before moving forward. Her abridged reaction disturbed him, but he knew all he could do was follow her. With only the pitch-black woods of whispering trees behind them, Hook and the beautiful woman entered a clearing surrounded by a multitude of mushrooms and crossed into the veil of the woodland fairies.

He couldn't help but feel a sense of relief walking into the well-lit area. The air was warm and soothing, though there was still a thin layer of glittering snow on the ground. The trees were full and lush with brightly colored leaves of orange-red and green. Music and lights filled the air while dozens of lanterns hung from the trees. There were two pavilions sat on either side of the large group of what looked to be a magnificent masquerade ball. Everyone seemed so graceful and enchanting with such possessed refinement that it stole his breath. They were all dressed so eloquent with masks of bright ribbons and pale colored feathers. The music was majestic and seemed to be coming from everywhere and nowhere at the same time. There were large tables under the pavilions covered with golden lace, and the most exquisite feast of food and wine that Hook had ever seen. There were magnificent centerpieces of shimmering crystals and floating flowers. There were brightly colored orbs in the air and golden luminescent lights that seemed to twinkle and flicker rapidly around them. The orbs were beautiful but somehow seemed different than everything else at the party. The dancing figures below laughed and gawked at them. Something about it felt cruel and wrong.

The beautiful woman held up a small golden chalice with wine. "Drink. You must be thirsty."

"No thank you," he replied politely.

Her face turned stern and cold. "I insist, James. Take a drink."

Hook could see he had offended her. His eyes squinted as he took the chalice and took a large sip of the wine with such confidence that it made her giggle. The mulled wine tasted strange, fanciful, and sweet like berries. Hook raised his glass to her smugly afterwards. But as the moment passed, her face went still with anger and confusion. She slowly raised her hand to take off her mask. Her skin now appeared livid and bloodless. It appeared that the wine had not affected him as she had planned.

Hook looked around; all eyes hidden a mask were slowly turning towards him. It wasn't a welcomed feeling, and the intangible tension only grew as the music started to fade. "What is going on?" He turned to ask the beautiful woman, but she wasn't there

217

anymore. His eyes quickly searched for her, but she was gone. Every figure began to take off their mask and walk towards him in an eerie pace. Their bodies twitched and jerked in an inhuman pace. At that, he quickly dropped the chalice and drew his sword from his belt. As he slowly swayed it in front of him, the figures hissed and chimed as they retreated backward. *The iron... they can feel it. It is time to do what I came here to do.* Within a mere second, he was swinging his blade in full force. The party of fairies began to scatter and scream. Many tried attacking. Rays of bright lights came blasting towards him, but they all fell. His skill and precision with a sword proved to be most deadly. Confusion and terror filled the air as their winter ball quickly turned into a massacre. Fairy blood and viscera poured out onto the glittering white snow. Hook started to realize that many were flying away. He had killed many, but not nearly enough. Soon his blade could not reach them, but he wasn't finished, for out of the corner of his eye he saw a tiny blue fairy hiding behind one of the trees. Acting quickly, he reached out and snatched the little creature tightly in his hands. Then that was it. There was nothing left; nothing but blood on the snow. He huffed heavily as he looked down at the small fairy that was struggling and screaming from inside the palm of his hand. "Stop that!" He demanded.

She shook frightened. "Please, let me go."

But Hook's deadly wrath had been unleashed with such little reward that it only left him with more hatred and anger. "I will not! I wouldn't have let any of you go! If only- If only..." Hook's face turned red and shook with fury, "If only you couldn't- fly!" He roared ripping her wings from her tiny body.

The Blue Fairy screamed in agony. When he looked down at the savage wounds that he had inflicted upon her, she looked up at him pleading weakly: "Please- just leave me here. I want to die in peace."

Hook gave her a pitiful look. "No, no, shhh. You are not going to die. I have just the person to keep you alive- for as long as I wish it!"

"Are you going to torture me then, mortal?"

Hook gave a vicious laugh. "Let us just see how helpful you can be as my prisoner."

The little fairy dropped her head and nodded silently.

"Now then, how do I leave this wretched forest? For I long to be back on my darling sea."

Hook and his small captive made their way out of the veil and down through the sun-kissed forest. Once they had made it into the center part of the woods, they were far enough away that he was already feeling much better and as he checked his compass, he saw that it was starting to work again. Suddenly, he could hear voices, but it wasn't like before; these sounded like men's voices: "Hook! ...Hook!"

He recognized one of the voices; it was his father and his crew. *But why were they out here*

219

looking for him? He wondered. But Catcher had beaten all of them. He jumped up upon his back and licked his face in a fit of joy. Blackbeard followed, smashing down trees and pushing his way to get to where his son was. Upon seeing him, Blackbeard lunged towards him, hugging him tightly. The rest of the crew kept their distance, just watching the reunion. Suddenly, the captain could hear a ringing sound coming from Hook's pouch. "What is that? You Didn't...?"

"Yes, I have captured a fairy. I need Mr. Smee to tend to her, right away. She has lost a lot of blood and will likely need a lot of his miraculous skills."

"Oh," Blackbeard said looking concerned.

"Father, why such a greeting? I was only gone for one night. Surely you have more faith in me than that."

Blackbeard shook his head interrupting. "Son, you have been gone for two whole weeks. I was losing my mind!"

"What! I was gone for fourteen days?"

Blackbeard nodded. "I have been looking everywhere for you. Where have you been all this time?"

Hook looked behind him towards the trees. "Beyond the forest. Where the snow is now red, and the music is now silent. But none of that matters now, because I bring with me a prisoner who is going to help me find *her.*"

Blackbeard's face was that of sudden realization. "*Her.* The Scarlet Fairy be the one you are after now?"

Hook grinded his teeth in anger, "I killed many, Father, but not her. But I will, and this nasty little creature is going to help me!" He said opening his pouch to look at her. "Aren't you?"

She gave a single weak nod before Hook covered the pouch again.

"Well then, I am off to my room. I need to get my new pet into a proper cage and give her to our own dear Mr. Smee. Come, Father, let us sail out to sea. I wish to be here no longer."

CHAPTER TWENTY-TWO

THE BLUE FAIRY

The captain and Hook made their way back to the ship in silence, the crew following a respectful distance behind them. Blackbeard couldn't stop looking at the flickering blue glow coming from Hook's pouch. Her light seemed to be dimming as her life within her weakened by the second. Blackbeard secretly wished her light would go out, that she would die before they reached the ship. For however much Blackbeard wanted to aid and support his son's vengeful ambition, the idea of having a fairy aboard his ship made his stomach curl. But as usual, Blackbeard's wish would not come true. They made their way aboard the Queen Anne's Revenge, and Hook made his way to his quarters, where Mr. Smee was waiting anxiously for his arrival.

"Oh, thank heavens! You're alive; thank god!" Smee let out a breath of relief so intense; you would have half thought he hadn't breathed in days. His eyes welled up with tears of joy, but the feeling was short-lived, for yet again- it would be his job to save another from the tightening grips of death's fingers. Hook reached into his pouch gently and pulled out the tiny pixie. Her back was drenched in blood. She was pale and unconscious. Smee looked down at her in shock. "Oh," he said as Hook gently placed her in his hands.

"I must ask the impossible of you again, Mr. Smee. And I assume I need not implore to you the importance of your success; do I, Smee?"

The doctor nodded nervously before rapidly laying her down on a fresh pile of rags before running across the room to get a bowl of water and his supply bag. But unlike Catcher, Hook did not care to watch Smee's process, but instead merely made his way over to his bed to read his books with Catcher lying next to him. But Smee didn't need his hovering glare to understand the severity of the situation. So, Smee hustled around, doing all that he could to save her, with just as much vigorous exertion as he had with the others. As the hours had passed, Hook had succumbed to his exhaustion and was now asleep on his luxurious bedding, while Smee used every extreme measure he could to save the small magical creature. He silently sobbed as he burned her back to stop her bleeding. Smee pitied her, for she looked so young and small. Once she was cleaned, he couldn't help but question her appearance. She looked so different than the ones he had seen in Hook's sketches and books. The Blue Fairy had on a long blue dress that sparkled so brightly, you could see it through the dark stains of blood. She had markings of strange symbols on her skin and a sweet tiny face surrounded by lovely long azure hair. He felt as if he was looking at a child- a child with wounds of such horrific gore that it made his stomach turn and his conscience riddled with guilt. As a doctor, he couldn't bear to see one so young suffer, but somehow this was different. Looking at her brought Smee to tears. He prayed silently for her eyes to open; giving him any sign of hope. As he gazed at her fragile appearance, he couldn't understand Hook's hatred for them. After all, Hook had never told Smee of his history with them, and all he himself had ever seen of magic was beautiful and serene. Still, he would never dare challenge Hook's motives or actions, no matter how cruel and deadly they may be. He wasn't sure why Hook had brought her on board, but he was internally grateful it was by his master's request to save her. The night went by unbearably slow, and the fairy seemed to show no signs of improvement. Smee was getting more nervous by the second, hoping that Hook would just sleep through the night, giving her more time for a miraculous recovery. As luck would have it, a terrible storm was rolling through the late hours of the night, bringing soothing sounds to Hook's ears, and rocked the ship back and forth helping him sleep as soundly as a baby.

Smee leaned down close and whispered: "Don't you worry, miss. I'm going to take good care of you. You are going to be alright- I promise." Smee had always thought that even when someone is unconscious, that hearing positive things was helpful. "Please, miss, open your eyes." But she didn't move. Smee's heart fell, but even as the hours passed, he did his best not to lose hope. But to his dismay, the storm passed, and the sun had already started to kiss the present morning. Smee felt panicked, he put his hands together and began to pray: "Please... please. I wish she would wake. I wish... I wish," he whispered again and again, but it wasn't the gods that would hear his plea, but magic. The Blue Fairy's skin began to brighten, shining a faint bluish glow upon Smee's face. He looked down in wonder and awe as her big eyes began to open. Smee was so overjoyed that he silently clapped his hands together, "Yes! Thank you. Thank you!" The tiny pixie looked up at him. "Shhh," he whispered. "Do not try to move; you are alright now. I am a doctor." He wasn't sure if she understood him, so he merely gave her a kind smile. To his heart's delight, she gave him a weak smile in return.

As the morning sun grew brighter in the sky, the rays of light shined in through Hook's large windows and upon his face. He let out a roaring yawn that startled Smee and the tiny pixie. Her body shook with fear as she felt his presence approach her. "Does it live?" He asked coldly.

Smee nodded uncertain and afraid what Hook might do next, for there was something sinister in his tone that alarmed him. "Yes, she does, but she is still extremely weak and unable to speak it seems."

Hook looked at him sternly. "Very well then, Mr. Smee. You have done well, I knew you wouldn't let me down, and under your care, I imagine she will be well enough- Very soon. Isn't that right, Mr. Smee?"

Smee nodded nervously. "Of course, Captain! Of course."

"Good! Be sure to inform me of her status thusly."

"Yes, sir."

Days went on with very little signs of change from the wounded pixie. She had remained silent but seemed very interested in Smee's strange behavior. Her eyes following him around the room and observing his task and manner to treat her. He had indeed done well, her pain had already started to diminish, but the pain of losing her beautiful wings was the worst torture of all. When Smee stood over here, she felt safe. Her family had always taught her that humans were evil, but maybe not all humans were.

"Captain?"

Hook looked up from the book he was reading. "What is it, Smee?"

Smee looked sheepish and afraid as he spoke. "I have a question about this little fairy; why... um..."

"Spit it out, Mr. Smee! Why what?!"

Smee gulped. "All of the fairies I have seen on your sketches and in your books have black eyes."

Hook waved his hand annoyed. "Yes... so?!"

"But her eyes are not. See for yourself," Smee said nervously.

Hook suspiciously walked over to take a glance at his tiny prisoner. She gazed up at him, absolutely petrified. He finally took a real look at her. She had one blue eye and one purple, not solid like the others but rather kind and human looking, except for their size. Her eyes were large and had beautiful curling eyelashes. Her hair was azure and was as long as her body. She had a baby blue dress on that twinkled, not by her movement but on its own. She was not wearing any shoes, which struck him to be especially odd. And as if he was blind to it before, she looked to be a child. *How old is a child fairy anyway?* "Her different appearance means absolutely nothing to me!"

"Bu-but, Captain..." Smee said sadly.

Hook shot over a vicious glare. "Have you taken pity on the creature, Smee? She is evil! They are all evil!" His voice thundered upon the shaking doctor.

Smee shook, hiding his face cowering down. "I'm so-ss-sorry, Captain. She just doesn't seem evil," Smee whispered.

Hook charged at him. "Why, you blubbering id..."

"Leave him alone!" The fairy screamed.

Hook looked down at her stunned. "What in the blazes happened while I was asleep?" He huffed glaring at both of them. "I guess I should not be surprised! Though I fear you may find your charms waisted on dear old Smee. You may have poisoned my doctor's fragile mind, but you will never change mine!"

"I know I cannot change your mind, but it is true. I am not the evil one- you are," the Blue Fairy said in a soft, shaky voice.

Hook could see she was frightened, but she had gained his interest. "So, I'm the evil one, am I?"

She looked up at him with despair, trying to hold on to what little bravery she had left.

Something about her luminescing eyes suddenly stopped him as if he was seeing them for the first time. They looked innocent and sweet. Somehow without the surrounding evil of the party, she looked completely different. It wasn't just her eyes, but her entire appearance had somehow escaped his notice until this moment. The others were all dressed in pale colors of golden champagne and rosy pink, with lace and various animal masquerade masks, but she wasn't. Her dress, though long and beautiful, was not extravagant and formal like the others. She did not have a mask, and her hair wasn't dressed in high fashion. It just laid freely down her scorched back. Looking at the brutal carnage, he had inflicted upon her suddenly caused a stirring of guilt. It was small, but enough to make him pause. He looked back towards his bed. Catcher was just lying there; he wasn't aggressive towards her at all. Come to think about it; he hadn't been since he found him in the woods. Letting out a frustrated sigh, Hook spoke: "You know that no matter what you say or do, you are going to die here as my prisoner. You do know that, right?"

She nodded sadly. "I do not speak to you on my behalf, but on his," she said looking at Smee, rocking back and forth nervously.

Hook looked over at Smee, rolling his eyes in annoyance. "And just why is that, if I may ask?"

She looked at Smee with pity. "Because of what this human has done for me. He was kind to me. Not for his own betterment or advantage, he did not seek wishes or reward. I have no doubt he saved me under your orders, but he did not have to be kind to me."

Hook looked at Smee with disgust. "Oh, he did... did he?"

"Yes, he did! And it has brought to light something that I have always believed. For that, I can and will die at peace knowing that I spent my life believing the right thing."

Hook's eyes squinted suspiciously. "How do you mean?"

"I have been told all my life that humans are evil; that the war against them was not only necessary but essential; that the only way to keep our kind and our realms alive is with the stolen souls of mankind. But I never felt that it was right. I thought it wrong and unjust. Eventually, my disinvolvement was viewed as rebellion. I was punished often, and my family was threatened. In the end, even my family turned against me," she sighed. "But I see now that I was right! Not all humans are evil and cruel- just some," she said with a stare that made him smirk.

"Hmmm," was all Hook said in response to her little tale; though her story hadn't seemed dishonest, he couldn't bring himself to feel anything towards her but hatred. Nevertheless, he needed to think about this new information. He looked over at Smee who had started to stop his incessant quivering. Hook let out another frustrated sigh, "Well if you are quite done, Mr. Smee; maybe you could remove this infernal creature from my desk so that I can work," he said as if firmly announcing his rigidity on the matter. Smee did as he was told and quickly scooped up the pile of rags with the Blue Fairy being tossed around on top of them, almost falling off. Luckily Smee came back to his senses upon seeing her and whispered a quiet apology before placing her on an end table across the room. "Wait!" Hook demanded. Smee froze in terror, afraid that maybe Hook had heard him. "If you are so despised by your kind, as you claim, then what were you doing at the party?"

Smee slowly turned around as she spoke: "I wasn't supposed to be there. I was trying to free the captured souls that are cruelly kept there," he answered peeking her head above the rags.

Hook turned to face her. "The orbs. They were souls," he whispered. She could see that it wasn't a question, but more of a realization. Suddenly it all made sense: why she was hiding and why she looked different. *Maybe she is different.* "What is your name, fairy?"

"Ainsel."

Their eyes met, and suddenly it hit him: he had captured and tortured a good fairy. He was the evil one here. He had harmed an innocent. Hook turned around quickly, closing his eyes and taking in a breath of genuine sorrow. His shame and guilt suffused his mind. *How could this have happened?* "Are there others like you?"

"Not many I'm afraid."

Her answer made his stomach twist with remorse as he turned his back to her commanded Smee onwards. As the hours drew on, Hook's heart grew sore from the sounds of her misery and pain behind him. Each moan or sob was another vivid reminder of what he had done to her: the image of his hand ripping off her wings from her body, the innocent blood he had spilled; it was all so evil. *How could I have let this happen?* Hook hadn't known everything about fairies after all, and such lack of knowledge was just another slice of guilt and painful regret he would carry with him forever. The following day, when Smee was not tending to the fairy's wounds, Hook asked him to leave the room. He didn't want Smee around to see what his sorrow; just like Blackbeard never wanted anyone to know of his. Demons were to be suppressed and private. Both his actions and memories would be for him to suffer and no one else. But he did need to talk to the fairy; there was much to say. Once they were alone, Hook made his way over to the table where she was. He cleared his throat gruffly as if nervous. "So, Ainsel, why are your eyes not black like the others?"

231

"The eyes are the windows to the soul. If you look hard enough, you can see exactly who someone is through them. Even one's emotions can be seen through them. Humans will never live long enough to have their souls so tarnished by evil like my kind. Dark fairy's eyes are black because their soul is just that: *black*. They feel nothing about their evil deeds. How they get what they need and want requires heinous crimes. It is not right; I just never could bring myself to do any of those terrible things."

"Ainsel, I know what you must think of me; and I guess after what I have done to you and the massacre you witnessed; I couldn't possibly hope to change your mind. But maybe if you heard my story, as I have heard yours, you might find it in your heart to forgive my mistake. I pray you find that I am not evil, though I admit I am filled with wrathful vengeance. I have never in my life thought to harm an innocent. I guess somewhere in the bloody euphoria of my rage that night, your appearance and purpose escaped all my logic and reason."

She looked up at him with kind eyes. "What did they do to make you hate them so?"

Hook took in a deep breath, for this was the first time he would tell someone the whole story, and he hoped it would be the last. "Well, it started before I was born. My father Blackbeard had the unfortunate crossing with the Dooinney Oie."

Ainsel's face scrunched up. "That is bad."

"Yes, it was. He was cursed, and with no hope for an end to his misery, he went to a witch who offered to change his curse in exchange for his first-born child. My father agreed."

Ainsel's eyes open wide in shock. "Oh my."

"After I was born, my parents tried to hide me. My mother even put me in an orphanage, but that devil creature still found me."

"Who found you?"

"I must have sketched her out a thousand times," he said spreading the papers on his bed. "But I do not know of her true name. I have been calling her the Scarlet Fairy since she came into my life."

Ainsel looked at his sketches, studying every detail of her character carefully. "What did she do?"

Hook looked over to his mother's old book. "She killed someone I cared for, and then she took her soul. I have been hunting the Scarlet Fairy ever since. I want her to pay for what she did. I'm afraid my hatred towards her and your kind have caused me to..." He looked at her wounded back and lost his breath.

Ainsel could see his sorrow. "Do not worry, for I have always believed in second chances. I forgive you. And maybe fate has brought us together for a reason. I think I may be able to help you. I know a lot about my kind, and I may be able to find this: Scarlet

Fairy. For while I believe in second chances, true evil has no bounds. There must be a stop to it."

"I thank you for your forgiveness, but I cannot ask of such a dangerous task of one so kind. No, I am going to set you free. I only wish there was a way to give you back your wings."

Ainsel smiled joyfully. "But, James, do you not see? It was my purpose to help others. If I find my wand, I can use its magic to give me my second chance. The chance to do what I was meant to do, and by the laws of magic, if I honor that: I will have my wings."

He let out a large breath of relief. "Where is your wand now?"

"It is in the woods where you found me; I must have dropped by the tree when you grabbed me."

He shook his head slightly, not wanting to relive that moment. "I will take you there, and maybe then we both can have our second chance."

Hook was not one to spendthrift time, he had made his decision, and he intended to execute it quickly. Blackbeard was more than happy to turn his ship around, heading back towards Yorkshire if it meant that the fairy would be leaving his ship. But Blackbeard wasn't the only one who was feeling unnerved, for the news of the massacre had already spread across the realms.

After escaping the human's wrath, the fairies told the Elders in great detail what had happened in the forest in the hours past. "I am sorry to disturb you like this, Majesty... but I bring the most terrible news. A mortal came into our woods and it..."

"Oh, what is it?! Humans stumble into our woods all the time; we take care of them simple enough. What could have gone wrong?"

The Ellyon looked up nervously. "This was no ordinary human, sir. He killed hundreds, leaving only vast traces of scarlet agony upon the glittering frost below."

The Grand Elder's face was still. "I have lived longer than all, as old as the sky. I have seen many of my kind's lives ended by the hands of mortals. They are vicious beasts but should any of them venture into our realm; we take care of them!"

The shaking worried fairy spoke again: "Yes, but our charms and magic failed to touch him. It was as if he was shielded in some unnatural way. We tried everything to stop him, but he was just so fast. I do not believe he simply stumbled into the veil as all the others have done. No, this was planned. He knew where to go, what to do, and he knew we couldn't harm him."

The tale was an interesting one, and yet the Elder needed to know more. "This is a matter of the utmost importance. Let us bring all those of magic gathered to your forest. There is much to say, and all must attend by my rule. That is my word, go now: tell them. I want to know who this mortal is."

CHAPTER TWENTY-THREE

THE THREE LORDS

After a few weeks, Blackbeard's ship was heading back to Whitby, and Hook's temperament changed by the hour. For however certain he was in his unrelenting obligation to Ainsel, the very thought of entering those woods. It wasn't the fair folk that caused him unnerving terror, but the forests itself. Something terrible and malicious guarded fae territory and Hook was horrified to cross paths with them again. Though he dared not admit his condemning vulnerability, his thoughts and feelings consumed him with great unease. His thoughts had somehow projected from him and into the sight of the Blue Fairy's kind heart.

"You do not have to take me back there. You may leave me upon any step of land. I know of the danger you face entering woodland's path, and it is far worse than you could imagine."

Hook closed his eyes shaking his head as he tried to swallow the lump in his throat. "No." He knew she wouldn't survive should she try to make her own way to the forest. She had never been without her wings, and even though she had healed a great deal, she was still weak from the wounds he had inflicted. No, he had to do this. She could see that he would not be moved on this, so she decided if she could not persuade him otherwise, she would do what she could to aid him while they were still in the safety of the ship. But she would have to hurry, for alas, they were not far, and time was passing quickly.

His anxiety overwhelmed him; not even Smee could be permitted into his chambers short of tending only to Catcher. However badly he desired to bring him any cheer or comfort, he could not brave his captain's walls. The Blue Fairy on the other hand no longer feared the man at all. They understood each other now, and she knew as she watched every tortured thought he tried to force out of his mind, that he was doing it for her.

"James, please swallow your pride, for it will not serve you well now. I can help you if you would only listen. Heed my words, do as I say, and I promise you survival. You are strong, but I know of what the guardians can do and will do to you. The fact that you are alive now is because the fae had other plans for you."

Hook let out a breath of defeat, after all: she was right. *How was he to survive them again?* The events that happened that night in the black forest flashed through his mind. It was the girl, the beautiful woman that saved him from their attack that night. Had she not, he would have most certainly died there. "Alright, Ainsel, tell me. How do I survive the guardians?" He asked kneeling on the floor in front of her, as to look her in the face. She smiled a comforting smile as she gazed into his fearful eyes.

"We call them the Three Lords," Ainsel said.

Hook looked stunned. "Lords! Lords of what?"

"Lords of everything in the woods: the ground, the animals, the trees; they are all under their rule. There is not a single thing that happens out there that they do not know about. They stand still and watch; that is until an unwelcome stranger strays too close to fae territory. That's when things get bad. But if you heed my every word, you might be able to leave the woods alive."

Hook nodded. "What do I have to do?"

She smiled as if proud of him. "There are three very important things to know about all magical creatures: First, bring an offering. Each creature has its own pleasures. Most people think to offer blood just as you would for the gods, but it is actually a very dangerous offering for magical creatures, especially if it's your own. It makes them want the rest of you. Second, most magical creatures including the fair folk are obsessed with cleanliness. Many people have been taken out of a forest for simply moving a stone that had been perfectly placed. And three, the best thing you can do is wear your clothes inside out."

Hook looked up at her with a suspicious smirk. "Come now... an offering I understand, and I have heard about their obsessive cleanliness, but why wear your clothes inside out? That just sounds ridiculous."

Her face looked at him sternly. "Actually, it makes more sense than you think. In a world where summer is winter, the old is young: an irrational act within irrationality may flip the coin for one in our mundane world. Wearing your clothes inside out will not stop them, but it will confuse them, thus slowing them down. You must bring rocks with you, and when you think you see one or think there is one chasing you, start throwing the rocks in opposite directions. The creature's unbearable need for tidiness will compel them to find the rock and put it back in its proper place. When it has done so, and you can hear them charging you again, throw another and another. It may keep them busy long enough for you to escape their deadly grasp."

Hook nodded. "And what sort of offering pleases the forest?"

She sneered at his disdain, "The forest likes breadcrumbs, berries, and flowers. Again, these acts of trickery will not make them stop, but it will buy you time. Throughout the ages, many have survived the Three Lord's wrath simply by luck or under some sad circumstances; they were simply saved because they wandered into the forest with a dog. The human may return out of the forest safely, but the dog will not get out alive. Most magical creatures despise them. Dogs are the most suitable offering for the Three Lords," she said setting a slight gaze at Catcher and Hook spotted her.

"Well, I am not taking him into the forest with us then. I will not be offering my dog!"

She giggled sweetly. "I know that. You care a great deal for your little creature, don't you? I have watched you together; you treat him as a friend, even though you are two very different species."

Hook remained silent.

"And what of Smee; is he your friend?"

Hook turned to look towards the door to his chambers, knowing full well Smee was never far from it. But as Hook thought about it, he shook his head. "I do not think so; though I haven't given much thought of what makes a true friend. The one thing I do know is you should be able to trust them completely, and I do not place trust in people lightly. People are too easily changed: for money, for fear, for gain; I cannot put such trust in anyone that could do that. So, no, I guess I do not have a friend."

Ainsel's heart dropped, somehow what he had said hurt her deeply. Somehow, she thought after everything he had shared with her; something had changed between them. "What about me?" She asked sadly. "Do you not trust me?"

Regretting his harsh words, Hook looked over at her and suddenly realized there was something different about her appearance. She still looked just as lovely and kind as she had before, but she somehow seemed older... less childlike. They had only been sailing a little more than a couple of weeks. *How could she look so different? When did it happen? How had Hook not noticed it?* He thought about the past week;

241

he had barely even looked at her. His thoughts had swarmed his mind, blinding him from all. But her question had forced him to really look at her. She still had her lovely turquoise hair that tumbled down to her feet, her skin was milky white, and her beautiful blue and purple matched eyes were as enchanting as ever, but she no longer looked like a child. Instead, she appeared to be the age of a young lady. "What is happening? Why do you look to be aging so rapidly?"

She looked herself up and down and giggled. "Time can be a funny thing for my kind. Mortals think us immortal, but that is only half true. Time moves differently in every realm. Here in the mortal world, my aging process has been corrupted, forcing me to age more rapidly."

Hook looked at her concerned. "Why?"

"When the realms were divided, our magic was bound to the other side of the veils. The effects of this world are not like ours and can be quite dangerous for us if we stay in it for too long. Without my wand, I have no magic to stop the rules of time that were not meant for me."

"But you will be alright, won't you? I mean, it will still be a while before I can get you back to the woods."

"I will be alright. It will not be much longer at the fast rate Blackbeard likes to sail."

He could see she was trying to make light of the situation and not cause him further guilt, but if she thought Blackbeard was sailing fast now, she could fathom the great haste he would force upon the ship to save her; even from time itself.

Once the ship was docked Hook wasted not a single moment, he grabbed his bag full of rocks, scooped up Ainsel, and called Catcher to the bed. "Now you stay here, boy! I will back before you know it," he said turning to look back at the door. "Smee!"

The nervous doctor came stumbling in the door. "Yes, Captain?"

"Take care of my dog, Smee. No matter what happens, promise me you will take good care for him!"

Smee nodded. "I promise."

Hook grabbed his coat and turned it inside out before putting it on. He brought various pieces of iron, his belt, his boot tips and heels, and two of his sharpest blades. He braced himself once more before leaving his chamber, and off the ship to venture into the woodlands again. Without much more than a single word of goodbye to his father, Hook stepped down to the town of Whitby with the Blue Fairy hidden in the palm of his hand; only this time it was to protect her. Making their way into the area of Scarborough, Hook could see the giant area of woods up ahead. It looked just as it did before and yet somehow, it didn't. It made Hook nervous. Everything in his body told him to turn around.

He took his first step upon the path when suddenly he heard Ainsel's muffled voice yell: "Stop!"

"What is it? Is something wrong?"

"I can feel them in there: the clan of fairies is in those woods, which means that all of the Three Lords will be there. You must leave me here; I fear for your life if you dare cross into their territory. You mustn't," she pleaded desperately.

Hook shushed her. "Nothing is going to happen to me. I am ready for this, and it is all thanks to you. I will not leave you here like a coward, where something awful could still happen to you in your weak state. No, I must be sure you found your wand and have your wings again! I just have to."

Ainsel let out a hopeless sigh. "But James, this is not what we planned. Once I am there, and I find my wand, others are likely to see me. With so many fairies there, I will not be able just simply to leave. Without my help, the Three Lords will kill you," she sobbed. "No, let's just leave right now! We can come back once they have gone."

"But we don't know when that will be, and mortal time has already begun to change. I did this to you, and this is my only chance to fix it. I would rather die saving you, then live having killed you!"

His words made her soul ache. "James... please."

Hook shook his head sternly, "Enough! You are not to come out of the veil once you are inside. If they see you with me, the other fairies might harm you, and that I cannot allow. You must stick to the plan. I am a survivor; please believe in me."

She gave a weak smile, "I do believe in you," she said before they both looked on to the forest. The sun was still up, allowing every detail to be seen in the light. The trail went all the way into the steep center slopes that Hook remembered. The ground was still covered in a thin layer of snow. The forest was quiet; each hard-pressed step he made in the ground seemed to remain when he turned around to check. Everything felt fine, normal, even comfortable, but this moment of peace was quickly shattered as the sudden sound of an icicle fell from a nearby tree. Just the one sudden sound of something braking was enough to make Hook sweat. He decided to take a few more steps forward, keeping his footing hard and pressing in deeply with each step, and still checking every few seconds to be sure they were there. To calm his nerves, he breathed calm and steady as he moved forward down the same path he had taken before; the one that seemed to change as you crossed it. It was if this part of the forest had vast amounts of gardeners. Everything looked like a serene painting. And something else had changed as well: the calmness in the air was now so oppressive. There was this overwhelming sense of being watched, and Hook knew they were. Suddenly: *crash!* Another icicle fell, then another and another. Ainsel popped her head out from Hooks tight grip to look up at him.

"It's the trees; they're moving," he whispered.

She looked up at him and whispered: "Run."

His feet were flying before she could even finish the word, but it was no use. Whatever the things were, they were much faster than humanly possible. He could hear them hastily shuffling in their pursuit to grab him. The tree bark groaned and creaked with every move they made charging at him. His legs were on fire; his body felt like it should have shut down by now. He knew he was pushing himself too hard, but the adrenaline coursing through him kept him going him; that is until... *Slash*! Something had clawed at his coat, lunging him far forward on the ground. He was sure his back was cut. The pain was agonizing, but there was something else that mattered more, he looked down in his hand. "Ainsel are you alright? Are you hurt?"

She shook her head no. Suddenly there was the creaking sound as if a bough had broken behind him. "Don't look back, James. Just run," Ainsel whispered urgently. Hook got up from the ground with all the strength he had and started to run again. He reached into a bag he brought and started grabbing stones. He threw the first and then another, and sure enough, the charging shuffles seemed to be suddenly interrupted, but within mere minutes they were back to a rushing attack. This time he reached into his pocket for breadcrumbs, but before he could throw them out:

246

Slash! He was clawed again and lunged hard upon the frosted ground. This time the pain was too much; he didn't think he could move his legs, but instead lifted the rest of the breadcrumbs out of his pouch and turned to face them. The sight that greeted his eyes made it hard to breathe. There they stood: the three gargantuan wooded figures of twisted, knotty bodies and jointed with antlers and sinew. The head looked like a moose head, except it had hallowed black eyes. It sniffed the air looking for his scent. Hook remained perfectly still, with his warm blood running down his cold back.

There was a smell of rotting death about the wooded figures. The giant monsters didn't say anything, but he could hear their deep laughter. The tallest in the middle bent its limbs and contorted as it stretched out its neck bringing its head closer to him. Fear struck Hook's vitals as he watched in absolute horror as the thing opened its mouth to reveal the face of his mother. She looked pale, bloody, and eyeless. The vision was enough to stir his rage. Then a crunching sound of bones met with the wailing screams of a woman came from within the Lord's wide, crooked smile of splinters. The horror of their trickery made him wince, but hearing their following laughter, sparked a flicker of anger inside him. He forced himself up and turned to continue walking away from them. If this were a game, then they would want to take their time in killing him, and time was all he needed to get Ainsel back to the veil. They were nearly there; even if they were to get a few more slashes in, he would survive. He just needed to hurry. One steep slope down was the tree by the veil. They were here. He quickly turned to look back at the Lords, just in time to see one charge at him on all four legs of wooded twine. *Slash!* Knocked to the ground in agonizing pain, Hook pulled out Ainsel and slid her down the slope to the veil. "Go get your wand and get your wings back. I will peak an eye in to make sure you are successful."

Ainsel welled up crystal-like tears in her eyes, "James, you have already lost all your breadcrumbs, your coat is shredded... what are you going to do?"

"You said you believe in me, right?"

She nodded.

Hook smiled. "Alright then, do not weep. Go get your wand. We will see each other again very soon," he said wiping her eyes.

She gave a pitiful sniffle that made Hook smile as she composed herself as crossed the veil with throttling music carried on the wind behind her as it closed. Sparkling dust flew into the illuminated light with the wind from the cracks of the veil. Hook turned his face away from it angrily, as if not wanting even a sliver of their magical world to touch him, but alas the bestial grunts and laughter awaited behind him. Hook remained still, picturing the land beyond the veil, trying to figure when Ainsel should reach the tree where he found her, hoping that her affliction goes unnoticed long enough for her to reach her magical remedy. But the burning impatience wasn't the peak of his agony, for the malicious Lord's cruelty hadn't abated, the voice of his mother's call still echoed the chilling air.

He knew it was all a cruel trick, but as always, when sadness dared to grasp at his soul, it arose a scorching fire within him. His anger grew more fiercely with each breath of their vile being and word spoken. He just needed to wait a bit longer, he thought. He had to be sure Ainsel had her wings. Still, their antagonizing pierced through his heart like spikes burning from Hell's fire. They tore through all his power of will, his heart pounding harder as time was once again adding itself to his torture. He couldn't contain himself any longer; he looked back to look into the eyes of the devils, turning his head slowly and gazing at them with such hatred that for a moment a silence struck the forest Lords. But the moment was shortly shattered by the sight of their grins and the sound of their laughter. It was too much. He screamed in a fury, drew his iron sword and charged at them rapidly with brutal force.

The next few minutes were a blur of the slashing dark silver of his blade and a mist of splintered wood flying, but the laughter never ceased. The Three Lords towered above him, amused by his arrogant rage. Unlike the creatures, Hook's spark of adrenaline had peaked, and through all his physical excursion, his motions had slowed: diminished by exhaustion. As the night drew its surrounding blackness, the creatures seemed to change, becoming even more frightening somehow. The smell of burning flesh and rotting corpses filled the air; becoming so nauseating that it became difficult for him to breath. Their wicked smiles that had before been full of spiking splinters now looked to be large yellow teeth, jagged, and sharp. Their eyes were glowing with something intense and evil. Their antlers reached higher and sharper than before. Their moose like skull was now bare and skeletal, bringing even more horrific attention to every deep-rooted tooth high within their long jaws, but the real terror lied in the change to their bodies, in the sun, their limbs appearing like twine and spindling branches as now covered in long black fur; like giant bodies of bears. One swipe from their giant bear-like claws with long thin fingers slashed at Hook, sending his iron sword flying far away from his grip and another slashing him hard into the ground. His breath had left him; paralyzing fear filled his soul as the three guardians surrounded him. He looked up at them. They were still for a moment, sniffing the air and licking their teeth as if preparing themselves for something delicious. There was nowhere to run, nothing he could do; he was going to die. But he wasn't going to wait around for their sadistic torture. The Three Lords bent their heads back in laughter once more, only this time, Hook quickly reached down into his boot, grabbing his smaller iron blade and shoved it down into one of the Lord's legs as far as it would go. A wailing scream of pain echoed throughout the air. Hook had never heard anything like it. His ears rung painfully, but he didn't remove his grip from his dagger. Instead, he rapidly ripped it out with a cruel twisting motion. Gushing blood poured out covering the king's black fur, dripping down upon Hook as he rolled to his left, quickly sending the blade into another Lord's leg. Again, the forest echoed with the sound of the guardian's wailing howls. Through their pain and blood, Hook had a sliver of hope in his eyes. If he could just injure the third, maybe he could make a run for it, but it was too late. For in a matter of seconds, the Third Lord swung at Hook's arm with deadly force. Hook was sure his arm was going to come clean off, but in great haste, he let go of the dagger; dodging the blow but losing his only hope for escape in the process.

The Three Lords towered over him, deadly silent. He had pissed them off; he could see it in their wicked glowing eyes. It pleased him. Looking up at them smugly, "What is it? Do you not find this little hunt funny any longer?"

The creatures scowled in a fury, raising their claws above him, ready to strike their final deadly blow. Hook closed his eyes accepting his fate, he knew this would happen, and he didn't regret it. Suddenly a shining blue burst of light blasted through the woods. The Three Lords howled more loudly than ever before, then all of a sudden, there was silence. Hook opened his eyes to find he was back in his room on Blackbeard's ship, and Smee was in the corner with his mouth gaping open and his eyes struck with utter shock. He froze, unsure of what happened, maybe it was just another cruel trick, but as the warmth of the room touched him, and Catcher happily approached him licking his face, bringing him back to reality. *Am I really here? Am I alive? But how?* He tried to stand up from the bed in a daze; he was bruised, beaten, and tired. His vision began to tunnel in darkness and in a moment his body collapsed with only the faint sound of Smee's voice calling his name before everything went black.

CHAPTER TWENTY-FOUR

HEAR MY CALL

Back in the woodlands, the blast of magic that had saved Hook was now gone, yet the effect of such a cause laid still beyond the veil. Ainsel could feel Hook's distance; He was safe. She quickly turned the wand towards her back and whispered a magical spell:

"Magic, please
Hear my call
Grant my wish
Make me one and all
I swear to you now
the fae's Absolute Law
Of honor and purpose
I shall not fall
I will never alter or waver my stance
Please give me
My second chance."

Big sparkling fairy wings slowly appeared on her back, even more, beautiful than before. She looked at them smiling with immense relief and complete joy, waving them slowly, rising slowly into the air. She could fly again. How she wished James could see her now. If It eased even a piece of his guilt, it would be everything. And yet a part of her just wished she could see him. She was so happy that she had found the wand in time to save Hook from the guardians that she had failed to keep her wounded form hidden. Most of the fairies hadn't seen or felt the blast of magic she had sent outside the veil, but the Elder did. He didn't know who's it was. He just gazed out at the mass hilltop full of fairies, as if suspiciously trying to find the one among them. The Grand Elder had always prided himself a most powerful and wise leader. There was nothing he didn't know and very little he didn't control, but this catastrophe was made even more frightening by the fact that this had happened by a human. A human with an extraordinary power that no fae could hope to touch- and that made him very dangerous. *But how did he know of the veil? Does he know of the others?* The Elder thought as his eyes scanned over the twinkling crowd below him. But Ainsel wasn't the only one hoping to go unnoticed, for another caught her eye. She was sitting under one of the pavilions alone. Her glow was dim, as it is typically when a fairy is down. She had come here tonight as the others did, to follow orders and as to not appear as if hiding something. Every other fairy had circled around the Grand Elder, eagerly waiting for his words of strength, wisdom, and comfort, but Ainsel wasn't interested in what the Grand Elder had to say. She was far more curious about the fairy hiding under the pavilion, for as she drew closer, she could see that her glow however faint- was *red*!

Ainsel grew nervous as she approached her, unaware of what to do or what to say. The Scarlet Fairy looked up at her; her pitch-black eyes were large and round. Her hair was long and as red as the striking dress covered in bright crimson lace. Her shoes were covered in ruby jewels. A pendant of her importance and rank hung on her neck. It was a pendant well known to all the creatures of Nine Realms. They are called the *Unblessed Ones*, known as the allegiance to the Snow Queen of the Unseelie Court. James was right; she was undoubtedly a monster, for the Unseelie Court held only the most malevolent and evil fairies. Their trickery knew no bounds; to be their victim meant certain death. And the most treacherous and ruthless villain of all was their queen. The Snow Queen was said to be cold-blooded, cruel, and pure evil. With long silver hair in three long braids covered in stars going down to her dainty bare feet and skin so pale it made the brightest of winter snow sparkle in her presence. Her beauty is said to have no equal, her lips as red as fresh dripped blood and eyes as purple as blooming lavender. Always dressed in fine shining silver, and jewelry made entirely of pristine crystals. Desired by all, she had gained her power with ease, as it was not only mortals who couldn't deny her charms, but magical creatures as well. It is unknown how many souls she has taken within herself, but her thirst for power was as unquenchable. Consumed with greed and hate for all humanity, she found the Elder's subtle methods of stealing souls to be weak, minuscule, and unsatisfying. She rebelled against their control, taking over the realm beyond the wardrobe, and under her irresistible charming rule, others followed. It is said that only the Grand Elder himself had the ultimate power to banish her from the magical lands beyond the wardrobe. For while he bore no love or empathy for humans, he could not condone her blatant malicious methods. She had started to consume souls unto herself instead of for the magic of the realms themselves. Her power was so great that it took all the Elders to overpower her, entrapping her in a small citadel in a forest beyond the troll bridge. Though she remains banished and exiled, her undesirable charm would still consume the hearts of many. Rising as her army, the Unseelie Court was born. Creatures of the night: trolls, dark elves, and fairies formed to steal souls for their beloved queen. The Grand Elder had used his own blood to bind her to her prison, but she was much younger than he, and her bitterness and powers would only continue to grow until there would be no one left to stop her deadly wrath upon all the realms.

Ainsel shook in fear within the Scarlet Fairy's presence, for it was vile and frightening. How James had survived such a target was indeed a miracle. Though Ainsel was sure the queen had consumed the poor nun's soul long ago, it was just the first link in a chain of deadly proportions. This fairy may have thought she had merely given a little boy a shield, but in fact, she had handed him an extraordinary weapon. Looking into her eyes, Ainsel could see her fear. *She knows who did this, and she is afraid.* Ainsel gathered a breath of courage, "Were you there that night?"

The Scarlet Fairy looked up at her sadly, "No. My clan is not invited to the parties, but he didn't know that."

"*He?*"

There was something hopeless in her eyes. She didn't answer at first. She just sat there staring off in the distance in a daze. "But he will. He will find me- I see that now," she spoke as if no longer aware of Ainsel's presence. Ainsel couldn't allow herself to feel empathy for her; for though she was a forgiving soul and believed above all things in second chances, she knew the awful things her kind had done, or maybe she just couldn't forgive what she had done to James. She had broken his heart, and that was something she couldn't forgive, no matter how deeply she tried. The Scarlet Fairy rose up from the table, turning her gaze away from the crowd above and flew away into the darkness. Ainsel watched as she disappeared, knowing full well where she would be going; where all the Unblessed lived: in the forest trees of the citadel.

A loud striking clash of thunder and lightning roared through the night sky, waking Hook up sweating in a panic. He quickly put up his hands, as if still in a fight, only to find Smee and Catcher struck with alarm beside him.

"It's alright, Captain. You are back on the ship, though I know not how," Smee said in a sweet yet shaky voice. But Hook didn't hear him, for suddenly he felt something small moving around on his back. He tried to move, but his body writhed in severe agonizing pain. "I'm so sorry, Captain. I don't understand what it is, but I have been removing pieces of wool and fish bones from your wounds, but it just isn't closing. I am doing all I can to keep your wounds clean. Once I am sure there is nothing left within them, I will stitch you up."

Hook froze in disgust and fear. *Wool and fish bones?* He thought as Smee helped to roll him over and attend his back, he smelled something. It was the same smell of rotting death that came from the Three Lord's breath before his escape. *My escape!* His mind flashed back on the bright blue color that blasted him out of the forest. *Ainsel.* "It was Ainsel; she saved me," he whispered.

"That's what I thought," Smee said leaning in close with a tiny tool and cloth drenched in what smelled like whiskey. There was a soft whisper of, "*Sorry,*" before an unbearable burning suffused him.

Hook screamed in agony as Smee reached in, pulling out the pieces of wool and bones within his flesh. The smell of death filled the room, but Smee focused intently until the slashes across Hook's back were once again clean. He placed another bandage over the gaping wounds to help with the bleeding, but something about the way he shook his head made Hook's eyes well up. "Is it over?"

"I'm afraid it is not, Captain. For in a matter of hours, the wounds will be once again saturated in filth and debris, and I will again have to go in and remove it before this unholy infection kills you."

Hook nodded his head in understanding as tears of pain welled up in his eyes.

The next few weeks were slow and torturous, leaving only the company of Catcher and Smee as any comfort. But the near-death experience had left Hook an even more bitter angry man than before. He wanted to go back to those woods and set them all on fire. Their taunting sinister laughter echoed in his dreams, reminding him of his brutal defeat. *Was Ainsel still out there?* How he wished he could see her now- to know that she had her wings back. *What if something awful had happened to her?* The thoughts of terrible possibilities raced in his daily thoughts. She had saved him, but at what cost? *Did the others see her? Was she in trouble?* His thoughts and nightmares had become their own form of unbearable torture, challenging his sanity once again, with only the terrible feeling of something crawling under his skin to wake him.

It was now early April, and a collection of terribly beautiful storms were rolling in almost every night. Smee looked as if he was going to unravel any second, but because of the need for his constant surgical skills, he never permitted himself the comfort of the bottle, even in the most wicked of weather. After the final cleaning for the night, Smee took the slim opportunity to catch some sleep while Hook laid awake reading on his bed as usual. Looking out his large windows at the beautiful strikes of lighting was almost enough to make Hook smile. Then suddenly, just as his eyes were about to fade again into the dreaded darkness, a burst of blue light appeared in front of the window, and he heard a voice: *"James."*

Hook opened his tired eyes, seeing the blurred image of a beautiful woman surrounded by a blue hue. "Ainsel?" He said jolting himself out of his daze wholly shocked by the sight of her. She wasn't the tiny little fairy he had previously seen. She was older and as tall as a mortal woman. She was indeed the most enchantingly radiant and beautiful thing he had ever seen. Her long hair was bright azure and wild. Her skin was pale and flawless. She wore a glittering long blue gown that sparkled as if it were made of the stars, and of course, her telling blue and purple eyes; both without even a touch of darkness within them.

She smiled at him. "James, I am so happy to see you." Her eyes drifted down to his bandaged back. She began to well up with tears, "Oh! You are hurt! Those nasty beasts!" She said with a hint of anger as she lifted her hand. A long silver wand appeared in it, as she made her way towards the bed.

"Don't!" He yelled, mortified of the rotting smell. "I have a physician. I do not need the help of magic, though I am grateful. I will heal in time," he said as kindly as possible, as to not offend.

She understood and kept her distance as he had asked, but gently shook her head, "No, James, I am afraid these wounds will not heal. They were inflicted by magic and therefore can only be cured by magic. But I need not get any closer. I can do it from here, and it will be painless, I promise. Do you trust me?"

Hook nodded his head. "Yes, I trust you."

A small ray of light came from her wand towards his back. A tingle buzzed through his wounds, and he knew that it was in that moment that all the fish bones and wool were gone completely as his slashed wounds slowly closed. She lifted her wand upright as the light began to fade. "May I come towards you now?"

The smell of rotting death was gone now, and yet the word that came out of his mouth was: "No."

She looked surprised and hurt when suddenly he stood up from the bed with a smile. "For I will come to you," he said in a charming voice, approaching her. Looking her deep in the eyes, he wrapped her up in his arms, hugging her tightly. "I am so glad you are okay," he said looking down towards her beautiful shining wings.

She let herself go in his warm embrace, laying her head down upon his shoulder. "I am glad you are now too."

Another clash of lightning struck the night sky, waking up Smee in a sudden panic. Catcher ran over to him, licking his face as if trying to console him. "Stop that!" He said, rubbing his face and adjusting his glasses. He looked towards the bed as his vision came into focus- It was empty! He jumped out of the chair with his heart pounding, when suddenly he saw them. "Ainsel? Is that you?" He asked, shocked to see her.

She giggled as she let go of Hook and walked towards him. "Yes, my dear Smee. It is me."

Smee looked her up and down, stunned. "How long was I asleep?" He asked, taking off his red cap, scratching his head in confusion.

Ainsel giggled again.

Hook walked towards his table and pulled out a chair for her. "Come, Ainsel; let us talk," he said. She walked over and sat down. Hook then proceeded to pull himself a chair to sit across from her. "Smee, please tend to my blood-stained sheets while I speak with Ainsel privately."

Smee quickly stood up. "Yes, sir," he said politely and hastily began to change the bloodied sheets, tripping over himself and Catcher prancing around his feet.

Hook merely shook his head and turned to face Ainsel. "So where have you been all this time? No one hurt you, did they?"

"No one hurt me, yet I must tell you something I did discover while I was away."

Hook leaned forward inquisitively. "What is it?"

Ainsel's face went still. "That night, behind the veil; there was a large gathering. It was about you. The Grand Elder was there to make a speech concerning our safety, though it was also clear he was there to spy upon any who might be responsible, as no mortal has done what you have done in our realms. I was searching for my family; I knew they were there as it is the law that all fae must attend when the Elders call a gathering, but..." She paused.

Hook was about to burst with anticipation. "But what?"

"But I found someone *else* there," she said hesitantly.

"Who?"

Ainsel cleared her throat to answer: "The one you call the Scarlet Fairy. I know what she is, and better, I know *where* she is. I have done what I promised I would do, but she is no ordinary fairy. She is under the rule of someone far more villainous than any other creature in all the Nine Realms. The guardians that surround her will be strong, and I fear you will need my help once again."

"You found her! What is her true name?"

Ainsel shook her head. "I'm afraid I do not know. She is an Unseelie- an unblessed one that works under the rule of the most ruthless queen."

Hook rubbed his face, taking it all in. "But this... queen, you said she is, in fact, a fairy, correct?"

Ainsel nodded. "Yes, she is called the Snow Queen."

Hook's eyes squinted in recollecting thought. *The Snow Queen.* "Is she the one behind the wardrobe?"

"Yes. She is bound to her Frosted Citadel in the Third Realm. She was stripped of her wings; still she grows more powerful every day. She is extremely dangerous, as are the ones that follow her."

Hook nodded trying to understand everything, "Alright, so this *queen* is bound to a castle, unable to leave?"

"Yes."

"Who are the guardians?"

"They are the guardians of the Goat Bone Bridge- the three trolls. I will help you get across the bridge, but from there is the worst kind of fairies. If I should dare cross them, I will most certainly die, and the Snow Queen will consume my soul for her own power."

Hook raised his hand to stop her and stood up. "Wait! You said that the Scarlet Fairy is an Unseelie. So, does that mean that the Snow Queen has my mother's soul?"

Ainsel felt afraid; she could see how mad he was. She knew she had to answer, but she couldn't bring herself to say the word. So, she closed her eyes and gently nodded.

Hook didn't say anything, just grunted deep under his breath as he paced the room floor. He had always known his mother's soul had been taken, but this... Somehow knowing it was all for the greed and power of one malevolent queen was worse.

Ainsel stood up to console him. "James, I understand."

Hook yelled interrupting her: "No, you don't understand! How could you?" He said sitting back down in the chair with his head hanging between his legs.

Ainsel looked down, feeling pity for him. "Well then, help me understand."

Hook looked back up to her beautiful eyes. He hadn't meant to lose his temper. He knew she must have dreaded bringing him such news. "Because, Ainsel, this means that my mother's soul was all just for one queen. And that makes me not only want to kill the Scarlet Fairy for taking it, but I want to kill the queen that devoured it also."

"Alright then, let us come up with a plan to get past the guardians of the bridge and off to the Frosted Citadel." A pause came over her. "I am sorry about your mother, James. I hate that I upset you so."

Hook let out a sigh to calm himself down. He suddenly felt like a monster, yelling at her as he did. "No, Ainsel. It is I that should be sorry. I shouldn't have lost control of my anger like that. Please forgive my abrasive temper. I am most happy to see you. You look so- lovely," he said so charmingly nervous that it made Ainsel blush.

Smee, on the other hand, felt especially awkward in the following moment of pause; reminding them of his presence with a subtle clearing of his throat. Hook and Ainsel looked over at him standing in front of them holding a giant pile of bloody sheets. "Uh, I'm sorry, Captain, but I need access to the door, so I may go and clean your bedding."

Hook scowled at his annoying interruption but moved out of his way. Smee waddled out the chamber door with Catcher tugging on his shirt dragging behind him. Ainsel and Hook's silence broke with abrupt laughter as Smee tripped, yelping as he fell to the ground. It was just like clumsy Smee to lighten the mood. After the door was rocked shut by the ship, Hook and Ainsel sat back down at the table together, ready to plan his next deadly adventure.

CHAPTER TWENTY-FIVE

THE TROLL BRIDGE

The storm had settled. The waves were calm, and the ship swayed slow and steady, rocking all those aboard the Queen Anne's Revenge into a deep sleep- all except for two. Ainsel and Hook stayed awake talking for hours, though it did not take long for Hook to realize the grave danger he was about to put himself in. For while there were those who may stumble upon a far sighting of a troll may survive, all mortals who have dared try to cross their bridge have never been seen again.

Trolls have been found dwelling in isolated mountains, caves, and then there are the most notorious of all troll's dwellings: under bridges. But in the lands of Scandinavia, there lay a place where you can find the bridge of all bridges: The Goat Bone Bridge. Underneath lay the lives of three Jotnar trolls: the king, queen, and their foul son, the prince. And within the surrounding woods are the little Hudrefolk trolls.

The Jotnar are large, dim-witted, with the strength and size of their ancestors, the ice giants. They are known to be extremely ugly and gross in appearance, with large cycloptic eyes the size of plates, giant ears as big as its head, and long hair growing on various patches on its deformed body. They have sharp claws on their plump bulbous fingers and fangs the size of tusks that protrude from their oversized mouth filled with large jagged teeth. Covered in burlap, leaves, and dirt and their smell of rotting flesh, trolls are considered the filthiest of all creatures, mostly due to their uncontrollable fear of water and rain. The Snow Queen's guardians are the three most vicious of them all. No mortal has ever made it across the bridge. Many have tried to fight their way across, hoping for the fame that would surely follow such a legendary victory, but all have failed. They can smell the blood of the meat they do so desire; even far away. For the sense of smell is the Jotnar's greatest sense and only skill. The only chance to cross troll territory safely is to do so during the brightest hours of the day, for if a troll should dare enter the smallest touch of the sun's rays, it will turn to stone. Many trolls over the ages have lost their lives in such a way, unable to resist the alluring scent of a human. But not all trolls are so easily lured to their death, for the smaller trolls, the Hudrefolk, have their own ways of luring trickery to entice mortals to their caves. Magically using the sensual call of a woman, or the simple promise of a great treasure hidden within the caves. The Hudrefolk are far cleverer than their giant relatives. They can cast magic and even have the ability to shapeshift, making them nearly impossible to spot should they not be in their true form. But much like the Jotnar, they are not immune to the sun, and will die should they fail to reach underground or a deep cave in time. But while most believe these creatures to be vicious and cruel, they are not without the ability to love. Trolls love one thing, and one thing only: family. Late at night when the moon shines, the strange sound of howling can be heard in the mountains. It is not a wolf, but the sad mourning cry of a troll's discovery of a loved one turned to stone. No life discarded, the stones of the lives lost will remain safe, carefully placed nearby.

The time it would take to arrive in the troll mountains of Myrdal was coming soon. Hook wasn't sure how ready he was, but instead, put on a brave convincing face to Ainsel of false confidence. But Hook couldn't fool Ainsel; she saw right through him, always able to read what was truly in his heart, not by magic, but by something else. There was something special between them that allowed her to reach him in a way that no one else could. She had prepared him as best she could. The plan wasn't trying to survive the trolls, but to kill them. But there was only one way to kill a troll- You must keep them outside long enough for the sun to come up. But the bridge Hook needed to cross was broken by ways of magic until the sun had set and darkness covers the lands below. Only then will the bridge magically become whole enough to walk across.

The next few weeks Ainsel and Hook had gone over each possible scenario in their minds, but no matter how many ideas or strategies they had, they found that there was always something that could go wrong. Ainsel couldn't bear the thought that she was sending Hook off into danger- or possibly his death.

The idea alone awakened some strong feelings inside of her. She had prepared him as best she possibly could, and now all they could do was wait for Blackbeard's ship to reach its course. Blackbeard often requested his son to dine with him in his quarters as they used to, but things had changed between them. Hook had changed. He was distant and quiet. Still, Blackbeard never ceased his efforts. After every complicated thing in Hook's life, whether it be a past memory or a dreaded future, the one thing he could count on to be unconditionally simple was Catcher. Hook loved Catcher immensely. Ainsel warned Hook about the danger Catcher would face should he bring him with him to the mountains. For while trolls detested the taste of the animal, their sheer loathing hatred for the man's loyal protector brings out the monster's rage. Still, Hook assured her he would never intentionally put Catcher in danger, and besides- he wouldn't need Catcher's gift of sight to guide him to a veil since Ainsel would be telling him exactly where to find it. When the ship docked in the beautiful lands of Iceland, the crew and Smee were more than excited to enjoy their days on land.

At the edge of the mountain's trail, Hook and Ainsel exchanged a moment of silence. A feeling of goodbye held deep within their eyes. Uncertain of what to say next, Ainsel simply gave a slight wave of her wand. A shimmering gold scroll appeared in Hook's hands. He looked down to discover it was a map of magical detail, with a blue streak of light leading him straight to Goat Bone Bridge and beyond to the grand Citadel palace. "This magical map will help you on your quest should you be in danger," Ainsel said sweetly.

Hook looked at her confused. "How?"

"When the time comes, you'll know what to do. Just remember the plan, hide until the right time, and I will use all my energy moving time forward."

Hook nodded and rolled the scroll together once more, and hugged Ainsel tightly in his arms, both fearing they may never see each other again. She had saved him from the guardians before, but she couldn't do it again. Her tears began to fall as Hook headed into an open clearing leading deeper into the woods.

It didn't take long before Hook's dread overtook his mind. He hated the woods. Tiny animals scattered in his presence. Bushes and trees shook with the wildlife around him, but Hook knew it was only a matter of time before the silence came; it always came.

Hours had gone by when Hook stopped to gaze at the large overgrowth. He noticed something hidden behind the tall grass. As he squinted his eyes to focus; he saw that It was a sign. Hook moved the grass away to read what it said. The wood was damaged and worn from age and weather conditions, but the letters were large, two words written in red paint- *BEWARE TROLLS!!!* Hook bent down and used his knife to remove the sign from its hidden location and stuck it in the ground outside the overgrowth in plain view.

The sun was beginning to set its orange glow between the trees. Hook looked down upon his magical scroll. He was only a few miles away now. He could be at the bridge before dark if he hurried. Keeping the scroll in his hand, he followed the blue streak of light that guided him as he ran through the murky amber woods. The sounds had already begun to change: the air, the trees, and the animals. *The animals. They're gone now.* He had finally entered troll territory. Small various stones of dead trolls perfectly placed around like flowers in a garden. This was the place, the place where he would wait until the late dark hours of the night. He was close enough to draw them out of the cave, but far enough away to be safe until it was the right time to attack. Hook was no fool, he knew he couldn't fight the trolls and win, but if he timed it right, he could keep them outside long enough for the sun to come up.

The sun had set its last glowing rays upon the wood's shadows. Hook could see the broken bridge up ahead. Covered in moss, dead leaves, goat skulls, and human bones. There was no sound now. It was eerily silent, the part that always made Hook feel so uncomfortable. Finally, the moon welcomed the night with its glowing presence upon the mountain below. Hook quietly slumped down between a group of tall sycamore trees. Hiding in the overgrowth, Hook watched as large pieces of rock and stone rose into the air away from a large cave under the bridge. Hook hadn't noticed it before, for it was completely closed off, but one by one, the cave was opened magically by the removing of the covering boulders.

The cave was pitch black; he couldn't see anything inside. The bridge was now whole. Suddenly, a loud, shocking thud reverberated through the forest. Hook felt it shake his bones. He was knocked off his feet as his sight was greeted with the terrifying sight of a gigantic foot stepping out of the cave. His vision could barely reach the range of their height. Their bodies were ugly and deformed, each covered in hair and large boils and warts. Their legs and arms looked disproportioned on their bodies, and their ears and noses looked to be too large for their heads. Hook froze as he could hear the distant sound of the creatures sniffing the air. They know I am here. He didn't move, for if he did, they would surely hear him. The massive trolls began to frantically thrash their heads around sniffing the air wildly in utter frustration. Grunting at one another, they began to stomp around, never straying too far from the bridge. Though the smell was unbearably enticing, they knew the danger of wandering too far from the safety of their dark cave. Their movements had become hostile and angry; stomping upon the earth harder and harder, tossing Hook around and bringing more of his sweet scent into the air. Hook was sure they were about to lose control and come for him, but then something happened. The gigantic trolls began to howl loudly in the air. Drool dripped from their salivating mouths as they splashed upon the ground below. They couldn't stand it any longer; they were going to come for him now. But they didn't move; instead, they howled louder, this time with more desperation.

What are they doing? Then a noise came from behind him. He rapidly turned his head to look when suddenly others were coming from four different directions closing in on him. *The Hudrefolk.* They were coming right for him. Hook urgently looked down upon his scroll: it was time. "Come on, Ainsel! Now!"

The forest went dead silent once more, but Hook knew they were all looking right at him. Suddenly something yanked him up from the ground. Hook looked down to see it was a smaller troll. He tried to break free from the troll's strong grasp, but he couldn't. The tiny troll's body was as sturdy as a rock and looked as if it didn't feel it at all. Instead, his efforts were met with only their malicious laughter. The troll continued to hold Hook up in the air as the three others began to race around the area in an inhuman speed collecting wood and setting up a fire. They were preparing to roast him like a pig.

When it was all ready, the troll proceeded to carry him towards the pit. The other three grabbed long strips of twine to tie him up. The Jotnar trolls eagerly circled the fire. Stomping and pushing each other in excitement as Hook was placed carefully above the flames. Sweating in panic, he squirmed around trying to reach the scroll. It came loose and fell into the fire. Hook lifted his head, giving the laughing trolls a sinister smile. A drop of rain hit the sizzling wood below. The trolls gasp as another fell upon the hissing flames. Each looked up in fear as sudden rapid rain began to fall from the dark sky. The trolls screamed as they scattered for cover. In their mist of panic, the trolls had left the bridge, running into the underground cave. Hook had almost begun to laugh when the realization of his entrapment came back to him. Yes, the fire was gone, and the bridge was free to cross, but he was still stuck, and the trolls were still safe. The rain Ainsel had cast would eventually stop, and the trolls would have their chance at their feast once more. Hook tried again to wiggle his way out of even one thread of twine, but it was no use, the twine was too strong and thick.

He had just dropped his head in defeat when suddenly he heard a familiar voice: "Did I forget to teach you how to get out of a hogtie?"

"Father?"

A slash ripped the twine apart, releasing him completely, his body hitting the pit of wet wood below. Hook thrashed around to see Blackbeard, giving him a confused chuckle, "What are you doing here?"

Blackbeard jumped down reaching out his hand to his son, lifting him off the ground. "After you left, your fairy told me of your plan, and I thought I might be able to help. It appears I was right." The trolls were standing on the edge, moaning and growling into the rain with anger. There was now the smell of two mortals in the wind agonizing their hunger, and they had steered too far from the bridge. "The sun will rise soon. You better get going, my boy."

Hook looked at the greyish hue rising in the sky. "But—"

Blackbeard raised his hand in objection. "I know what this means to you. The Scarlet Fairy awaits you just across that bridge. I will stay here and fight off the trolls until daylight. What good is being immortal if I cannot help my son?" He asked, placing his hands upon his shoulders.

Hook looked at the bridge. Pieces of stone were already beginning to detach but he still felt uncertain.

Blackbeard jolted him back to attention, "Look, I may not be able to enter portals reaching other worlds, but I can do this! Trust me! Now go!" He commanded.

Hook nodded and ran. The trolls began to panic watching a mortal heading towards the bridge. The rain stopped pouring just as the sun was about to rise into the sky. The trolls ran out to stop him, but it was too late. He jumped off the bridge, landing on the other side just as the last boulder crumbled. The trolls howled as the sun cast its blaze upon them, turning all of them into stone. Hook hit the ground rolling, looking quickly behind him. The bridge was gone, and his father had been there to see him do what no other man had done. Blackbeard waved his sword in the air before smashing the stones of the dead trolls into shattered pieces across the ground.

CHAPTER TWENTY-SIX

THE SNOW QUEEN

Catching his breath, Hook walked up a steep summit. At the top was an invisible door framed with blue frosted ivy and black twine. It stood completely alone in the silent wood. He drew his sword, anticipating what may lay on the other side. The air began to change as he drew closer, becoming cold and crisp. He reached out his hand to touch the invisible doorway when he felt something. It felt like a thick cloak. He took it in his grasp and slowly pulled it to the side. A gush of harsh freezing air rushed upon him as he walked through the veil. Wild flurries and large snowflakes of the most enchanting design danced in the chilled wind around him. He had made his way into the veil of the Third Realm, and the sight of what lay ahead stole his breath. Looking down from the top of the hill was a land covered in sparkling ice and winter snow, tall sycamore trees covered in frost, with large decorative garden ornaments, small hanging icicles, and silver lanterns that flickered upon the beautiful terrain ever so perfectly. Standing taller than the trees, was a giant crystal fortress in the center of the entire realm. Along the trees were random little windows, and at the bottom there looked to be various types of tiny doors. It was a little village.

"How cute," Hook said sarcastically under his breath. All of the sudden, one of the little doors opened, revealing a tiny redcap gnome. His hat hung down his shoulder, and he had a long white beard that laid upon his chest. He couldn't see his eyes or his feet as each step he made sunk into the deep snow. He carried a crooked holly staff for balance on the unstable snowy ground. Hook chuckled at the old gnome's difficulty when suddenly it stopped; as if it could hear him somehow. *That's impossible.* He was far enough away, and no one knew he was here. But as he looked around, he noticed something peculiar: It was quiet- too quiet. He thought there would be whimsical chimes ringing or ominous music dancing upon the cold breeze, but there was absolutely nothing. Hook didn't move an inch but rather gazed up at the trees. He hadn't noticed before, but there were doors higher up in the trees as well. They were open and floating before them were fairies- many, many fairies. His eyes wandered in the great winter circle, glaring at their shocked porcelain faces. Their eyes were pitch black, and each wore colored long robes that matched a glorious jewel that hung around their pale necks. Hook raised his iron sword gripped tightly in his hand, lifting his head with a menacing glare, he spoke: "Let it begin."

Brightly colored strikes and blast shot towards him. Hook stood still, waiting for the magic swarming around his sight to fall short upon the invisible shield surrounding him. Laughing as their failing efforts continued, Hook could hear frantic bells echoing upon the air. It didn't take long before the Unseelie Court knew something dreadful was wrong. Ceasing their fire, many flew away to hide or take cover within their homes high above in the trees. Others rushed towards the Frosted Citadel, likely to report the great danger that had been laid upon them to their queen. Hook watched every fairy that crossed his view intensely, searching for the one that mattered most. Slashing his sword aggressively through them, horrific screams filled the bitter cold air. As the fairy blood fell upon the glittering snow, the deep red taunting his ravenous hunger.

"Where are you?! I know you are here!" He screamed in raging fury, making his way down the ravine towards the Frosted Citadel. "You, cowardice wretch! Come face me now or I will kill your beloved queen!"

Gasp and cries overtook the realm, but still, she did not come. Hook huffed in anger, saying no more, but instead fiercely stepped forward to the frosted crystal fortress ahead, when suddenly the two tall doors to the entrance slowly opened before him. He grabbed his second blade as he entered expecting another attack of defense, but there wasn't. The Frosted Citadel was tall and wide, covered in majestic mirrors and brightly lit lanterns. From the inside of the walls, you could see everything on the outside perfectly. Hook looked up at what appeared to be a giant grizzly bear standing tall next to a crystal throne, upon which was a beautifully malevolent creature. She sat with such poise, with the posture of the most elegant royalty. Her dainty small hands rested so precisely upon the throne's arms. Her glimmering silver gown hugged her perfect figure flattering her every inch, with a long train flowing down the stairs to her throne the way water falls in a painting. Her hair was as white as fresh winter snow, in four flawless long braids under an elaborate headdress decorated in enchanting crystals that shined and twinkled like stars from the greatest of heavens. But the most mesmerizing part of her was her face. Pale as the twilight, shaded only by the high frame of her cheeks around her delicate nose, and full red lips that would shame the most exquisite ruby. Her lavender eyes were perfectly symmetrical to her astounding beauty and illuminating glamour of fiercely profound power. She stared at him silently, allowing her otherworldly beauty to intoxicate him. She waited for Hook to drop his swords, falling victim to her seducing trance. But he didn't. Hook stood still, glaring back at her with threatening hatred. The Snow Queen tapped her long red nails against her crystal throne, growing impatient.

Hook snarled in return. "Are you waiting for something, your majesty?" He asked harshly. His rude manner astonished her, for it had not been done before by anyone in any realm. Even the Grand Elder could not deny her charms on his own. She gracefully raised her right hand as a high jeweled staff began materializing in her grasp. She slowly stood up from her throne and started floating towards him. Hook tightened his grip on his weapons, unsure what she would do next. She proceeded to circle him curiously. "You look mortal. You smell mortal. Yet you do not behave like one. What exactly are you?"

"I am human. And you are the notorious Snow Queen I presume," Hook replied sternly.

The Snow Queen giggled to herself. "You have heard of me. Well, I'm afraid you have me at a slight disadvantage."

Hook smiled, "You have no idea."

She hissed at him, "Well you certainly have the smug arrogance of a human. So then, what brings you to my palace? You must be incredibly brave to have come this far. What is it you seek?"

"I am looking for a fairy," he answered plainly.

She laughed at him again. "Awe, poor young man. If you have come here seeking wishes, I'm afraid you came to the wrong place."

Hook chuckled before abruptly slamming his sword into one of the mirrored walls. The glass shimmered as it shattered to the ground. The Snow Queen stood up with rage in her eyes as he took another step forward with a sarcastic face of remorse. "I'm sorry about that. There's something about moronic laughter that just brings out the worst in me."

The Snow Queen's eyes grew wide and fierce with fury, huffing deeply in violent anger.

Hook smiled at her again, "Now that I have your attention, let me say again- I am looking for a fairy! And she is here in your court!"

The Snow Queen shook, glaring at him with immense anger as she sat back down. "I see. And just what do you intend to do with her?"

Hook looked behind him at the visible carnage he had left upon the wintered grounds of her realm. "I seek to destroy her, of course," he said slowly, as if to a dense child. "Surely, you could see beyond your walls; there is nothing you can do to stop me."

The queen raised her lavender gaze to the massacre outside her palace. She knew he was right, but she was too proud to admit a mere mortal could have the upper hand on her. "And just what did my Unseelie do to cause such devastation?"

"She- took- the- wrong- soul! A soul that now resides inside of you, which is the only reason *you* are still alive!"

The queen gave him a wicked smirk, twisting her jeweled staff in her small bony hand. "Very well then. Who am I to stand in the way of vengeance? Who is she? Say her true name."

His face twisted in frustration, his words slithering through his clenched teeth. "I do not know her true name."

"Then describe her if you can," she said in a demeaning tone.

"Her eyes are black as night; her skin is pale and tragic. Her emaciated body is covered only by a long red dress and a scarlet cloak."

Suddenly the queen's movements went still, and the air around them turned crisp as the mirrors and lanterns on the walls became cold and covered in frost. "Amara," she whispered under her breath.

"*Amara?* That's her name?"

The queen suddenly seemed to snap out of her momentary daze and stood up. "No! No! You cannot have her! You can take anyone else in my court!" She exclaimed as she began placing her fingers on the colored gems on her staff. One by one, various glowing fairies started to appear in the Frosted Citadel, each with a necklace holding a gem that matched the ones on her staff. They were all still and afraid, but none were the one he wanted.

"No! I want Amara! Call her here now, or you all die!" He shouted. Suddenly a red glow began to materialize in the middle of the room. It was her! The Scarlet Fairy! The very sight of her made Hook's blood boil. He circled with his blade pointed at her. It had been many years since he had seen her. She looked different somehow- frail and broken. "You! I told you I would find you! Are you ready to die, Amara?"

The Scarlet Fairy looked up into his fiery eyes. "I have known you would find me for some time now," she sighed, "I am ready, but please don't do it in front of my kind. Let me die quickly and with dignity- and I will give you what you need to reach the other you seek through the stars."

Hook's eyes widened "How?" He asked sternly with suspicion.

"Fairy dust."

Hook nodded, pacing back and forth deep in thought for a moment. "If you try to escape, I will come back here and kill them all."

The Scarlet Fairy nodded slowly, "I know."

Hook snatched her in his hands, looking her dead in the face. "Then we have an accord," he said taking a step towards the door when suddenly he hesitated. "I did this to the wrong person once, but I am only too happy to rectify that mistake now." At that, Hook rapidly ripped off her beautiful wings and tossed them aside like trash. Her screams echoed throughout the citadel. Blood rapidly began pouring down her cloak, when suddenly the queen rushed upon him.

"You cannot take my daughter! If you do, I will kill you and everyone you love!"

Hook shoved her off him. "We both know you can't, confined to your frosty little prison!"

She looked him straight in his eyes, seething with anger. "Then I will find someone who can!"

Hook walked out of the palace leaving the roaring queen behind him. As the bleeding fairy cried in his hand, he made his way back up the snowy hill, turning to take one last glance at his bloody carnage before lifting the invisible cloak and leaving the Third Realm.

Outside the veil, the air felt warm again, but as Hook kicked the broken pieces of stone out of his way, he heard a tiny voice below: *"Please."*

Hook looked down. The red glow that had once tormented his dreams as a small child was fading fast. Her face appeared so sad- so beaten. "How dare you act like a victim! You- who laughed at my pain, who reveled in all my suffering, and who laughed at her death. Well who's laughing now? You hear me?! Who is laughing now?!" He shouted shaking her violently in his grasp, "Just give me what you promised and die already!" Tears rolled down his heated cheeks. Sparkling red dust poured off her weak thrashing body as he shook her. Hook reached down to grab one of his pouches on his belt and held it up, tilting his hand to release the sparkling dust into the tiny bag.

Again, he heard a faint plea.

"What is it?"

She raised her hand, pointing weakly: "There."

Hook looked over to see a short stump off in the near distance. He walked over to it and placed her gently down upon it. She remained quiet as she curled up. "I do not feel pity for you! You are a monster!

God only knows how many souls you have stolen and destroyed before my mother's- after my mother's, or how many souls you would continue to take if I didn't kill you now! Tell me I'm right! Tell me you don't feel any remorse for what you have done! Tell me you whimper now only in despair for yourself! Tell me I am right! Tell me now!" He roared in utter rage.

The Scarlet fairy opened her pitch-black eyes once more upon him, "You are right."

Hook nodded, crying as he stood over her until finally, her red glow faded away. He walked away knowing he had done the right thing. He had stopped a horrible monster and maybe he had even saved a few souls as well. As he made his way through the woods in the calming daylight, he admired the beautiful fairy dust that lay sparking still in his little pouch. This was it; he had all he needed. *It is time for the Jolly Roger to set sail for Neverland!*

CHAPTER TWENTY-SEVEN
OFF TO NEVERLAND

Hook eagerly sped with fast pace back to his father's ship only to learn that he had once again been gone from this world for a matter of two long months. Blackbeard had made it back to the ship shortly after the destruction of the stones, pleased and proud to relay Hook's victory of the three troll's death to Ainsel waiting anxiously upon his ship. Smee too was overwhelmed with immense relief.

Though Blackbeard always felt uneasy in the presence of the Blue Fairy and didn't quite understand the odd relationship between the magical creature and his son, he couldn't help but notice the agonizing concern written upon her face. Her sadness poured out of her eyes with such deep sorrow, Blackbeard quietly commanded Smee to console her. Smee had tended to his request right away, and for two months, Catcher and Smee never left her side.

Hook arrived in high spirits, eager to tell his tale, and even more so to set sail upon his own ship that should be completed in only a matter of days. When the sun had set upon the horizon, the Queen Anne's revenge was already well out to sea. The captain and crew cheered in vigorous triumph to be back on the mysterious waters, but poor old Mr. Smee spent his first night on the sea with his head hung over the railing, purging his waves of unrelenting fear. After such a day of celebration, Hook was eager to spend the evening talking with Ainsel, with sweet Catcher laying peacefully on the bed nearby.

"Tell me of your travels. I have never been to the Third Realm. Is it as beautiful as they say?" Ainsel asked.

He smiled at her. It was so like her to inquire in the most pleasant way possible. "Indeed, it *was* truly a beautiful place."

Ainsel nodded slowly. "Was?"

He hated reporting such terrible things. He knew she supported him, and she had known of his deadly ambition before he left. Yet, he felt uneasy about painting such a bloody picture to such kind ears as hers. "Ainsel, let us not dwell on such things. I did what I went to do. There is nothing more I wish to say on the matter," he said kindly as he walked back towards his desk. Ainsel watched as his behavior seemed so curiously secretive. As he opened one of the top drawers, he placed the tiny sparkling pouch carefully inside it.

"How did you get that?"

Hook turned back around to face her but didn't say a word.

"James, how did you get that?" She asked more persistently.

"The Scarlet Fairy gave it to me."

Ainsel looked at him suspiciously. "She just gave it to you. Why?"

"Well, she did not just give it to me. We made a deal."

"What kind of deal?"

Hook let out a small huff of frustration, "She didn't want to die in front of the court. So, in exchange for a peaceful death, she offered her fairy dust to help me reach Pan through the stars."

She reached out to him gently. "Come here."

He looked at her hesitantly, "Why?"

"Please."

He grabbed her dainty hand, and they made their way over to his table in the big room. Her calming touch of spring warmed the deep ice inside him.

"Are you happy, James?"

He looked at her confused. "What do you mean?"

"Do you know how fairy dust works?"

"Well, I assume it makes you fly."

Ainsel smiled at him and nodded. "Yes, but do you know how?"

Hook felt annoyed, laying his head on the back of the chair as he answered: "No, Ainsel, how does it work?"

Ainsel leaned forward to pull down his chin. "You must think happy thoughts- only happy thoughts! If there is one smidgen of darkness or sorrow inside you, you will fall. Humans have so much room for emotions within them: doubt, fear, sorrow, shame, guilt, anger, and any single one of these will make you fall. In your world this fact is not quite as literal, mortals do not always realize the damage that these thoughts cause, but with magic, it's simple. Happiness brings you up, and *everything* else will bring you down. So, I ask you again; are you happy?"

He looked down to the floor, his thoughts racing through his troubled mind: The Scarlet Fairy. If anybody in this world knew how unhappy he was, it was her. "She tricked me," he said, rage boiling under his hot breath.

Ainsel looked at him with pity. "I'm afraid it was her last attempt to..."

Hook interrupted. "-To kill me."

Ainsel looked down, feeling sad. It seemed she was always giving him such distressing news. "I am sorry, but even if you were able to be happy enough get into the air, I fear your thoughts would cause you to fall."

"Even in death, she still threatens to kill me!"

Ainsel leaned in to hug him. "But she didn't succeed, and she never will again. Do not let her wickedness haunt you forever. You must take your ship across the sparkling sea, and into the land of your enemy," she said, staring deeply into his eyes, gently placing both her hands upon his face. "What would it take to make you happy?"

Hook had never really thought about it. He shook his head, trying to remember if there was ever a time that he was happy, but nothing came. "I fear I do not know if such a thing is possible for someone like me."

Ainsel looked at him confused. "Whatever do you mean- *someone* like you?"

Hook looked off in the distance, "I have been angry for so long. They have filled me with such hate- I fear I can never hope to feel anything else. Maybe I do not deserve to be happy."

"They? You mean the Scarlet Fairy and Pan?"

"Yes!" He said with seething anger.

"You have already come so far. And when you are done, and your enemies are gone- so too will be your hate. You have love around you. Catcher loves you, Smee is your friend, and you have been reunited with your father. If you would only let them in, the light will purge out the darkness that consumes you, and there will be room for love in your heart."

Hook looked up at her with hope. "You really believe that?"

She smiled gently, "I do." They paused intensely, overwhelmed with such burning fire and sorrow. Somehow, she had made him feel everything, but it was now at this moment that he couldn't fight it anymore. Instead, he closed his eyes, falling into it all-with a kiss. The moment was that of pure magic, lighting a spark inside the young pirate's dark soul. He felt it surge through him. A feeling, unlike anything he had felt before, bringing the first true smile of genuine happiness to his face. Ainsel whispered softly, "After this evil man is gone, you must let your dark past go. Only then will you truly be happy."

He looked up at her with an odd face.

"What is it?"

Hook took a deep breath as he stood from his chair to face her, knowing that what he was about to say could change everything between them. "Pan is not a man; he is a child."

Ainsel gasped, placing her hands upon her face in shock.

He pressed on urgently. "Ainsel, please understand; if I do not stop him, then he will take the lives of the innocent for all time. But once I kill him, all the guilt I carry from each soul he takes will be lifted from my shoulders. I created Peter Pan! And it must be me that destroys him!"

Ainsel stepped back. "But he is only a child? You cannot kill a little boy! There must be another way!"

Hook merely shook his head at her. "Do not be deceived by his young appearance. Peter is older than I, remaining a child only by fae magic. He was a murderous child, thriving only on his devious behavior and overwhelming those around him with fear. With powers- he has become unstoppable. I am haunted by every life he destroys. I am sorry, Ainsel, but I will not be moved on this. If you do not wish to stay, I will understand. You are so kind and sweet. You are the fairy that believes in second chances but believe me: there is no hope for him."

"But maybe he could change!"

"No! This sadistic child will never change! He was born evil!" Instantly, he could see that he had scared her again. He let out a deep breath as his guilt began to calm himself. "I am sorry. I do care for you, but you cannot stop me... the boy *will* die," he said with a voice most definite.

Ainsel's eyes welled with sparkling tears, but she said not another word. She took out her wand, and with a spark of blue radiance, she began to shrink back into the small fairy form she had once been before. Hook turned away from her, unable to say anything further. Out of the far corner of his eye, in the glimmer of sadness that loved her, he watched as she flew away. Hook stepped towards the large pane of windows and watched as her glowing streaks of sparkling blue flashed in the night, reflecting upon the sea like beautiful lightning. Peter had managed to destroy the first spark of light he had felt in his dark existence.

"Goodbye, Ainsel," he whispered, then turned to walk back towards his bed, picking up a book and laid down, sinking deeply into the bed.

Word had finally arrived that Hook's new ship was ready to port. And his new growing concern had been whether he would be able to acquire a crew, brave and worthy of what deadly adventures lay ahead. With such promising danger in its course, he feared finding such willing pirates would prove to be rather difficult, as he could not offer missions seeking treasure, but alas he was very much mistaken. The fame and glory of Captain Hook's name had already become notorious. At first notice of Hook's need of a crew, every ruthless, greedy pirate came from far and wide hoping to step foot or peg upon the glorious Jolly Roger. And what a magnificent vessel she was indeed. *No doubt she will be feared across all the seven seas in no time.* But being on the ship itself was another treasure of its own. Far from the regulations of Blackbeard's ship, Hook's ship had its own set of rules. But the same brutality and wrath of his father would befall anyone should they dare break one. Most of the rules made sense, though they were all things pirates hated like matters of hygiene or keeping the ship clean and organized. There were times you may be permitted to drink and gamble but only in what he deemed a suitable hour. Hook explained that the crew would have to face the unholiest of creatures on their journeys, and it will not do well to be drunk when you need to be using your head. To be aboard the Jolly Roger meant that you had to always be ready to fight and kill. But within no time, he had set to port three times, and had left with more and more men, prepared to serve and fight with him. Each were offered with only one promise: that they would see wonders beyond all imagination and would likely not survive to tell the tale. Luckily for Hook, a pirate's life meant living with two dangers: one was in the eye of the law, and the other was through an adventure, and that was something Hook would surely provide.

Hook had his new crew, his first mate, and his loyal companion, Catcher. He was ready to set his black sails upon the chilling air of the new year. The night of the next full moon was upon them, and Hook was finally ready to cross the veil beyond the sparkling road, and the monstrous demon that awaited him. The skies proved to be in Hook's favor: clear as crystal. Each star mirrored perfectly upon the still water. One would believe there were two moons that night, they were both so full and bright, bringing the sparkling road to life. The glittered ribbon lay upon the graceful flowing streams with brilliance, carved under the twin luminance of the two Luna sisters, like two different worlds coming together to dance amongst the stars and sea for one night. The crew awed at its radiant beauty, the sight bringing a song to their lips. Suffused by its wonder, the night brought music to the air, leaving only Hook and Catcher untouched by the magic clawing its way aboard the ship. The feverish recognition sent chills up Hook's spine then. He wanted to shout at the men to stop, but he knew it was no use, for the grip was stronger than any siren's and more malevolent than any evil they had ever encountered. Hook took his hold to the wheel, for the ocean's surface no longer resembled that of its other half. The stars painted upon the sea were now escaping their prisoned cast of mere reflection and began dancing, coming together along the path, shining and singing. As he attached the ship perfectly upon the glittering ribbon beneath them, a jangle of fear and electricity gripped at his spine.

The men's drunken singing and dancing grew louder and more irritating with each inch forward. Each thrash of the sea trying harder and harder to push the ship off its narrow course. Still, he held it firm and steady. The surrounding water soon turned black, threatening to swallow them whole should they dare fall from the shining path. Its shine was almost blinding, and the previous pristine reflection of the moon was gone, leaving its twin alone in the sky and in its place now looked to be a glowing stoned doorway. Hook could suddenly hear thrashing below him. Something was striking the ship with incredible force. But the ship remained strong, causing whatever it was below anger and frustration. The striking came harder and faster. He knew what it was the guardian, and it was fighting like hell to push the ship off the road. Suddenly an awful growling sound filled the air, but the music continued to grow louder as the ship approached the door. But the growling never ceased, and it seemed it was the guardian that the sky could hear, not the enchanted musical stones that sang bringing them forward. Suddenly a gust of dark clouds appeared in the air. They slowly drew closer to the moon above, as if trying to mask the door below. Hook didn't know how, but he knew it was the crocodile. The clouds began to fill the sky, casting multiple shadows hiding the view of the stars and smearing their obscured darkness across the full moon. Suddenly the path beneath them began to weaken and narrow. The ship started tilting strongly to one side, then the other, making it more and more difficult for Hook to control the wheel. It now appeared there was no water around them. The black sea now looked like an open void, waiting to consume the ship should it fall. The shining ribbon had now become a narrow line, forcing him to maintain perfect balance, lest falling into the dark oblivion below, like a giant mouth waiting to devour them. The blasting hits from the monster below continued to strike harder with more urgency... letting him know he was close; if he could just hold on a bit longer. The ship began to sway out of control as the weather threatened to take them down. The masking clouds surrounded them, making it impossible for him to see the path ahead, but the singing stones were calling him forward. Suddenly, there was one last strike that hit below. The crushing sound stole Hook's breath, and the ship began to fall. This was it: he needed the men's help at the ropes. He screamed his orders, but the men couldn't hear him. They continued to dance and sing, completely oblivious to all around them. He used all the strength he had left to hold the wheel steady, but his hands were shaking, and his arms felt like they were about to fall off. Hook screamed in fury and frustration; he was about to lose his grip. The thoughts swarmed through him, weakening his hold; when suddenly his left hand fell. A tear from his vengeful soul began to fall down his cheek as his right hand started to lose its grip. Each striking blow to the ship brought down another finger, but he held on with everything he had: until the last finger slipped.

"No!" He screamed as the final blast from the crocodile hit, sending him tumbling across the deck of the ship when suddenly it stopped. Everything went silent. The clouds began to clear, and the waves were still and calm. Hook looked around him curiously. The crew stared at him confused, suddenly ripped out of their spellbound state. Smee looked down in shame once again, knowing full well what had happened. But Hook wasn't looking at them; his eyes searched for something far more important. *Where is Catcher?* He brought his shaky hands to his lips and whistled for him loudly. To his relief, his call was immediately followed by a loud bark and the sight of his loyal companion running right towards him. Catcher pounced in playful delight, bringing Hook's heart back to a regular pace. He stood up and slowly made his way to the front of the ship, and as the clouds and mist faded, it was the warm sun that greeted his sight. And what laid straight ahead was none other than the Lost Island itself. The men looked out at the beautiful tall trees towering over the sparkling golden sand that laid upon the open beach.

"Where are we, Captain?" One of the men asked looking through his spyglass with awe. The men all looked at Hook as he remained strangely quiet for a moment, for the sight was both one of terror and longing for him. But somehow through both, the vision brought a sinister smile to his face. Suddenly another strike hit the ship. Hook looked down to the sparkling blue water, and there staring up at him with large yellow eyes was the crocodile: every scale shined in the sunlight, his tail slowly swaying, and his beaming eyes floating just above the surface. As their eyes met, it was as if the monster realized who he was. No doubt he could smell each of the crew's scent, clouding any chance of deciphering his own... but now as they looked eye to eye. The recognition gleamed within his eyes with yearning desire. He lifted his head, opening his massive jaws, grazing his snake-like tongue slowly across his crooked smile. Hook took out a pistol from his belt and slowly pointed it towards the hungry monster. But upon the first click, the crocodile broke his gaze and quickly swam away. Hook hit his hands upon the front railing at his sides as he laughed with chilling malice.

"Captain?" The men inquired again.

This time Hook quickly whipped around to face them with a sudden villainous flare. "We are in a land of great magic and wonder, men! A place haunted of lost and devoured souls! A place ruled by true evil! It is the home of the devil himself! Welcome lads... to *Neverland!*"

"*Hook! Hook! Hook!*" The men cheered and roared.

It was just as Hook remembered it: a beautiful nightmare that never steered too far from Hook's dark mind. It was one of two places he and Peter had shared a long time ago, and now it felt they would share a home again. There was nowhere to port the ship, leaving Hook with the unsettling decision to leave the ship poorly unguarded as he and some men dropped into a small wooden boat to row ashore. Hook wasn't sure if he should take Catcher at first, but in the end, he felt it would be better to bring him upon the island than to leave him with just Smee and a few men left on the Jolly Roger. After all, Catcher would likely be able to find Pan and his little friend more quickly than by his own tracking skills, clever as they were. Hook took the few men who at least pretended to heed his warnings about what awaited them upon the sand, though Hook knew that he would likely lose a few men due to their selfish ambition and greed. But Hook couldn't and wouldn't waste his time babysitting his crew; a mere warning would have to suffice, and should their doubt not prove not to be enough, Hook could always count on their fear of him. Hook had somehow become even more of a cold and harsh captain than his father before him. Hook's wrath and anger had become a vast aura he couldn't contain or control. Even poor Mr. Smee had fallen victim to his fury and become as afraid of him as he ever was of

Blackbeard. The days passed and losing Ainsel had proved harder on Hook's soul than he cared to admit. Somehow losing her had simply and completely become Pan's fault, and Hook was more ready than ever to kill him. The water below sparkled like diamonds glittering in the sun, but then Hook noticed something strange: there was no sun.

There was light and warmth, even a calm ocean breeze that filled the spring air... but no sun in sight. There were clouds in the sky, but unlike any he had seen before, a detail that had escaped his sight during his last visit. The clouds were full and white, and the sky around it was the purest color of baby blue. Hook looked again at the water, anxious and paranoid he held up his pistol ready to fire at any sudden movement rippling through the sparkling sea.

Then suddenly all the men were struck in awe by the sound of a woman's voice. *She was singing.* Hook quickly looked around trying to see where it was coming from.

"What is that, Captain?"

"It sounds so beautiful."

Then as the boat drew closer, Hook noticed three beautiful mermaids sitting upon the rocks singing. The men wanted to drop out of the boat and follow them under the water. One of the mermaids came down from the rocks and swam gracefully towards the boat, with her beautiful melody echoing through the air. But as Hook turned his gaze rapidly towards them, all the men had already covered their ears and closed their eyes. One of the men spoke loudly, as to overpower the spellbinding song around them. "Cover ye ears, Captain! For that be the call of a siren out there!"

Hook smiled in relief; grateful that pirates lived by legends, tall tales, and superstitions. Within minutes, the young mermaids were circling the boat, but what had once been a plan of alluring lust had now become more aggressive and malice. Hook wasn't sure what their next move was; for their vulture behavior had not yet dispersed. But as the boat came to shore, Hook looked down to find the beauty and melody was no more. They were just gone. "Remember men; this place is cursed. If you dare try to take from its wonder and riches, you will die," Hook said before a single foot touched the golden sand.

Catcher excitedly jumped out of the boat and pranced around Hook gleefully. He looked up at the tall trees, never two the same, covering the entire island, making everything underneath seem dark. The island seemed larger somehow as if every step you took you into a whole world: Peter Pan's world. And like the last home, he and Peter had shared, Hook would be the one to watch it all burn!

CHAPTER TWENTY-EIGHT

THE PICCANINNY TRIBE

As Hook entered the sprawling forest that encircled the darkness within, the all too chilling frequent silence of the woods was novel to his disturbed mind. There wasn't a single scuttle through the bush, the obnoxious chirping of various species, nor even the slightest buzz from an insect could be detected. Hook gave his men behind him the gesture of silence as the uneasiness grew thicker in the air. Putting his index finger to his lips, the men's steps upon the invisible sun-soaked grass seemed as silent as the constant warm breeze of spring around them.

As they made their way through the tall brush and trees, Hook noticed that there seemed to be no sense of direction, for despite the outward appearance of the island, to be inside it was the very definition of lost. No step left a trail; no mark could be made then left, and with every turn before and after- there was something new and unknown. He took out his compass, but the needle lay dead as if science itself didn't exist in this place. There was no sun, no constant direction of air, and worst of all: they couldn't hear anything.

The crew was growing tired, though no one dared utter a breath of discomfort. The shipmates had no idea how long or how far they had been walking, but it appeared they were no closer to finding whatever it was Hook was after.

Suddenly there was a piercing scream of a child in the distance, followed by a manic burst of laughter. His heart fell to his feet. The men behind him froze in fear, and white-hot panic burned in Hook's mind as the sound of clawing and crunching clenched their vitals, but it wasn't the cracking sound of bones breaking; it was the unrelenting images of it vividly surging through all their minds. All of the sudden, there was an ominous thrush of air that came through the gleaming trees revealing a dark figure rapidly whipping through them. He had never seen anything move that fast.

The laughter echoed as if drumming off the walls of a cave. Hook suddenly got a sense of where it was coming from and rapidly burst through the woods as quick as his feet could carry him. The crew sped fast behind him trying to keep up; when all the sudden, it was back: the silence. He stopped to catch his breath and listen, his men coming up urgently behind him. Then all of the sudden, one of his men only a few feet away was abruptly struck ill, vomiting upon the grass below.

Hook was furious. "What is it?" He demanded in a loud whisper. But no one answered. Instead, the men stood there gawking upon the ground. Hook burst through them, shoving them out of his way to see what it was, but as he looked down, what greeted his sight made his words die in his throat. Hearing the splash of blood beneath his feet was the skeleton of a small child. It was fresh, with only the remains of thin bits of skin on various parts of the body and long blonde hair stained in blood upon its bashed skull. It was horrific.

Hook's hand clasp over his mouth as he turned around in shock. The dead silence in the air left only the sound of their hurried heartbeats and gasp of terror to surround the crew. Suddenly the wind began to chill, and the terrain around them started to change to the color of autumn. The tree branches whipped in the wild fall air, the red leaves curled and flew past them as the tenebrous atmosphere began to close in.

He weakly lifted his eyes as the rays of fading light revealed the horror of more skeletons of youth upon the ground ahead. The sky was darkening, and a beautiful moon had quickly risen into the black above them.

None of the men, nor Hook knew how long they had stood there staring down at the ground unable to move, but as the shadows from Luna's magnificent shine moved about the island, Hook was taken out of his trance of vivid horror. He lifted one foot in front of the other, and the sound of his men's footsteps behind him began to follow.

Dark imagination surged through them with every dead corpse they passed. All tried to ignore the random strips of flesh and ripped tendons found on the ground, each struggling to keep their view up and their food down.

Then through the darkness, he spotted the orange glow of fire up ahead. The flickering light illuminated what appeared to be demolished wooden houses. But hidden behind the thicket was the smell of burning wood filling the air, and the sight of smoke rising high above the tall strange trees.

The sounds of drums reverberated through their bones as they drew near. The crew drew their swords and daggers high, but Hook held up his hand for them to lower their weapons as he slowly made his way closer. The fire shined its warm glow upon an unusual sort of camp. The haze of smoke was too thick for him to see anyone, but something about the aura around them was a sense of anger and war. He carefully reached out for each base of thick bark that stood between him and the beating drums of battle.

Suddenly a burst of shrill wails came from the dark distance beyond any reach of light. The scream sent chills up his spine. *What was doing this?* He thought as the agonizing screams continued. Hook tried to escape the graphic thoughts running through his mind, but it was as if it was impossible to fight them. Images of such horror weakened his knees. He clawed his way through the thick smoke, moving closer towards the camp.

Once he made his way into the clearing, he saw a circled group of Indians. He had heard of Indian rituals and their knowledge of magic, *but why were they in Neverland?* All eyes glared towards him, but the drumming never ceased. Hook slowly reached for his blade feeling their threatening oppression, when suddenly he noticed something: a smell. It wasn't a bad smell; in fact, the scent was rather intoxicating. The smell of meat roasting on the fire filled the air.

His eyes finally began to adjust to the thinning smoke, seeing the fine details of the tribe surrounding him. Their vision sent a surging chill through him. They were eerily slender and tall; with inhuman muscles showing through their dusty grey skin. They had long raven black hair, each with a leather band of feathers. Their eyes were glowing with the fierce stare of a predatory animal.

He could hear them breathing; it was hard and fast like they had been running for miles. So little of them still looked human, but somehow the sense of humanity was still dwelling inside.

Suddenly a quiet cracking branch from the woods sent the Indians on high alert. They hunched down as if ready to charge when suddenly a figure came through the largest tepee in the camp.

As the thick cloth opened, he was shocked to see a tall, stout Indian step out onto the ground. He looked entirely human. His skin was red and tan; he was dressed in fine cloth covered in beads and wore a giant headdress of long beautifully colored feathers. His eyes were small and beady on his large round face, but Hook could see no evil in them. "Peace," he said raising his hand slowly.

The tribe of beast quickly seemed to come to their senses and sat back down on the ground by the fire. It became clear that this was their chief, yet he had somehow escaped the horrific fate of those in his tribe.

"If your offer of peace is true and you or your men value your lives, then tell them to drop their weapons!" The chief roared.

Hook hesitated, but as he looked at the beast around him, he gave a slow nod. The sound of pistols and blades dropping came down like a wave of surrender that made him uneasy.

The chief then nodded in return. His eyes wandered at his emaciated tribe, but Hook couldn't help but notice his eye never took the glimpse of the mysterious glow from the fire. Ravenous hunger struck his yearning soul. The intoxicating scent of the cooking meat seduced all within its reach; the savage tribe licked their teeth and growled under their breath. They slowly started to make their way towards the roast, when the chief pointed at him.

The chief didn't say anything for a moment, he just pointed to him, causing Hook's heart to pound and his body to sweat. "Come!" The chief said turning to walk back into his tepee. Hook raised his hand gesturing his men to come forward when he heard the chief speak again: "Alone."

Hook turned to look at the forest again. His men's faces now revealed in the amber glow from the flames. There was fear in their eyes as they stood. "Stay in the woods. No matter what you see or hear, do not come any closer. That is an order from your captain!" Hook commanded. He knew his men needed that. To see their leader be brave and show no fear.

As the cloth closed behind him, the thought of the tribe attacking his men swarmed through his mind. "Your men are safe! You must not think about those things. It is dangerous to let your imagination run wild here. My tribe will not hurt them, but I cannot help you if you do that," the chief said as he sat down on a round throw.

"I cannot seem to control my thoughts! These images are-"

The chief raised his hand to silence him, then picked up a long pipe. "Here, take this. It will help."

"What is it?"

"It is magic. It will help cloud the mind and keep your imagination at bay."

Hook hesitated. "Thank you, but..."

The chief's eyes grew fierce. "It would be unwise to reject my help. Neverland is a place where imagination can create reality, and it is the *imagination* that will drive you mad!"

Hook gulped, gently reaching for the pipe. He took in a small puff, and as he exhaled, he watched as the purple smoke slowly flowed out in the collected forms of his thoughts. Each breath made Hook feel stronger and more in control.

The chief placed his hand upon the burning ash and shook his head. "Not too much. For a man without fear is simply a fool."

"What of my men? They will need your help too."

But the chief shook his head and put the pipe away in a stone box marked with five ancient symbols. "If I am to help your men, then you must do something for me."

Hook craned his head inquisitively. "What is it that you need?"

The chief cleared his breath, "There is a boy here who has taken my daughter."

Hook swallowed deeply. "I am sorry, but if her soul was taken, I do not think I can do anything to help her now."

"The boy did not need her soul to bring her here! My daughter has magic in her blood. She is safe!" The chief let out a deep breath. "I remember the night he took her. She had been sneaking out of camp to meet with him in secret for days. I wasn't sure what he was until she described the boy's green friend. I knew then that he was amongst the little people and shared their powers. I tried to warn her, but she wouldn't listen. The night before she was to marry and take the role as the following leader of our tribe, she met with him by the water. He promised her immortality and forever youth if she came with him. I tried to stop her, but I was too late. So, I too made a deal with the boy. I sold my soul to bring my tribe with me to this realm. But the game they had once played together in secret had become a game for all of us. The boy hides her, and should we fail to reach her in time, his children come for one of my people."

"How long have you and your tribe been here?"

"We do not know. Time is so different in this place. The boy alters the appearance of the island making it impossible to track where you are or where you've been."

The twisting path in the woods now made sense. "So, have you ever found her?"

"Yes, many times, but he always takes her again," the chief said looking down to the ground, struggling to continue: "Or she runs out on her own to find him."

"What? Why?"

"She believes she loves him and worse, she believes the little demon loves her."

Hook could see his heartbreak. "What about your tribe? What has happened to them?"

The chief looked out through the small crack in the fabric that cloaked them. "I have no soul now, but they came here with their soul untouched. I thought the deal I had made was only damning myself. Had I known the truth... I would have never-" His voice broke.

"Known what? What has happened to them?"

"When we got here, it was quickly realized that there was no food here and the water contained magic that would leave them bound to this land forever. Their desperate thoughts of hunger and thirst overwhelmed them. Day by day their sanity slipped farther out of their reach. I didn't know then what I know now of the magic of this place. Had I, then I could have stopped them. But when the first of our tribe died from starvation, the others couldn't help themselves."

Hook looked at him curiously. "What are you saying?"

The chief looked up trying not to choke on the words falling from his lips. "They ate him."

Hook placed his hand over his mouth in disbelief. *The meat, the skeletons, those children were all...*

Suddenly Hook hunched over, vomit expelling from his twisted stomach. The chief reached in the box once more and handed it to him. Hook wiped the sickness from his mouth and inhaled the smoke deeply into his lungs. The images and wailing cries left his mind and into the purple clouds that filled the air.

"It is too late for my tribe. They are something more than human now. For them, nothing else matters but their desire and hunger. But even the most predatory of animals have a leader. I still control what they do and *who* they eat."

"Pan's children," Hook said in realization.

The chief looked at him sternly. "Do not pity them. Those children are forever lost. They are empty vessels, mere shells doing their masters bidding. They are monsters that will kill who they are told to kill. There is a war going on in those woods; you must be sure to set your men upon the right side. My tribe might be monsters, but they will only kill Pan's lost boys!"

"And what does Pan do about all this?"

"To the boy, it is all just..."

"A game," Hook interrupted, remembering the psychotic laugh he had heard earlier in the woods, just after one of the children was killed. "If your daughter keeps going on her own, then how can I help?"

"Because her soul has not been taken, you can take her back to our world."

Hook let out a sigh. "I will find your daughter, but you must understand my purpose here is to kill the boy. He and I have some unfinished business, and I

313

intend to finish it. Help my men, help me kill Peter Pan, and I promise- I will save your daughter."

The chief handed the box to Hook. "You will only be able to find her at night."

Hook stood up from the ground. "Why?"

The chief grumbled as he struggled to stand up. Facing Hook with his hand upon his shoulder he replied. "Remember this...

When the trees are full
And the grass is green
When diamonds are sparkling
Upon the blue sea
When the breeze is warm
And the clouds are all still
That's when he is here,
And the lost boys will kill.
But when the light disappears
And the moon rises high
When the two stars twinkle
Up in the black sky
When your footprint can be seen
On top of the ground
When the silence is gone
And hidden shadows are found
That is when you know
That he is now gone,
Because in Neverland,
Peter Pan is the sun."

The slow thumping of his heartbeat resonated in perfect unison with the ominous beating drums outside. The sounds of ravenous tearing and chewing filled the wintery night air, but Hook's mind seemed to be perfectly calm. The purple smoke had put him at ease; so much so that it was until this moment that he had forgotten one significant thing: "Catcher!" Hook burst through the cloth that separated him from the tribe of hungry creatures eating around the fire. Hook's eyes frantically searched for his small companion, whistling his call; but he didn't come.

The chief calmly walked out behind him, placing his hand upon Hook's shoulder. But Hook angrily shoved his hand off of him. Suddenly everything went dead silent as every creature rapidly set their lurid glare upon him. It was a moment that would have scared anyone in their right mind, but Hook didn't care; all he could think about was the one thing that was missing.

The silence was rapidly broken by the retrieval of the crew's dropped weapons as the tribe began to growl. Strips of hanging meat stuck in their inhuman jaws of teeth. But this time, Hook took notice. Quickly gripping his blade, he prepared himself for an attack; not from the tribe, but his own.

"If your monsters have hurt my dog!" Hook roared, huffing under his breath.

But the calm chief simply shook his head. "Man of the sea, I do not think you fully understand what my men are. Your dog is safe. He had wandered lost during the day, but when the moon raised, he was able to track his way back to your boat. The Piccaninny tribe will now and forever be the wendigo tribe of Neverland. They will not eat anything other than human skin, because they *cannot* eat anything other than the meat of a human. A wendigo is cursed with an insatiable appetite, forever hungry. They hunt and kill as I command, but I must implore you to hurry back to your furry friend. For if the lost boys find him first; well, let's just say they have a truly evil imagination."

Hook quickly set his gaze on the woods behind him shouting: "Back to the boat, men!" The crew rapidly began to run, whipping through the trees heading back towards the ship beneath the moon. "How long do I have until the *sun* comes back?"

"In your time... I would say he is never gone more than three days."

Hook turned around curiously. "Why three days?"

"Because like I said, there is no food on this island. If Pan is to keep Tiger Lily, he must bring her food and water from our world. But I fear you will find that time here is very different. Three days there could feel like a mere minute here. I have found that time here is unpredictable, but none the less, I hope what I have shared with you tonight will help you on your journey. We are allies now, you and I. Trust in me and I will trust in you."

Hook ran making his way through the marked trail back to the shore. Strangely the time and distance it took to reach the camp now seemed to take only mere minutes to return to the beginning; back to the golden beach where his ship and his dog lay waiting under Luna's glare.

The crew must have gotten to him fast, for it wasn't long before Hook was within earshot of Catcher's bark of excitement. The sound brought him instant relief, but now that the moment of manic worry had passed, all he could feel was immediate disgust with himself. *How could I have put Catcher in so much danger, how could I have not noticed him missing when they were in the woods, and how could my thoughts of Peter have overtaken him so severely that he had failed his most loyal companion?* The feelings of guilt were immeasurable as he finally made his way through the last of the encircled trees and onto the sand, where Catcher quickly raced towards him. Catcher's overly happy greeting only made Hook feel worse; he had put his dearest friend in danger, yet Catcher still loved him.

The crew rowed the boat back to the Jolly Roger. Their minds twisted and filled with panic and fear. Hook knew he should tell them what had happened; what they had just witnessed, but he couldn't: not yet. He needed them to smoke the pipe of purple magic. For he feared telling them what about the wendigoag would only enhance and escalate their vivid imagination and could likely break them mentally. For as Hook looked around the boat, he noticed three of his men were missing. The poor souls frozen in the woods, stuck in a nightmare that would never fade from their minds. They were gone, and Hook couldn't risk losing any more men before battle.

They safely made their way back onto the ship, with Hook's orders to join him around his large dining table. The men sat, unable to utter a single word. Each lost in a faraway gaze as Hook reached into the chief's box. He looked for whatever it was he needed to fill the pipe, but there was nothing there: nothing but the pipe. He looked at it curiously for a moment. He hadn't noticed before, but there was nothing in it. Hook stood up from his chair suddenly suffused in anger, but before he could storm out of the room in a deadly rage, he thought back to everything the chief said. *Nothing is what it seems in this place.* He looked back down at the empty pipe, then over to all the confused faces staring at him. He tilted back his head, gaining back his composure of fierce control. Then strolling the room in a circle around the table, Hook cleared his throat before speaking: "Alright men, after meeting with the Indian chief I have gained some knowledge about our where we are and who we face. The chief and I have come to a mutual understanding, and after gaining his favor, he bestowed upon me a bit of magical medicine crucial on this island. Filled inside this pipe is a purple plant that will eliminate your fears and ease your imagination. Now, I know this sounds strange, but I have smoked the plant myself and believe me: it works. I want you all to take the pipe and take a deep inhale before passing it around to the next man beside you. Believe," Hook commanded as he reached the pipe down to the first man.

He watched the pipe fill with bright purple as the pipe touched the man's hand. The room was soon filled with the vivid purple puffs of horror of each man around the table. One by one, every thought dispersed into thin air, and Hook was finally able to explain the truth of what lay hidden behind the shadows of the Lost Island. Only this time as he looked about the room, what was staring back at him was a group of fearless men.

The timeless night's events had been weakening for everyone. Hook was anxious to drop scarlet rubies upon the sand with his itching blade, but he knew that if he and the crew did not collect some rest, they soon would be useless in moments of battle. So, two men of the crew that had lingered behind with Smee upon arrival were to stand guard and watch the beach while the others slept. There was to be a four-hour rotation for the entire duration of their journey. Should daylight return, Hook wanted to be informed immediately. As the men retired below deck, Hook and Catcher made their way to the captain's quarters, but before Hook climbed into his bed, he decided to ease his mind with a bit of reading.

Before he could grab a leathered spine, the quiet air was suddenly shaken by the chilling howl of a wendigo. Hook looked out his window at the distant smoke still rising above the tallest trees. He closed his eyes, preparing himself for what he knew was about to come next: the scream of a hunted child.

Once the screaming came to an end, Hook opened his eyes and went through his books, knowing now what book he should be reading. He flipped through the pages of ancient lore rapidly, looking for the one word that would sever his knotting mind: *wendigo*. It didn't take long to find tales of the cursed creature; though unlike most stories of such vicious monsters, this one struck Hook as sad.

The legend traces back to two native tribes. Long ago they referred to the creature as the stone coat bears. But somehow through the ages, the name wendigo meaning *'evil spirit* is what most call it today. Some believe the first wendigo made a deal with the devil to save his tribe, but most have come to believe something else, something far more sinister. The natives believed that should a human consume another; it invokes the evil spirit with itself. The host is then infected, tormented slowly as the voracious hunger and plaguing nightmares melts away their sanity. Overcome with strange odors that only the host can smell and enduring agonizing burning sensations throughout their limbs and feet. The heated pains would overwhelm them, usually causing them to strip down, running naked through the forest like a madman. The creature is soon suffused with its urges for human meat, constantly devouring, yet never sated. The gluttonous morphing creature grows with everybody it consumes, making it impossible to ever be full. The once human being is then forever frozen inside the host; most believe it dwells within the creature's heart. Legends says that the only way to kill a wendigo is to destroy the heart; freeing the prisoned soul within. Should the creature be allowed to wander without control, its mortal form will change completely. The putrid body covered in matted hair over its decaying skin, the sallow eyes glowing over its elongated jaw filled with large teeth and its unusually long tongue. Though the figure will always appear frail and slender, the wendigo is in fact anything but weak. Strikingly faster than any animal, and extremely tall with giant sharp antlers; the creature becomes the perfect predator. Time and age only seem to strengthen and add to their more than human powers, the oldest even having the capability of mimicking human voices. Hook's eyes searched for a way to help the cursed tribe, but alas- *there is but one cure for the wendigo: death.*

CHAPTER TWENTY-NINE

SKULL ROCK

Hook wasn't sure how long he had slept before the next piercing scream from the woods woke him, for hours meant nothing in this place. The moon was still full and high surrounded by a black blanket illuminated by two twinkling stars in the sky. The wailing of their unholy cries sent chills up his spine and every nerve standing on end.

When he sat up from his bedside, the view of the Lost Island shined beautifully off in the distance. Hook wondered how many poor souls had dreamed of its magical splendor, all unknowing of the blood and evil that hid within its shadows. As his eyes wandered, so did his mind. He looked down at the table beside his bed and reached into the drawer for the chief's box.

Before inhaling the pipe, he opened one of his largest windows. He exhaled the thoughts from his mind, watching as the clouded visions of purple figures floated through the night air. But as they did, Hook noticed they weren't simply disappearing as they usually should, but rather that the smoke was traveling. Curious, he squinted his eyes, narrowing his focus when suddenly he spotted something he hadn't seen before; there was a tiny area of dark stone a short distance past the island. Hook quickly walked over to his desk to retrieve his golden spyglass.

When his sight found the stone, he saw that the smoke was entering a cave, but not just any cave; this cave was in the shape of none other than a giant human skull.

Hook couldn't help but sigh and rub his face in annoyed frustration. "Really!... What the hell?"

Suddenly there was a loud scraping noise coming from just outside his door. Catcher's ears perked up suspiciously from the bed. The sound of something heavy being dragged across the ground cringed his sensitive hearing as he quickly approached the door with his blade ready in his hand.

Hook whipped open the door to hear a girlish yelp and the sight of stupid Smee dropping to the floor with his arms across the top of his head. "Blast it! Smee! You idiot! What in the hell are you doing?!"

Smee looked up fixing his foggy glasses as the sight of his furious captain came into view.

"Oh, Captain, I am so sorry. I thought you were sleeping. And then I guess my imagination got the best of me because I heard the door and thought someone was coming to kill me."

Hook let out a fuming sigh and shook his sword in anger. "I was! I still might!"

Smee shook in fear but said not another word. Hook suddenly noticed what was making such a wrenching sound; next to Smee was a large domed chest. Hook saw right away that it was one of Blackbeard's. "What are you doing with that?" He demanded.

Smee peeked open his eyes, squirming where he stood, he tried to open his mouth to answer: "I...uh... well, Blackbeard asked me to-"

Hook stomped his large boot upon the wooden floor. "What? He asked you to do what, Mr. Smee?!"

Smee suddenly stood up straight, putting his hand to his head in saluting form as if abruptly whipped back into reality. "He asked me to give this to you after we reached the island. I fear I was not able to approach you with it before you sped out into the woods, and I knew you would not have permitted me to come out there after you, and then when you got back with the crew, everything was just so..."

Hook rose his hand to stop him. "That's quite enough now, Smee. I think I understand. Do you know what is inside?"

Smee shook his head rapidly. "No, Captain."

"Then I wish to take it from here and open it privately in my chambers."

Smee nodded his head as Hook lifted the giant chest with ease and carried it into his room and closed the door.

As Hook carefully placed the domed chest onto the floor beside his bed, he began to wonder what his father could have possibly put inside. When the chest opened, it revealed two large boxes sitting next to each other. The one on the left had a small letter on top that read:

It is the duty of a good captain to protect his crew.
Just as it is the wish of a good father that his young
learn from his mistakes and become better than
himself.
Do what you can to protect your men,
and though I am not as clever a man like you,
I hope what I do know of such warding
protection can be of some help.
You must always know who you can trust.

Hook opened the box under the letter. Inside was a diverse assortment of bright and dark red objects: earrings, bandanas, shirts, belts, straps, and hats. Hook smiled, it made sense now why Blackbeard could only trust Smee with the chest, for as long as they have known him, he had never once taken off his red nightcap. Then Hook glanced at the second box. There was no letter on top, but as Hook opened it, he saw that there was a small note pinned to a silky black wrap. Hook carefully lifted the small letter and read:

But most importantly my son,
as it was your wish to do this alone,
I pray you also project my greatest
treasure,

-You.

Hook lifted what was in the box and unwrapped the silk fabric. Underneath was a folded red cloth. A gulp went down his dry throat as he let the fabric drop. With the collar still in his grasp, Hook gazed in awe at the most exquisite coat. Designed in the French fashion, the red velvet fabric was embroidered with marvelous golden stitching. Down the front and around the sleeves, were shining gold buttons. It was glorious, and for a short moment, Hook became lost in his marvel.

"Smee! Gather my crew!" Smee obeyed, and in no time the entire crew was in formation on the main deck. Hook circled them, opening the box from Blackbeard, and handing out a single red object to each as he passed. The crew looked confused at first, but as Hook explained it was for their safety in this place, every man wasted no time in putting it on. Once Hook felt he had their attention again he invited them into his dining quarters to talk and smoke.

They all agreed happily ready to clear their minds, but before Hook could provide that, he also needed to explain the current situation of rationing their food supply equally and very little for fear of running out. He also revealed who and what exactly they will face: the wendigoag, the lost boys, the Green Fairy, and of course Pan. It seemed that after every detail Hook could think of, he soon had covered, the crew, fearful as they were, appeared to understand the consequences if they should fail.

"Alright, now assemble your weapons, Pan may not be here, but the lost boys are still out there. I think I only need a few of you to come with me. Have nothing to fear, the wendigo tribe is on our side after all, and Pan will not be back until the sun comes up. It has come to my attention that there a poor helpless little girl out in those woods, and I must find her. For surely, she knows where Peter's hideout is; and then, men- that is when we attack!"

This time leaving Catcher behind with Smee and the crew, Hook and his three best climbed into the small boat again, but this time they followed the purple smoke to the Skull Rock. As they drew closer, Hook could suddenly hear someone singing; it was the voice of a little girl.

The song was sad and beautiful and yet it did not carry the same power and control as the surrounding sirens. Hook gestured for his rowing men to be silent, allowing the small boat to enter the gaping skull's mouth undetected. The voice grew louder, echoing off the black wet walls of the cave as the figures of smoke rose higher into the air. The cave was filled with various sized stones that stacked high into what could only be thought as the paths to the skull's eyes. The purple forms climbed their way up, each stone glowing with a strange carved symbol. He didn't know what any of the symbols were or what they meant, but something about the smoking fear was somehow enhancing their fiery glow.

The splashing water shined on the wet stone as he carefully placed his boot upon the first rock. Every note in the girl's song brought the animated air rising towards her. His movement upon the grounded rock, however, did not cause any magical spark of reaction. Hook looked back towards his men and gestured for them to remain in the boat quietly while he went up the rocks alone. He wanted to be sure that if any lost boys came, he would not be caught off guard. Two of the men turned to face the outside entrance while the other kept an eye on his back.

The glowing stones were slippery and wet from the growing tide of the sparkling sea, but Hook's careful footing remained perfectly at ease. But as he climbed higher, he noticed something strange. The dry stones appeared silver, weathered, and broken. The ancient markers carved by a legendary age forgotten by humanity, broken beyond recognition yet proclaimed such power as they fed, bringing back its vibrant brilliance. He climbed carefully until reaching the top, where there seemed to be another surface of solid ground. Suddenly the source of the throttling music obscured by the clouding purple smoke finally came into view: it was a young Indian girl. Hook took one step creeping towards her in silence, but the moment the melody stopped, he knew he had been spotted.

"Tiger Lily?" He whispered, hoping not to frighten her. "It's alright... I am not going to harm you."

The girl's eyes elevated him in suspicion. "Who are you?"

He took another step towards her cautiously. "Your father, the chief, sent me."

Tiger Lily burst with panic, but before she could run, Hook rushed her, wrapping his arms around her tightly. She fought and screamed out of the skull's eyes, bellowing a horrid call for the lost boys, but his strength overpowered her immensely. He clasped a hand over her mouth and carried her down the ancient stones to the small boat. It took all four pirates to hold her down the whole way back to the Jolly Roger.

Hook had to admit for such a young girl; she was quite fearless. She had fought him the whole way, and even as a large crew of ruthless pirates surrounded her, she remained fierce and unafraid. Irritating as she was, one couldn't help but be impressed by her. Hook ordered the men to tie her down. She squirmed, fought, and even tried to bite as five men struggled to restrain her. Anger illuminated in her eyes as Hook squatted down in front of her. There was a long, tense pause between them as he analyzed her.

"You are a tough girl, Tiger Lily. I can see why Peter likes you."

She widened her eyes in surprise.

Hook gave her a sly smile, "Oh yes... I know Peter. We go back a long time; I am most eager to see him again. Would you kindly tell me where he dwells

329

upon this little island?" He asked with sinister charm. But Tiger Lily merely squinted at him with suspicion before letting out a shrill scream that pitched through their ears. "It is no use, girl. The lost boys will not be able to reach you here, for if they land a single foot aboard my ship, my men will kill them all. Do you understand me?"

She gave a slow single nod before spitting in his face.

His anger began to boil inside him, "Come now, Tiger Lily. Where can I find Peter Pan?"

But she just looked at him plainly and shrugged her shoulders smugly. "How should I know where he is?"

Hook nodded clicking his tongue at her noticed sarcasm. "Surely, you of all people would know of his whereabouts- or maybe I have merely overestimated your importance to him, and you are simply not privy to such information," he said bluntly. But she merely chuckled at his ever so weak attempt to outwit her. "You can trust me, Tiger Lily. I am merely an old friend of Peter's."

Tiger Lily shook her head. "I do not know who you are or why you are here, but I know you are a liar! You are no friend of Pan's! He hates grown-ups! But fear not, for when Peter Pan returns, you will not need to seek him out. He will find you!"

This time Hook chuckled as he bent down towards her, seething through his teeth. "Ah, but will he be able to find *you* before you starve to death?" At that moment, he finally saw a glimmer of fear in her eyes. But when she turned up her nose and looked away, he finally left her alone. She remained silent for endless hours, never uttering a word when questioned.

It didn't take long before the chief, and two of his tribe appeared on board. The chief was eager to see his daughter, and as it happened- she was happy to see him as well. Hook expected some objection to his daughter being tied up like she was, but he didn't so much as show the slightest disapproval, leaving him with the fair assumption that the chief has had to resort to such an attempt himself.

After their loving greeting, he pulled the chief aside for a word. "Pardon me, sir, but as I have respectfully fulfilled your wishes and found your daughter, I now ask for something in return."

The chief squinted at him suspiciously. "The trade was my pipe and protection in return for my daughter's safe capture. What do you ask of me now, Captain?"

"You are right, my friend. Yet, I fear I do need something else from you. Please talk to your daughter. I believe it is you and you alone that could get any information out of her."

The chief craned his head curiously. "What is it you need to know?"

331

"I need her to tell me where to find Pan on the island. I must kill him! I must! She is the key. I can feel it! She must know where..."

The chief raised his hand to holt Hook's words. "She does not."

"What do you mean? How do you know that?"

"I know because I can walk through her dreams. It is the only way I can be sure she is safe. I know what is in her heart and what lies within her soul; just as I have also seen what dwells inside the twisted mind of Pan. She cannot tell you where he lives, because he hasn't told her. Peter has control of the island and everything on it, making it nearly impossible for her to find him during a game. Nevertheless, she has never failed to do so. Pan moves his hiding spot around. It has never been seen in the same place twice. She hasn't even told him her secret."

Hook looked at him curiously. "What secret?"

"Their game, of course. Tiger Lily always finds him, but the boy has yet to discover how."

"Do you know the answer?"

"I do. It is his shadow. See, there are two pieces of the boy: Peter and Pan! While he has not fully realized it, the animation of his lively shadow reveals the true spirit of the boy's former self. Still alive and playful, the shadow often plays its own game, giving Pan away in moments of hiding."

Hook nodded, his thoughts stirring wildly in his head. Looking towards the door where Tiger Lily sat waiting, he got an idea. "So, his shadow is tied to him by magic; interesting indeed. What would happen if he were to be *separated* from it?"

The chief thought to himself for a moment. "I suppose the shadow would be forced to return to our world from once it came. Without it, the essence of the boy he once was would be gone, and Pan would be lost in this place forever."

The next span of hours felt more torturous than ever. Hook spent much of his time looking out the window, hoping to see the faintest gleam of sunlight. The crew spent most of their time maintaining their sanity with the pipe and cleaning the deck. Most of the men were already feeling their hunger. The shrill wailing of children and howling in the distance reminded them of what should happen if they succumb to temptation. The smell of meat often swept through the air, enticing all within its reach.

Staring at the moon, his eyes fell and as his dreams of Pan washed over him. He wasn't sure how long he must have slept that night, but it was Catcher's alarming bark that woke him. He stood on his feet, rapidly grabbing his red coat and hat from his wardrobe. Smee suddenly screamed and came pounding on the door. "Captain! It is daylight! The sun is here!"

Hook whipped opened the door. "I know, you idiot! I know! Get the men together! Everyone on deck! Go now!"

"Aye, sir," he said before rushing off to do as ordered.

Quickly, the men ascended to the main deck; each wearing their own bit of red as ordered. Hook turned to Smee and whispered: "Get the Indian girl."

Smee rushed to the dining quarters and dragged out Tiger Lily, still sitting in her chair.

Out of breath, Smee returned to Hook's side when the captain suddenly turned to him again. "Good, Mr. Smee. Now go below deck and hide Catcher. Lock the door and stay there!"

Smee nodded nervously before running beneath the ship.

The Lost Island was soon bright green and vibrant. The surrounding sea glittered like diamonds, and the golden sand on the shore flickered in the light. The silence was soon broken as the sound of chiming bells wisped through the summer breeze. Hook ordered the men to their stations. He knew Peter would notice the ship right away and wouldn't dare approach a full crew of pirates without some help.

A quick burst came across the sky, followed by a glowing green light, and several other dark figures. They were heading towards Skull Rock, where Hook was sure Peter would be looking for Tiger Lily. It didn't take long before a hooded figure flew out the cave's eyes and streamed quickly towards the center of the island. Hook watched as a large brush of movement swarmed throughout the forest heading straight towards the location of the Indian grounds.

He watched through his spyglass, waiting for that moment of splendor when Peter realized the young girl was not there. The trees whipped wildly as the flying figure rushed across the island... Hook knew Pan was desperately looking for the girl and was likely collecting his devil minions for a trip to the sea. He sat idly in a chair with his iron blade laid across his legs. The flying form of a young boy rose high above the trees, followed by his little green friend and what appeared to be over two dozen hollow-eyed children.

Each of the figures was dark as if the sun were directly behind them. Hook remained still, ordering his men to stay at holt until he gave the orders. As the flying children came closer into view, the glimmering reflection of their blades and arrows shuffled through their hands. Hook chuckled to himself; these small creatures didn't stand a chance. They were clumsy, ill-formed, and untrained. One by one, the group of lost boys landed upon the main deck, and through the clearing appeared a young boy in a dark hood.

When his feet touched the deck, Hook watched as the boy slowly removed his hood, and revealed the face of the one and only: Peter Pan.

"Who are you and what are you doing here?!" Pan demanded. Hook's men remained still and quiet.

"I said! What are you doing on my island?!" The moment was growing tenser, yet if Pan had any fear, he was sure hiding it well. His eyes burned with profound anger, "You will answer me! I am the ruler here!" This time Peter floated up into the air. But the main deck was soon echoing with the crew's roaring laughter. Pan's face grew red with fury, "How dare you! Why do you laugh at me?" Then the men's laughter was suddenly silenced as the sound of a loud thump came from behind them.

Peter turned to see what it was as a man leaned in close and whispered: "We laugh because you are *not* in charge here!" The pirate said bluntly. Pan turned his head to face the man when suddenly another thump came upon the deck, then another and another until finally, Peter set his gaze upon the ship's captain. A strange feeling washed over him as the crew roared, "Hook!... Hook!... Hook!" Something about the name stirred through Peter's mind of flashing memories. Images of the past coursed through him as the tall fearsome pirate approached. As Peter gazed into the captain's blue eyes, a feeling of thrill, joy, and brilliant fear suffused him entirely.

"What is it, Peter? Has it been that long? Don't tell me you have forgotten me?" Hook's voice was certain and calm.

It was in that moment that the revelation came upon Pan as he silently uttered the word that brought a smile to his face: "James," he whispered before looking up at Tink. She was trembling in shock. But

336

Pan merely glanced back to Hook with a sly grin. "Wow! I must admit, I had given up on you a long time ago, old friend. I must say, you are looking- old," Peter said mockingly. Circling him in the air, he spoke again: "Ah well, you are finally here. Don't tell me you have really spent all this time still sore about the past."

Hook glared in silence. Slowly gripping his blade, he resisted the urge to kill Peter right then and there. But god, did he want to do it; to watch his blood drip down upon the wood beneath their feet. Seeing his fury, Pan continued: "Aww, that is just so- pathetic. You *have* spent all these years looking for me?"

Slash!

Peter opened his eyes abruptly bringing his hand up to his cheek. When he looked down at the blood on his hand, a surge of pure excitement and thrill overtook him. He laughed again, "See, that's what I love about you, Hook! You are simply too much fun!"

Hook chuckled rudely in return. "Yes, yet I hear you on the other hand, have become quite the bore. Why, you cannot even beat a silly girl at a game of hide and seek? Pity!"

Peter was suddenly jolted with a striking realization. *Tiger lily!* "What have you done with her?" He asked, dropping to the deck.

Now it was Hook pacing him around like a tall vulture. "If only the world knew what became of the famous... Oh, that's right! No one knows who you are,

Peter Pan!" Hook rubbed his fingers across his chin sarcastically, "Hmm... you do have the lost children. No wait, they don't have souls. They cannot ever really admire you. They are empty. They feel nothing. It's too sad, isn't it, men? This boy used to be something! Now look at him! Just a little fairy imposter, hated by his own kind and forgotten by his own world. Why, there was a time that this boy could beat you at any game, but now he is unable to beat a little girl. Now who is pathetic?" Hook said bending his head back with laughter. "See, Peter, the truth is... much *has* changed over the years we've been apart. I have charted countless journeys, finding treasures of gold and silver. My name is known across all the seven seas. I have conquered not only the lands from our world, but also in yours! Both mortals and magical creatures have come to cringe at my name, and now I am here for the crown; to claim Neverland as my own! And as for you, Peter Pan! Well, you will be to history what you are now: absolutely nothing!"

"I am not nothing! I am still the great Peter Pan!"

The men laughed mockingly as Hook continued, "Fear not, Peter, for before I kill you and send you on your journey to Hell, I will embark upon you a little going away present: I know your little friend's secret."

Peter's eyes widened with shock and curiosity.

"The key to her success is very simple... It is your shadow. Yet, I wager here and now, men, that even without it... he would still fail."

"You're wrong!"

Hook smiled, "Shall we see?"

"What?"

"Rid yourself of it and let us find out who is truly the best- once for all!" The crew roared, cheering their captain on, making Peter feel small. "So, what do you say, Peter? One last game, or are you afraid?"

Peter sneered at the thought. "Peter Pan is not afraid of anything!" He screamed, lifting a double-edged blade from his belt. He gazed at Tiger Lily, winking at her as he bent down to his feet. And in the blink of an eye, Pan sliced away the dark shadow bound to him. The pain caused him to scream in agony. Once separate, the shadow quickly tried to fly away, but it was suddenly snatched! Holding the squirming shadow tightly in his grasp, Hook began to bellow with victorious laughter.

"You see that, men?! I now hold in my hand the shadow of Peter! Without it... Pan will die!" Laughing along with his crew, the arrogant captain had failed to notice the Green Fairy's absence. But as Hook steered his gaze upon his fallen enemy, the smile on his face quickly fell as the sound of Pan's chilling laughter reverberated across the ship. "What are you laughing at, Peter?!"

The boy should have been in great pain, but his laughter only elevated as sudden figures of purple smoke began to appear circling around his head. "You see, old friend, you spoke to me of fear and well, it got me wondering- what you are afraid of? I had wondered if you had met the others on the island. I figured you had since I can think of no other reason why you should have Tiger Lily, and I knew that the only way you and your men could be found as anything other than insane... is if the Indian chief bestowed upon you his lovely little antidote for my paradise of true imagination. The figures of smoke dancing around are formed of every fearful thought you have had since you've been here, and I must say yours are interesting, to say the least." With a quick snap of his fingers, there was a sudden splash as if something burst through the water below. Hook hurried to gaze over the side of the ship to find the giant crocodile in a bloodthirsty rampage; only this time with the sound of a loud clock ticking as it moved. The sheer volume was overwhelming. It took everything he had not to let go of the shadow to cover his ears. But the worst was yet to come. Pan lifted into the air, slowly moving towards him.

"Give it back, Hook!" Pan demanded, pointing the sharp dagger.

But Hook remained strong, holding the shadow tightly and rapidly whipping out his sword to Tiger Lily's throat. "Back off, Pan! Or I kill the girl!"

With that, Pan charged at Hook, screaming with full force. Hook tossed Pan back down to the ground. With his full weight on top of him, he held Pan down by the tip of his blade. "The game is over, Pan! You lose!"

Then suddenly the face of Pan's struggling fear turned into a wicked grin, "Ah, Hook... If you are going to play a game, you should always make sure that it is you that holds the winning hand!" At that, Pan snapped his fingers, and the wailing cries of Catcher began wailing from the captain's quarters.

Hook rapidly turned his frantic gaze towards the door. "No! Catcher!" His moment of distraction was soon met with a burning surge of pain slicing through his left arm. He watched in horror as his severed hand dropped into Pan's grasp. Peter's shadow was released and quickly went flying into the air. Pan rose from the ground, juggling Hook's hand like a toy. With blood gushing onto the deck, he watched as Pan dwindled his severed extremity above the water, shaking it enticingly for the scaled beast below.

Finally, Pan dropped the bloody meat right into the devouring crocodile's jaws. With the loss of so much blood, Hook fell weakly upon the deck. But as his vision tunneled, it was Pan's victorious grin he saw before everything went black.

Tinker Bell rushed to Pan, reminding him that he needed to find the shadow before it was too late. But before they flew off, Pan took one last look at his dying rival on the ground. "Such a shame. That was the most fun I'd had in years! Alright, boys, I killed the famous Captain Hook, and I want you all to kill his crew! Get creative- make me proud!" Then Pan and the Green Fairy hurried into the sky, believing that the captain aboard the Jolly Roger was dead: *they were wrong.*

CHAPTER THIRTY

THE DARLINGS

As Pan and Tinker Bell burst through the stars, taking all light from the Lost Island, a full blue moon rose into the night sky shining its luminance upon Neverland. With the absence of the sun, so too was its power. The magic controlling the crew fell, and a swarm of wendigoag soon overtook the ship. Hook was taken to his quarters under the urgent charge of Smee while the surviving crew fought along the tribe of the beast to kill Pan's soulless army.

Some of the children fled, escaping to the island amongst the darkest of trees. Though many of the crew died of their wounds and suffering, their bodies were nothing compared to the fileted children that laid upon the deck. The vicious tribe quickly took their carnage with them back to their camp; no doubt the air of Neverland would soon be filled with the scent of smoking flesh upon a smoldering fire. The captain laid within his bedchamber. His arm singed to stop the bleeding. Soon Hook would wake in agony once again, as Smee worked frantically to save his life.

As Pan and Tinker Bell entered the Tenth Realm, the hour was still that of an early day, causing Pan much difficulty. His shadow traveled towards a terrible place of his past; to the earth's mark of the old

343

orphanage in Wales. But the building was gone, and so too was any tie Peter had to this world. The shadow grew frantic, flying abroad to other lands, always too far ahead for Pan or Tink's reach. Chasing Peter for days had grown frustrating for both as finally, Pan watched the shadow slither through the only open window of a beautiful home in London, England.

A thick fog clouded the tall gargantuan buildings, gothic and intimidating in both size and riches. Massive, elaborate Victorian features and darkened wooded beams held the golden frame of the window. The sheer white curtains that slowly waved in and out upon the soft wind were somehow inviting. Pan felt the hewn roughness beneath his grasp as he crept, hugging the walls carefully. He kept his feet off the pane and his hands off the two open doors of windows, lest they creak and betray his presence.

There were other windows below, and though they were closed, one could not ignore the refined elegance of the home. Each room lined with vibrant regal wallpaper that was lit by the most magnificent chandeliers. Each appeared like floating gold with large crystals that were centered so perfectly within each room and hall. The rooms themselves were framed with elaborate marbled design, and each seemed to all be a different color. The finely crafted furniture was polished and shined with every speck of light in the house. There were shelves as tall as the ceiling among some of the walls, each with various books or trinkets placed precisely in its proper place.

Everything within the home seemed to conform to some convoluted form of wealth and etiquette. These people seemed to have more money than they knew what to do with, but to Pan and Tink, it was merely a disgusting display. For it was only a few feet down that the hungry still roamed the streets, dirty and cold.

But once Pan creeped his way back towards the only open window, both he and Tink cautiously peered inside. This room was wholly different than the others; it was certainly not laid out according to the same archaic rules. It appeared to be some sort of nursery. There were three oversized beds. Next to each of them was a tall chest of drawers, and a floor covered in children's toys. But just as Pan was about to make a daring attempt to enter, a sudden burst of three young children came running through the room.

Pan quickly ducked around the window ceil unnoticed. It was clear they were going to have to wait until nightfall. Once the three children were asleep in their beds, they could safely enter and retrieve the hidden shadow within. But time was slow, leaving Pan and Tinker Bell at the mercy of the entertainment made by the playful children inside.

The oldest of the three was a young girl. She had brown locks of curls that were hung tightly with a bow that perfectly matched her baby blue nightgown and shoes. Her pale skin was beautifully complemented by her large hazel eyes and the natural pink shade of her lips and cheeks. The middle child was not much younger than the girl, though he appeared to already understand his high status in the world. The boy wore round crafted glasses upon his stale features and was dressed in a white nightshirt and brown slippers. And finally, the youngest child of the playful three was a boy no older than three years of age. Unlike his older brother with smooth brown hair, the youngest seemed to favor the features of his sister; with eyes that were hazel and curling blonde locks. Keeping up with his siblings in footed pajamas, the tiny child was accompanied by a worn teddy bear half his size.

Their games were silly indeed, but there was one detail where Pan couldn't resist his interest. The oldest of the three children created such imaginative stories as they played. Acting out her characters were the most thrilling and lively storytelling Pan had ever seen. Not alone, the shadow of Peter eagerly lent a fascinated ear hidden within the room. But when a large furry dog dressed in ridiculous nurse attire started to sniff around suspiciously, Peter's shadow was soon cornered, slithering into a locked drawer.

The dog soon forgot the matter due to the pressing involvement of the children's playtime. It seemed that the young three had convinced the hairy creature of their dependence. Treating to their mess and attending to the youngest with worry when he fell from the bed, the dog was very busy. Still, with the creature so close, Tink took extra care to remain hidden. Pan, on the other hand, was simply too enamored with the young girl. To his great surprise, the girl spoke of the most exciting adventures, famous explorers, mermaids, and magic. It seemed she had some keen sense to it all, but with one word, everything changed.

The two younger boys in the nursery picked up what appeared to be toy swords. They wrapped small clothes around their heads and stood upon their beds as if they were ships. The boys begged the girl to tell them stories about pirates! But not just any pirate, the most fearsome pirate known to man: Captain Hook! The theatrical young girl obliged and was soon playing the role of the famed pirate herself, fighting with swords in all matter pretend. The boys loved every second of it.

It seemed that above all others, the stories of Hook were the most thrilling. The young boys created a secret treasure map, and with every fragment of their imagination, Pan could feel it was their deepest wish to be a part of such an adventure.

Each word tore through Pan like a blade. There was no mention of fairies; how he wished it was his name spoken upon their lips with such admiration and awe. The painful truth of what Hook had said upon the ship earlier that day, was now becoming a torturous revelation. In this world, Peter Pan *was* nothing. In Neverland, the ones who fell under his command and fame were also nothing. Earth had forgotten him, and within the Nine Realms, he was merely the boy who tricked a fairy, punished to remain on the island as their servant for as long as he lived. He was nothing more than a slave of the Elders; for the sake of his soul and Tink's, he had never broken a single rule. He had lost what he once was, while his enemy's name would be known throughout history.

Jealousy overtook him. If only they knew, that it was he who had defeated the famous pirate they loved so much. If only they could see what *he* could do. If only...

Suffused with anger and annoyance, Pan snapped his fingers. A spark of glittering dust flew through the window and into the mind of the young girl playing in her blue nightgown. The boys looked upon her sudden striking silence with confusion, but the girl simply responded with a sly grin. It was thus that the girl began to tell stories of the boy who fought the dangerous pirate and cut off his hand.

Instantly, the boys were amazed, playing along as the girl described the most thrilling battle between pirates and the lost boys of Neverland. But even as the children played in his name, Pan knew it wasn't real. To them, Peter Pan was merely a fragment of their imagination, but the name *Hook* would remain unbearably real.

Pan's agonizing thoughts were suddenly interrupted by a sudden burst through the nursery doors. A large man and woman came into the room, both formally dressed. The man looked incredibly angry, while the woman looked kind. The man began his sudden rant, raving and yelling about the room. It seemed that the treasure map that the boys had made was a critical piece of the man's wardrobe for the evening. The girl, however, proclaimed all fault as her own, explaining that the boys had merely acted out of excitement during one of her stories. The man charged at her with irritation.

But as Pan watched the young girl defend her actions, it was his own imagination that unfolded. The man demanded that she stop her insufferable behavior, and with the final act of ripping away the dog's nurse clothing, he declared that this would be the girl's last night in the nursery. It was time for her to grow up and remove her foolish notions from the company of her two younger brothers. The woman and children had only a moment of objection before cowering to his tyranny. And after a quick dismissal of the dog, the man and woman sent the scolded children to bed.

Pan then eyed the parent's movements throughout the lower windows. The man escorted the dog outside, while the kind woman said a few words to an elderly woman sitting by a fire. The old woman waved a farewell as the man proceeded to assist his wife with her coat. With a quick wrap of his own coat, the topping of his hat, and the grasp of his cane, the man and woman left their home in discussion.

Pan made his way back up to the open window. The children were neatly tucked asleep in their beds. He whistled for Tinker Bell, and in the dark of the night, they entered the silent room to retrieve the shadow from the chest. Tink flew through the small lock to recover it, but Peter's shadow made a quick escape, flying out of the drawer. But before it could slither out the window, Pan grabbed it by the foot and the two went tumbling loudly throughout the room.

With the final loud thump on the floor, the young girl burst wide awake, gazing down at the floor to find him trying to rub his shadow back onto to feet. Pan was shocked as the young girl approached him as if she were star struck. Confused at her extensive knowledge of him, it seemed he had placed more of himself in her susceptible imagination than he thought.

Instantly overwhelmed with the girl's jabbering, it seemed she had somehow conceived false past encounters with him. Rushing to help with his shadow, the girl went to the chest of drawers for a needle and string, insisting that sewing the shadow on was the proper solution. But Tink was still inside the drawer, and with a hard thrust, the girl sent the Green Fairy and other small trinkets hurling backwards. After a swift hard landing, a tiny brass thimble came twirling upon her head. The little pixie glowed red with rage.

Overwhelmed with the girl's aggressive flirtation, Pan flew sitting upon the air above the bed as she sat upon the floor, ready for sewing. As the girl excitedly rambled on, Pan lowered himself slowly and shook his head, "Girls talk too much." Reaching his leg out rudely, he waved his shoe for her to hurry up. When she continued to talk to him, he materialized his pipes, performing musical magic to overpower the volume of her voice.

The girl took a minute to understand the offense, but the momentary pause wasn't enough to holt her adoration. "My name is Wendy. Wendy Moira Angela Darling."

But Pan waved his hand, rudely brushing her off, "Wendy it is!" He interrupted.

Surprised by his crass tone, she proceeded sewing quietly. But once Peter and Pan were bound together again, a chilling spark of cunning brilliance echoed through his twisted mind as she said the words both she and her brothers would live to regret: "I am quite happy you came tonight, or I might never have seen you. My father is removing me from the nursery. He insists I start behaving like a proper lady!" She cried, whimpering into a tissue, "Oh, how I wish I did not have to grow up."

CHAPTER THIRTY-ONE

AN ACT OF BETRAYAL

As Peter Pan led the three happy children flying playfully around the grand clock tower of London, the three waved their arms like free birds through the clouds to enter the blue blanket of glittering stars. Little did they know that something truly sinister was at play.

The Darling three would be entering Pan's realm with no contract. Flying far and fast ahead was Tinker Bell, still stunned by the night's events. It all just didn't make sense, and yet Tink seemed to be the only one fearing the inevitable consequences should Pan bring mortals freely to the island. *Was Pan willing to forsake both our souls for mere fame and glory? For if it was so, then Hook had already won and both he and I will die due to his jealousy and arrogance.* The very thought was more infuriating than the image of that stupid girl trying to trick Peter into kissing her.

Reveling in the silly girl's shameless flirtation with behavior well below one of her status was only more glory for Pan. But having created such a delirious illusion of himself in the children's mind was not something Tink admired, but instead found pathetic.

The Green Fairy's rage charged as she sped far beyond the others. It seemed that all was falling apart, and it appeared that it was both Hook and the girl that would be their undoing. She wished she could make Pan understand, but it was clear when she broke out of the drawer and charged the young girl that he was just too lost in his own scheme. Something changed within him when the shadow was cut from his body. *Pan would have never chosen anyone or anything over me before, let alone a prissy young girl. Ugh*! Tink thought, slamming her arms swiftly at her side, blasting through the veil's portal. She had to get to the island before the others. *Pan would take both the boy's souls soon enough; he had no use for them. But the girl, he had plans for. But this wasn't like bringing Tiger Lily to the island. This girl had no magic in her blood and would thus cause a tide of death upon both of us when the Elders find out. The girl has to die! But Pan made it clear back in the nursery that I was not to harm the girl. The lost boys! The lost boys are the key!* They were Pan's vicious puppets, but Tink had the same magic that was needed to control them. No doubt the blood under the full moon was still warm in the sand.

If she got there quick enough, she could give them the order, and it would merely seem like an accident. *The little wretch would be dead long before the Elders would know of her arrival. Once Peter sees that the captain and the crew are all dead, we can go back to the old games and Peter will be back to his old self.*

Hook had lost a lot of blood on board before the crew could reach Smee. But with hours of tireless work and a wish upon a star, Hook awoke.

Despite his burning pain, his eyes instantly searched in a frantic sweat for Catcher. But the moment of panic quickly faded as Catcher popped his head up upon the bed. The captain threw his head back in relief. "What happened?"

Smee spoke lightly: "No one knows what happened in the final moments of the battle between you and the boy, but you were found nearly bleeding to death on the main deck when the moon rose into the sky. I regret to say, sir, that you lost your hand."

Hook's mind flashed upon the last moment he and Pan had on deck before the world went dark. He looked down at his deformity with anger. "That little bastard hurt my dog and then fed my hand to that bloody crocodile!"

Smee patted the air trying to calm him. "Captain, I was with Catcher the whole time. He was never in any danger."

Hook looked at him with frustration. "But I heard him! I heard him whimpering in great pain. That is how..." Suddenly it all made sense. "That is how he was able to cut off my hand. He tricked me! Where is he? I want to kill him now!"

Smee suddenly rushed over to retrieve a small French chest. "It is not my place, sir, but I just happened to have here the perfect weapon for such a purpose." Lifting open the chest revealed a red velvet pillow with the finest prosthetic hook ever made. The piece itself was beautifully crafted, with a golden engraved base and a shiny curved hook made of solid iron. It was not only perfectly symbolic, but in some strange way, it seemed to complete the captain's being.

Gazing upon the weapon's shiny reflection, Hook smiled wickedly as the vision of Pan's blood dripped down its blade. Smee trembled at the blazing madness in the captain's eyes.

"Where did it come from?" Hook asked, staring at the weapon's perfection.

Smee smiled kindly. "I wasn't sure I would be able to save you in time. So, I...."

"-You prayed?" Hook interrupted.

Smee shook his head. "No, I made a wish upon a star," he answered nervously. Hook looked at him sternly as if upset by such an act, but Smee spoke again before he could erupt. "It was Ainsel, Captain. She told me long ago that if you were ever in any trouble, to wish upon a star and she would hear it. The chest appeared in your room shortly after."

Thinking about Ainsel was simply too difficult for Hook, so he quickly changed the subject: "And Tiger Lily; is she alright."

"Yes, Captain, she is well. The chief came for her."

Hook slammed his fist down. Tiger Lily was the only card he had, and now due to his loss in the fight with Peter, the chief might no longer see him as a strong ally.

Smee pleaded for Hook to inhale the chief's pipe, but Hook refused: "I will not have my thoughts used against me by that villain again. For however torturous they are to me, they will do far less damage in my head than in his!"

Smee hadn't the faintest idea of what had happened with the young fairy boy, but he could see there would be no changing the captain's decision, though he feared if they should not get off the island soon, the captain may lose more than his disturbed mind. Smee stood upon the main deck looking out at the two bright stars twinkling above in the sky.

Suddenly, there was a quick stream of flashing green light. Glittering like a thousand emeralds, it was Tink alone that came bursting through the dark realm, bringing not the faintest glimmer of sunlight with her. The sight came and went in a matter of seconds, leaving Smee with the doubt that he had seen it at all. The stress of the captain's violent rage had left him in desperate need of a drink. Tired and unnerved, Smee decided since the captain was now on the mend, that he should now get some much-needed rest.

He wobbled carefully below deck. He didn't want to be found in his chambers, so he headed towards a small little corner amongst the rest of the sleeping crew. He laid his head down quietly, but just as soon as he shut his heavy eyes, chaos struck the ship. Falling out of a worn hammock in full panic, the entire crew charged to the main deck ready with arms. Smee tried to cowardly crawl across the floor unnoticed when suddenly he was snatched up to his feet by the back of his striped faded shirt.

"To the deck, Mr. Smee! The captain demands your presence!" Shouted one of the men. But Smee was too exhausted to focus. Nevertheless, the weary doctor was dragged up the wooden steps and across the main deck by the back of his collar. The clouded white noise of the chaotic rustling of the crew fell on deaf ears until the sudden sting of a slap struck across his round cheek, and the raging scream of the captain roared through his ears.

"M' Sorr- sorry," Smee stammered, but what Hook said next wasn't to him, but rather a command to all.

"Fire!" Suddenly a booming clash shook the ship. Smee closed his eyes and held his ringing ears as the crew loaded the cannon again. *Boom!* Again, the cannon fired. Smee slowly opened his eyes trying to spot the target. Up in the sunny sky, hidden behind one of the perfect fluffy clouds were three small children screaming, and the young boy in green clothes was flying around them. The cannon fire aimed for the fae child, but it appeared with each shot, the boy would move just in time.

Though his placement put the other children in danger, the fae boy seemed to enjoy every second.

That is, until a single figure caught his eye: "Hook! No that's impossible!"

Hearing his words, the two boys cheered in excitement! Their star-struck behavior ignited Pan's murderous rage. Everything inside of him wanted to rip out their wretched souls right then and there, but something stopped him: Wendy. He needed the girl. He needed to separate them, and after a few days apart, she would forget all about them. Once she had long forgotten her family, she would be entirely at his will.

With a sly crooked smile, Peter Pan gazed down into the eyes of his greatest foe. *The girl will witness and let the story be told that Peter Pan killed the great Captain Hook!* Snapping his fingers arrogantly, Tinker Bell appeared before him. "Tink, take the girl to the tree. Keep her safe until I return. I will take the boys."

Tink nodded and began to lead the frightened young girl through the sky, heading straight towards the Lost Island, but she wasn't heading for Pan's sacred tree; she was heading into the land of the lost boys, and every one of them was waiting, standing beneath the trees to kill the girl. Wendy struggled to keep up with the small fairy's incredible speed. But every desperate plea from the girl only annoyed Tink farther. *How dare that teacup human behave as if I am working for her; that I should aid her after parading around with the pixie dust that was forced out of me. And now she thinks she can tell me how to fly!* Tink whipped in zags barely staying in Wendy's view at all.

It was not only making her nervous; she was also becoming afraid as she started imagining falling to the ground. But as far as Tink was concerned, the girl's worst imagination was no match for her own.

Whipping through the tall fresh trees covering Neverland's darkness, Wendy ultimately lost sight of Tinker Bell. Wobbling with striking panic, a sudden mist of whistling arrows came piercing through the brush towards her. In a blinding second, she was shot, and her screams of pain and terror echoed throughout the island. Tink smiled wickedly, watching from one of the higher branched trees. No doubt Peter had heard the young girl's horrific cry, but it was too late. The girl had fallen to the rocks below. *Pan would kill the lost boys responsible before any fault or blame could possibly be tied to me. With the girl and her brothers' dead, both Pan and I will be safe once again.* Tink had never betrayed Peter before, but after the danger, he had put her in- her treachery seemed to be fair game. As Tink flew down, sparkling with smug pride, she was suddenly struck with more anger then she had ever felt in her entire life. There, below the trees, floating just above the rocks, was Pan holding an unconscious Wendy in his arms. Pan slowly lowered her to the ground, seeing her blood upon his hands as they left her.

The two younger brothers rushed to her in panic. "Save her, Peter Pan! You must save her, please!" John begged. The youngest child, Michael was in tears, weeping into the small teddy bear he had brought with him. Peter had rushed to the scene so quickly; he had no choice but to bring them along. Reaching down, Pan touched his right hand upon her. The brothers watched in awe as a glowing light shined upon her, healing her wounds and waking her instantly. Tink's rage burned right through the leaf that hid her.

"Thank heavens! What happened?" Michael asked.

Pan stood holding one of the bloody arrows in his hand. "That is what I would like to know!" He shouted, snapping his fingers, commanding the lost boys into his sight. Normally, Pan wouldn't have hesitated in just killing them, but there were too many mortal eyes upon him, and he needed answers. "Why did you do this?" Pan demanded snapping his fingers again.

The lost boy closest to him replied plainly: "It was an order."

Pan's eyes widened in shock. "Order! I gave no such order! And the only other that could... *Tink!*" It was suddenly clear. He knew Tink. He knew why she did what she did. Eyeing through the surrounding green, he spotted her emerald glow, "Tinker Bell! You dare go against me after all we have been through!?"

Tink burst through the leaves with fury, and while the others could only hear intense bells and gestures of madness. Peter could see she accused him of the same treachery. She demanded he choose between them, but he had made his choice in London.

He had a plan for Wendy. *She will make me immortal, not only in his world but in Hook's. She will make me a real legend, and all Tink could offer was a life restricted by fairy law. How could she take this away from me? How could she go against me so intensely?* And with a final sigh, he gave her his answer, "Tinker Bell, I hereby banish you from me forever!"

Wendy and her brothers watched as the heartbroken fairy flew away, and even though she had tried to kill her, Wendy felt sorry for the small pixie. "Oh, Peter. Please, you mustn't banish her forever!"

In truth, Peter had regretted it the second the words left his mouth. For he and Tink, the word forever is so much crueler than any human could conceive. Pan couldn't imagine his life without her, but she needed to be punished, and more importantly, he needed her out of his way. But if his decision proved anything, it was this: if he was going to have to choose between his happiness and loyalty to Tink- well, that was a game she was always going to lose. Without Tink, the plan would have to change. Luckily, Peter was always quick on his feet. Wendy was healed, but still so overwhelmed with fear, she was incapable of flight. But Pan still needed to separate the siblings from their sister, and with one beat of a distant drum, it was obvious what he needed to do.

"What was that?" John asked.

Peter answered with a sinister smile: "That, my boys, are the Indians."

John and Michael looked at each other with thrilling excitement. "Did you say Indians, sir?" John asked adjusting his glasses upon his face.

"I did indeed. See, the lost boys and I have a little game with the Indians on the island: a hunting game! Would you like to play?"

Wendy herself was not keen on the idea. "I cannot go hunting, Peter. I am a young lady. I would ruin my gown and tangle my hair. No, I'm sorry. It just wouldn't do."

Though Pan found the girl to be whiny, prissy, and boring, she had said exactly what he wanted to hear. "Oh, don't worry, Wendy. I will take you to go see the mermaids!" And with that one word, Peter had Wendy gushing in his arms. "Alright boys, take our new guest on a true Neverland adventure!"

The lost boys lined up, though Pan wasn't surprised that John had placed himself at the front as the leader. No doubt the brat felt entitled. And while Pan thought arrogance on everyone else was something to challenge, he found much more joy knowing that John would be leading them to their deaths.

Wendy urgently proclaimed for Michael to be careful, and as John led his younger brother and the lost boys through the wood, Tinker Bell watched as Peter and Wendy flew away with her dainty hand in his.

But the smitten young girl had made a dangerous mistake, for there is nothing more frightening or deadly as a scorned fairy's wrath.

CHAPTER THIRTY-TWO
VOICE OF CAPTAIN HOOK

Tiger Lily had already escaped the hold of the tribe, but her father happened to know exactly where she was going. Since they all knew there be no finding Peter on the island during the day, Tiger Lily's only hope was Skull Rock. It was the place they could always find each other, and she would surely be on her way. Seeking Hook's assistance again, the chief wanted the captain and his first mate to go searching for her but Hook no longer wanted to involve himself with him or his mischievous daughter. Hook had another idea. He would find the young Indian girl, but this time- she would be his bait.

Hook took Smee aboard the small boat out on the sea. It didn't take long before they spotted the young Indian girl's wet feathers floating on top of the water. She was swimming quickly, with the large crocodile following behind her. No doubt Pan had enchanted the guardian of the island to be her guardian as well. The monster's tail pierced through the surface, ticking like a clock with each swift stroke through the water. It seemed Pan's magic would fall into Hook's favor, as now he would always know when the creature was nearby. Closing in on the girl, Hook drew his pistol and fired at the slithering reptile. The creature growled and snapped violently, as blood began to spread within the sparkling water. Tiger Lily panicked, swimming harder and faster towards the cave, but it was no use. Smee scooped her up in an urgent haste, fearing the loss of his own limbs. The wounded monster whipped around the boat fiercely, just waiting for the chance to attack. Smee apologized silently as he tied up the young girl. Hook did not know if her lack of raging defense was because her captor was Smee, or if she had simply exhausted herself in the water. Defeated as she was, Tiger Lily lacked no manner of arrogant stubbornness. With her eyes closed and her nose high, Hook could do nothing but shake his head at the deviant girl that Pan had grown to treasure.

Smee didn't like it; something about this ominous mission felt wrong. "Erm... Captain, something about this doesn't sit well with me. What are we doing with the Indian girl?"

Hook smiled, looking to the dank cave ahead. "Pan has come for her before and he will come for her again."

The excitement of the lagoon had hit its peak, though the mermaids were not the mystical creatures Wendy had imagined; they were enchantingly beautiful but ruthless and cruel. They all seemed to be enamored with Peter, each shamefully smitten and even more blatantly flirtatious with the boy then herself. They treated him like a king, and somehow Pan had lost himself so much in their mist of seduction that he failed to care or even take notice of their obvious attempts to drag her into the water. When more of them surrounded her, and Wendy could no longer contain her balance on the surfaced rocks, she cried for Peter's help. But to her great surprise, the boy didn't come to her aid. Instead, he was overtaken with manic laughter. Now shocked and afraid, she desperately reached for one of the nearest stones. Taking it into her small grasp, she slammed the rock down with great force upon one of the hands that pulled on her gown.

The mermaid screamed in pain, causing Pan to rush upon Wendy, snatching the rock away before she could do it again. "Wendy, stop!" He yelled. She couldn't believe it. Feeling angry and confused, she watched as the cruel mermaids swam about calmly as if completely unaware that they had done anything wrong. When she shot a furious glare back at Peter, he laughed again. "You need not be so upset, Wendy. They were only having a little fun."

The mermaids nodded and giggled.

"Trying to drown me! You think their deplorable actions to be that of playful fun? My life is not a game! And I am not a toy that can just be..."

Peter suddenly clasped his hand over her mouth. "Shhh." Coming up in the distance was a small boat. "It's Hook!"

The mermaids quickly fled, for whether they were in this world or the next, a boat was always something they needed to avoid. Upon a closer glance, he saw her. "They have captured Tiger Lily." Taking his hand off Wendy, it seemed his attention had been completely diverted. Wendy didn't know who the Indian girl was or why Hook had taken her, but something about the way Pan looked at her made her heart ache. Peter cautiously followed behind them as they entered the cave. Wendy had little choice but to follow him into what appeared to be a giant stone skull, for otherwise she would be stranded in Mermaid Lagoon. Weighing the options, Wendy suddenly realized how afraid she really was and how much she wished she was at home. She had nearly been killed twice, and she couldn't shake the feeling that maybe Peter Pan wasn't the hero she had imagined. Entering through the open jaws of the cave, Peter flew Wendy up to the highest stone overlooking the entire rock.

Hook had tied up the Indian girl with rope and an anchor. He carefully placed her on a boulder below the tide, and in no time at all, half of her body was already submerged in water. "Tell me where I can find Pan's secret hiding place?!" He demanded. She looked at him confused, but Hook didn't need her to answer, for he and Smee had strategically rowed the boat all the way around the island. There was no doubt in his mind that Pan would learn of her location, but waiting in that cave swirling with purple smoke, something inside him snapped. Gripping his hook under the rope, he yanked her small body to his face screaming, "This is your last chance!" But both Tiger Lily and Hook knew he wasn't talking to her, he was speaking to himself. The thoughts bringing him to the brink of madness was suddenly shoved by the sound of a strange voice echoing within the cave's stone walls. Afraid it was all in his disturbed mind Hook asked, "Do you hear that, Mr. Smee?" Convinced it was some sort of evil spirit, Smee crumbled in a frantic sweat, leaving him to investigate the matter on his own. "Watch her," Hook ordered simply. Smee nodded slowly as he rapidly looked about the cave. Hook drew his sword and began to wander the shallow rocks, but upon further distance, the voice began to change to his own.

Leaving Wendy upon the high rock, Peter dove down closer to Smee. He brought his hat to his mouth and spoke again, "Mr. Smee!" The voice of Hook echoed.

Smee shook in fear because if there was anything that could make the sound of the captain's voice more terrifying, it was being in a dark cave with it echoing off the walls. "Captain? Is that you?"

Peter looked up at Wendy, sharing a small snickering giggle before he answered: "You must release the princess and take her back to her people!"

Smee stumbled in confusion. "But, Captain, I thought... Yes, sir," he said, lifting Tiger Lily out of the rising tide and placing her on the boat. But before he had successfully breached the cave, Hook stopped the small boat with his foot.

"Mr. Smee, just what the hell do you think you are doing?"

Smee tried to explain he was simply obeying his orders.

"I gave you no such order, you fool!" Hook screamed and kicked the boat violently back to the center of the cave in volcanic anger. But as Smee began to put Tiger Lily back into the water, Hook's voice commanded again in an unbelievable rage for Smee to let the Indian princess go, but this time, Hook heard it too. He suddenly understood what was happening. It wasn't that he was losing his mind, but instead had his own plan being played by another: Pan. While Smee shook in absolute panic and terror, Hook spotted Peter sitting arrogantly on top of a long rock overlooking the water below. He quietly crept towards him. Peter had his pointed green hat over his face to help his voice deepen. It was the perfect opportunity to strike, but there was one thing he hadn't counted on: Wendy was there too. She shouted Peter's name in warning, allowing Pan to quickly evade Hook's sword, and fly up into the air with a smile on his face. The boy was thrilled, for there was to be a battle at Skull Rock with three sets of eyes as their audience. Smee was rather excitable, cheering Hook on as he swiped his sword through the air, but Pan managed to always be just a little too out of reach for him. But while Pan was having fun, Wendy couldn't help but notice Peter's insufferable cheating. Hopping along the stones, Hook was forced to attempt proper footwork upon the most impossible of surfaces. Yet even as he was climbing upon wet rocks that were steep or even crumbling, Hook's performance was both brave and gallant. He was everything Wendy had ever heard of and more, but Peter behaved with bad form and dreadful underhanded arrogance. The battle had become excruciating for Wendy to watch. Fighting with nothing more than a small dagger, Peter flew around Hook, stabbing him in the back. The captain didn't stop, even as the boy stole his hat and blood was running down his exquisite red coat. But with one final act of conniving trickery, Pan lured Hook across a false illusion of a stoned path causing him to fall.

Barely holding on by his newly equipped hook, the captain was consumed with both extreme anger and fear. "You best be sure to kill me this time, Pan, because if you do not, I will use my hook to rip out your heart!"

Skull rock echoed with Pan's laughter then. As Hook began to sweat in an agonizing struggle, Peter did the one thing that brought everyone in that cave to utter horror. With a quick snap of his fingers, there was a new sound reverberating off the walls. "Do you hear that, Captain?" Pan asked mockingly.

It was the ticking of a clock. Hook looked down in terror as the giant hungry crocodile was now waiting with open jaws below. Peter lifted his foot above the sliding hook. Wendy begged him to stop as the crocodile jumped from the water, but it was too late. The hook finally fell from the crumbling rock. But as

Wendy gasped in horror, an unlikely hero came to the rescue: Mr. Smee.

Rowing the boat in full force, Smee managed to slam into the unsuspecting crocodile. The monster's charged, and the attack turning into a frenzy as Hook wrestled for his life. Smee panicked, turning his back with his hands over his ears to muffle the horrid screams of his captain when suddenly something caught his eye, something Hook had left on the boat. *Bang!* Smee fired a shot from the captain's pistol. The bullet splashed as it went through the dark water. Smee shook afraid, unsure what he had shot as Hook and the crocodile had become grisly chaos of water and blood. Smee's eyes searched desperately for his captain, but he didn't see anything.

The cave fell silent, as the echoing the sound of the ticking crocodile faded. The creature was gone, though whether the crocodile had died or just swam away, Smee wasn't sure. He reached his arms beneath the surface of the sparkling black water crying out Hook's name, but the tide was rising, and Smee had failed to notice Tiger Lily was starting to drown. Suddenly something came bursting through the bloody surface onto the boat; it was Hook.

"Row to the ship," Hook whispered weakly. Smee obeyed, taking both rows into his hands and urgently made his way out of the cave. Despite Hook's survival, Pan's boisterous cheers of victory came to a halt as Peter remembered Tiger Lily and rushed to her rescue. Wendy watched as Pan dove into the water and carried the exotic princess out of the cave in his arms, leaving her behind.

"Peter, wait! You have forgotten me!" She screamed, but it was no use. They were gone, leaving her to fly back to the island on her own. She sadly flapped her arms like broken wings, cautiously leaving her thoughts to her brothers and their safe return home, lest she falls from the sky and be lost within the bloody sea below.

CHAPTER THIRTY-THREE
A DARK TURN OF EVENTS

As Pan returned Tiger Lily to her tribe, he was shocked to find that Wendy's two younger brothers were not just alive, but enchanted. The chief changed their sight so that the children wouldn't see the gut-wrenching monsters that they truly were, but rather appeared as a normal Indian tribe that was healthy and heap glad.

Unable to speak the words of man, the chief used unknown gestures to communicate. John arrogantly translated as if completely fluent in the secret language. But in truth, it was only Pan, the master of such communication that understood what the chief really said. There was to be a momentary truce on the island between the lost boys and the Indians, due to the recent rescue of his daughter, but both parties knew such peace was not to last.

To show a sign of good faith, Pan whisked all light away from his lost island of mirrored trees. For one night, all that stood upon the island would stay in one place, and direction would exist. But Pan had his own motives. With his sunlight gone, Hook would surely think him absent from the realm, giving him a false sense of security. But not all sight would be fooled that night, for though the company of the Indians wasn't that of horror, Wendy was a young lady of high status and didn't find the redskin's actions to be that of adequate respect. She had heard stories of the savage race of Indians before. They were wild and strange.

Suddenly, as if they had heard her thoughts, one of the Indians' came over and gestured for her to go collect more firewood. Wendy was furious. If her parents knew about this... "No! How dare you!" Wendy shouted. It was time to go home, but as her eyes searched for Peter, what she found made her sick to her stomach. Sitting next to a clothed platform, Peter Pan was watching the young Indian princess dance. His face lit as if mystified by her charm. All this time, Wendy had been smitten with the fairy boy.

How could he love the Indian girl? It just doesn't make sense. For though she could see that Tiger Lily was beautiful, free-spirted, and deathly loyal to him, Wendy's past encounters of Peter simply didn't seem to mirror this one at all. In fact, she didn't like the boy she had come to know on the island. *He had always been so sweet and charming before. He had wooed her heart the way a prince behaved in her stories. Every time he had visited me, he was just so romantic. Why did he seem so different now? Why did he bring me here?* Struggling with her thoughts, Wendy tried to reflect on their previous encounters in the nursery, trying to make sense of it all. *Had his flirtation been all in her head?* But as Wendy thought about it, she suddenly realized she couldn't remember the appearance of the nursery. Shaking her head in confusion, she thought about her home: the rooms, the halls, the doors, the walls, they were all just *gone.*

She couldn't remember any of it. She tried to think of Nana, her sweet dog that had been there since she was a baby, but somehow, she couldn't picture her. Wendy suddenly laughed, the way one does when they can't believe the absurdity of a situation. Trying to calm herself down, she told herself that she was just tired and distressed. She went to find her brothers for answers. No doubt they could bring her back to her senses and they could all go home.

As Hook lay in bed exhausted after Smee had finished tended to his many flesh wounds, both Smee and Catcher were sound asleep within his room, leaving Hook alone with the view from his window and the two twinkling stars in the blue sky.

Whispering weakly, he spoke: "I know the second star on the right is for him, but I believe now that the first star up there is for you. If it is, I hope that you can hear me. I need you, Ainsel. I feel defeated. I am lost in a fog full of fear and anger. I know you left in fear of my vengeful actions and that of my soul, but please hear me now, my soul is never gone if I can feel you. Please know that I will be sorry for the rest of my miserable life for causing you pain, but you must understand, without one's destiny, life simply does not matter. This place is poisoning my mind. I can feel it bringing me back to my childhood; my mind free to play and dream again. My sanity is wandering each dusty corridor of my memories trying to find the one door that remains open. I fear what will happen once I enter the one room of nightmares where the vivid memory I shall never be rid of lives. I can still see her face- the image of true horror that never quite left me. My vengeful heart is what made me what I am today, but please don't think me the villain. I just wish it would stop. Please, Ainsel, help me make it stop." With no answer, Hook cried himself to sleep that night, dreaming of a grand storm. But just as Hook had wished, a spark of bright blue did come through the night sky of Neverland- and it *wasn't* lightning.

It was both the shortest and the longest night there had ever been in Neverland and no one was more eager for it to end than Wendy Darling. After leaving the Indian camp, the Darlings followed the lost boys to their hideout in the thicket. Wendy found it odd how after such an exciting evening, her brothers had exhausted themselves, but the lost boys seemed to have lost no source of energy. Feeling uncomfortable and afraid, she looked for somewhere that her tired brothers could sleep, but there were no beds.

"Wendy! Wendy! I'm hungry. Please get me some food." Little Michael cried. It was then that she realized that she hadn't seen a single person eat or drink on the island.

"Yes, Wendy, and I would very much like a cup of tea myself," said John.

She looked to Peter for an answer, but all she got was a crooked smile that twisted her stomach. John was too self-involved to notice any threatening nature, but Wendy didn't hold it against him, for the Darlings had lived a very safe and comfortable life without even a shred of danger before now. Wendy had always found their life in London boring. Every day of her privileged respectable life had lacked the excitement and fantasy of her stories. That is- until she met Peter Pan. But she learned the hard way that in every great story, there lies betrayal, deceit, and true love. And it seemed now that Peter had shown her just that. He was indeed a boy in love, but not with her. She didn't know why he had really brought her to Neverland, but she did know that it was time for she and her brothers to leave. To get their minds off their hunger and thirst, she simply and quietly gathered nearby materials to make a suitable bed for them. "It's been a long night; you both must get some sleep. We will be going home in the morning," she said in a calm nurturing tone, so as not to alarm them.

Like most toddlers of his age, Michael whined and fought in childish temperament. John however was rather eager and willing to get back to their finer lodgings and his private studies. Though he hadn't known the cause for his sister's sudden change in mood, he was quite used to his sister's more authoritative role. His father had always proved it was but a gentlemen's duty to be in all manner agreeable to a lady, and though his sister had on certain occasions

377

behaved improper, he had never ceased to see her as such. "Very well then," John said politely.

But Pan flew into a burst of rage. "No, you will not go home!"

Wendy rapidly turned to him in shock and fear. "Why do you say such things, Peter?" She asked, but no words of comfort came from his lips, only a flicker of evil that sparkled in his eye. Wendy began to tremble, for though Neverland had proved to be full of many dangers, she had not thought to be kept prisoner here. "Peter, surely you do not mean to kept us here forever. What about our parents? Our mother will be greatly worried."

"What is mother?" Michael asked sweetly. John was normally quick to answer any spoken question arrogantly, but in this case, he was struck with a rather odd void.

Wendy turned to her baby brother with sadness. "Michael, our mother is someone who loves and cares for us above all others. Have you forgotten everything?" The question had scared the little boy to tears. "Oh, Michael, I am sorry. Do not worry," she whispered and picked him up into her arms. He wrapped his tiny legs around her and laid his head upon her shoulders. It was then that Wendy realized she had to be brave. She had brought them into this danger, and it was up to her to get them out. "Peter Pan, we are leaving for London this instant, and you can do nothing to stop us!" She said sternly. "Come along, John. We are going home!"

John nodded and followed quietly as she walked out of the tree house carrying little Michael still in her arms.

CHAPTER THIRTY-FOUR

DESPERATE SOUND OF A BELL

Hook awoke to the sudden sound of ringing bells. Springing from his bed, he expected it to be Ainsel in an answer to his desperate plea... only to find there was a little green pixie standing upon his window ceil. Rushing upon her, quickly placing his hook's iron blade at her throat he spoke, "You must be incredibly brave coming here alone."

Tinker Bell raised her burning chin above his iron blade, glaring at him intensely.

Gazing into her cruel dark eyes, Hook couldn't deny his sudden interest in her dangerous query. Pulling away his hook with an impressed chuckle he asked, "So what do I owe this unexpected visit of Pan's own fairy?" His words struck her like poisoned arrows to the heart. The sudden mark of distressed pain and heartbreak came across her small face. Hook wasn't one to put it past a fairy to try to trick him, but it wasn't fae behavior to express weakness in such a way. "Have I said something that upset you?"

She nodded.

"I see. Well then... my apologies, my dear, though I fail to understand my offense. Is such sadness due to my mention of Pan?"

Again, Tink nodded.

"And when I said Pan's fairy, I take by your reaction that you are no longer?"

A tear fell from Tink's eyes as she nodded again.

"Interesting, but why come to me about it? Do you seek my pardon now that you no longer belong to my enemy?"

This time Tink shook her head as if offended.

"Then why may I ask are you here, Ms. Bell?"

It was then that Tink made a rather rude impersonation of a prissy girl, using her dust to materialize the image of a long gown and a bow on the back of her head. Hook didn't understand the small pixie as well as Pan, but as he watched her movements and frustration, he remembered the new young girl amongst the three new children he had seen upon Pan's last arrival.

Overwhelmed with her theatrical jealousy and anger, Hook raised his hand to stop her. "Alright, I believe I understand. You want this girl to be gone, but correct me if I am wrong here... how can a girl who is destined to lose her soul be any threat of yours?"

Tink shook her head, glowing red with fury.

Hook chuckled as he suddenly understood, "Ah, so the purpose of your mission emerges. Am I to understand you are here to seek my help?"

Tink looked up into his eyes, and with a serious and direct glare, she nodded.

Hook laughed at the thought. "I would rather lose my other hand than help you!"

But to his great surprise, the small pixie did not look the least distressed by his immediate rejection. In all honesty, he had rather hoped she would lash out in anger, giving him indisputable cause to strike her down dead. But instead, she just stared at him, slowly raising her tiny hand and pointing her finger to his nose in a scolding manner. Ringing bells filled the air as she told him: "You *will* do it."

Hook scoffed, disgusted at her arrogant certainty. Leaning in closely, he responded harshly: "Let me be plain, Ms. Bell- why in the hell would I?"

It was then that Tinker Bell did something that made him cringe. With a wicked smile, the Green Fairy snapped her tiny fingers. Suddenly, a long glowing parchment appeared through a sparkling green mist of pixie dust.

Hook was furious, "I do not make deals with fairies!"

But the Green Fairy merely raised a sly eyebrow before bringing the fine print closer to his eyes.

He couldn't deny his curiosity, for there was only one thing she could offer that he would want: Pan's beating heart on a plate. He snatched the glowing parchment from her hand and made his way over to his desk, reached for his glasses, and took a closer glance at her proposal. As he reached the bottom of the page, he felt enraged. "You offer the healed return of my hand in exchange for the malevolent task of the kidnapping and cold-blooded murder of three innocent children!" Hook tore the parchment in half. "I do not kill the innocent! What I kill are evil monsters like you!"

Tink twisted her face in annoyance, causing him to charge at her, but just as he raised his hook high above his head ready to slice her apart, a mist of sparkling dust appeared before him in the form of three small children. The glittering figures cried, begging for food and drink, each whimpering weakly for their parents- for their *mother*. The last desperate plea caused him to slowly drop his hook. He suddenly understood. If he did nothing, it would be the cruel fate of Neverland that would kill them.

Taking in a small puff of purple smoke, Hook could finally begin to think straight, and through such clarity, he was struck with an idea. "Allow me to make you a counteroffer, Ms. Bell. Tell me where Pan's hideout is, and I will take the three children under my charge- where I will take them back to my world and return them safely to their home."

Tinker Bell squinted at him suspiciously before shaking her head.

But before she could finish her chiming movements, Hook answered the pressing question for such a bargain. "And in return, I want you to restore the Piccaninny tribe back to their human forms with all of their souls safely and sanely intact. Freely untie them from this realm and send them back to their land in the mortal world. That is my offer! Take it or get the hell off my ship!"

Tinker Bell was stunned. Looking to the glittering mist, the three forms conformed to one. It was a question that given the wrong answer would bring both she and Pan great pain. The sparkling form slowly came into the form of a young Indian girl.

Hook nodded, "Yes, I mean Tiger Lily as well. After all, I may leave this wretched island defeated in battle, but I will take great pleasure knowing that I caused my loathed enemy the worst pain there is. For whether you exist in this realm or the next- a broken heart is by far the cruelest fate for one that must live forever. And as Tiger Lily grows old having had her own children and grandchildren, she will have forgotten all about him. I will die one day a happy man with he and I both knowing that it was I, Captain James Hook, that took everything from him!"

A tear fell from the Green Fairy's eyes, but ultimately, it was her head and not her heart that agreed. She would rather Pan live on broken hearted, then for both of them to die the eternal death at the hands of the Elders. At that, another glowing parchment appeared, Hook took up a feathered pen dipped in fresh black ink, but before he could sign his name upon the page... Tink suddenly remembered something. Ringing in rapid alarm, she snapped her fingers together, bringing another line of fine print upon the bargain. Hook squinted his eyes and read the words aloud, "I, James Hook, am not to lay a finger or a *hook-* on Peter Pan." Hook's eyes lifted from the words to the black eyes of the pixie, and with a sinister smile, he slid the feather's final mark elegantly across the page. "We have an accord," he whispered, suddenly snatching the small pixie within his hand and slamming her into an iron lantern above his desk. "I am sorry, Ms. Bell, but as I said, I will be taking everything he loves and that includes you! The deal is struck, though I must say that you did not choose the words of your last condition wisely."

CHAPTER THIRTY-FIVE
AN UNLIKELY HERO

"They'll be back." Peter chuckled to himself. After all, how did they expect to get home on their own. The very idea made Pan laugh. Swinging upon a hammock hanging high inside the hidden tree, he played his magical pipes. His music coursed through the night air like a menacing lullaby to be heard by all of Neverland. Hook's new prisoner had kept her end of the bargain, there was a marked map laid upon the captain's desk with the markings of two tiny footprints leading towards a large tree upon the island. It was the perfect time to act, for as long as the moon remained in the sky, the land would remain still and everything upon it could be tracked and therefore could be found. Hook assembled his men and descended upon the dark path into the woods. When the crew made their way deeper into the thicket, one of the men noticed a trail of small footprints upon the ground. A soft whistle into the air caught Hook's immediate attention. Upon closer examination, it became clear that not only were the children not in the given direction of the hidden tree, but unlike the barefoot tracks of the lost boys- these tracks were made by two sets of small defined shoes, and one set of tiny clothed footprints. It was them: the three children, and though Pan was not one to travel on land- the noticeable urgent pacing of the tracks struck Hook as a sign of attempted escape. Pan had been clever disguising his presence on the island with all evidence to the contrary, but Hook was not a foolish man. Though his eyesight had never been as perceptive as some, his hearing was impeccable. The faint sound of musical pipes proved that Pan was not only in this realm, but he wasn't with his three latest conquest. Hook and his men quietly followed the tiny tracks, and soon it was the faint cry of little Michael that brought them to their location. Sneaking up behind them, each of the children were suddenly grabbed and silenced. With a large hand over each of their mouths, none of the three children were able to shout for help, though Wendy privately knew that Peter wouldn't have come if they had. The Darlings were taken aboard the small boat where Smee was waiting to row them to the ship. Bound and gagged until safely secured below deck, the three children were each sat and tied to three tall chairs. They each wiggled in fright until the sudden sound of large boot steps came across the floor. The tall presence stood behind them, causing their hearts to pound hard and fast within their chest. None were able to move or see this figure, but they knew who it was. It was the very man they had all heard about in England. He was the most feared captain in all the world... Hook.

"You must accept my most sincere apologies children. It was not my wish to capture you in such a way, but I fear I had no choice in the matter. Strictly business, I assure you. But alas, please believe me when I say that you are safe, and I have only brought you here so that I can take you home. Though I fear I must keep you bound, you must understand that I am doing so for your own safety. I am James Hook, the captain of the Jolly Roger, and this is Mr. Smee, my first mate and personal physician. Please allow him to attend to any reasonable desire or request that you may have whilst you are here on my ship. I do have plenty of food and drink aboard," he said politely as Smee stepped out in front of them. Wendy's eyes slowly raised upon the two men before her. Hook was tall, dark, and fierce. His posture was perfectly symmetrical with his poise and rich fashion. He was more magnificent than the Darlings had ever imagined. But the odd man that stood shaking next to him appeared short and unbearably anxious. His clothes were ratty and torn, and while most pirates were known for their dirty appearance... this little man didn't look like a pirate at all. Wendy's thoughts were suddenly interrupted as Hook spoke again: "You are safe children. It is my sincere hope to make your stay on my ship as comfortable as possible. Mr. Smee is going to remove the cloth from your mouths now, though I urge you to remain quiet. Do not scream or cry for help, for I assure you that while I mean you no harm, if Peter Pan finds you- all of you *will* die."

Each of the children nodded in unison, and with a clear understanding, Mr. Smee released each of their gags from their face. Just as promised, none of the children screamed, though whether they had believed him or not, Hook did not know, but he had a few questions for the young girl that had made this all possible.

"What is your name, my dear?"

"I am Wendy Moi-... Wendy is enough," she answered in a shaky voice.

Hook chuckled at her reluctant reply. "I see. I suppose it is for the best. Names are a funny business where we are from. My mother told me once to keep such a thing to myself."

She craned her head curiously. "Why?"

He smiled and stepped closer towards her chair. "It was one of the fairy rules she told me when I was a young child."

Wendy felt even more confused. "That is ridiculous, for I myself have read many books, sir, and yet I have never seen or heard of such rules."

"I liked books growing up as well. I inherited my mother's books after she died, though I fear I only have one left."

She suddenly felt awful. She had only thought of her parent's death once, after a horrible nightmare. But such an idea seemed too dark and tragic for her already imaginative mind. "How did she die?" The words fell out of her mouth as if beyond her control.

Hook hadn't spoken of it in years, nor did he ever want to again, but it seemed the truth of the matter might help the girl understand the gravity of their dangerous situation. "She was killed by a fairy."

The words were difficult for her to swallow, though no part of her could deny the truth of it. Her mind suddenly flashed back to Pan's fairy that tried to kill her upon her arrival. Though her mind was swarmed with questions, she didn't say another word. After all, how could he really know what she so desperately needed to hear: *why had Peter Pan brought her here?*

The sound of the door behind them creaked open, and a raspy voice whispered something to the small doctor across the room.

The doctor nodded. "Captain, the cook has prepared a meal for the little ones as you requested. Should I have them brought to your table, sir?"

"Yes," Hook replied. All three of the children were moved to his private dining quarters, where they each ate quietly. Now with a warm meal and hot tea filling their stomach, all three of the children were suddenly feeling very sedated. Michael had almost fallen from his chair from exhaustion. Hook chuckled; it was all kind of precious really. He hadn't ever really spent time with kids, not even when he was one himself, but somehow these three children brought something out in him he never knew existed. They were innocents, and he suddenly felt intensely protective over them. "Mr. Smee take the children to your chambers. They will sleep there tonight. You will go below deck with the rest of the crew."

"Aye aye, sir," Smee replied with his hand to his forehead. Smee's chambers were by no means as nice as the captain's, but it was pleasant enough. It was large and very tidy. In truth, the space didn't look very lived in, for Smee hadn't spent very much time in the room at all. Wendy lay next to her two brothers on the bed. Little Michael lay in the middle. Snuggled under the thick blanket, the Darlings fell peacefully asleep. They may have been on a dangerous island within another realm beyond the farthest reach of their home and parents, but somehow, they felt safe. After all, they were aboard the most famous pirate ship known to man, and under the sworn protection of the most fearsome captain in all the world.

Lost in a deep sleep, Wendy suddenly awoke to a strange wet sensation on her face. It was a disturbance she had awoken to many times before. It was the feeling of a dog licking her face. "Nana, stop that," she whispered. But as she opened her eyes, she realized it was not nana that hovered panting above her, but an entirely new dog. "Oh. Down, boy. Down."

The dog jumped down from the bed, still looking at her from the floor. Wendy sat up, still lost in a sleepy haze, she suddenly remembered exactly where she was. The room was dark, and she could see the full moon through a nearby window, it was still night. The ship was quiet, but as she looked towards the door, she could see an orange light flickering from behind the cracked open door. Wendy slowly stepped down from the bed as to not wake her brothers. Approaching the sweet dog, she reached out her hand to pet him when suddenly he bolted. "Wait, come back. I am not going to hurt you!" She exclaimed in a loud whisper. But the dog went through the thin opening of the door. "Please wait," she said again following him out of the open door into the light.

When she stepped into the hallway, she could hear the soft pitter patter of the dog's feet going around the corner. As she came around, lightly balancing upon the tips of her toes, she spotted the long fur of the dog's tail enter another open door. Once the dog entered, she heard a ringing bell. It sounded chillingly familiar somehow, and it seemed to call her forward. Overwhelmed with curiosity, Wendy slowly peeked her head inside. Across the room, above a finely crafted desk was Tinker Bell in a dark metal lantern.

Hook looked up as he suddenly heard a quiet gasp. "Who goes there?" He asked harshly, rushing towards the door. Wendy froze as she came face to face with the captain. "What are you doing in here, child? I thought you were all asleep. Is something wrong?"

"I- I am sorry, sir. The dog woke me, and I followed it in here," she spoke unable to take her eyes off the prisoner in his room.

"I see. Well since you are awake, would you like to come in?"

Wendy couldn't move. She had not seen the small pixie since the attempt on her life, but something about the way her black eyes stared at her left her terrified.

Hook could see the fear painted across her face, "You needn't be afraid, my dear. She is imprisoned by iron. Though she may wish it, she cannot harm you. Come in," he said, reaching out his hand to guide her through the doorway. Still, it seemed her mind was beset by too many horrors to truly hear him.

Hook suddenly realized what was wrong. She had been in Neverland too long, and her imagination was not only turning dark, but it was consuming her. It was true, Wendy could no longer fathom a happy thought. It was as if her dreams had stolen the last of her memories of home, and now all she could see or hear were the creatures of Neverland. Each of her thoughts were more terrifying than the last: the mermaids dragging her below the sparkling sea, the lost boys shooting her with poisoned arrows, and with every picture painted by her own blood and dying breath was echoed by the psychotic laughter of the fairy boy she thought loved her.

Then suddenly, a miracle happened. Hook interrupted her manic thoughts. "Take a breath of this. You will feel better," he said calmly as he handed her the chief's pipe.

Wendy looked at it utterly confused. "What does it do, sir?"

"A purple smoke will take away the nightmares that haunt you."

She hesitated for a moment. "My father told me something once about smoking, though I fear I do not remember what it was."

Hook gave her a pitying smile. "Should your father be cross, I shall be the one to answer for it. Please, take it."

Wendy did as she was told. And with a small choking inhale, the evil thoughts that suffused her came out through her mouth. Purple smoked figures of mermaids, the lost boys, and the murderous pixie came through the air. She watched blushing in both wonder and embarrassment.

"It is alright, my dear. To have ones fears out in the open can feel rather exposing, but do not feel alone- for we all have them," he said as he took a puff himself. As he exhaled, the figure of another fairy came into the room. "See?"

It was nice. Wendy hadn't ever known adults share such things. She had rather believed them to all be fearless, but he was the most ruthless pirate across all the seven seas, and he had just shown her his truest fear. Though Wendy wasn't sure who the fairy was that haunted him- she had a good idea why.

"Sit down, child," he said as he pulled out two chairs across the room from the furious Green Fairy. But now with her mind cleared and her manner unashamed, Wendy bravely sat down to talk with the arch-nemesis of Peter Pan. "Would you like some tea?"

Wendy nodded, in truth the smoke had made her throat scratchy and dry. As he poured her a cup, her eyes glanced upon Tinker Bell again. "May I ask, sir, why do you have Pan's fairy?"

Hook wasn't used to the ways and manner of how to speak to children, and while he never saw the truth as harmful, he answered her carefully: "She came to me to make a bargain... It is what fairies do, though not all are as forth coming as she was."

Wendy was stunned. *What did she come to him for? And if they did make a bargain, why was she imprisoned here?* "May I ask what it was?"

Hook scrunched his lips crookedly, unsure if he should say. "Well to be rather frank, miss. She sought my help in the hopes that I would be your family's executioner. Though I do not know exactly why, for the Green Fairy lacks verbal communication. She was quite desperate to be rid of you."

Wendy gasped, suddenly hoping for the magical pipe again.

Hook could see he had scared her and quickly spoke again: "Do not fear, child. I made no such bargain. For unlike her kind, I do not kill innocent children. Though I did not know of your rather strange circumstances here, once I knew I could save you- I changed the bargain. Though I would normally rather die than make a deal with a fairy, it was one that could save many lives and only destroy one."

Wendy felt like she had swallowed a sharp piece of glass. "You mean to destroy Peter?"

Tinker Bell started to buzz. Green flashes began to glow within the swinging lantern, and inside it she was furiously ringing like a rapidly rung bell.

It was then that Wendy had another thought. "Why do you hate him? Why do you hate Peter Pan?" It was the kind of question that only a child was brave enough to ask, and she was the only child that he would give such an answer.

"I have known Peter since he was just a boy. We were brought up in the same orphanage together."

Wendy was shocked. "I do not understand. Peter Pan was human once?"

Hook chuckled. "Oh yes, I am younger than him if you can believe it."

She scarcely could. "What was he like?" She asked, her mind filling with more questions.

"He wasn't much different. He was born a mischievous spirit... I remember the first moment we met, though I cannot remember my life before him. I think you'll find that even when Pan isn't there- his spirit never quite leaves you."

Wendy smiled at his rather dark sentiment. "Were you ever friends?"

Whatever answer she had hoped to hear was instantly crushed under the weight of pain and hate upon Hook's face as he shook his head. "No, Wendy, we were never friends. We have always been enemies. He was a bully, a trickster, and he was and forever will be an evil soul."

She suddenly felt awful. "Oh. But how did he become a..."

– "A fairy?" Hook interrupted.

Wendy nodded.

Hook let out a sigh of regret. "The world can blame me for that. I brought the power of fae into his life in hopes they would destroy him, but Peter was clever. He made a deal with a fairy; I imagine the same one that you see above my desk right there and made an exchange for the powers of the fae." His voice began to break with sincere regret.

"What did he *exchange*?" She asked though she intensely feared to hear the answer.

Hook cleared his throat, unsure of how to say what he was about to say: "Well, you see... Peter knew that the price for such a bargain with a fairy could only be met with one thing. It is the thing that the fae are always after- a soul. But Peter was too cunning, and beyond all expectations, he came up with a devious idea. Instead of offering his own soul, he would use his new powers to do their bidding. He would spend his immortal life stealing the souls of others."

Wendy suddenly couldn't breathe. Tears welled in her eyes, each falling in long shiny streaks down her flushed cheeks. Choking on her soft sobs, she suddenly understood. "That is why you have been trying to...."

Hook reached out his hand and wiped her tears from her tiny face. "Yes, I have tried to kill him, and I am sorry to say that I have failed. But I will save you and your brothers, along with the tortured lives of the Indian tribe. I will take you home where you and your family will be safe," he said, smiling at her. He truly believed that all of her questions had been properly answered, but the moment was far from over.

Wendy was suddenly struck with more terror than ever before. "How?"

"How what my dear?"

"How will my family be safe? He knows where I live. What if he comes back?"

The room was suddenly filled with the sound of chiming bells. Hook didn't have to look back to know what it was. Tinker Bell was laughing. It seemed she wasn't the only one that hadn't been completely thorough on the bargain. It was true, Pan could simply go after her family again. The simple fact was that as long as he was alive, he would always be a monster. Wendy began to cry harder, and it was enough to break Hook's heart. It was then as he looked into her sad little eyes and the reminiscence of all he had shared with her, that he realized he had lost sight of his true purpose. It wasn't to hurt Pan- it was to *end* him. "You are right, child. Do not weep, for I will make it

398

right, I promise," he said with a new redefined tone. Wendy looked up as he stood up from his chair. "Mr. Smee!" Hook shouted.

Instantly, the thudding of rapid footsteps came towards the room. Smee burst through the door in his usual fright. "Yes, sir?"

Hook looked down at Wendy and then to the lantern. With his deepest tone of command, he declared for all to hear: "Wake the crew! Tonight, I kill Peter Pan!"

As Tink looked about the crowding of Hook's crew within his chambers, she listened intently to each of the men's deviant plan to destroy her dearest friend. The more she heard, the more she felt frantically ill. She had made Hook promise not to touch Pan, but there was absolutely nothing she could do to stop one of his crew. And while Hook knew it would be easy enough to give such a deadly charge to one of his more ruthless mates, the chance of magical interference was a risk he just couldn't take. He had only one shot. For once light shines across the Lost Island again, the boy would be all but impossible to find. No, this had to be now, and it had to be him to do it. *But how?* The excited voices around him clouded into a distant blur as Hook thought of his options.

"No, men! For though I am honored, Pan must be killed by me! Now, there are many weapons upon this ship, but I fear using a sword or even a pistol might be too close and could be slyly mis-construed as death by my hand. Besides, my history of late has proved that confronting Pan directly gives him the chance of escape by flight or by other means of magic. Yes, it must be a surprise- an *inescapable* surprise. There has to be a way!"

The crew continued to yell out their own colorful ways of murder, but all were deaf to what Hook needed until a sudden tiny polite cough came from underneath the towering crew that hovered over the table. It was Wendy. She stood up from her chair to stand amongst them. The crew went silent, all were rather stunned and dismayed at her blatantly rude interruption. After all, like most pirates, they believed that a lady's presence on board was bad luck... but this was no *ordinary* girl.

Finally, after an awkward pausing stare, one of the crew spoke: "Look here, little girl, one'd have to be blind and deaf to not see where you come from in our world, but you have no rank on this ship, and you got no right to speak among the likes of us."

In truth her actions were a great surprise to herself as well. But the purple smoke had a rather strong effect on her fear, and any restrictions that had been controlled by them. She had stood by them bravely only to be scolded and thrown back down. The man was right, in London she may come from a high name, but here in Neverland on Captain Hook's ship- she was nothing. But as Wendy slowly began to sink back into her chair, the man that had scolded her so, suddenly hit the floor. Wendy gasped as she saw that it was Hook that had come up and struck him on the head. The man was still conscious, though suddenly deathly afraid. "How dare you speak to my guest like that!" Hook shouted, bending over to look the swollen pirate in his bloody face.

"But, Captain, she is just a *girl*," the pirate said.

Hook kicked him. "Feel lucky for that, you fool, for the matter of forgiveness you require to keep your miserable life is for her to decide. Get up and apologize to the young lady this instant!" Hook demanded. The battered pirate rose from the floor, while all the others stood silently. It was then, in front of the entire crew that one pirate begged for a young girl's forgiveness.

Wendy of course did forgive him, just as Hook had expected her to. The punishment wasn't the point, but rather the statement. And as the intense moment simmered, it was clear that not a single man on board would dare speak ill of Wendy or her family again.

"I also apologize for such a rude interruption, my dear. What was it you were going to say? We would all love to hear it. Wouldn't we men?" Hook asked suggestively. All the crew agreed in unison, the man that was still bleeding from his head was more energetic than the rest. Hook was glad to see his words and actions had comforted her, though like most adults, he wasn't truly prepared to hear anything of substance from the child; it was merely the common act of humoring a young one's thought or idea.

But Wendy was about to surprise everyone within the room. With a tiny sweet voice, she spoke faintly: "The raid of the Walrus."

Hook felt suddenly stirred. "Pardon me, miss. What did you say?"

Wendy cleared her throat, collecting her bravery and calm breath as she looked up into his eyes. "I speak of the weapon used to win one of your many glorious battles- a bomb."

Hook remembered the battle well. It was a victory he had shared with his father, Blackbeard. A siege to overtake Long John Silver's ship had been won with the powerful blow of a bomb, though in this moment it felt as if he himself had just been suddenly hit by one. "How do you know of this?"

"As I told you before, sir, I am very fond of stories. My brothers and I cherished yours above all others. After our studies, when we were given our time of play in the nursery, we loved nothing more than to pretend we were a part of your crew. It was John that enjoyed pretending to be you. Silly really, I know, but we only wished..."

Hook whipped up his hand to silence her. "Do not ever say that word in front of a fairy, for they will try to use it against you. Do you understand?"

Wendy nodded, trying hard not to look at Tinker Bell, and failing.

Hook began to pace the floor of his chambers feeling overwhelmed. "Everyone out!" He shouted. Each of the men began to leave through the door, "Except you, Mr. Smee! You stay!"

The door shut with only Smee standing behind it. "Yes, Captain," Smee said shaking. Wendy still sat at the table, unsure of what would happen or be said next.

"Wendy, how often did you play these games?" Hook asked.

She thought for a moment; her memories fading in a hazy blur. "We played all the time. The story of the Walrus just came to me when I wasn't looking for it. I find that whenever I try to remember anything about my life at home, all I can see clearly are my memories of Peter."

The very thought of it all was suspicious to Hook. "May I ask what you were doing when you first met Peter?"

Wendy suddenly couldn't think straight, "I don't..."

Growing uneasy and crawling with impatience, Hook cracked, "Wendy?!" His commanding voice shook her to her core.

"I- I do not remember."

Hook could see she was scared and confused, but he was beyond the point of coddling. "Well, what do you remember?"

She closed her eyes. She thought as hard as she could; her mind desperately racing through the thick fog that clouded the doors to all her memories. But the more she stretched her efforts, the more things seemed completely lost; the way one feels when waking from a dream and entering reality. Now that she was forced to think about it, the more the memories of Peter no longer seemed to make any sense. "I am sorry, but all I can remember is playing with my brothers in the nursery. We were all pretending to be pirates- playing out my stories about you. My brothers love to hear me tell stories. Then suddenly, I started to tell them stories about Peter Pan. He would come to visit me at night, through the open window. But he was different then. He was charming and sweet."

Hook scoffed. "Charming and sweet? Doesn't sound like the Peter I know at all."

Wendy covered her face, sobbing into her hands. "It is all so strange. The night he came to get his shadow, he behaved so differently."

This time Smee popped his head up. "But, Captain, I do not understand. If she made a deal with Pan and he brought her to the island, why hasn't he taken her soul?" It was the question on everyone's mind, and Smee was just drunk enough to ask it out loud.

"Why did he bring you and your brothers to Neverland, Wendy?" Hook asked.

"Well, when I told him that I couldn't tell stories about him anymore because I had to grow up, Peter suddenly became quite insistent that I come with him," she replied.

"What about the boys?" Smee asked.

"I regret to say that it was my idea to bring my brothers," Wendy answered sadly.

Hook shook his head still frustrated. "But why would you do that? Most of the children he takes are enchanted and have no choice. You are telling us that you came here of your own free will? Why?"

"Because he made me believe that he *loved* me! I thought he would take me on an adventure, and we would have that kind of love that ends in happily ever after like in all my stories. Instead, I get here, and everyone tries to kill me! And instead of saving me like I believed he would, Peter treated it all like some sort of twisted game. And Tiger Lily..." Wendy's sobbing voice had become completely muffled by her hands.

Hook sat down to console her. "Alright, come now, my dear. Yes, he tricked you. It is what the fae do, and it is what *he* does best. But it is not the worst thing that could have happened. I know that you are feeling spurned and hurt right now, but this could have been far worse. Though I must ask, why did Peter say he wanted to bring you? It was not for love, because as we all now know- Peter loves Tiger Lily, so if it wasn't for your soul, then why?"

Wendy thought for a second. "Well, he said he loved my stories about him. He told me I was the one, and that he needed me to come to Neverland with him so that my stories about him could become real."

Hook nodded, finally understanding. "Like your stories about me?"

Wendy nodded.

The captain suddenly burst with laughter, startling both Wendy and Smee. "That pathetic fool! And your brothers? How did has he treated them?"

"Oh, well I do not know really. We have been separated for almost all of the time that we have been here."

"Why?" Hook asked in suspicion.

Wendy shrugged. "I hadn't really thought about it before. It all seemed quite innocent enough."

But Hook rapidly raised his hand to silence her. "Shhh, I was not asking you, my dear. I was asking her!" He shouted pointing at the green pixie. But Tinker Bell crossed her arms and turned her back to him. "You will answer me, fairy, or so help me I will tear you apart- limb by limb! Do not tempt me!"

Tinker Bell believed him. She turned to face him slowly and with a red face and with dramatic movements, she filled the lantern with sparkling green dust. Through it all, Tink told Hook of Pan's plan to have the boys killed.

"Kill them! How?" Hook asked inquisitively.

It was then that with a wicked smile on her face and eyes locked with Wendy's that she brought her hand to her mouth and did the dance of the Indians.

Wendy gasped in horror. "Why would the Indian tribe kill my sweet brothers?"

But Tinker Bell just rolled her eyes, annoyed at the girl's ignorance.

"Ah, I see. Pan thought or rather expected the wendigo to kill the boys, taking them as merely more lost boys. Clever Peter- clever."

Wendy was terribly confused. "Wendigo? What is a wendigo?"

Hook shook his head and smiled as he gazed out the window. There was no smoke from their fire in the night air above the trees as it had always been before. "It is no matter now, they are free."

Still, Wendy felt overwhelmed. There were still too many questions, and it seemed that every answer she was given only brought about another question. But the answer she so desperately sought above all others remained a mystery, though it seemed she was the only one left who did not know the key. And while she could live with forever being in the dark with all the others... there was one she just couldn't simply let go. "Please, sir, I need to know. Why did Peter Pan bring me here?"

Hook turned away from the window and with a single glance at the sadness in her eyes, he told her the truth. "Peter brought you here to use you to gain fame back in our world. I am certain he had every intention of returning you to London, though without even the faintest memory of your family- not even your brothers. With everyone that holds any sort of importance in your life gone, you would be at his disposal. Coming to Neverland and seeing the magic for yourself made it more real than anything you could possibly imagine... that's what Pan has always wanted, and he was willing to deceive you and destroy all you love and care for to get it."

Wendy stood from her chair in a gasp. "That is why he brought me? So, all those times... he tricked me. He never loved me at all! It is no wonder he found my smitten girlish behavior so funny. I feel so cheated- so used. I have nearly died three times, I almost got my brothers killed, and all the while watching the boy that I thought loved me- prove to love another right in front of my own eyes. And through it all, after everything I have endured, I find out it was all for the sake of his fame. You were right, Captain Hook, he is evil!"

He smiled at the young girl. As if he wasn't already especially fond of her, she goes and sings his favorite song. "Well, do not fret now, my dear child, for I believe I have decided to use your rather ingenious idea. I shall kill Peter Pan with a bomb, and rest assured he will never do this to anyone ever again," he declared. Wendy smiled as Hook clapped his hands. "Good, then let's get to it. Smee, get the crew to bring me a bomb from below deck! Now!"

Smee raced out of the room screaming his usual: "Aye aye, sir," as he ran down below deck with his hand still saluting at his forehead. Once the bomb was ready, three of the men carefully placed it into a small box and wrapped up in netting and rope.

Wendy stood up. "No, it cannot look like that. If Pan thinks that the box came from a pirate, then he will suspect foul play and the plan will fail. The box must look like it is from someone else. Here..." Wendy said, reaching her arms out for the box. Taking her sash from around her dress, she perfectly tied the baby blue silk around the box. But Wendy had a final touch of her very own. On a small parchment she wrote the words:

To Peter.

With love, Wendy

She folded the paper and slid it carefully under the fancy blue bow. Hook wasn't sure what she said, but he could see it was something she needed to do for herself. After a small pause, she lifted the box and handed it off to Hook in silence.

"Wendy, I need you to stay here and look after your brothers now, alright?" She nodded as tears

409

began to well up in her eyes. Hook and Smee slowly made their way towards the chamber door. But just before he took his first step outside, he turned to the young girl once more. "I do not pretend to know what you are feeling right now, my dear, but please believe me when I say that what you have done here- helping me, I do not ever what you to regret it. Because what you have truly done tonight was not out of jealousy or vengeance. You are not evil. You are no villain. You must always remember that you did not destroy an innocent life, but rather helped save thousands or more. I was prepared to leave the island forever content with only the cruelest of intentions; selfishly satisfied with Pan's everlasting suffering, but it was you that reminded me of my true purpose. Thank you, Wendy Darling. You are the real hero of this story." Hook's last words before leaving the room left Wendy with a slight smile and Smee an emotional wreck. With the loudest sobs of his first mate closing the door behind him, Hook stepped out onto the main deck rolling his eyes. "Smee, would you kindly get ahold of yourself!"

Smee nodded trying to quickly wipe away his tears from his reddening face; suddenly aware that he was still holding a bottle of rum in his hand. He carefully placed the bottle upon the deck, hoping desperately to escape the captain's notice. Hook instructed the majority of his crew to remain on board and guard the children, taking only three of his men in addition to Mr. Smee onto the small boat ready to row ashore the Lost Island. The men were still and silent.

Their path was lit by only a single flamed lantern held by Smee himself. Hook stood with his left boot at the head, and his hand carefully holding his weapon tightly within his grasp. Smee looked up at the man he had come to devote his life to, and he wasn't sure if it was the light of the flickering flame shining upon his vibrant red coat and long dark hair, or if it was because of the soft sentiment he had just witnessed from such a hard-walled soul, but Hook had never looked more magnificent than he did at this very moment.

The captain led the crew along the path given by Tinker Bell herself into the dark terrain of the woods. With only the flickering light held by Smee's shaking hand to guide them, Hook and the crew carefully crept through the thicket. Finally, as they reached their destination, Hook could see there was one large willow tree centered amongst all the rest. It was very round and appeared almost invisible, cloaked by the blanket of black darkness around it. The men would have likely walked right past it without seeing its morbid shape, but there was a light shining from high inside the willow tree. There were circular openings on the outside, likely so that Pan could fly out whenever he so desired. There was a large sculpted stone in the shape of a door blocking the bottom base of the trunk. *This must be the entrance for the lost boys*, Hook thought. The door was cracked open enough for the light from inside to come shining out. There was a swinging sound coming from inside the top area of the tree. It was quiet. It was as if the only sound left on the island was the whistling squeak from Pan's hammock that was

411

swinging ever so slightly from the inside. It was an eerie kind of silence; one only made more ominous when the music from Pan's pipes started to play again. Hook knew this was his chance.

He quietly slid the stone door open, peeking within. The inside of the tree seemed to be magically larger than its appearance from the outside. It was deep and very wide. It looked as if there were thirteen floors. With his heart racing wildly within his chest, he put down the boxed present on the ground and quietly slithered the deadly gift inside before carefully placing the stone back over the bottom of the hidden tree.

Hook turned to his men and whispered. "Alright men, on the count of three I want you to quietly make your way back to the boat. You must take great precautions to not be seen or heard. Wait for me there."

Smee was the first to very adamantly shake his head in reluctance. Something about being out in the woods in the dark again had brought about the worst fear in him. The very idea of crossing through it again without Hook was more than his panicked mind could handle. Unable to contain himself, Smee began to cry, mumbling gibberish, and causing the crew's only source of light to sway unsteadily.

Hook quickly took away the lantern with his hook and clasped his hand over Smee's mouth. Hook let out a sigh of frustration. It was his own fault really. But he had brought Smee, and with only one source of light, he could not send his men off with the lantern.

With his bad eyesight, the idea of Smee being his only guide back to the boat in total darkness was inconceivable.

"Alright, change of plans, everyone! Listen to me closely. I am going to knock on this door. Pan will surely hear it and believe it is the Darlings coming back to him. Once we hear that the music has stopped, we are all going to run back towards the boat. Do you understand? And Mr. Smee, if you so much as let out another whimper, I swear to the gods- I will kill you!"

The crew and Smee nodded, but just before he could knock on the door, Smee made a tiny sniffle. Hook turned in a rage, but the crew already had their hands all over him. Huffing in frustration, he turned towards the door again. *Knock.* But the music continued. *Knock.* Still, the magical tune echoed through the air, and with a final boom, Hook knocked again. This time the tree fell silent. The men all bolted carrying the clumsy Smee through the black woods back to the water with their fearless captain racing behind them.

CHAPTER THIRTY-SIX

A SECOND CHANCE

As Pan reached the bottom of the willow tree feeling pretty smug, Tinker Bell was feeling absolutely panicked. The idea of Peter dying was heart breaking enough, but knowing it was about to happen stole her breath. She realized now why her banishment had been so hurtful. Though the fae kind are not often known to understand the feeling of abandonment, Peter's actions in such felt like it was killing her slowly.

Being in the lantern while others conspired against Pan made her realize how much the young boy meant to her. From the very beginning he understood her and she him. Her own kind found her strange, but with Peter, she had found a friend that completed her soul. She would be punished till the end of time for the deal she gave him, but they all just didn't understand. She really had made the right choice. She couldn't lose him, she wouldn't!

Now alone in the room, she pushed on the lantern as hard as she could, going from side to side. The pain from the iron burning through the skin on her tiny hands released the first sound ever uttered from her mouth as her true voice screamed in brutal agony.

Finally, after what felt like hours of torture, the lantern fell- crashing to the floor. The weak Green Fairy then used her singed hands to pull herself up and fly through the broken glass and out of Hook's bedroom window, rushing with all the strength she had left to save Peter Pan.

Wendy and the boys had been gone for quite a while and were likely frantic by now to rejoin him, but as Pan approached the door, he was surprised to find a small wrapped box upon the ground. *That is strange*, he thought. But upon a closer glance, Peter recognized the blue ribbon that was tied around it. He picked up the box but before flying back up to his hammock, he decided to take a quick peek outside the door.

No one was there. Peter smiled, he had to admit... he was rather intrigued. He had all but taken Wendy for a complete bore, but maybe she would surprise him. He flew back up to his hammock, swinging slightly with just one leg hanging off the side. Sitting on top of the beautifully wrapped gift was a small card.

Pan slipped it out and read the words of endearment from the smitten young girl. It was yet another declaration of love from Wendy and was tossed aside with nothing more than a scoff and a chuckle. Peter was rather excited to see what was inside. No one had ever given him an actual gift before. And if it turned out to be just another token of her affection, then at the very least he would get a good laugh out of it.

415

But upon opening the box, what he found inside was rather peculiar. It was a round golden clock ticking ever so quietly.

"That's odd. The hands aren't moving," Pan said as he gazed into its delicate face. Then suddenly the tree was filled with a silence. Pan shook the little fancy clock, bringing it closely to his right ear. Then suddenly Tinker Bell came bursting through one of the high openings of the tree. Sparkles of bright green dust flitted rapidly behind her as she flew towards him. "Tink, what are you doing?! It's a gift from Wendy! Stop it!" He screamed as Tink tried desperately to pull away the clock with her singed hands, but Pan wouldn't let it go.

Then all the sudden, the clock began to zing and rattle uncontrollably with smoke already beginning to rise. Struck by surprise, Pan let the clock go and within a mere second, Tinker Bell snatched it away and bolted down to the ground. But before she could slip through the door, the silence was broken: *Boom!* The clock exploded, causing most of the hidden tree to come falling in on itself.

Fire and smoke began to fill the air as Peter urgently searched for Tink. But through all the debris and falling ash, it was behind a large wreckage where Pan spotted her green glow flickering faintly with only the weak sound of a ringing bell. Peter was immediately consumed with worry and fear as he raced to her aid. "Tink! Tinker Bell? Answer me please!"

It was then that a weak chime of desperation fell upon his ears.

"Wendy?" Peter didn't understand. "Forget about her! She means nothing to me! Please don't go out! I need you!" But it was too late. The sound of the Green Fairy's enchanting bells fell silent and the last glow of her light faded into the darkness. "No! Tinker Bell!" The hidden tree was dead silent with only the living breath of the lost little boy who thought his only fear was growing up, but as he sat there in the darkness, both the essence of Peter and Pan had their greatest fear realized.

It was then that his cold heart fell deep into despair. For whether he lived in this world or the next, from now until forever, he would be completely *alone.* It was too much for him to handle, he felt something human inside of him and it was more sadness than he had ever felt since he himself was nothing more than a mere mortal.

Caught in a haze of absolute desperation, Peter suddenly began to rip through the fallen wreckage screaming Tink's name- the very name he had given her all those years ago. But there was no answer. A single tear fell from his eyes, and whether it came from the fae or human part of him didn't matter, for it was the broken heart inside of him that loved her. She had been his one true friend, and she had died to save him.

As he dropped his head, the sparkling tear fell down his face upon the broken relic stones and splintered fragments of the magical tree. Then suddenly the sound of beautiful bells chiming came from behind the wall that divided him from her.

"Tink! Tink? Is that you?" Pan asked suddenly struck with desperate hope.

"No," said a beautiful voice.

Peter was stunned, but before he could say another word, the glow of magical dust began to surround the cracks of the wall, removing the stones and wood- piece by piece. But this glowing dust wasn't green, it was *blue*. The pieces of the piled wreckage were not only moving but were also coming back together as if fixing itself, and behind it all, standing above the dead body of the green pixie was the lovely fairy with azure hair. "Who are you?" Pan asked rudely.

"My name isn't important in this matter, nor is it what you truly want. I can help you," she said sweetly, gazing down at the sad sight that lay before her. Peter looked down at Tinker Bell; without her light she looked completely different. It was as if it was her youth and beauty that made her glow. Peter stepped closer to look at her. She was now a small grey form, her wings crushed, and much of her skin burned. "It is quite a ghastly sight indeed, Peter. Though I imagine you have likely seen much worse, since you have designed such horror yourself."

Pan looked up at her with suspicion. "What do you know about me, Blue Fairy? You don't know anything!"

"Oh, I know more than you think."

Pan whipped out his dagger, quickly glancing at Tink and the mysterious Blue Fairy. "Get away from her! Why are you here? Did the Elders send you?"

"Child, you need not raise such petty weapons at me," she said before waving her hand causing the blade to magically fly across the room. Peter was shocked. "Sorry to alarm you. I fear you mistook me for a fairy with a range of power like your own, so allow me to tell you now... Do not make such a mistake again. I am far more powerful than you or your late friend here. I have abilities that far succeed any that you could ever hope to achieve. But fear not, for I am not here to harm you, Peter Pan. I am here to help you."

Normally, Pan was a boy with many words, but in this moment, as he looked at his loved friend laying ravaged upon the ground, he could only think of one: "How?"

"I shall like to make a bargain," she said starting to circle around the dead pixie.

Pan felt like he was crawling out of his skin every time she got close to Tink. His blood began to boil beneath the shaky surface as he asked: "You mean to say you have the power to bring her back?"

"I do."

Suddenly, Pan felt like he couldn't breathe. He didn't need to hear anymore. "Do it! Do it! Whatever it is you want, it is yours! Just do it! Bring her back to me! Please!"

"I will bring her back, but you must do something for me. You must understand what I ask and agree before the magic can begin."

Peter was getting anxious, "Yes! Yes! What? What do you want?"

"I want you to promise that you will allow the children to sail back to London and I want you and your friend to promise you will never bring another child or their soul to Neverland again. That is my offer. Take it and I will bring back your pixie and give her a second chance. Do we have a bargain?"

Pan was astonished at how much she knew about Wendy, the ship, and what he and Tinker Bell did on the island. But all those questions running through his mind gave him an idea. "That is quite a bargain indeed, but not entirely fair. You ask me for so many things, while I receive only one wish..."

The Blue Fairy warily stared at him. "Is not the life of one worth more than the others I wish from you?"

Peter laughed and shrugged his head. "I am a child, Blue Fairy. I care not for quality as much as quantity. I want more or no deal at all. Besides, I am starting to get the feeling that this little deal of yours is just as important to you as it is to me. So, work with me a bit, and I shall concede your request."

Ainsel was flustered by his arrogance, but he was right. This *was* important. "What else is it you seek?"

Pan smiled crookedly. "I want answers."

The Blue Fairy hesitated for a moment, but time was running out and she needed this to work if she were to save Hook. "That is all?" Ainsel asked But Pan shook his head.

"No, you see, I need Tink's counsel before I ask, so if you please."

This time the Blue Fairy glared at him unamused.

Pan crossed his arms and sat down comfortably. "I got all the time in the world, but those kids will start to starve to death soon."

The Blue Fairy sighed. "Fine, but you must understand, should you break any of my rules, the deal is void and your little friend falls dead. Do you understand me?" She asked in a scolding tone.

Pan nodded sarcastically. "It is a deal then."

The Blue Fairy pulled her wand out of thin air and with a single tap and a beautifully spoken charm- a ray of stardust fell upon the cold creature, bringing the color of life back into her cheeks. Peter watched in amazement as his dear friend who only seconds ago was in the Realm of the Dead was now as alive as she ever was. All he could do was smile as she opened her round dark eyes searching for him, and as a smile came across her rosy pink face, he knew she had found him.

But the moment of nostalgia was short lived as Tink saw the other fairy in the room. And though they had never met, unlike Pan, a true fairy can feel the strength and power of another. The fact that she was able to rip a soul from the Realm of the Dead and restore her back to life should have been a clear demonstration of her power, but it didn't even come close. She didn't know why she was here or why she had saved her, but alive or not, Tink was suddenly very afraid. Quickly flying behind Peter, she asked him what was going on.

Pan smiled. He had feared he would never get to hear her bells again. "Don't worry, Tink! She is here to help us."

Tink chimed, *"But who is she? Why is she here?"*

Peter giggled as he looked back at the Blue Fairy. "See, I told you I would need her. First question, what is your true name?"

The Blue Fairy nodded with her eyebrows arched highly upon her face. "My name is Ainsel."

Pan and Tink looked at each other and then back towards her. "Well, Ainsel, what are you really doing here?"

This time Ainsel looked very hesitant about her answer. She couldn't lie, for if she did, it would void the bargain and the children, the Green Fairy, and possibly even her love would die. No, James needed her. She had to do this. "You are not the only true mortal here with a fairy behind you."

Her words caused Pan's eyes to widen.

"Yes, I am here to help James. He believes you deserve to die, and with or without my help, I am sure he will succeed. But no matter what happens, as long as I am around, he has my protection. And due to our bargain, it seems your fairy's restrictions will prove rather useless in such schemes. So, I suggest that you accept what I have offered and let those children return home on the ship and you remain here to live out your immortal life with the companion I just so graciously gave back to you. Are we finished?"

Pan chuckled rudely, flying through the air, circling around her. "Almost!" He shouted as he rapidly pulled out the Blue Fairy's wand and zapped her down to her pixie size in a small binding cage. "Do not feel bad, *Ainsel!* Powerful as you are, I always was good at stealing things. It's a gift really," he said looking down at the shocked fairy.

"No, you can't do this!" She screamed.

But Pan quickly silenced her with his waving finger, "Tisk. Tisk. That is where you are wrong, my lovely Ainsel. See, I have heard all your terms and though I am unable to lie, I will always find a way to *cheat*."

Ainsel shook her head in disappointment. "There is no cheating out of this one Peter Pan, for what you fail to understand is the absolute binding of Fairy Law. If you ever bring another life to the Ninth Realm of the Lost Island again... or the Darlings do not sail back to their home in London- your fairy will die!"

Peter smiled in amusement, but Tinker Bell on the other hand was suddenly feeling completely panicked. She chimed in frantic alarm about the Elders. It was a detail that she feared had been forgotten and one that had trapped her fate to an inevitable death. For if they failed to collect souls for the Ninth Realm, the Elders would come and deliver upon them the eternal death of the fae, but if Pan broke his bargained vow, she would fall forever lost in the underworld- a place most horrible for magical creatures.

Tink had already seen where she and Pan would go and what they would face due to their heinous crimes. Pan turned to her. "Don't worry, Tink. I have every intention of keeping my word," he said plainly. Tink ringed in frustration. Peter glared back at her, "I know the Elders will come for us, but they will not find us here." Suddenly, Tink understood. They all did. For there was only one place for those who went against the Elders: The Third

Realm of the Snow Queen. "And I know exactly how to get there."

Ainsel glared back at him bravely. "I am not afraid of you, for no matter what you do, James will come for me. You *will* lose."

Pan's eyes lit as he flew out one of the high circular windows, leaving only the sound of his malevolent laughter echoing within the hidden tree with Tinker Bell following closely behind him.

CHAPTER THIRTY-SEVEN

ONE LAST WISH

Pan had only one last thing to retrieve before leaving: Tiger Lily, but as Peter flew towards the Indian Camp, he found that everyone was gone. It was completely silent, without even the scent of smoke in the air. Pan didn't understand. "Tink! Where is...?" But as Peter turned to look at his fairy's face, a sudden clutch around his heart began to twist. "Tink!? Where is she? Where is my Tiger Lily? Tell me now!" Peter shouted in frantic anger.

It was then that Tink reluctantly admitted she too had made a deal recently to save his life, but the cost was tragically high. She tried to explain as best she could as to what had truly happened, but Pan couldn't hear anymore. He charged through the air towards the ship with more vigorous anger than she had even seen. All who stood upon the Jolly Roger had been there to witness the bomb's explosion. Though it was Wendy Darling's own idea, seeing the weapon's erupting destruction was a whole other matter. It seemed that somehow through it all, even the crew had come to accept Smee as their own as the small drunken doctor skipped and danced around amongst the rest. But Hook stood at the wheel alone, with only his loyal furry companion at his side. Wendy turned and

426

looked at him curiously, for he looked troubled. It was as if what he was looking at disturbed him somehow. He should have felt proud and victorious, but something about the ominous moon shining upon the sparkling blue horizon had left him with a bad feeling. Gazing at the Lost Island through his golden spyglass, he suddenly felt a tiny tap on his shoulder. As he looked down, he saw that it was Wendy.

"What is it, my dear?"

Wendy looked down at the deck floor shyly. "I was just wondering, sir, if we might be going home soon?"

Hook couldn't place his uneasiness, but he didn't want to scare her. "Yes, of course. At your stations, men! We set sail for London!" The Darlings clapped and cheered happily as the ship came to align itself with sparkling road on the blue sea. The steadfast ship was sailing towards the moon at full speed, with only the crocodile guardian attacking the ship below. The sounds of the booming thuds upon the hardened wood felt as if the creature might tear right through the ship. They needed to hurry if the vessel was going to make it in one piece. The attacks were getting harder and more violent, but they were close. It was only a bit further before they would reach the cloaked door hidden behind the glorious moon. Wendy looked nervous standing before it in astounding awe. Hook smiled at her. "It is alright, Wendy. We are almost out of this world. I promise you and your brothers will be taken home safely."

She smiled and nodded, but just as the ship was about to reach the moon, it began to fade in the dark sky causing the road on the water to break. Hook struggled to control the ship, not understanding what exactly went wrong, but in a mere moment, it would all become clear.

"Not so fast, Hook!" Shouted Peter from high above. It was then that the captain spotted the young boy's shadow and that of the little pixie he had until this moment believed was still inside the lantern above his desk. But Hook just chuckled, for while he didn't know how Tink had escaped or how Pan could have possibly survived such an explosion, he wasn't the least bit surprised.

"Back up, children! Get behind the crew," Hook commanded. The crew and Smee did as ordered, but Catcher never left Hook's side. The dog barked at the two green figures that threatened his master's ship. "Come to say goodbye, Peter?"

Pan chucked harshly. "I have, my old friend! And it will be a bloody goodbye indeed."

Hook smiled. "You seem angry, Peter?"

Pan pulled out his long dagger and pointed it towards him. "I will kill you for what you have done!" Pan shouted as he turned and pointed his dagger in the direction of the old Indian Camp.

It was then that Hook understood and began to laugh. "Ah, I see. I took your love. Well, don't worry,

Peter! I will happily rip out your cold broken heart so that you won't have to feel this pain any longer."

Wendy and the boys looked panicked, sobbing behind the crew as Peter flew down close to Hook's face. "Oh, you still haven't learned, have you, Hook? See, I too have something you love- or rather *someone.*"

Suddenly, the captain's heart felt as if it would run right out of his chest. Trying to suppress any fear on his face, he instantly pulled out his sword to kill the boy right then and there, but as always Pan quickly flew high into the air. "I do not believe you! It is not true!"

Pan smiled wickedly, "Oh, I am afraid it is!" He giggled, snapping his fingers. Low and behold, the small cage of magic appeared on the ship with the Blue Fairy laying sadly inside. "Poor, Ainsel," Peter said mockingly.

Hook rushed to the white vibrant cage, but when he got to the bars, he saw that there was no door or lock, just bars of magic holding her in. He tried to lift it, but his hand simply went right through them like a mirage. He got down on his knees to look into her face. "I will get you out of there, my love!"

She reached up and touched his hand. "You cannot, James. This cage locks me in by ways of the most powerful of magic."

Hook shook his head in desperation. "How did this happen?"

Suddenly, there was an echoing whistle coming from above them. It was Pan tapping the Blue Fairy's wand upon his knee.

Hook rapidly turned back to Ainsel. "How did he get your wand?"

She looked down shamefully. "He stole it from me and then used my own powers against me. I am nothing without my wand."

The captain rushed back towards Peter. "Give her back her wand, you devil!"

"James, please stop! The boy and I have made a deal. He has promised that the children will be returned safely on the Jolly Roger to their home in London, and he can never again take a life to Neverland."

Hook shook in a livid rage, unable to stop desiring Pan's blood pouring down from his blade. "But..."

Ainsel spoke urgently: "James! Listen to me! You got what you wanted! You don't have to kill anyone! Peter, please, it is not too late to change! I can give you your second chance!"

Pan hunched over with malevolent laughter. "Did you hear that, Hook? She is going to give *me* a second chance! Me! Hahahaha! My poor Ainsel! Always believing in the good in people. Didn't sweet James tell you? There is no good in me! I am the most ruthless of them all!"

Suddenly, his dagger had been struck by Hook's sword. The vengeful captain then looked up with a sinister gaze. "Let's see about that!" Hook said, quickly slashing Pan's cheek with his blade. In an instant, Pan and Hook were whipping through the air, crossing their swords upon the ship. But even as his body was being slashed through the air, Pan's devious laughter echoed throughout the realm.

Ainsel tried to stop them, but it was no use. Hook wasn't going to cease his attack until the boy laid dead upon the ground. Climbing the main mast Hook screamed, "Men, grab him!"

The crew snatched the boy and brought him down to the ground. Peter struggled in a rage. The sound of Hook's boots reverberated upon the wooden deck as he stepped towards the boy that he had hated his whole life.

Raising the sharp tip of his blade to the boy's chest, he spoke: "Peter, this is it! Men, get the wand!" Hook ordered. The crew searched franticly, but they couldn't find it. It was as if it had just disappeared.

Pan chuckled as he gazed up at Tinker Bell. Hook looked up at the Green Fairy. It was then that her black eyes twinkled as she waved the Blue Fairy's wand in her hands. With a swish and a zap, the very power Ainsel had used to bring her back from the dead raised up every lost boy that had ever died on the island of Neverland.

The undead children quickly swarmed the ship, forcing the crew to let go of Peter and unleashing a full-blown battle upon the Jolly Roger. As the violent bloodshed on the wooden deck below unfolded, the black silhouette figures of Captain Hook and Peter Pan could be seen high on the mast behind the dark sails lit by the sunlight that shined its orange ominous glow down upon the realm.

The warm breeze in the sea air was no longer filled with the sound of Pan's benevolent laughter, but rather the horror of the undead's wailing cries. With the white noise of the ocean waves, the once silent army of soulless children were now somehow more alarmed and afraid then they were before. The whispers of their suffering crept under your skin as if their fear was somehow contagious. The scent of decay was overwhelming as their jutting innards spilled out onto the deck covered in the island's hidden branches and sharp stones from the terrain.

Unable to fight the invisible shackles that controlled them, the children wailed in transcendental agony as they battled the crew against their suffered will. Hook was repulsed by them. "Why don't you come down here and let us end this horrific massacre!"

Peter flipped through the air in play. "Why would I do that? I'm having fun!"

The captain reached up and snatched Peter down with his sharp hook, bringing him close to his face. "I am done playing your game, Peter Pan! Stop being such a pathetic coward and fight me like a man!"

Hook's words had taken command of the ship. All that stood below stopped and stared at their masters above. Even Tinker Bell and the Darlings stared at Peter to see what would happen next.

Pan looked at all the faces watching him, and somehow this time- the matter wasn't so funny. He had been challenged in front of everyone and as he looked into Wendy's eyes, he knew what he had to do. "No man calls Peter Pan a coward and lives to tell the tale! I will fight you fairly! I will even put one hand behind my back."

Hook scoffed at the ridiculous overreach of boyish arrogance. "You mean... you won't fly?"

Pan looked down at his audience once more before looking back at Hook, answering through his seething teeth: "I give you my word!"

Hook looked down at him with a sinister smile. "Good form, Pan! Now let's have at it!" He screamed, kicking Pan down to the ground. He jumped down raising the sword above him ready to drive it into the boy. Pan was trapped under the weight of Hook's long blade, "Alright, Peter, give Ainsel back her wand and I will let you live." He demanded. Pan smiled and suddenly Ainsel began to scream in paralyzing pain. Hook looked up to find Tinker Bell had used the wand against her. He rushed to his love's aid, but he couldn't make it stop. The agonizing torture that was coursing through her was by magic. There was nothing he could do. He felt powerless. "Stop! Stop! Stop hurting her! Please!"

Pan stood up on the deck with his arms on his hips and a wicked grin across his face, "You know what! There sure are a lot of deals going on around here. Tink made one with you, Ainsel made one with me, and now you ask me to make another here with you. So here is my one and only offer, my dear old friend. I am willing to set Ainsel free, and all I ask is one tiny little favor. I want you to walk the plank, jump off the ship, and let your soul be the last given to Neverland."

Hook looked into Ainsel's sad eyes, her tiny body shaking in absolute pain. She tried to shake her head, but they both knew what he going to decide. He got down and reached his hand through the bars to wipe her tears away and whispered: "Listen to me, Ainsel. Everything is going to be okay. Like you said, the kids will be taken home safely, and Peter will never again take another innocent soul to this island again."

She wanted to tell him the truth... that Pan, and his Green Fairy would be escaping to the Third Realm and would likely be stealing even more children than before for the evil Snow Queen, but the pain had overtaken every inch of her body. The only thing that could escape her mouth was her cries of pain.

Hook spoke softly: "You have always said you believed in me, so now it's my turn to tell you something. You are a fairy with extraordinary powers, and I do not believe that they only come from your wand. You have magic inside of you. I have felt it since we first met. You have saved me. Now, let me save you!" He stood up and walked towards the wooden plank the crew had perfectly placed for him. His men stood in perfect lines on either side with their hats and bandanas off as they looked down to the floor in respect.

Smee rushed up to him, crying. "Please, Captain, do not go! Don't leave us!" The small doctor pleaded. Catcher rushed up to Hook not understanding what was wrong.

The captain patted him on the head. "Good boy, Catcher. You will always be my sweet boy. Take care of Smee, okay?" He said kindly. Smee called the dog to him, holding him as he wept. When Hook stepped up onto the plank, he looked behind him at all the faces he would never see again. "Wendy, you and your brothers will be taken home safely just as I promised. Stay brave for your little brothers, alright. Men, it has been an honor being your captain. You have served me well, and when you are returned to our world, I know you will honor my memory well. Now, Peter, you have yourself a deal. Set her free now so that I can see for myself that she is okay. I want to say goodbye."

Peter scoffed. "Like I got the chance to say goodbye to Tiger Lily?"

But suddenly there was a shining zap that struck the cage releasing the Blue Fairy from her prison and her pain. Peter glared up at Tinker Bell, but she didn't care. It seemed like the right thing to do. After all, it was the Blue Fairy who had brought her back to life.

The magic from the wand had freed Ainsel. She dropped to her knees heartbroken. "James," she whispered weakly. "You would really sacrifice the Jolly Roger, your life, and your soul for me?"

Hook smiled and replied: "Of course, I would. I love you."

Ainsel smiled just as Pan walked up to Hook, "Well, my old friend, I guess this is goodbye. But do not worry for in Neverland your soul will live forever. A fact that will keep me sated. See I know something now."

Hook took his first step on the plank. "What is that, Peter?"

"You and I complete each other. Before you I was just an orphan named Peter and before you met me, you were just a little orphan boy named James. Don't you see? *I* made you what you are: Captain James Hook. And *you* made me Peter Pan! Without you, I do not exist and without me, you would not exist. I know that we hate each other, but I just want to say now that I thank you for this amazing adventure. And because of Wendy, the world will know our story and it will be heard for years to come."

Hook took another step further, "Wendy knows the truth about everything, Peter! The world will know the truth about you; that you are an insane psychopath that steals children and collects their souls. You are no hero in her eyes, Pan. You are the villain!" Hook said taking another step forward.

Peter's face lit up with a crooked smiled. "Oh, but see, that is where you are wrong. Wendy *will* remember her little trip to the island the way I want her to- after I alter the memories in her pretty little head. In fact, the world will know through her that it was *you* that was the evil villain. And I think that makes me the... what is the word? Oh yes, the *hero*," Peter whispered in his ear before shoving him off the end. *Splash!* Hook hit the water. The sound of the ticking clock that followed the crocodile drew in closer ready to devour its favorite taste. The sound of crunching bones and the smell of blood filled through the sea air, the entire crew and all the children cried in horror as the sounds of their beloved captain was taken under water. The sea had taken him, but it would be Neverland that would keep him forever. After a long moment of mournful cries for most, and thrilling victory for Pan, it was time to leave before the Elders arrived. "Tink if you would please," Peter said in a commanding tone.

Tink whipped out the wand and waved it slowly over the ship. The undead children and the crew disappeared, and with a final zap of pixie dust that sparkled like stars and diamonds, the children's sad faces were instantly transformed to ecstatic happiness and cheers. Pan grabbed Hook's hat and red coat while Tink used the wand and her pixie dust to cover the ship in solid gold and lift it high into the air to sail away.

As the flying Jolly Roger headed back to London, Smee had escaped, rowing away in the small boat with Catcher, a large bag of treasure, and Hook's favorite book placed carefully upon the seat beside him. Though everyone on board the Jolly Roger would return to the world with Peter Pan as their hero, the Blue Fairy was still in Neverland standing on the edge of the sand looking out into the water. "James, you said you believed in me. I pray now more than ever that you were right." She closed her eyes and reached out her arms. "The true power is within *me*.

Magic, please
Hear my call
Bring my love back
Body, heart, and soul
I swear to you now
the fae's Absolute Law
Of honor and purpose
He shall not fall
He will never alter or waver his stance
Please give my love
His second chance."

The Sun was gone from the island of Neverland. The golden sand now shimmered in the dark. The sea was now black, with only the moonshine that glittered upon the slow waving surface. But there was no ripple, not a single splash. "Come on, James. Please, come back to me."

Ainsel slowly began to drop her arms and fell hopeless on the sand below as her whispered wish went out into the night. Tears welled within her